THE

HURRICANE

BLONDE

Halley Sutton

Allison & Busby Limited
11 Wardour Mews
London W1F 8AN
allisonandbusby.com

Published by arrangement with G.P. Putnam's Sons, an imprint of
Penguin Publishing Group, a division of Penguin Random House LLC.

First published in Great Britain by Allison & Busby in 2023.

Discussion guide and interview with Halley Sutton © 2023 by
G. P. Putnam's Sons

First Edition

ISBN 978-0-7490-3062-9

Typeset in 11/16 pt Sabon LT Pro by
Allison & Busby Ltd.

By choosing this product, you help take care of the world's forests.
Learn more: www.fsc.org.

FSC
www.fsc.org
MIX
Paper | Supporting
responsible forestry
FSC® C171272

Printed and bound by
CPI Group (UK) Ltd, Croydon, CR0 4YY

For Paul Vangelisti, who tells the best stories.
I took one and ran with it.

CHAPTER ONE

The pretty blonde would be dead in three minutes.

She stood in front of the Biltmore Los Angeles hotel, wind snapping her black linen dress against her waist, revealing shiny Spanx and spray-tanned thighs. Ringed around her, a dozen true-crime junkies baked under the September sun, leaking electrolytes but not enthusiasm. Not yet. For three more minutes, Beth Short – better known as the Black Dahlia, Los Angeles's most infamous unsolved murder – was alive to tell her story.

'I hitched a ride up from San Diego with a travelling salesman,' the Black Dahlia said. 'A "nice guy," married. You know the type.' Melany Grey, the actor embodying the Dahlia, pantomimed *handsy*, skimming her palms over her bodice. My murder tourists laughed, nudged each other. *Yes, yes, we know.*

Stars Six Feet Under wasn't the only tour company in Hollywood that promised an insider's look at the macabre underbelly of fame. But we had something that set us apart. We had my Dead Girls. For four hours every day of the week except Mondays and holidays – though you'd be surprised how many people preferred spending Christmas with murdered starlets over their own families – I could bring the dead back to life.

'I told him I was meeting my sister. But he wouldn't leave me alone. A *gentleman*.' The Dahlia rolled her eyes. 'I sat in that lobby trying not to play footsy with him for hours.' She gestured to the Biltmore behind her.

I'd heard the story hundreds of times, but I couldn't help myself. I turned on cue with my tourists and stared at the hotel, glittering in the white sun.

In 1947, when the Black Dahlia was murdered, the Biltmore was the largest, fanciest hotel west of Chicago. She was class, and money, and all the promise of Los Angeles – that mirage of fame and success and good fortune – rolled up into one.

Now, nearly a hundred years into her residency – ancient in this city, which preferred its buildings like its women: shiny, new, *young* – the Biltmore was starting to show her cracks. Sumptuous carpets a little threadbare. Gilded frescoes dingy and studded with grey gum patches old enough to vote.

In the end, she *had* brought the Black Dahlia fame.

'By the time I got rid of him,' the Dahlia said, blonde strands escaping her black wig, 'it was night.' Her voice fell to a hush, leaving us to imagine 9th January, 1947, when Beth Short wandered from the lobby of the Biltmore into the dark, dangerous cold of downtown Los Angeles and disappeared. A week later, her body, cracked open like an egg, would be discovered across town by a young mother and daughter out for a sunny morning stroll.

Melany paused, letting us sit in our imaginations, wondering. Then she shivered, fluttering her fingers over

8

actual goosebumps raised on her bare arms.

I peered closer, impressed. Actual goosebumps – a good trick. All the girls I hired from my mother's acting school for my tour came with the Vivienne Powell guarantee of excellence, of course. But goosebumps on command – even Vivienne's magic didn't usually extend that far.

'Who knows what might have happened to me if he hadn't been such a *gentleman*,' Melany said. 'Maybe I would've left while it was still daylight. Maybe I would've lived a long life. We'll never know.'

I nibbled on the edge of my thumb, biting deep into cuticle and sucking on the pain. Like every tour, I wanted to stop her there. Keep Beth Short alive a few more minutes. But that wasn't the way the story ended. You couldn't cheat the past.

I knew that better than anyone.

Melany finished the monologue I'd written, sharing theories about the Dahlia's fate: the sons and nephews who came out of the woodwork with stories about bad daddies who might've killed her. Thousands of suspects. Never solved. I didn't think it could be any more, not really. The Black Dahlia meant something to Los Angeles, but only as a mystery. Even if they didn't know it, people preferred it that way.

Melany stared at me, eyebrows raised.

Earth to Salma. I cleared my throat. 'Any questions?'

In the back, a woman with sunburned shoulders and a puffy purple fanny pack raised her hand. I tried not to roll my eyes. I could guess her question. She'd want personal details about the Dahlia. She'd have her own theories about who she was, what happened to her, *why* it happened to her. I'd come to think of Beth Short as something of a litmus test: you tell me what you see when you look at the Dead Girl, and I'll tell you what's missing in *your* life.

'Yes?'

'Didn't the brochure say we'd get a cocktail?' A low rumble of laughter moved through my group. Emboldened, Purple Fanny Pack smirked. 'I mean, this *is* the Salma Lowe tour, right? I'm surprised we don't get drinks at every stop.'

The laughter was louder this time. I scrunched my face into an almost-smile. 'Funny,' I said. 'I haven't heard that one.' I gestured at the hotel. 'Upstairs, the bartender has crafted a real treat – a Black Dahlia cocktail, special for our tour. Be back here in twenty minutes, or the bus leaves without you.'

My tourists lined up for their drink tokens, jabs at my tabloid past long forgotten as they held up their palms for the promise of lobby air conditioning, the phantom taste of Chambord and Absolut citrus already on their tongues.

When I'd first started my tour, I'd made the mistake – oh, what a mistake – of believing my guests wanted to understand my own obsessions: the shadow side of the Hollywood spotlight, the darkness that beckoned for women who burnt too brightly. *She had everything until she didn't.* The Marilyn Monroes, the Jayne Mansfields, the Thelma Todds and Jean Harlows and Dorothy Strattens – none of whom lived past thirty-six.

But after five years, I knew what my riders really wanted: photographic evidence of being interesting – dark, complicated, ever so slightly twisted. They'd gladly fork over seventy-five dollars to let tragedy crinkle the edges of their cookie-cutter, basic-bitch lives, sprinkling Dead Girls over their Instagram feed like a game of brunch, brunch, murder.

Melany hovered near my elbow as I handed out the final token. I let the doors slide shut – that air con *did* feel good – then said, 'Goosebumps on command. Impressive.'

'Really?' Melany's face lit up, pink as a shrimp. 'You were impressed?'

I winced. Actors were like puppies, eager to soak up praise and attention. And like puppies, there was something appealing and dangerous about all that *tell me I'm good and I'll follow you anywhere* trust. It could get a girl in trouble. 'You made Vivienne proud.'

She bounced happily on her toes, dress swishing around her knees. I rummaged through my purse, looking for the check I owed her, along with a tip – goosebumps deserved a tip – when Melany said, the words all in a rush, nasal Texas twang creeping in, 'Then would you put in a good word with her? There's this part I'll die if I don't get – well, actually, I *already* didn't get it, but maybe there's *another* part, and if Vivienne freaking Powell tells him I'm a good actor, Cal will reconsider—'

'Cal?' My purse dropped onto the asphalt. A lip gloss and a tampon, identical shades of pink, bounced onto the street. 'Cal Turner?'

Melany bent down, gathered the tubes for me. 'His new super-secret project. The casting director won't even release the full sides for auditions. It's on an' – her fingers made bunny quotes around my tampon and lip gloss – "as-needed basis".'

Restricting sides – script excerpts actors used for auditions – was not the worst rumour I'd heard about

11

Cal. *The most dangerous director in Hollywood*, one magazine had dubbed him – like it was a good thing. When I'd known him, he'd been a fledgling auteur with a leading man's face and a bad temper. And my sister's fiancé.

'So? Will you?' Melany's face was eager, like a little girl promised a toy.

I'd always been a coward when it came to conflict.

I dug through my purse again, stalling as I fished out a floppy worm of orange sugar-free gum, thinking of Cal's face as I chomped it. 'Sure,' I lied. Even if acting wasn't high on the list of things my mother and I no longer talked about, I wouldn't have done it. Not for Cal's film. 'I'll put a bug in her ear.'

Melany gripped my arm. I couldn't look at her. 'Oh my God, I can't thank you enough. Salma, you're a lifesaver.' When I looked up, Melany's head was tilted as she watched me, her cornflower-blue eyes wide. 'Don't you ever miss acting?'

The gum fell to the back of my throat. I coughed. 'Miss it?'

'I used to watch *Morty's House* as a kid, you know. You were good. You were *funny*.' She hesitated for a moment, then said, almost shyly: '*Iron Prayer* is my favourite film.'

If I had a dollar for every time someone told me my parents' film *Iron Prayer* was their favourite movie – well, in a way, my family *did* have a dollar, more than a dollar, for every time I'd heard it.

But *Morty's House* wasn't anyone's favourite show, except maybe mine. Playing plucky Polly Parker hadn't required much acting talent besides mastering a salty sprinkle of one-liners, like: *Gosh, Mr Morty, don't you know what to say to make a girl feel special!* with an eye roll so big, I had to ice my forehead between takes. *Morty's House* left me with a permanent bald spot behind my right ear from years of a pulled-too-tight-ponytail, meagre residual checks from our brief flirtation with syndication in the early aughts, and a taste for amphetamines in the form of producer-mandated diet pills.

It had also been the only time in my childhood when I'd had friends, real sleepover-truth-or-dare-MASH-until-morning friends.

Melany wasn't done. 'You can't tell me Vivienne Powell and Dave Lowe's daughter doesn't have acting in her blood.' Melany must have seen my face, because she clicked her tongue, shook her head. 'I'm sorry. That was thoughtless.'

Even though it had been almost two years since my father died, every mention of him was like a tiny punch still, another reminder he was gone for good. I still expected him to pick up the phone when I called. It was a shock to remember – like I'd carelessly misplaced him somewhere. But it was death that had been careless with me.

How you stop acting: never live up to your family's expectations. Delight the tabloids with a never-ending stream of bad angles and bad choices, the merry-go-rounds of rehab to red carpet and back again, the box office bombs and black sheep antics that sell more glossy covers than good news can. *You won't believe what Sloppy Salma did now!* You stop acting when you sell more magazines than movie tickets.

And in the end, when you needed it most, fame meant nothing. It couldn't protect you from the things that go bump in the night. It couldn't protect you at all.

Melany just didn't know it yet.

'I'll put in that word,' I said. Behind us, a few of my tourists staggered down the lobby stairs, cherry-cheeked and loose. 'Thanks again, Melany.'

I turned on my heel, blinking into the smoggy sunlight as I crossed the street to my bus. I folded my arms against the steering wheel, ignoring the leather scalding me through my sleeves. Melany gave the hotel one last look, then slid the wig from her head, shaking out her long blonde hair underneath it.

She didn't need my good word anyway. She was Cal Turner's type exactly.

I closed my eyes as the tourists mounted the steps. I didn't want to watch them swaying into their seats like big drunk babies, yelping and giggling as they leant against scorching windows, making a show of fanning themselves with a Stars Six Feet Under brochure. Ready to devour one more Dead Girl before the ride home.

I was always jumpy at this part of my tour.

As the bus rocked, I practised my final monologue of the day. *Tawney Lowe – an actor you might also know as the Hurricane Blonde – died twenty years ago, in the hours between 10:30 a.m. and 1:17 p.m. on 16th June, 1997.* But no, that was pulling a punch. *Tawney Lowe was* murdered *in the hours between . . .*

Murder. The word stuck in my throat like a clot of phlegm.

I counted backward from ten before I tried again. It was an old trick from the Betty Ford Centre for Clean Living and No More Fun, where I'd served two tours:

14

a longer stint from 2001 to 2002, as a teenager, and a shorter stay in 2004, a refresher course on the appeal of court-mandated sobriety.

Twenty years ago, my sister, Tawney Lowe – also known as the Hurricane Blonde – was strangled to death. Her murder has never been solved.

I'd said it before. What was one more time?

I opened my eyes. 'Okay, everyone,' I said, glancing at my sun-mottled crew in the rear-view as I nosed the bus back onto the glitter and rush of Los Angeles streets, backward in time to 1:17 p.m. on 16th June, 1997, when my mother and I discovered Tawney's lifeless body steps from her pool. 'One last stop and then you're home free.'

CHAPTER TWO

In Hollywood, there are blondes and there are *blondes*. There are the breathless baby-voiced *Gee whiz, mister* Marilyn blondes, held up high like empty trophies. There are the platinum-hued Harlow blondes – striking and remote, never natural. There's the Blonde Next Door, who everyone loves as a child when she's friends with an alien, or the little kid sister. But then she grows up, a trick no one asked for. There are sunny, friendly blondes everyone likes to see happy but *loves* to see dumped, those *poor little never could keep a man* blondes whose heartbreak always makes the front page. There are Hitchcock's icy blonde sufferers, the curves-everywhere blonde spilling out of her bra, the butt-of-the-joke blondes, the power blondes begging to be taken down a notch, the blondes who go out like a light, not a survivor's bone in their bodies, the blondes who make the prettiest corpses.

None of them held a candle to the Hurricane Blonde.

'All right, everyone,' I said, my voice froggy as I jammed the bus into park, releasing the hydraulics with a friendly sigh. 'Last stop.'

As my riders descended the stairs – still giggly and

tipsy – I checked my lipstick in the rear-view mirror, thumbing away little clumps of red as I avoided eye contact with our destination: the three-story Spanish Colonial down the street.

The June my sister died, the trees lining her street flowered in one last splendour before summer set in. Twenty years later, the jacaranda still stood guard over Tawney's Olympic-size swimming pool, drooping with the purple blossoms. All these years later, and it still looked as it had when she lived there. It made it possible to believe Tawney might still pull up in her white Porsche, cranky and snappish after a fourteen-hour shoot. The Jacaranda House was waiting for her to come home.

That made two of us.

The bus swayed as my final rider made his way down the stairs, grunting as he half-hopped to the pavement below. I took one last glance at myself in the mirror, fingers tracing the slight lines around my mouth. Tawney died before ageing had become a concern; no sisterly words of advice for the best tricks to keep time at bay, *Pond's cream, Salmon, I swear by it. Trust me.*

'Showtime,' I whispered, yanking my keys from the ignition, trying to put a bounce in my step I didn't really feel as I descended from the bus.

My group formed a semicircle on the sidewalk in front of the Jacaranda House, and two of the younger riders turned to snap selfies in front of it, pink tongues extended. Everyone avoided the faint fuchsia stain on the pavement, a leftover from the early years when fan-brought bouquets rotted in the sun until they were etched on the asphalt.

'Here we are. Our final stop.' I paused, glanced

17

around. A few tourists watched me with varying degrees of discretion. One, a white man in his forties wearing a baseball cap, who had come by himself – fucking creepy – stared at me with naked curiosity.

I'd learnt long ago that part of my tour's appeal was an experience with Salma Lowe: daughter of Hollywood royalty, former wild-child starlet, tabloid fixture turned upclose confidante of murder. They didn't want the truth. They wanted their money's worth.

They wanted a show.

I cleared my throat. 'On 16th June, 1997, Tawney Lowe, also known as the Hurricane Blonde, was murmurd' – I coughed twice, *spit it out* – '*strangled* to death by persons unknown. No one has ever been charged with her death. At 1:16 p.m., after lunch with our mother, I rang her doorbell – *there.*' I craned my head over the top of my riders, gesturing at the front door. Every head turned with my finger, as though tugged.

The top of Tawney's Juliet balcony above the front door was visible over the privacy hedges my sister planted after a paparazzo made five figures off a shot of her sunning topless. I could picture her stepping onto it, frowning down at me in her favourite mismatched bikini, mouthing, as she had a million times: *Door's unlocked.*

For a moment, the feeling was so real that my throat closed, the wind knocked out of me.

I ran through the rest of her life on autopilot, impersonal as a Wikipedia entry: growing up famous, the daughter of Dave Lowe and Vivienne Powell Lowe. (*Oh,* Iron Prayer *is your favourite film? I haven't heard that one before!*) Tawney's star rising in Hollywood. The handful of films she'd left behind, which I'd watched often enough I could quote her every line. On the set of one of those films, *Love's Long Midnight*, she'd fallen in love with then up-and-coming director Cal Turner. A few months after the film came out – bombed, rather – Tawney called off their engagement, infamously leaving only a note: *I can't love you when I don't even know who I am.*

Three months later, she was dead.

The details I didn't share: the strangulation lasted probably less than five minutes. No neighbours heard her scream or cry for help, or noticed anything out of the ordinary. That because she'd been lying out in the sun when I found her, it had initially made determining a time of death difficult.

As I talked, I noticed the two selfie queens nudging each other, pointing behind me. I turned my head, but before I could see, Baseball Cap asked a question.

'Who do you think killed her?'

I took a deep breath. An old warning: *Salma, this fixation of yours is not healthy. It's not helping you heal.* 'No one was ever arrested. The investigation is still ongoing,' I said carefully.

There was a smugness to his expression, like he knew what I was thinking. He hooked his thumbs into his belt loops, tilted his head. 'You must have a theory.'

I gritted my teeth. 'I really can't say.'

No one can stand an open-ended mystery. Theories were everywhere. There'd been the serial killer in the early aughts with a yen for busty blondes who turned out to have been incarcerated during Tawney's murder. There was the anonymous tip that my sister's death was a mob hit, that Tawney had *seen something she shouldn't have*. And it was true, she'd been antsy the last few weeks before her death, distant and moody. But the tip hadn't given any leads to chase, only vague mentions of something *bad-bad* at a nightclub, no details.

Then there were the fake confessions, the crank calls – *I chopped your sister into little bitty pieces; Charlie Manson did it, people think he can't hurt anyone, but I'm telling you; Jesus punishes whores with fake tits*. The more terrible the details, the less plausible the tips. It didn't matter. Each one turned me inside out.

There were a thousand open-ended possibilities.

But Baseball Cap was right; I'd had my own suspicion, once. But I knew better than to dwell on that. 'Any other questions?'

One of the selfie girls raised her hand, then without waiting, called out in a strangled voice: 'Is that another actress in the pool?'

Actor, I wanted to correct her, not *actress*. I held back. 'For this stop, we don't—'

She jabbed her finger behind me. 'Right there. *Right there.*'

I turned. In the sunlight, Tawney's pool shimmered blue and white. White? A towel, I thought, blown into the water. That was all. I was about to say as much when it moved again. Something waving. Something underneath the surface.

Not *something*. A hand.

'Oh fuck,' I said.

Baseball Cap stepped forward – *man in charge here –*

but I ducked under his arm, already streaking past him.

My heels sank into the ground, and I stumbled, didn't stop. If anyone was going to investigate, it would be me.

I had my hand on the iron gate, punching in Tawney's twenty-year-old code without thinking – 07/21, the date of my sister's cancelled wedding to Cal – shoving at the handle as it buzzed. Dread spread from my stomach to my toes as I pushed it open.

There was a body at the bottom of the pool.

I closed my eyes, squeezing so hard I saw neon splotches. It had happened to me before. Minutes slipped out of my clock, rearranged themselves to an internal logic that didn't have any use for time. I'd catch sight of a long blonde ponytail, or a mole on the back of the neck like Tawney's, and I was fifteen again. It passed. It would pass when I opened my eyes.

There was a body at the bottom of the pool.

She was suspended in the water, twisting gently like a ballerina in a music box. Hot pink bikini straps, skin bluish in the chlorine. Reaching, reaching for the surface.

Oh God oh God oh God oh my God oh God oh God.

I kicked my shoes off, and then I was half-falling, half-jumping in, icy rush filling my nose, my throat. I opened my eyes and shoved myself down, four, six feet, until I could grab her hand, crinkled and cold.

Even as I kicked hard for the surface, I knew. The dead feel different, even in a pool, even warmed by sunshine. Your fingers know the truth before your heart does.

I was screaming for help before I surfaced, gagging on mouthfuls of chlorine. The man in the baseball cap grabbed underneath her arms, grunting as he hauled her dead weight backward. I flopped myself onto the pavement like a fish, gasping for air, too stunned to cry.

When he flipped the body over, I could see mascara smudged in a little half-moon under her closed lashes. Early twenties, maybe younger. Dark blonde hair made darker by the water, which had also turned her swimsuit dark pink.

'Call 911,' I told Baseball Cap, who gaped down at her. When he didn't respond, I clapped my hands in his face. 'Hey! Call 911!'

Then I was starting CPR, not sure if I remembered it right, pounding on her chest and blowing hard into her mouth. Over and over, I repeated a promise that wasn't mine to keep: 'You're going to be okay, you're going to be okay, you'll be okay.'

I kept it up until I felt faint, way past the time I knew it was useless. Then I remembered – for drowning victims, weren't you supposed to turn them on their side, to help expel the water in their lungs? Wasn't that what I'd seen in the movies? *Stupid, Salma, stupid, you've wasted time, maybe you killed her, maybe this is* your *fault.* My fingers trembled as I rolled her, thumping her gently at first, then harder, willing her to cough, sit up, thank me, breathe again, live again. *Jeez, that was a close call!*

Finally, my arms burning, I gave up. The dead girl slipped down my thighs, eyes open wide. I reached down and brushed a lock of the dark blonde hair from her forehead. I was thinking, *who were you?* and *how did you get here?*

But mostly, I was thinking, *I'm sorry. I'm sorry I couldn't save you.*

Behind me, I heard a click. Ten feet away, Baseball Cap, his call to 911 completed, snapped photos of me on his phone, the dead girl splayed over my knees. I blinked again, time collapsing, the flash of the shutter like the blinding pop-pop-pop – *Salma, Salma! Look over here!* – of the red carpet from years past.

Thirty-four years of training kicked in, and I couldn't help myself: I smiled pretty for the camera.

16TH JUNE, 1997

'No more arguing,' my mother said, hands flexing on the steering wheel like she was choking it. She glared at me in the passenger seat, her lips a prim line of La Vivienne by Dior. 'Go.'

I glared at her, fifteen and moody. It wasn't *my* day Tawney had ruined by bailing on lunch. But Vivienne was in full movie star mode, and I knew she wouldn't crack. We wouldn't go anywhere until I complied.

'Fine,' I muttered, slamming the door so hard behind me it rocked the car.

In the five minutes we'd spent arguing over who should knock on Tawney's door – me pointing out, rather reasonably, that since *they* were fighting, *she* should go – my sister was dead or dying less than a hundred yards away.

I tromped up the steps. If the *adults* couldn't behave like adults, why did I have to? How freaking unfair was that?

But at her gate, I hesitated.

In a bad mood, Tawney's acid sarcasm crossed the line quick-quick into casual cruelty. She'd apologise later – sometimes *much* later – hugs, kisses, *Dinner's on me,*

Salmon. But she'd been especially snappish since she called off the engagement. The week before, she and my mother had fought worse than usual, a real lung buster. The lunch had been a white flag attempt. But after an hour and a half of waiting for Tawney to arrive, my mother paid for our twenty-five-dollar salads in silence, then drove us straight to the Jacaranda House.

I looked back. At the curb, Vivienne fluttered her hands at me. *Go inside, go.*

I punched in the gate code: 0721. She hadn't changed it. Maybe she still wasn't sure about the breakup. I felt my heart lift a little. Maybe Cal wasn't really gone for good. Maybe she'd give him another chance.

No answer to my knock. I turned to my mother, shrugged. I could see her bent over the wheel, sunglasses blotting out her eyes. I knocked again, called Tawney's name. When she still didn't answer, I pushed the door open – my sister left her front door unlocked, *Tawney, how could you be so stupid* – and in the sunny glare, the Jacaranda House stretched dark and unending before me.

The next part comes in blips and snatches.

Whir-chop of her ceiling fan. Snowy leather sofa in the centre of her living room, a blanket kicked to one side. Curving marble staircase up, up, up. Open French doors out to the pool, Tawney's happy place. Greasy shimmer of my sister's tan legs behind the glass.

Of course she stood us up to catch rays, I thought, sliding through the doors, glaring at her polished-pink toes. *Bitch.*

Tawney was half in the shade of her yellow-and-white sun umbrella, her legs long and brown in the sun. The coconut smell of her tanning oil. Then I saw all of her.

Tawney still looked like herself, not yet completely a corpse, despite the unnatural angle of her limbs, the purple tinge at her lips. Eggplant bruises already settling in around her neck. Sun bounced off the pool, throwing shards of light over my sister's eyes, open and staring straight up at the sky.

It didn't make sense.

At her hip, a still-damp, crumpled towel. She would've used it to rub her long blonde mane dry after she swam thirty laps, her morning ritual. Weeks later, we'd discover it was the murder weapon, the terry cloth scratching her throat as she struggled. I stepped closer, my shoe slipping on the puddle of overturned suntan oil slicking her legs, and leant over her.

In my memory – a kid's memory, it couldn't be right – Tawney's marble eyes looked through me, but her lips crooked up in a tiny smile and I thought: *she's asleep. When I touch her, she'll wake up. This is a scene study, that's all.* I reached out, threaded my hand into her hair, and then I heard my mother behind me, screaming.

That's when I knew.

CHAPTER THREE

Detective Mykella Watkins wasn't like other cops I'd met. For one thing, she was a woman. I watched her take statements from my tourists, silver earrings tinkling as she scribbled in her notebook. She made a point of shaking hands, thanking them for their time, before moving on to the next. In her tan suit, her polite professionalism, she was a world away from the crew-cut-and-aviator-sunglasses cops who interviewed me when Tawney died.

I kept my back pressed against the scorching metal of my bus while I waited to give a statement. If I didn't have to look at the Jacaranda House, I wouldn't have to imagine what was unfolding behind the yellow caution tape ribboning Tawney's front yard.

Had the dead girl lived there? On my tours, I'd sometimes catch a flicker in the window, the warm feeling of being watched. But no one had ever come out to say hello. That was fine with me. I could pretend it was still Tawney's home.

While we waited for the cops, I called Dale, who owned Stars Six Feet Under. He kept asking me to repeat what had happened – *Just one more time, Salma, run me through it one more time* – until I finally snapped.

'Get here and see for yourself,' I said, hanging up.

Across the street, Watkins flipped her notebook shut, making eye contact with me before she sauntered over. I straightened my shoulders, pushed myself away from the van. *Here we go again.* As she introduced herself, explained the questions she'd be asking, I realised she thought I'd never seen a dead body before. I didn't correct her.

No recognition on her face when I gave my name.

I walked her through the events of the afternoon. Watkins nodded as she scribbled, dark head bent so I was looking down at the white zigzag of her part.

Had I noticed anything unusual? Had I seen anyone on the property before I found her?

They were the same questions detectives had asked twenty years ago. *Tell us again, miss, where you found the body. Did you touch it? You can tell us if you touched it.* My sister's body, her famously coveted, photographed, gossiped-about body, an *it* already.

I still didn't have any good answers.

The sun was starting to go down, and I crossed my arms over my chest, shivering in my damp clothes. Watkins finished jotting a thought in her notebook, then looked up at the Jacaranda House.

I stared with her, looking at Tawney's glimmering blue pool. It had been my job to fish out the leaves and jacaranda blooms from the pool with a large net – Tawney's toll for keeping my secrets, my mother's Belvedere vodka bottles that started to go watery, the after-the-fact late-night alibis.

'The Hurricane Blonde murder,' Watkins mused. 'My first few years on the force, I got called out here once or twice to shoo away looky-loos.' Then she peered at me. 'Lowe. Relation?'

I licked my lips. Bringing my sister into it would change things, I knew. There was no way around it. 'My sister.'

Watkins made a sympathetic face, didn't say anything. I hated that look. She knew things about me now, private things.

Behind her, EMTs bumped a black bag on a stretcher down from the curb to the street. We both stared at it, each of us with our separate, silent thoughts.

'Anything else you think might help? Any guesses as to what happened here?'

My sister's death all over again, I thought. But no, of course the two weren't connected, except by location.

I had a flash of Cal's handsome face, his arm snug around Tawney's waist. The golden couple.

'No,' I said. 'No idea.'

Watkins's waist crackled, her walkie-talkie lighting up. She frowned, tilting her head to listen, then sighed. 'Salma, will you excuse me for one second? Don't leave, please.'

Saved. I nibbled my thumb, watching Watkins duck behind the yellow caution tape. I closed my eyes, rubbing slow circles over my heart. But with my eyes closed, all I could see was that poor girl six feet deep in Tawney's pool, the blue twist of her lips. My eyes snapped open, roaming over the Jacaranda House. The sun passed behind a cloud, and the white house took on a grey, dingy look. Suddenly, it was no longer the friendly refuge of my childhood, and I shivered.

Down the street, a car door slammed, and I jumped, then shook my head. I needed to think about something, anything else, or I would unravel. I'd unzip my own skin and climb out and never find my way back.

From the car – a van – a woman with too-bouncy hair emerged, adjusting a lavaliere at her cleavage, followed by a man with a handheld camera. I squinted, reading the print on their van: KXLA CHANNEL 7.

Shit. Double shit. Salma Lowe finding another body would be a story. I hoped Watkins would hurry. I angled myself more closely to my bus, keeping my head down.

I almost screeched when someone tapped my arm.

'Excuse me?'

I turned. Not the reporter. Instead, a white woman with dreamy, wide-set eyes and silver-blonde hair – a little younger than my mother – had her hand on my sleeve. She'd crept up on me.

'You almost gave me a heart attack,' I said.

I studied her. She wore a baggy linen sweater, an eco-friendly shopping tote on her arm. She didn't look like a reporter, but you could never be sure. Maybe there was a tape recorder hidden in that bag. It wouldn't be the first time.

'What's happened?' Her eyes darted to the Jacaranda House. EMTs had angled the ambulance to block any potential gawkers from view, but the tape was a giveaway.

I knew that look. A rubbernecker look. A nosy neighbour look. Not a reporter's look. I tamped down a flare of irritation: every day was the worst day of *someone's* life. Those details belonged to this girl's family, not a stranger.

'I'm not sure.' I pointedly pulled out my phone and scrolled, hoping she'd get the memo. I could feel the presence of the reporter pulsing like a sonar at my back.

Where the hell was Watkins? I'd exhausted Instagram and Twitter before it became clear the woman wasn't leaving. I snuck a glance underneath my lashes.

She stared at the caution tape with patient focus. A blue vein pulsed at her temple. There was a dry patch of skin on her cheek, a faint collection of freckles dotting her nose. Her scrubbed-raw prettiness was at odds with the uncanny symmetry of so many Angelenos, who paid to have their faces cut and tucked and pinched and folded, always ready for the prime time.

I couldn't stop looking at her. I wasn't sure why.

She turned and caught my gaze, like she expected me to stare. Like she was used to it. My cheeks flared with embarrassment.

'I think it was a medical emergency,' I said, gentler this time. I wasn't exactly lying.

I'd expected my words to put an end to her curiosity, that she'd drift back to whichever McMansion she called home and stalk the evening news for an update like a normal person. Instead, she drew in three quick gasps, a prelude to hyperventilation, and clutched my arm. The colour drained from her face, and I had a terrible thought: *is she this poor girl's mother?*

'Somebody was hurt at the Jacaranda House?'

I blinked twice, my chest buzzing. I stared down at her whitening knuckles, clutching my arm. The Jacaranda House. That had been *our* private name for it, Tawney and me, our little nickname.

'How did you—'

'Salma? Salma Lowe, is that you?'

Both of us stopped in our strange ballet, her hands

31

wrapped around my forearm, me trying to pry her off. Down the street, the reporter shaded her eyes, squinting. I saw her give one sharp wave to the cameraman, and then her heels were click-clicking on the pavement as she jogged over.

'Fuck,' I said under my breath. 'Lady, let go of me.'

Instead, her fingernails dug into my skin. Her eyes narrowed, her mouth a moue of horror. 'You're Salma? You're Tawney's sister?'

'What the fuck?' I tugged on my arm, feeling a frisson of fear. There was a dead girl not a hundred feet away. An accident, maybe.

Maybe not.

The reporter was almost to us. 'Salma! Salma, my name is Samiyah Jones, I'm a reporter for KXLA, I'd love to speak with you—'

I liked reporters even less than cops. I shoved the woman so hard she stumbled. Across the lawn, Watkins ducked under the caution tape, headed for me. I knew I should wait. I knew I should finish giving my statement.

But the blinding glare of the camera, its red light swaying back and forth as Samiyah and her cameraman panted for my statement, my tears, my trauma – I couldn't take it. Once again, time collapsed on itself, a barrage of bad headlines ticker-taping across my eyes.

Slow down, youngster! Dave Lowe's teenage daughter spotted dancing on table at nightclub.

Sloppy Salma: sources tell us child star is a 'raging alcoholic' who likes coca-not-cola.

Here she goes again: Salma Lowe enters rehab for the second time, cites 'exhaustion.'

Fuck that.

Watkins had my name. She had more than my name; she knew who I was.

I'd get an earful from Dale. I didn't care. I grabbed the bus keys and launched myself into the driver's seat, slamming the door. Not a moment too soon; I could hear the reporter pounding on my window. *Five minutes of your time!* I ignored her and I burnt rubber, headed for the anonymity of the freeway.

But at the end of the street, I checked the rear-view. The silver-blonde stood in the road, staring. *You're Salma? You're Tawney's sister?* I could feel her eyes on me as I pulled away, even as I turned the corner down the street and left it all behind like a bad dream.

CHAPTER FOUR

The Stars Six Feet Under bus picked up a few appreciative honks and stares as I glided in and out of traffic, foot heavy on the accelerator. Northbound on the 405, I thought: *they're telling her family now*. When I made the exit for Hancock Park, I pictured her arriving at the morgue, bagged and tagged, where she'd be swabbed for evidence, soaked in fluids and powders, her body a clue to be solved.

I hadn't realised where I was driving until I exited the freeway, slowing to a crawl in the evening traffic. At a red light, I rested my forehead on the steering wheel, closing my eyes. I took two deep breaths in through my nose and counted the beats of the exhale.

Breathe, Salma. My mother had repeated that as she drove us home from the Jacaranda House, following the ambulance that had taken its time pulling away. By then, we all knew there was no reason to hurry. I kept my eyes screwed closed as my mother took the curves of Mulholland slow, her hand on my knee like without an anchor I might vanish, too.

Behind me, a friendly Angeleno laid on the horn, letting

me know the light had changed, and I gasped, eyes jerking open as I slammed my foot onto the gas, jumping forward.

I was transposing one trauma onto another. Two dead women in the same place, years apart – my brain was rewriting one scene with the other, because that's what brains did, found connections, even in the grimmest of circumstances.

I parked the van alongside a lovingly tended lawn in Hancock Park. In the time since I'd found the poor girl's body – whoever she was – in Tawney's pool, the sun had started to go down and twilight was turning the neighbourhoods' well-tended grass a sleepy shade of blackened green. The houses along the street – mansions, all – settled into a private evening glow. It was a zip code that looked too expensive for death, but I knew better. Every place has its secrets.

I picked my way across the wide limestone slabs of my godfather's driveway, leading up to his pearly two-story French Mediterranean villa. Bougainvillea bushes and gnarled cypresses protected it from view, while also announcing: *Someone famous lives here.* Jack Parlato, once known as 'the Production King' for his string of hits, valued his privacy – but not at the expense of his glory.

I was grateful for the hedges now. I didn't need any suspicious neighbours calling the cops about a drenched woman trying to break into Parlato's palace. The front windows glowed; Jack was home. I kicked my shoes off – my kitten heels rubbed against my still-damp feet, threatening blisters – and hurried up the drive.

At the front door – ten feet tall, a doorbell that would play the drumroll jingle for Twentieth Century Fox, if I tapped it – I knelt to run my fingers across the bricks of Jack's front stoop, searching for the false one to pry up the spare key. My fingers scraped against the grout, stinging, then a corner of a brick wiggled enough for me to lift it an inch or two, slide the key out.

I stood up, dusting my knees off. I slid the key into the lock, holding my breath as I tumbled it slowly, then pushed the door open.

Jack's foyer was dark. On a console, I could see a photograph of my father and Jack from April 1974, arms around each other as they held up twin Academy Award statuettes for *Iron Prayer*, beaming at their golden good fortune. My mother hadn't been there that night – Tawney was born weeks later – the only leg of the trio without a matching trophy. My eyes lingered on my father. The whole world in front of him. I pressed a kiss to a fingertip and smudged it against the glass over his face.

I closed my eyes, swaying lightly. I smelt lemon and garlic, the faint trace of a rich floral, Miles Davis streaming from the living room. Nothing bad could happen here, in Jack's house. As a child, it had been a second home to me. Tawney and I even had our own individual guest bedrooms. I'd stayed with Jack when my parents were away on shoots, or enjoying movie premieres and long drives up the coast to Santa Barbara to bring us back grapey, slurry kisses. Those had been the fun times. It had also been home to me in darker times: the two of them on another trip to Tahiti or the Maldives to *try again*. To *start fresh*. There'd been a lot of that, over the years.

Soon, I'd call Jack's name, tell him everything. But not yet. I wanted one more moment of feeling warm and safe and far from the Jacaranda House first.

From the living room I heard a husky feminine laugh, then the rise and fall of Jack's voice.

My eyes snapped open. I knew that laugh.

I crept to the edge of the foyer, my damp sweater and jeans leaving a trail of droplets behind me. I'd peeled my top off in the car, dried it over the air conditioner as I drove. It hadn't helped much; now I was cold *and* wet.

I peeked around the corner. My mother sat on Jack's carpet, a nearly empty glass of wine in hand. In front of her, a sprawl of photographs. She leant toward Jack, who sat on the couch, hands clasped between knees, then held up another photograph for inspection. This time they both laughed.

What a cosy family scene. Missing only one member.

Jack stood up, collecting my mother's wine glass. He'd have to pass through the foyer to get to the kitchen, I realised, and I backed up – slowly at first, then more quickly, trying to make it to the door before he saw me.

I wasn't ready to see my mother.

My hand was practically on the doorknob when Jack rounded the corner and saw me, stopping short.

'Salma?'

Jack wore an apron stamped with winking green olives over a crisply pleated yellow-and-orange silk shirt. He had an empty glass in each hand, a gentle ring of red wine in the bottom. He was in his mid-seventies, though he could pass for younger: perpetually too tan, a shock of bright white hair, and eyes such a light blue they were practically transparent. I felt an ache, as always, seeing him without my father at his side, bourbon rocks glasses in their hands.

A matched set. 'I used the spare key,' I said. I considered bolting, telling him I'd explain later, then thought better of it. 'What are you wearing?'

'A present,' Jack said automatically. Jack's head was tilted, and I realised he was scanning me: the damp clothes, the stringy hair, bare feet. When he saw me notice, he forced his face into a neutral expression. 'From your mother. Salma, are you all right? What are you doing here?'

A hiccupping sob trapped itself in my throat. Jack took a step toward me, alarmed, and I opened my mouth to tell him everything when I heard my mother call from the living room, 'Jack? Is someone there?'

'Sorry,' I said. 'I didn't mean to interrupt. I'll go.'

Jack shook his head. I knew he realised I hadn't answered his question. 'It's Salma,' he called to my mother, turning back to the living room. I knew he meant for me to follow.

I hesitated, giving the door one last longing stare, before I padded after him down the hallway. I'd never known how to say no to Jack, not since I was a kid faking a sore throat to watch cartoons on his couch while he made soup from scratch and answered my parents' calls from Tahiti with soft assurances that I'd be all right. *Don't worry, she's in good hands.* And then he'd hang up the phone, wink at me, and ask what time the patient required ice cream for her sore, sore throat.

Jack rounded the corner and said brightly, making a show of the good news, 'Look who I found!'

My mother's long legs were drawn up underneath her as she sorted through the contents of a half dozen boxes of photographs in front of her. When she saw me, her eyebrows lifted, and I was a kid again, straining to remember my lines. *Again, Salma. Give it real feeling this time.*

It passed. My mother stood, looping an arm around my shoulders in a soft hug. I breathed in her perfume – tuberose and neroli, the scent I'd caught in Jack's foyer. Jack excused himself to the kitchen, holding up the wineglasses, and then it was just the two of us, sizing each other up. 'What a surprise, darling.'

She stroked my hair once – her creamy white hand not waterlogged or puckered with death – and I tried to laugh but it came out strangled. 'A good one, I hope?'

Vivienne's eyebrows drew together. From my mother, I had inherited thick black hair, a nose most generously described as *patrician*, and a wide mouth that took well to lipstick. It was easy to divide our family up: Tawney and my father with their golden hair, easy smiles, easy charisma. Then my mother and me, pale and dark and *handsome*, not *pretty*.

'Don't be silly,' she said, voice film-noir smoky, silver-streaked hair pulled away from her face. She plucked at my top. 'Why is this wet?'

'Sprinkler malfunction at work,' I lied. I nodded at the photographs, eager to change the subject. 'What's all this?'

Vivienne's face fell at my mention of work – *Darling, isn't a bus tour a bit . . . déclassé?* – but she lit up looking at the photographs. 'The American Film Institute is hosting a retrospective for your father in a few weeks. They've asked me to speak. Jack and I were going through old photos to donate.'

Ah. And they hadn't thought to include me, his only

living daughter. My mother smiled at me, oblivious. I stuffed down the hurt, the anger. It was my fault, really, for all the grief I'd caused her over the years. Salma the addict couldn't be trusted. The trustworthy daughter was dead. 'Excuse me,' I said. 'I should go freshen up.'

I hurried to the bathroom, locking myself inside. I stared at myself in the mirror: round, doughy face. My mascara had bloomed into an uneven smoky eye, my bangs drying in spiky black clumps. Next to the sink basin, an amber bottle caught my eye – perfume. I sniffed delicately at my damp sweater, made a face – an unholy mix of dried sweat and panic and chlorine – then sniffed the perfume bottle.

Tuberose. Neroli. Jack kept a bottle of my mother's perfume in his guest bathroom. I set it gently back on the counter, massaging my forehead. I'd call my mother and Jack later to apologise for the intrusion. But I needed to leave. Now. Whatever comfort I'd thought I'd find here, I'd misjudged.

When I swung the door open, eager to escape, my mother was standing in front of me, holding a box. I flinched, and she caught it, her smile wilting. She thrust the box at me, and I could see it was packed to the brim with old photos. A cardboard peace offering.

'You don't have to do that.'

Vivienne shrugged, played it lightly. 'Jack has fifteen boxes in there. I need help.' Her eyes roamed my face. 'My beautiful girl,' she murmured.

I blushed and shook my head, wise to her tricks but letting them work anyway. For a moment, her approval washed over me, and I forgot I'd held another dead woman in my arms not hours before. Then her eyes landed on my damp sweater, and her expression shifted, just slightly. 'You know, darling,' she said, choosing her words with such pointed delicacy my spine stiffened, 'if you were having your . . . issues again, you could talk to me. I hope you know that.'

Once an addict, always an addict. Even to the people who loved me best. Maybe especially to them.

'I'll keep that in mind,' I said curtly, stepping past her to the front door, slamming it behind me.

CHAPTER FIVE

I wedged the tour bus into my parking spot, jamming it into park and sliding out with the box under my arm. In the not-too-distant dusk, I could hear the whoops and screeches of children playing, the horns of ranchera music. No sirens. No rush.

Whatever had happened in mid-city today, it hadn't reached my home in Glassell Park. I hadn't brought it with me.

My bungalow was one of five nearly identical buildings set on one concrete foundation: clean white stucco, tiled roofs, trimmed in a cheerful teal. When I'd first seen it, I'd liked that the one-bedroom, one-bathroom home was the size of a shoebox. It made me feel like I was playing a role again: *normal girl, not famous, lives paycheck to paycheck.* I'd filled out the application on the kitchen counter, the butter-yellow vintage tiles cool against my hip.

Inside, I downed a glass of water, then another. Then I looked around my kitchen, hoping for a forgotten Xanax hidden in the dark caverns of my drawers. No such luck. Not even cooking sherry. I ransacked my purse, found my last strip of orange gum, and popped it into my mouth.

One thing I'd learnt in rehab: you're never truly clean. You just swap. Alcohol for cocaine, Coca-Cola for alcohol, minty orange gum for a whole cocktail of rich girl vices: vodka, Percocet, Xanax, bad men who remind you too much of Daddy. Sure, aspartame will give you cancer, but it takes a little longer to kill you, and it annoys your family members less. Some choices are better than others. Marginally.

I set the box down on the coffee table and clicked the television on, settling on a grainy noir. When I couldn't sleep as a kid, I'd creep downstairs. Most of the time, my father, an insomniac, was still awake. I'd crawl into his lap, navigating my way around the slosh of his ever-present whiskey, until I was snuggled under his chin. He'd have his eyes glued to some black-and-white classic that we'd watch together: *The Man Who Shot Liberty Valance*. *Sunset Boulevard*. *It Happened One Night*. He'd whisper notes into my ear about the best scenes, teaching me to love his favourites: *Watch John Wayne now, see how long he stays relaxed? The little smile, tells you he's in control? Then . . .* pop. *Kicks him in the face*. My father laughed, took another sip of the whiskey.

I flipped the channel. I'd had enough grief for one day.

I settled on the news. I wanted more information about the girl in Tawney's pool. As I watched, I leafed through the photos my mother had given me. There were my parents in their youth, haunting the set of *Iron Prayer*. Me as a chubby and solemn kindergartner on class picture day. I set aside a photo of my father in short swim trunks at the Beverly Hills Hotel, gnashing his teeth and flexing for the camera, then another of my mother peeking through her long, dark curtain of hair, smiling shyly.

I paused. A more recent photo of my parents book-ending Tawney on the steps of the Jacaranda House, soon after she'd bought it. I'd taken that one. In it, Tawney flipped me the bird.

I set it to the side. That one, I'd keep.

My hands stilled only when I caught sight of a reporter in a cream suit – not the journalist who'd chased me – standing in front of the Jacaranda House, ballet-slipper nails clutching the mic as she ran down prime-time facts: *The body of a young woman found in a swimming pool at this address today . . . If the house behind me looks familiar, it's because it's the site of one of Los Angeles's most notorious unsolved murders: that of the young actress Tawney Lowe, in 1997.*

I wasn't the only one slipping backward in time.

Police have identified the young woman as Ankine Petrosyan, 23, of Tarzana.

Ankine. Her picture flashed on the screen. I paused the live show. A headshot: Ankine against a white pillar, blurred cityscape behind her. She wore a blue halter top and her hair – dark brown, almost black, not the dark gold I'd seen today – blew gently away from her prom-queen-pretty face. Her eyes stared through the camera, like she was trying to pin me into place. *Don't look away.*

I clicked play. The reporter sped into motion: *Investigators tell us they have not yet ruled out foul play.*

I shuddered.

The rest of her report returned to my sister – *Tawney Lowe, also known as the Hurricane Blonde and ex-fiancée of A-list director Cal Turner* – and the picture of Ankine was replaced by Tawney and Cal. In it, my sister wore a skimpy white bikini, straddling Cal's tuxedoed knee, her mouth open in a truly pornographic O.

I recognised it right away. Their engagement photo shoot at Chateau Marmont. I studied the photo, scanning their faces. Tawney in profile – the curve of her cheek, the insouciant glare. Cal, leading-man handsome, even in his brooding pose.

The day Tawney died, he had been interviewed by *Vanity Fair*'s correspondent to the stars, Cherry Partridge, for his latest film. He'd been on a photo shoot all day. It was a solid alibi. A perfect alibi.

I hadn't spoken to Cal in sixteen years, although our paths had crossed on occasion at premieres or awards shows, my attendance dwindling with my career. I'd kept tabs on him, though. He'd been a temperamental director – a temperamental *man* – when Tawney was alive. But since her death, the rumours about him had only gotten more, more extreme: he'd dosed a leading actor with Sudafed to get an unhinged performance out of her, packing her away in an ambulance to have her stomach pumped as soon as he yelled *cut*. (She'd won a Golden Globe for the performance.) Allegedly, he'd tried to film an entire feature with a fully hypnotised cast and crew, producing something so dreamy and surreal that his distributors refused to air the final cut, relegating it to urban legend status in fanboy corners of the internet.

Keeping tabs on him was an old habit. For years – most of my addict years – I'd blamed him for Tawney's death. The first few gorounds in rehab, and in therapy for years after, I'd spent most of my time jonesing for phentermine and vodka and obsessing about Cal. Yes, he had the perfect alibi. Yes, he'd seemed devastated by her death. But who else would want her dead? Who else could've possibly wanted to hurt her?

It had taken years of therapy, and getting clean, to put that behind me. To understand that my suspicions were really a manifestation of my own grief and guilt about Tawney's death. About Cal, and everything that happened after her funeral.

And yet. I wasn't the only one who suspected Cal: every few years, a petition circulated calling for his boycott, his arrest by the LAPD. I knew there were actors and producers who refused to work with him. But still, another awards season, another Cal Turner blockbuster graced the marquee. Another A-list cast, burbling about what an honour it was to work with him. *A genius.*

I couldn't even blame them. I'd seen every one of his movies in theatres.

On TV, the reporter was snagging back screen time from the walk down Lowe family memory lane. *In a true Hollywood twist, Ms Petrosyan's rep confirmed yet another eerie parallel to Lowe's life: Petrosyan had recently been cast in Cal Turner's latest film.*

The control slipped out of my hands, thunked against my shin, pain blossoming up my leg. I didn't move. I barely felt it. Instead, I stared at the television screen, wondering if I'd heard right.

The girl in the pool was connected to Cal. Another dead woman in Cal's orbit.

Foul play has not yet been ruled out. I don't know how long I sat in the living room, thinking no good thoughts, things that didn't lead anywhere but trouble. Thoughts I'd put away with my addiction, or thought I had.

Rosy dawn was streaking the sky, warming my windows, when I finally wandered to bed, doubting the possibility of sleep. Ankine's family was probably awake, too. I hoped she didn't have a sister. I knew what this night would be like for them.

As I turned my face into the pillow, closing heavy eyelids, I pictured Ankine's headshot, her dark hair, the hunger in her eyes. The starlet that would never be.

I knew that hunger. I'd felt it myself. Maybe I still did.

Don't, Salma. Don't look too far back. The past was trouble, and pain, and a version of myself I didn't want to be again.

But as I finally drifted off, I knew one thing was true: the ghosts that haunted me had increased by one.

DECEMBER 1996

The Chateau Marmont had been my mother's idea: the bastion of Old Hollywood glamour the perfect setting to anoint Cal and Tawney as the new Hollywood It Couple.

We found them entwined on poolside chaise longues when we arrived, padding down the steps to the Marmont's pool. Without missing a beat, the *Vanity Fair* photographer snapped my mother, who flashed a smile. Vivienne never took a bad picture, and even if she had, it never would've made it to print. Weeks later, that candid shot would be published in the article – Vivienne radiant and composed, me glowering behind her.

It was eighty degrees, and the sickly green palms and banana fronds that lined the pool were wrapped in white Christmas lights. Tawney's hair was slicked back with gel, and she wore a skimpy white bikini – bridal by way of *Playboy*. Cal glared at the camera in a full tuxedo, a young Brando for the new millennium. Every place they touched – her hip glued to his side, fingers fiddling with his loose tie, cheek against his – crackled with intimate electricity, like we'd opened a bedroom door midflagrante.

Watching them, I felt an ache spread in my chest, a

feeling I didn't have a word for.

Sprawled nearby, leopard-print pumps kicked off, Cherry Partridge barked commands in between sips of champagne. A tape recorder was balanced on her lap, next to a scribble-filled notebook. Her photographer was a lank-haired Swede with dishwater-blond hair and a genius for selling expensive photos of naked women who posed on the trampy side of tasteful. Jack owned a volume or two. The photographer stretched himself into various acrobatic contortions to get the right angle.

The camera loved them. Cal was so handsome people assumed he was a leading man. Tawney, at twenty-two, had graced no fewer than four magazine covers, was on lock for a Dior beauty campaign. The year after she died, *People* magazine would run a story that reported plastic surgeons voted Tawney's nose the most sought-after cosmetic alteration. *Frankly*, one was quoted as saying, *I'm getting tired of all these ski-slope noses.*

Cherry drained her champagne, then waggled the flute in the air. An assistant rushed to refill it. 'Tits forward, darling – that's it! Think, "blushing bride" but also "debauched honeymoon"!'

Next to me, my mother winced.

At Cherry's prompting, Cal pulled Tawney onto his lap, straddling him. Her white bikini hiked up, revealing another inch of long tanned leg. I could count her ribs under her bikini top. 'How about this?' Cal called, deferent only to Cherry.

'You're gorgeous.' Cherry tipped her champagne in salute. 'Don't worry, Tawney, we'll airbrush that cellulite right out.'

Tawney's smile fell. My mother cleared her throat. 'Perhaps a less revealing pose?'

Cherry waved her off. 'Give the people what they want, Vivienne. They're a young couple in love. Sex sells.'

My mother's lips zipped together into a sharp line. She let the photographer take another few snaps, but then Vivienne walked to the wardrobe cart and yanked a filmy caftan from a hanger, draping it over my protesting sister's shoulders. 'This isn't a *Penthouse* spread,' she chided Tawney, who glared.

'It's *our* photo shoot,' Tawney said. She pushed the caftan off her shoulders onto the ground. Cal readjusted her on his lap. 'Not another happy family publicity stunt.'

I crept around the other side of the pool, watching my mother eye the discarded caftan like Tawney had soiled it. 'I'm a little old-fashioned. You looked . . .' She let the pause hang in the air, so we could fill in the blanks. 'Cheap.' Vivienne supplicated to Cherry, 'You understand, don't you? A mother's worries?'

Even at fifteen, I got it: she could afford to piss off Tawney, but not Cherry. *Keep your enemies close and the tabloids even closer.*

Cherry's lips were pursed, her eyes narrowed. She and Vivienne studied each other; Cherry annoyed and trying not to show it, my mother collected but angry. Then Cherry tittered. 'Of course, V.' My mother winced. 'Let's move on to our interview, shall we?'

Cherry clapped her hands, and the assistant reappeared with champagne flutes for everyone, even me. Tawney scowled at me and I could read her expression: *Why didn't you stop her?* With Cherry's back turned, Cal slid me a wink. I smiled.

'Anything to say on the record about the engagement?' Cherry had her tape recorder ready, practically under my mother's nose.

'Oh, we're thrilled,' Vivienne said, smiling at Cal. 'Cal feels like family already.' My mother tickled my hair. 'Doesn't he, Salma?'

'You could ask *me* if I'm happy about it,' Tawney snapped, glaring at Cherry.

My mother tugged at Tawney's hand, displaying her enormous halo diamond engagement ring as proof. 'She's happy.'

Cherry flashed her teeth, pearly white against her hot pink lipstick – a smile, or a snarl. 'How rare, to see such a gorgeous couple so genuinely in love,' she gushed, and my sister glanced at Cal, her smile a sunburst. 'Especially when your courtship was plagued with such . . . indelicate rumours.'

Cal's hand in Tawney's hair stilled, trapped in the golden strands.

Tawney smiled. 'Rumours keep the tabloids in business.' She flashed Cherry a pointed look. 'Libel's still illegal in this country. As you know.'

I held my breath, watching Cherry's face. The year before, Cherry – and by extension, *Vanity Fair* – had been sued over a breaking story of an underground Hollywood honeypot brothel targeting rich producers. Cherry had named names, claiming she had sources on the record; the sources claimed otherwise. The courts narrowly ruled in Cherry's favour.

They might not be so kind next time.

Cherry took another leisurely sip of champagne, bobbed her head to one side, acknowledged the hit. 'What's that expression about photos and a thousand words? You *did* look rather cosy with that co-star of yours.'

This time, the tension over the Marmont was like a thundercloud ready to burst.

Tawney and Cal had never been camera-shy about their volatile relationship. Their public fights were chum in the paparazzi waters. A particularly bad lung-buster landed a pap a six-figure shot of red-faced Cal outside the Viper Room as my sister wailed behind him. The paycheck probably made up for the black eye Cal left him, connecting less than two seconds after the shutter clicked.

And then, a month ago, the *National Enquirer* published The Photos. My sister's hand on Eric Wainwright's knee, the two of them twining into each other over sushi. A long hug goodbye in front of her distinctive white Porsche, my sister's eyes closed against Eric's shoulder. When they broke, Tawney called me, crying, complaining the paparazzi wanted to pick a fight between her and Cal for the story. And I believed her, even though my first queasy thought was: *I've only seen you look at Cal like that.*

On the chaise, Cal's face darkened. He yanked his hand out of Tawney's hair, blonde strands still threaded in his knuckles. Tawney flinched, biting her lip hard.

Click, click, click.

The Swedish photographer looked down at his camera, satisfied, nodded. I wasn't the only one who'd caught Cal's anger, Tawney's pain.

Cal shoved my sister off his lap. 'You can't use that.' He appealed to Cherry, 'Tell him he can't use that.'

Cherry's photographer smirked, made a show of bringing the camera to his face again. Cal knocked my sister off the chaise when he lunged. I darted to Tawney's side, helped pull her up. In the fall, she'd scraped her knee on the pavement, dots of blood welling, and she winced, holding it, as the cameraman danced backward, nearly slipping into the pool as Cal chased him, sputtering expletives.

'Georg.' Cherry clapped her hands twice, *Bad dog, bad*. Both he and Cal stopped in their tracks, Cal's chest heaving with anger. Cherry didn't say anything else. She didn't have to. Georg huffed, dropped the lens, popped open the lid, and pulled out a thin strip of film, then made a show of showing Cal the absence. Tawney sank onto the chaise, a thin line of blood snaking down her leg. Cal stalked back to the chaise and plopped himself into it. Tawney set her hand on Cal's knee. He flinched it off.

In the stunned silence, Tawney cleared her throat. 'Eric's a dear friend, that's all. Besides, I'm a happily committed woman.' This time, she took a cue from our mother and waggled the sparkling diamond under Cherry's nose.

'Happily . . . committed . . . woman . . .' Cherry repeated, scribbling in her notebook, then underlined it so hard it nearly ripped the paper. When she looked up, she was smiling. 'It's so lovely to hear that, especially given your parents' own fairy-tale marriage. I hope your union is blessed with such happiness.'

Tawney's smile slipped, just for a microsecond.

Cherry lobbed a few more softball questions before clapping her knees. *What wonderful footage to work with, thank you, darlings!* Blowing kisses into the air like confetti as she told us goodbye, her assistants packing up behind her.

As she climbed the stairs up to the Marmont, Tawney called after her – unable to stop herself from snagging the final word – 'Cherry, if you ever want someone to help you cover those greys, I know an excellent colorist. You deserve better than a box.'

My mother clamped her hand onto my sister's arm, shushing. I watched Cherry pause, a hand drifting to her hair before she walked away as though she hadn't heard.

I knew she had.

When the cover went to press, Tawney's bikini-clad ass took up more than a quarter of the shot, her long brown legs hugging Cal's hips, while he reclined on his hands, a haughty look on his face. It fed the daytime talk show circuit for weeks. *I wouldn't want my daughter looking up to Tawney Lowe as some kind of role model . . .*

Nowhere did Cherry mention Cal's outburst, my sister's bloody knee. *The conversation turned tense when I brought up the photographs of Lowe and co-star Eric Wainwright*, Cherry wrote. *'I'm a happily committed woman,' Lowe snapped at me. Doth the lady protest too much? One wonders. If Cal Turner is America's next great auteur-in-the-making, Lowe is a busty flash in the pan. Art and commerce make for an uneasy marriage: just ask Polanski and poor Sharon Tate.*

A year later, my sister barely in the ground, Cherry

would publish *The Hurricane Blonde: A Definitive Look at the Unsolved Murder of Tawney Lowe, America's Most Famous Starlet*. The book was translated into thirteen languages, an instant bestseller.

In the end, Cherry *had* gotten the final word.

CHAPTER SIX

T he next day, I returned the bus to Stars Six Feet
Under, intending to resume my tour. But Dale had
other plans, insisting I take some time off. I agreed to
three days, no more. Bad things happened if I stayed
alone with my thoughts too long.

I had time to kill and nowhere to bury the body, along
with a whole bunch of thoughts I was trying not to think.
Like how Ankine had ended up in my sister's pool. Or
how she'd been cast in Cal's film. Or how good the cool,
syrupy oblivion of a vodka soda would feel.

I spent the first day sorting the photographs from my
mother, plucking out my favourites. I wanted to show not
Dave Lowe, movie star, but Dave Lowe, dad. I snagged
a shot of him nursing a gimlet at Musso & Frank's, the
legendary Hollywood watering hole. The story went, a
producer discovered him there after my father picked a
fight with the bartender over the proper way to make the
cocktail (equal parts Rose's lime cordial and gin).

Another: my father and Tawney asleep on a couch, her
cheeks rosy with fever, golden curls tucked under his chin.
One more: Tawney's legs dangling in the blue pool at the

Jacaranda House, smiling into the camera.

The sight of the Jacaranda House reminded me of the older woman with the silver-blonde hair. Everything about her made me uneasy: the way she'd tugged on my arm, the intensity with which she'd gazed at Tawney's house, her use of the nickname.

You're Salma? You're Tawney's sister?

A Tawney groupie, maybe. Every few years, there was a new podcast, a new Investigation Discovery episode, a new psychic with a clue to crack the case. It always dragged the Tawney groupies out of the woodwork, mostly women but a few men. Some dressed up in Tawney drag – foam boobs, freakishly overinflated pout – and held gatherings at her grave, her home, her Hollywood star.

I told myself it was a privilege that so many people still mourned my sister.

It was less fraught to focus on Ankine. After the news that she'd been cast in Cal's film, I scoured the internet, searching for hints about the project, her part in it. A *Deadline* announcement for the film reported Cal had paid one million dollars for the rights to his *most ambitious and virtuosic work yet*. But that was all. Cal kept his actors locked under non-disclosure agreements so tight it'd be easier to tunnel out of Guantánamo Bay than talk to the press without getting sued.

I clicked on a recent interview for his last film, *Hardboiled. What sets a Cal Turner film apart?* the interviewer asked. I rolled my eyes. *Every experience is real*, Cal said. *I don't hire actors. I hire those souls brave enough to traverse the dark heart of human experience. My films change lives.*

His ego hadn't gotten smaller.

I tried Ankine's social media. On Instagram, she boasted a modest four thousand followers – not yet a star. I scrolled through her photos, pausing to watch her frolic in the Malibu waves, shots of the Hollywood sign. Nothing from the set – but then, I hadn't expected there to be. A few posts celebrating commercial or walk-on-extra spots. No features. Nothing in her background to explain why Cal cast her.

Five years deep, I found a photo of Ankine as a high school Juliet, beaming in scratchy cheap satin. She cradled a bouquet of white roses, wearing a goofy, unpractised grin that scrunched her eyes and showed her back molars. A boy, maybe ten, stood beside her, not smiling, but his eyes looked proud – or perhaps awed.

A little brother. Ankine had at least one sibling.

My phone buzzed. Jack. I declined it. I still wasn't ready to tell him about Ankine.

I tapped on Ankine's followers, searching for a clue about her connection to Cal. I scanned usernames, looking for anything familiar. I'd made it to the *H*'s when my phone buzzed again. Jack again. This time, he'd simply texted me a link, then *???* I clicked the link, then immediately regretted it.

In the KXLA news report from the Jacaranda House, Samiyah, the reporter who'd chased me, wore a lilac trench and white pumps. A chyron ran across the bottom:

MORE HOLLYWOOD CONNECTIONS IN POOL DEATH.

The broadcast switched to an amateur-quality photo. In it, a dark-haired woman, bangs plastered to her forehead, sat on her knees, Ankine's body half draped over her. She looked almost puzzled to see a camera, and her hand was curled protectively over Ankine's shoulders. A slight, sick smile on her face.

'Oh,' I said, one hand lifting to my mouth, shielding it too late. Baseball Cap and his stupid camera. I'd been so worried about paparazzi showing up, and I'd never considered him. He'd sold it to an outlet, maybe, or posted it to Instagram with a searchable hashtag (#murderbus #reallivedeadgirl #TawneyLowe).

I stopped the video. I knew I should call Jack. He'd be worried. I owed him a thank you for the heads-up, at the very least. But I couldn't bring myself to do it. I didn't know what to say. And even though it was different – *I* was different – I felt the same sick curl of shame in my stomach seeing the photo as I had when I'd called him for a ride home from the clubs as a girl, too loaded to drive.

Instead, I dialled Stars Six Feet Under. I told Dale I'd see him in the morning. I hung up before I could hear his protests.

Stars Six Feet Under was located on a low-rent block of Hollywood Boulevard, far enough off the strip that tourists didn't find us unless they were trying. Years before I'd joined the outfit, the stucco had been painted black, but the sun had faded it to a mealy grey. Los Angeles was a city that refused to commit to darkness. A curlicued neon green sign blinked STARS SIX FEET UNDER over a white hearse popping a wheelie.

Subtlety wasn't part of our charm.

The parking lot was already full an hour before my first tour. I threw the door open, wincing as the first few bars of Chopin's 'Marche Funèbre' pinged around the gift shop.

An older couple perused the Black Dahlia paperbacks (*My uncle's deathbed confessions!*) while a group of teenagers tittered over our collection of key chains, each with a different tiny snapshot of real crime photos. A slack-jawed woman had parked herself in front of the wallpaper, a garish pink-and-Marilyn print, all windblown skirts and cherry lips. Gold plastic stars had been hammered over the Marilyn wallpaper: Sharon Tate. James Dean. Natalie Wood. Tawney, of course.

At the back of the gift shop, there were two doors: one to Dale's office and one to Dale's pride and joy, a museum full of personal, morbid, *stars, they're just like us especially when dead* artifacts sourced from eBay, shady estate sales, and other avenues I didn't care to know.

The office door was closed. I didn't want to hear Dale's arguments about why I should take more time off. But I needed my keys. I knocked, steeling myself.

'It's open.'

I pushed the door. 'Full crowd today,' I said instead of hello. 'Who died?'

Even seated behind a desk, Dale was roughly the size and shape of a refrigerator. Hands like volleyballs. His mouth dropped open in surprise, then twisted into a frown. A half-remembered word of advice from my counsellor at Betty Ford: *You'll alienate people if you continue to process your grief as humour, Salma.*

'Sorry,' I said, putting my hands up, a bravado I didn't feel. 'Bad joke. How many today?'

Dale hesitated. I wondered if he would tell me to leave. But I was fine. Salma the addict wasn't reliable. Sloppy Salma couldn't have handled it. But me, I was strong. Unflappable. It was one of the differences between us now.

Dale must've seen the determination on my face. 'Twenty-five. Phone's ringing off the hook.'

I forced a smile, trying to ignore the queasy feeling in my stomach. It was what I'd wanted. But when I closed my eyes, I could picture Ankine, drifting in the pool like a slow-moving angel, her eyes open and unseeing.

Dale tossed me the keys, and I gave him a too-heartfelt thank you, then headed out to prep the bus. Without fail, my tourists left behind mountains of trash, crumpled handouts noting our stops, empty water bottles, purse

61

detritus. I could make order out of chaos in the bus.

I released the hydraulics and the doors swept open. I took a deep breath in, relishing the waft of stale sweat, feet, and cherry air freshener. *Ah, home.*

My mother thought the bus tour was purely to annoy her. My father, when he was alive, thought I was afraid of more failure as an actor. Jack thought it was penance for my sister's death, a way to keep her memory alive.

But the simple, pragmatic truth was Dale had been my sponsor in Alcoholics Anonymous. I needed a job out of rehab, both for money and as a condition of my plea deal after the second DUI. Back then, the job had been a solution to a problem.

I hadn't realised how much it would eventually feel like *mine*.

I spent twenty minutes brushing away crumbs and climbing under seats, retrieving gum wrappers, a pair of sunglasses for the lost and found. When I heard footsteps on the stairs, the clatter of the door opening and closing, I assumed it was Dale. I straightened with a smile, brushing my sweaty bangs off my face, a quick retort on my lips – *this place falls apart without me* – before I realised it wasn't Dale.

A man was bent over my steering wheel, examining the seat. I couldn't see his face – just a loose grey T-shirt, artistically threadbare jeans. We'd gained some mainstream fans with the discovery of Ankine's body, I could see.

'Tour doesn't start for another twenty minutes,' I called.

He looked up. He had his phone in his hand, and he

was clicking away before I realised who he was. Baseball Cap – the shutterbug from my tour. Back for seconds.

Not to be *that person*, but in my day, paparazzi, fiends though they were, didn't have the added incentive of social media. A pap had to be at least a decent photographer, had to sit and stake out an area, build relationships with the bar owners and valets who could tip them off to a celeb arrival. They had to *work* a little. Nowadays, any old nobody with a smartphone can make a few bucks by being in the right place at the right time.

I held a hand over my face. 'You're on private property,' I told him. 'If you don't leave right now, I'll have security escort you out. I mean it.'

But we were alone on the bus. No one to help. No one even knew he was here. I took a few steps forward, hiding my face, but he was between me and the exit, the narrow bus aisles making escape impossible.

When I first started at Stars Six Feet Under, Dale chased off the occasional pap. They'd been drawn by the obvious headline: *Salma sunk so Lowe!* As a kid, I hadn't known how to handle the attention – if I reacted, they'd hang around like flies, taking pictures until I could escape into a car, duck into a store. If I didn't, they'd take it as *carte blanche* to taunt me, trying to get their shot. I couldn't win.

But that was years ago. I was a different person now.

Baseball Cap's finger slid, switching to video. *Uh-oh.* 'Salma, do you have anything to say to Ankine Petrosyan's family?'

The democratisation of celebrity footage in the years since I'd been a news story meant a big payday required more than a few candid shots. It required a meltdown. I wouldn't do it.

'Move,' I said, one hand up now in front of his camera, close but not touching. I thought about calling for Dale, knew he couldn't hear me anyway.

'What was she doing at your sister's house? What's the connection between her and Tawney? Tell us, Salma.'

I gritted my teeth. I couldn't stand having my photo in the news again. But what I *really* couldn't stand was that I was the story again, not Ankine. The last thing her investigation needed was a washed-up distraction. 'Get a hobby,' I told him. 'Get a life.'

I tried to clamber over the seat to the door, but Baseball Cap moved fast, cutting me off. He switched back to photos and the *click, click, click* of his camera made the space between my shoulder blades twitch. It reminded me of bad nights outside of clubs, stumbling home, knowing that my shame would be front-page news the next day, the worst hangover. The whole world would know what I'd been up to. How I'd fucked up, again.

'Stop,' I said, my voice louder. I was no more than ten feet from the door, but it might as well have been a mile – Baseball Cap had wedged himself across the stairs, trapping me. I couldn't go around him. Only through him. I feinted one way, and he shuffled, blocking me. My breath ragged, my lungs tight.

Click, click, click.

Ankine dead. Tawney dead – eaten by the paparazzi when she was alive. No escape, no privacy. Then after she'd died, the coroner – Coroner to the Stars – had sold her autopsy photos. Four magazines ran them before my family's lawsuit. Which had been worth more: the engagement photos with Cal, or the pictures of her on a slab, little black stitches unzipping her body?

Click, click, click.

My temper building, building, bigger than me now, bigger than all the years of rehab and therapy and counseling. *'Stop that!'*

'Ooooh, "stop that,"' he said, a singsong playground taunt. 'Or you'll what?'

I reached out with both hands, trying to push my way free. That was all I wanted. It was an accident when he tumbled down the stairs, skull crashing against the door, which held – held – *opened*, then he was sprawled across the pavement, phone clattering to the ground.

Somehow – like someone else was doing it – I watched my leg pull back, kick him, once, twice. Baseball Cap yelped, gripping his ankle. I stepped around him and picked up the phone.

'Be careful with that!'

But I was done listening to shitty men who didn't hear me, who took what they wanted without giving anything back. Men like Baseball Cap, or Cal fucking Turner.

My skin buzzed as I hot potato'd the phone from one hand to the other. The volume turned up on his face, outrage climbing to true rage – *What the fuck do you think you're doing, you crazy bitch* – then I let it fly. Glass rained down onto the concrete where the phone smashed into the black stucco.

The door to the gift shop flew open so hard I heard a crack, Chopin on its heels.

'Salma, what the hell are you doing?' Dale looked

between the two of us, confusion on his face.

Baseball Cap started screeching – *Assault! What she did to me was assault! I'm going to sue your asses so fast . . .*

My heart sank. I knew how it looked. Dale hadn't heard the things he'd said, seen the way he trapped me in the bus. No. All he saw was me smashing some guy's phone to bits, no control, no calm.

All he saw was Sloppy Salma.

That bitch refused to die.

CHAPTER SEVEN

It had been more than five minutes. Dale still hadn't said anything. I made eye contact with the signed Angela Lansbury headshot behind his desk. Even Angela's smile seemed a little pained. Are we proud of our actions?

No, Angela. I couldn't say I was.

Dale had talked Baseball Cap down from pressing charges. A minor miracle. Baseball Cap kept squawking about his ankle, his First Amendment rights as an *American*, goddamn it. Dale let him wear himself out, then reminded him California was a two-party consent state for recording private conversations. Police weren't in anybody's best interests.

It helped that Dale was six foot nine, bodybuilder big, the kind of man you'd expect to see at an Ironman competition, not a seedy Hollywood strip mall.

After Baseball Cap limped away, still unhappy, Dale and I filed back into his office for the second time that day. Like I'd been called to the principal's office.

'This is all my fault,' he said finally, python arms crossed over his chest.

'I'm pretty sure I'm the one who broke his shitty phone.'

Dale sighed, scrubbed a hand down his face. 'I knew you weren't ready to come back.'

I felt a pang of irritation. 'You're not my keeper, Dale.'

Even when he was angry – and I'd never really seen him angry, although I'd heard his AA stories, knew it lived inside him – Dale's voice never got much above a whisper. Now it was silky, sorrowful. 'I should never have let you hang around.'

Hang around. Like a fruit fly buzzing over rotting apples.

I knew what Dale was going to say before he said it.

'I think you should take a little break. Just to clear your head.'

No. I didn't want that. Without the tour, I'd have too much time to obsess about Ankine and Cal and my sister. That would be bad. Very bad. I gripped his desk. 'If that's what you want, you'll have to fire me.'

Dale's eyes dropped to my knuckles, white with strain against his Ikea desk. 'Salma, when was the last time you went to a meeting?'

Oh God. I forced myself to let go. 'I haven't used in a decade,' I said, my teeth clenched. Which was true. I wasn't one of those addicts who felt the need to count the days, the hours, since their last fix. I'd been a kid with a murdered sister, and easy access to anything I wanted. Anybody would develop a problem under those conditions. 'You know I'm okay.'

'I know,' Dale said quickly. Too quickly. 'But your anger—'

I scoffed. 'It's been a stressful couple of days. Cut me some slack.'

'That's my point.' The track lighting overhead gleamed off his bald head as he nodded. 'You need some *time*, you need to process.'

I searched for my best self, couldn't find her. That cowardly bitch had fled the building. 'That's some paternalistic bullshit.'

Dale's face dropped. 'I'm trying to help.'

'Yeah, well,' I said, standing up, feeling fifteen again, 'don't.' I wasn't being fair, or kind, and I knew it. Tears seared my eyes, but I turned away so Dale wouldn't see them.

Behind me, he called, 'If you ever need to talk to someone – if you think this is going to compromise your sobriety—'

I slammed the door before he could finish.

Outside, the pale gold sunshine had the audacity to be bright and friendly – like I hadn't just assaulted a man. Cars whooshed past me on Sunset Boulevard as I remembered the feel of him under my hands, the swift bubble of surprise I'd felt as his skull connected with the bus doors. Not just surprise – I was *glad* to see him hurt. I hadn't meant to hurt him, but I'd been glad when I did.

That wasn't me. That lack of control – it wasn't me. Not any more.

I ducked my head into my purse, half-looking for my keys, half-trying to keep my eyes from overflowing. Goddamn wannabe paparazzo. Goddamn Cal Turner and his films, and goddamn Dale for thinking he knew what was best for me, goddamn Vivienne and Jack for leaving me out of my own *family*, and goddamn Tawney for leaving me alone, all alone . . .

'Salma?'

I looked up. Melany leant against my car, holding a plate of cookies. Her smile could've powered a small country, it was so electric.

It fell when she saw my face. 'What's wrong?'

I sniffled. 'Nothing. Paparazzi runin. You know.'

Her mouth quirked up. 'I don't, actually. Lucky you.' Melany looked down at the cookies. 'I'm sorry to bother you at work, but I really had to thank you in person. I promise I'll do right by the role—'

I shook my head. I'd missed something. 'What are you—'

'The Cal Turner film!' I winced – it was just short of a shriek – as Melany bounced on her toes so hard the cookies jumped. 'I'm his new leading lady! My agent called, like, two hours ago, and I knew, when I heard, I *knew* I had to come thank you. So! Thank you!' She thrust the cookies at me, and I took them, dazed, staring at their craggy chocolate chip peaks.

Cal's film. Right. Before I'd found Ankine, before everything, she'd asked me for a favour. Not that I'd mentioned it to my mother. 'Congrats,' I said, forcing a smile I didn't feel. 'Wow, his leading lady. That's . . . something.'

'It *is*,' Melany said, blue eyes shining. 'This is it, Salma. This is my big break.' She bit her lip. 'This is all because of you. I'll never forget it as long as I live.'

I would've made sure Cal never even knew her name, if I could've. 'Oh, I'm sure you earned it.'

'Well, given what the film's about, your endorsement mattered, like, a lot. The most, probably.'

Time slowed down. *What the film's about.* What was the film about? That my endorsement would matter most? I cocked my head, and Melany's smile drooped at my obvious ignorance. She stared at the cookies, like she wanted to take them back. 'I thought you knew.'

'Melany. Tell me.'

'Cal's adapting that book, the one by that old reporter, what's-her-name, with the cleavage and the *hair*—'

Oh my God. Cherry. She meant Cherry. I took two steps back, my hip bumping against my car. Bile rose in my throat, and I wondered if I was about to be sick. 'He's adapting *The Hurricane Blonde.*'

When I looked up, Melany was beaming. 'That's right! And that's me. I'm the Hurricane Blonde – well, that's what Cal calls her in the script anyway. But that makes us family, doesn't it? I'm your sister for the next two months or so.' Then her face dropped. 'Salma? Are you crying? Oh no, you dropped the cookies . . .'

I was bent over, hands-to-knees hysterical, great guffawing wheezes exploding through my chest. I tried to catch my breath, tried to explain I wasn't crying, I was laughing, although God knew why, God knew what was so fucking funny. I looked up, leaning against the scorching metal of my car, and then I saw it. Breaking through the clouds behind Melany, ghostly white and tacky in thirty-foot-tall plywood, the hungry spirit keeping watch: HOLLYWOOD. The most ravenous bitch who ever lived.

* * *

Detective Mykella Watkins wasn't particularly excited to see me.

Across the desk, Watkins's face was neutral. Her hair was tucked behind one ear and three or four small silver hoops stamped their way up her earlobe. Finally, hands folded demurely on her desk, eyes wide and polite, she said: 'Is that it?'

I'd driven straight to the precinct from Stars Six Feet Under, peeling out so fast I'd left Melany with a mouthful of dust. My laughter had freaked her out – fair enough – and I couldn't even begin to explain.

Watkins had been busy when I arrived. I said I'd wait. I'd already waited too long to tell her what I knew about Cal Turner. All the paths that pointed back to him. When she'd called my name, leading me through rows of desks, ringing phones – the police station surprisingly beige and corporate, like a regional office of justice – I'd been so sure she would believe me.

And yet. *Is that it?*

My mouth was dry. On the way back to her office, she'd grabbed us both lukewarm coffees in Styrofoam cups, little packets of powdered cream and sugar. I took a sip. It tasted like mud.

'Did you figure out why she was in the pool in the first place?'

Watkins' face was closed. 'I can't give out information in an ongoing investigation.'

Another detail had been bothering me since I'd found Ankine: the punch code to the gate of the Jacaranda House had stayed the same all these years. 'Who owns the Jacar—the house now?'

Watkins shook her head. 'They prefer to remain private. Is there anything else, Ms Lowe?' she said, putting one hand on the desk and pushing herself upright. Our interview was over.

But we couldn't be done. There was still so much I needed to know about what had happened to Ankine. About her connection to Cal. I blurted out: 'So you're looking into Cal Turner as a suspect, right? Because you should be. You definitely should be. He's already hired a replacement. Isn't that strange?'

Watkins lifted one brow. 'Being insensitive isn't a crime.'

My mouth was running away with me now. 'He was my sister's fiancé. He was a suspect in her murder, too. And he cast Ankine in his film.'

Watkins lowered herself back into the seat slowly, and I felt her watching me, giving away nothing. 'You have a personal beef with Turner.'

I swallowed. 'He's connected to two dead women. I think that's worth looking into.'

'So are you,' Watkins pointed out.

'It's *different*.'

Watkins's face was impassive. She pulled out her notebook, flipped back a couple of pages. 'Do you remember the events of the night of 3rd April, 2001?'

Pulsating jellyfish tentacles under a black light. Gliding high on a wave of champagne and vodka and pills, the bass so heavy it shook the club's walls. Then, later, the red and blue glow of the police car, the feel of Cal's grass in my fists. *Murderer, murderer, murderer.*

My face was hot. I was grateful I couldn't remember

73

much more. 'How is that relevant?'

Watkins flipped forward a page, began reading official documentation from the restraining order Cal had filed against me: '"Victim accuses suspect of stalking him, lying in wait outside his home, and harassing him. He says this has occurred multiple nights in a row. Victim claims the suspect is obsessed with him and harassment is starting to interfere with his life."'

'Stop,' I said. 'Yes, I remember.'

'Personal,' Watkins repeated, flipping her notebook closed.

I'd been a sad, lonely kid, drunk and high and trying to navigate an ocean of grief, I wanted to tell her. I wanted to explain. But the words wouldn't unstick themselves from my throat. She'd already decided what the story was.

Watkins took pity on me. 'I shouldn't tell you this,' she said finally. 'But we've had the latest ruling from the coroner. Petrosyan's death was accidental. Accidental drowning, aided by severe asthma. No foul play involved.'

For a moment, I couldn't take in what she was telling me. I watched her foot jiggle under the desk. An accident.

'But that doesn't make sense,' I said. 'What was she even doing in the pool in the first place?'

Watkins shook her head, *No, no, no.* 'It's the coroner's call. Case closed.' She paused, thought about what she was going to say next. LAPD sensitivity training at its finest. 'I can imagine,' she said slowly, 'that what happened the other day must've been hard. Brought up a lot of bad memories. Please trust me when I say you have my deepest condolences on your loss. But if you really want to help, stop meddling. Don't bother Mr Turner, or the Petrosyan family. You're only going to keep wounds from healing. And if you don't stop prying' – here Watkins paused, those almond-shaped eyes flicking up to me – 'we'll be having a very different conversation next time. Okay?'

Oh, I understood. Watkins didn't believe me. As far as she and the LAPD were concerned, it was perfectly normal for an adult woman to drown in a stranger's pool in the middle of the day.

No one believed me. No one had believed me about Cal all those years ago, either.

My legs felt leaden as I forced myself to stand. Watkins guided me to the door, and as we walked, I tried to avoid looking at the people giving statements to cubicle cops, their tearstained faces, their helpless or resigned or apathetic stares. Statistically, many of them were likely to be here for drugs, even if they weren't users themselves. Evidently, none of them had famous parents who could ask the cops to turn the other cheek – *Thanks, Officer, take a headshot with you for the missus* – escort you home instead of giving you a night in jail, write you a warning instead of a ticket.

Even the night of Cal's restraining order, no one put me in cuffs. Once the officers knew who I was, they'd driven me back to the Hollywood Hills. Maybe they'd received an enormous gift basket for the holidays: *Dave Lowe appreciates all you do!*

At the front, Watkins practically shooed me out of the station.

I stopped as she awkwardly leant out, hand splayed

over the push-lever. 'You don't really believe it was an accident, do you?'

Watkins rolled her eyes. 'It's not my call,' she said. 'Goodbye, Salma. Stay out of trouble.'

I wasn't sure that was possible any more.

3RD APRIL, 2001

We started at Las Palmas, where the neon palm trees lit the bar's darkest corners in Technicolor sweeps. Lines of coke in the booth, not bothering to hide in the bathroom. Dave Lowe's daughter wasn't afraid. Belvedere straight: bottle service, not cocktails. Transfixed by an aquarium of bright, stinging jellyfish undulating behind the bar. They'd been lit with a black light, electric turquoise and yellow-green and poisonous orange that burnt my eyes.

It was three years, nine months, and eighteen days since Tawney died.

A breath of fresh air late into the night. I stepped out for a cigarette and made two phone calls. One: to Cal. He didn't pick up. We hadn't spoken since the day after my sister's funeral. I don't know if I left a message. The second: to John MacLeish, the homicide detective working my sister's case. 'It's my birthday tomorrow,' I slurred into his voicemail (not true). 'Can't you arrest him? Pretty, pretty please?'

We piled into a car, headed to the Opium Den, my friends and I, back when I had friends still, or at least people who enjoyed my fame, the good drugs and good clubs that came with it. More coke off the streaky mirror I kept in my leather jacket.

The doorman at the Opium Den waved us through without asking for ID. *Dave Lowe's daughter goes where she wants.* One whirl around the bathrooms there, but we didn't stay too long because the leggy models and the want-to-be-seens crowded every square foot, made me walk elbows out just to carve a path.

Dave Lowe's daughter did not fight for a bartender's attention.

I left the bar again to call Cal. 'Pick up,' I screamed into his voicemail. 'You fucking coward.'

After the Opium Den, the black car dropped me back at my mother's Mercedes – she and my father were on location for another project together, trying to recapture the glory of *Iron Prayer*, and the years of their marriage that weren't tainted by murder and too many secrets.

Then I was driving down Sunset, my veins hot and pulsing with a mission, foot a lead brick on the gas, the darkened palm trees pinwheeling above me, encouraging me west, west, to Santa Monica.

It wasn't the first time I'd parked outside Cal's home in the dark, sleepless hours after a club closed. But because I was Dave Lowe's daughter, the judge would go easy on me, a *first-time offender*.

I nibbled my thumb as I watched the light in his bedroom upstairs wink on. I sat forward, crunched over the steering wheel, and wondered if he knew I was close. If he could sense me. It seemed impossible he didn't think of me as often as I thought of him. Before I'd decided to do it, I was out of my car and on his doorstep, knocking. Gently, at first.

Cal's neighbour was the one who called the police. A drunk young woman, out of control, was on her nice neighbour's lawn, the one who was a famous director, and she was screaming awful, *awful* things. *KILLER. MURDERER. I KNOW WHAT YOU DID. FUCKING TALK TO ME. JUST COME TALK TO ME.*

When the police arrived, Cal was on his doorstep, holding a baseball bat, a young, *young* woman in a T-shirt and a thong behind him. I was in his yard, crumpled on the grass, sobbing, still screaming.

'Call Detective MacLeish,' I kept saying over and over as the police officers marched me to the squad car. 'He can explain. He'll tell you.'

Later, at my parents' house, MacLeish *would* be there, blowing into a steaming coffee cup as he eyed me, trying to decide if I was too high to talk. But first I was loaded into the back of the police car, the officers delicate with Dave Lowe's daughter. The blue and red lights dancing over my face as I begged them not to call my mother, *please, just don't call my mother.*

Cal filed a restraining order, then retracted it one day later – on the condition I receive immediate substance abuse treatment. Everyone, including my mother, told me how lucky I was, how much worse all of this could have been. And what you say to that, as a nineteen-year-old addict, is nothing. Jail would have been worse. Hurting Cal, or the girl he was with, would have been worse.

When I went into rehab, Tawney had been dead for three years, nine months, and twenty-two days.

CHAPTER EIGHT

I spent hours that night and the next day researching Cal's film, then, when I couldn't find much, Cherry Partridge. She'd come down in the world a few pegs: she was no longer writing for *Vanity Fair*, hadn't had a steady gig at any reputable publication in years. I wondered if that libel lawsuit had finally caught up with her. Her blog, *Poppin' with Cherry*, counted dozens of followers. It wasn't paying the bills.

Cal was, apparently. A million dollars for her dreadful book.

I closed the computer, rubbed my eyes. As a teenager, I'd believed Cal had been responsible for, *guilty* of, my sister's death. Even though he had an unimpeachable alibi: a filmed interview with Cherry, discussing his newest film as well as his breakup. But didn't I know what he was capable of? In rehab, my counsellors told me I was redirecting my survivor's guilt and my shame about what happened between us. Eventually I believed them. I'd already made so many wrong decisions.

But what if I'd been right all along? Cal *was* dangerous. Maybe he hadn't killed Tawney – *maybe* – but deaths kept happening around him. He didn't even need an alibi for

Ankine's death since it was legally an accident.

No one looking at him. No one keeping an eye on him, or Melany. Melany, with her chocolate chip cookies and her wide-eyed eagerness for fame. Naïve. Impressionable. No match for Cal.

I reached for the phone and dialled a number I knew by heart.

MacLeish picked up on the fourth ring. 'It's late.'

I told him everything: finding Ankine. Cal, book-ended by dead women twenty years apart. My visit to Watkins.

Then I told him what I wanted from him.

When I finished talking, there was near silence, except for the faint roar of a faucet. Hiding in the bathroom, so his wife couldn't hear. But I wasn't MacLeish's mistress. Murder was.

Former LAPD homicide detective John MacLeish had worked my sister's case for ten years, starting less than twenty-four hours after she died. He and his partner were regular fixtures in our home. For a year, they'd been assigned exclusively to Tawney – another macabre privilege of stardom. The day he retired, he'd given me his cell number, with the instruction to call whenever I needed. I thought Tawney's death kept him up almost as many nights as it did me.

'Okay, kid,' MacLeish said. 'I'll make some calls in the morning.' He told me when to meet him – he didn't need to tell me where.

'Thank you, John,' I told him. 'I mean it.'

Another pause and then MacLeish said: 'It's not going to be pretty, you know. What you're asking for.'

I knew. But I had to see for myself.

* * *

I had an errand to run before meeting MacLeish. I needed to find out more about Melany, straight from the source.

Dave Lowe might have had a successful career, but the Powell side of my family, my mother's people, had Hollywood roots that stretched all the way back to its inception. There was the great-grandfather who sank a fortune into early studios, then blew his brains out after the stock market crash and didn't see his gamble come to fruition. His son, my grandfather, became a director, no stranger to the awards circuit.

And Great-Aunt Esther started the Powell Acting Academy in the 1940s.

Esther trained three Academy Award winners and one of the most bankable stars of the 1950s. She had an unerring sense of what an actor needed to succeed; she understood the art of acting as a full-body experience, not a coat you could put on and take off. She demanded excellence, total commitment, and bodily ruin, and in turn, she promised those women success beyond their wildest dreams.

But only if they were willing to sacrifice everything.

By the time my mother took over in the early nineties – when two kids and a face that could no longer *quite* pass for thirty-two meant the roles dried up – PAA had earned a reputation as a star-making studio.

It had been a given her own daughters would be trained there, as well.

As I clomped up the steps of the Craftsman bungalow that housed PAA, the box of retrospective photographs at my hip, the front door swung open. A trio of young women streamed past me in a sweaty phalanx of body glitter and glossy, swishy hair. They broke around me as easily as water, not noticing me at all. Suddenly, I was thirteen again, chubby in a black leotard, my mother pulling me aside while the other girls – not my friends, not one of them my friend – snickered: *Salma, honey. Your face always does the wrong thing. We're going to have to work on that, won't we, if you're going to be a movie star like your sister?*

I'd gone home and practised my emotions in the mirror. My smile was a snarl. My laughter looked like panic. My tears played like guffaws.

Not ideal for the screen. Not ideal for life, either.

I could count on one hand the number of times I'd dropped by PAA since I stopped acting – not counting the times I needed to hire a Dead Girl. But I wanted more information about Melany. I wanted to know if she was ready for Cal. And I couldn't stop thinking about all the connections between Cal and Ankine and Tawney.

I'd even tried to get in touch with Cal for the first time in sixteen years. I'd left two messages with his assistant. The first time, I lied and said I was from Powell Acting Academy, that I had a casting enquiry. The second time, I gave my real name.

He didn't call back for either.

At the end of the hall, sandwiched between the headshot of a Tarantino muse and an indie darling, Tawney's headshot loomed large, the patron saint of starlets. Next to her, a corkboard boasted pin-stuck notices for auditions. *Seeking statuesque blonde for minor speaking, three-episode arc with potential for series regular. Friendly, Julia Roberts type but more beautiful, ages 18–24. Curvy: not to exceed 130 pounds.*

Lovely.

One in the corner caught my eye. *Midas Productions seeking speaking role for upcoming film project, MAGNUM OPUS. Brunette, young, emotional. Great opportunity for character actor.* Which was another way of saying not attractive, I thought. Midas Productions was Cal's production company. I wondered if my mother knew her girls were auditioning for her own daughter's story.

Vivienne's voice drifted from the closed door of Studio B, the smaller of the two acting studios in the bungalow.

'*Jeté! Jeté*, Danielle! Turn those hips out!' The soft whumps of bare feet against the ground. I winced, feeling a phantom pain in my own foot, the split toenails, blood-filled blisters. That was the difference in a PAA girl: she was classically trained from the feet up. After one class, everything hurt.

I pushed the door open as quietly as I could.

My mother stood at the front of a line of girls. Even at sixty-five, her good legs looked strong underneath her leotard. Her attention was focused on the girl at hand – Danielle – who panted, red-faced, in the centre of the room, hands on her hips. I recognised one of my other Dead Girls – she'd played Dominique Dunne, a young actor strangled on her front lawn by a violent ex-boyfriend, who served less than six years for her murder.

I held up my hand in hello. Dominique looked away, pretending not to see me, as if failure were contagious.

'Give us another read, Danielle.'

Danielle gulped, sipping air like it was liquid courage, before restarting her monologue. *Scene choice matters,*

Salma. We must always highlight our strengths, mustn't we?

At the front of the room, my mother's eyes narrowed, a subtle sign she was displeased. 'Danielle, one more time.'

She leant over to another pupil and whispered something. The girl gave my mother a startled glance then nodded, circling around Danielle, still performing her monologue in the centre of the room. Danielle looked up, but she was a well-trained PAA girl – she knew better than to break her concentration during a scene study.

I had a flash of my sister as a teenager, the crown jewel of PAA, her hair a soft pile on top of her head, firm-breasted and skinny in a stretchy leotard, long neck bent down, nodding, as she listened to our mother's instructions in the front of class. *Now, everyone, see how Tawney does it? See how natural?*

I shook my head, trying to clear the ghosts.

The girl clamped her hands on Danielle's hips, started to pull her backward, only to push her forward. It was an exercise I'd seen before; I'd even been on the receiving end of it once or twice. It was a small adjustment, meant to break the actor out of her routine. As the girl's movements started to get more forceful, Danielle tried harder and harder to ignore her – with dwindling success. Her monologue shifted, became more desperate. She started stressing the syllables in the wrong places. Suddenly, she was interesting to watch.

Up front, my mother stopped the exercise, gave Danielle a few notes of encouragement, then clapped her hands. 'Let's break, shall we?'

The girls scattered, heading to the cubbies in the corner

to check their phones, their panty lines, their spandex-rolled waists. I stepped forward, feeling somehow more naked in my jeans and T-shirt than all these girls in their leotards.

A wide smile cracked over Vivienne's face as she hugged me, tuberose and neroli sharp in my nose. 'Twice in one week, darling, how lovely.'

I handed her the box of photographs, the ones I'd picked for the retrospective on top. 'For you.'

The expression on her face as she took the box was practically reverent. Since my father passed away, my mother had found her footing as Dave Lowe's widow – the greatest role of her life, surpassing even *Iron Prayer*. But the retrospective would be nice, an honour for my father's legacy – and the only type of showcase my mother allowed herself these days.

She flicked through the photos I'd picked out. I noticed she pushed a few forward – either highlighting my choice or editing it.

'You never did tell me why you stopped by Jack's,' my mother said. She kept her head bent when she said it, so I couldn't see her face. Making it seem like she wasn't prying.

I cleared my throat. 'We had a sprinkler malfunction at work. I thought I'd see if Jack had a change of clothes.'

'Mmm.' She pushed one of my selections to the back of the box. So, editing. 'Nothing to do with that poor dead young woman at Tawney's old home.'

I fiddled with my bangs. 'You saw the news.'

'Jack did,' she said. 'I can't imagine why you didn't feel like you could tell me yourself.'

The answer for that was too complicated, too much

86

water under too many bridges. I changed the subject. 'I saw an advertisement for a role in Cal Turner's new film on your board.'

Vivienne smiled. 'It's a career-making opportunity. One of my girls was just cast in it. Melany Grey.' She slid me a sly look. 'I think you know her better as the Black Dahlia?'

'You know about my tour?'

I'd never seen Vivienne Powell roll her eyes, but she came close. 'I'm not blind, Salma.'

Around us, girls were starting to fidget, get restless. I was always taking up too much time and space at PAA; that feeling wasn't one I'd left behind in childhood. They had things they wanted to ask Vivienne, pieces of her they wanted to claim. I was in the way.

'But do you know what the film is about?'

Vivienne sighed. 'Salma, if this is regarding your little vendetta against Cal, I don't want to hear it.'

My nails dug into my palms, stinging. 'It's not a vendetta.'

Unlike me, my mother had never, not even once, really thought Cal killed my sister. I wasn't sure if it was because the *why* of it mattered less than the finality of it – my sister was gone – or because she truly didn't believe someone could be a talented director and a murderer at the same time.

'So many people willing to tear down the reputations of great men – great *artists*.' Vivienne shook her head. 'Doesn't talent mean anything any more? You've seen what they've done to poor Clark.'

Clark Gable had been my mother's godfather – daughter

of his favourite director. But in recent years, Gable's reputation had taken a hit. Loretta Young, his co-star on the film *Call of the Wild*, accused him of date-raping her during the production. Pregnant and unmarried, Young adopted her own child to conceal the scandal. Terrified of the consequences to her squeaky-clean image – and undoubtedly traumatised by the experience, I thought – she'd even paid for cosmetic surgery for her eight-year-old daughter, pinning back the distinctive Gable ears. Cutting her daughter to keep her own secrets.

But my mother was loyal, wouldn't believe any of it. 'Tragic, the way some people will take any chance to tear down a good man,' she said. 'You even used to have a little crush on Cal once,' my mother went on, *flip, flip, flip.* 'Or don't you remember?'

My breath caught. An unwelcome memory surfaced: my face puffy and sallow in the yellowy overhead light of Cal's bathroom. Holding back tears as I stared at my swollen lips, my dress on inside out. Still drunk, my hair stinking of funeral lilies.

If Vivienne noticed my pause went on too long, she didn't acknowledge it. 'He's making a movie about Tawney. About *us*. Using Cherry Partridge's book as source material.'

Vivienne's fingers stilled finally and she looked up. As an actor, my mother was known for her lovely expressive eyes, capable of projecting her feelings across the screen with a look. But I couldn't read them now. Finally, she said, 'Good.'

'*What?*'

She shook her head. 'You heard me. Don't you think I

want your sister's life to be remembered? Why else do you run that' – she flicked her hand dismissively – 'little tour of yours? Wouldn't it be better for people to remember her alive, the way we do?'

I was speechless. But only for a second. 'You think *Cal* should be the one to do it?'

Vivienne *tsk*ed. 'He's more than up to the task.'

'What about Melany?' I knew better than to tell her I thought Cal might be involved in Ankine's death. 'You know the rumours about what he's like as a director. You know how he was with Tawney, even.'

On the set of *Love's Long Midnight*, their only film together, Cal had called Tawney a stupid cunt in front of the crew when she'd improvised a line. But the part of the story everyone remembered – one of the reasons for her nickname – took place three seconds later, when she threw a water bottle at his head.

Cal wasn't the only bad director out there, either. There was the time Tawney locked herself in her trailer in protest of the director who brought an ice bucket to her door to ice her nipples before takes. There was the director who asked my mother when I'd start menstruating, because I'd been cast as a child and he wanted the role to be realistic. 'I can't have her sprouting breasts mid-film,' he'd said. 'The re-shoots would bankrupt us.'

But no one gave them shitty nicknames. Good directors – good *male* directors – got to be exacting, mercurial geniuses. Sometimes rapists.

Maybe even murderers.

Vivienne avoided my eyes. 'This industry isn't perfect. That's a reality we all deal with, if we want to be part of it.' The implication stung – that I hadn't *wanted* it enough, that that was why my own career had ended in flames. She nodded at her students, waiting impatiently on the sidelines. 'Now, if you'll excuse me, Salma, my girls are waiting for me.'

I was dismissed.

On my way out, I grabbed the flyer from the corkboard, the one advertising Cal's film, and gave it a yank, tearing it halfway down the middle. It was childish, but it was the first thing I'd done that day that made me feel even halfway decent.

CHAPTER NINE

I met MacLeish at an all-night donuteria on the mangy side of Hollywood.

Nom-Nom Donuts weren't the best donuts in Los Angeles, or the most artisanal. But you could get a half dozen glazed for less than five dollars. And when MacLeish and I first started meeting, I'd been charmed by the enormous sculpture of a fifteen-foot pink frosted with sprinkles in the parking lot, the neon-green NOM-NOM sign. At least they were in on the joke.

The first time I'd suggested it, MacLeish had rolled his eyes. 'Cute,' he said, clearly not amused by my teenage sense of humour. 'Cops love donuts. Got it.'

I was twenty minutes early, but it didn't surprise me to see MacLeish already in his booth in the back left corner, the one with a visual on the door. A cop's instincts never retired.

MacLeish held up a chocolate-smudged hand as I sat down. I knew without looking there'd be two donuts waiting for me: a pink cake donut with white and purple sprinkles, and a maple bar, along with a ginger ale, my sober brew of choice.

I studied him as I cracked the ginger ale. Whatever he'd found out didn't show on his face. He wasn't ready to talk yet.

MacLeish was dressed in slacks and a blue button-down rolled up over his forearms. Sometimes I thought we kept the formality in our meetings because neither of us wanted to admit the relationship had become purely personal. It would be like admitting Tawney's murder would never be solved. I wasn't ready for that. I'd never be ready for that.

We made small talk as I finished the maple bar, an awkward non-intimacy between us. How was his wife? *Good, fine, you know. How's the tour?* Good. Fine. You know.

Finally, as MacLeish crumpled a napkin – every time, he ordered two identical chocolate donuts – I couldn't take it any more. 'So? What did you find?'

MacLeish sucked his teeth, cleaning one hand with the crumpled napkin. There was still one chocolate donut left, and he eyed it ruefully before he rattled off the things he'd discovered about Ankine Petrosyan. Unlike Watkins, he didn't use a notebook. He could keep the puzzle pieces straight in his head. When Tawney died, it had been a comfort, proof that my sister mattered enough to him to learn the case by heart.

'Born 2nd November, 1997, in the Valley. Mom died when she was a kid, dad remarried, she and the stepmom didn't get along. Two half-siblings, both younger, both boys. Her father was a stunt driver – may be how she got into the biz.'

The same year Tawney died – 1997.

MacLeish rattled off more statistics about Ankine, some pieces I'd tracked down, others I hadn't. No known connections to Cal before the film. Talent was hard to quantify, but still, I was curious why an unknown had spoken to Cal for his *magnum opus*.

Then MacLeish pushed a photo across the sticky table.

At first, I thought it was a photo of Tawney. It took me a moment to realise the truth, then goosebumps broke out over my arms. Fluorescent lights buzzed above us while I stared. 'Jesus,' I breathed.

'I know.'

I couldn't stop staring. It was a copy of a Polaroid. In it, Ankine was a bottle blonde shot through with caramel highlights, the exact shimmering shade of my sister's mane. Her face was slimmer than her Instagram photos, lifted by deeply contoured cheeks to recreate Tawney's sharp angles. Blue contacts gave her eyes an unnatural sapphire glow. She'd overlined her lips to recreate Tawney's pout, and I thought it was possible she was wearing dentures that snapped over her teeth, too.

The only thing that wasn't exactly right was her nose – Tawney's infamous ski-slope nose. Otherwise, I might as well have been looking at a picture of my sister.

I flipped the photo over, rubbing my temples. 'Cal's make-up artist is a terrifying genius.'

MacLeish shook his head, chewing on a chunk of donut. 'Taken more than a year ago.'

A cold prickle climbed up my spine. She'd been dressing up on her own time. A Tawney groupie. I'd been partially right.

When I looked up, MacLeish was watching the door.

But this was only half of what I'd asked for. 'Did you get the coroner's report?'

Reluctantly, he pulled an envelope from his jacket. I noticed chocolate fingerprints on it. 'Kid, I gotta say, I don't know about this. After everything you've been through – I can't recommend it.'

Not your fucking decision. What was it about men? In elementary school, when they separated us to talk about our changing bodies, were the boys getting lessons on how to gently insist they knew what was best for us?

'Give it.'

MacLeish sighed, passed me the envelope. I practically tore it open.

The police report was on top: *Decedent found in pool at 3:37 p.m. by Salma Lowe . . .*

I skimmed the page. No speculation about why Ankine was there that day. One surprise: the name of the owner of the Jacaranda House, listed as E. F. Wennick. I mouthed the name to myself, but it didn't ring a bell. Police had questioned Wennick but hadn't declared them a person of interest.

But then, no one was. Because it was an accident, officially.

I turned to the coroner's report. Official ruling: hypoxemia and irreversible cerebral anoxia due to submersion in liquid. In short: accidental drowning. Time of death: some time between 3 and 3:30 p.m., when I'd found her. She hadn't been dead long.

I scanned the rest of the report. There was norgestimate, ethinyl estradiol, and cetirizine in her system. A quick Google search brought up birth control, over-the-counter allergy medications. Nothing unusual.

I flipped to the photos, avoiding the ones of Ankine's body. All the questions I still had – how Ankine had come to be in the pool in the first place, her connection to my sister, to Cal – none of the reports offered answers.

I took a sip of my ginger ale, swished it around my gums as it fizzed, an almost-pain. 'He's connected to two dead women now,' I said. 'Don't you think that's strange?'

MacLeish sighed. I could almost hear him shift to procedural mode. *Just the facts, ma'am.* 'There's no reason to doubt the report. Sometimes shitty accidents happen.'

'An *accident?*' Healthy, sober young women didn't just drop dead in swimming pools. An accident. A fluke. Nothing to see here, folks. Bullshit. 'What was she doing there in the first place?'

MacLeish chewed on his lip. 'I know you want answers. I wish I could give them to you.'

'What happens now?'

MacLeish shrugged. 'The coroner ruled it an accident. Case closed.'

I looked down at the picture in my lap. Ankine/Tawney pouted back at me. I didn't need a Betty Ford counsellor to point out I was conflating the two. Cal had already done that for me.

I knew the statistics. When women are murdered, it's almost always by someone close to them. The picture got slightly murkier when fame was involved; like Rebecca Schaeffer, shot at her front door by a deranged fan, it wasn't impossible Tawney's murder was random.

But two deaths intimately connected to the same man

– that couldn't be coincidence. And soon there'd be a third Hurricane Blonde for Cal.

If the roles were switched, and it was up to Tawney to find answers about me, nothing would have stopped her. She deserved that. Ankine deserved it, too. And Melany – she didn't even know what she was getting into. I wasn't going to throw my hands up now, say, *there, it's fine, I did enough*.

I gestured to the photo in my lap, the police report. 'Can I keep these?'

MacLeish gave me a long look. Too long. 'Sure.'

'Thank you, John,' I said, standing up. He walked me to the parking lot, where we shook hands goodbye. It was the closest we came to physical affection.

Then he pulled back, squinted at me, and said: 'Someday soon, kiddo, you're going to have to start living in the present.'

Easy for him to say.

CHAPTER TEN

Midas Productions was housed in a squat brutalist building, blocks from Venice Beach. Rather than lean into the California beachy-bungalow aesthetic of its neighbours, the building was all sharp square lines and poured concrete, a fortress against the balmy breeze blowing off the Pacific. The front door was a slab of burnished gold coating. I tinked a nail against it, felt the softened give of sun-warmed gold.

Of course Cal had an actual goddamn golden door.

'Subtle,' I muttered, then shoved my shoulder into it and pushed it open.

In the years since Tawney died, Cal had built a catalogue of films featuring a dead blonde, even if she was only an extra. His reviews still threw around words like *genius* and *visionary* and *auteur*. But the recent box office returns hadn't been what they once were.

You wouldn't know that from his production office. The mazama floors had been buffed to a reflective gleam. In one corner, a waterfall burbled over artfully arranged pebbles and green glass. Bowls of floating jacaranda petals rotted at the front desk.

I tried to shake off my nerves. I hadn't seen Cal up close since I was nineteen years old, when he sneered down at me through the windows of the cop car, blue and red flashing lights creating an inconsistent eerie glow behind him.

Not a life high point.

He wouldn't want to talk to me. He'd made that abundantly clear, over the years. But I had an ace up my sleeve, and I was willing, finally, to play it.

I gave a pseudonym – Beth Short – to the receptionist, along with a long-outdated headshot from my last-ditch attempts at stardom in my twenties, my real name scribbled out. I gathered the sides he shoved at me and followed his extended finger down the hall to casting.

It was unusual for a director to sit in on castings. But Cal wasn't *any* director. Nearly every interview with him mentioned, in fawning detail, how the *exacting genius* spent hours making sure every detail of his film was letter-perfect to his vision. He had to approve every person on set, even the extras. He was known for ripping apart costumes – literally – because they were one button short of his specifications.

Directors and cult leaders: praised for their control.

I glanced down at the script. It had been decades since I'd had sides in my hands, let alone read for an audition. I should've been nervous, and it was there, the old Hollywood tickle. But something else, too. A flicker, a return to myself – me before Tawney's murder, before Sloppy Salma.

The cover sheet read *MAGNUM OPUS*. No scene number, no way to tell how deeply into the film it took place. *INT. Funeral chapel, middle of the day. The HURRICANE BLONDE in a casket, a fuchsia spotlight on her in a surreal glow. The LITTLE SISTER, 15 but looks 19, Bettie Page haircut, fat but wears it well, stands up to eulogise her sister. Visibly drunk, she stumbles up the aisle . . .*

What the fuck?

I stopped in my tracks, the burble of the water feature barely louder than the pulse beating in my head. I blinked twice to clear my eyes, hoping I'd misread it.

I knew Cal was making a movie about my sister. I didn't realise he'd put me in it.

I crumpled the papers in my fist. I only realised I was bleeding when one edge of the sides flared red. I popped my left index finger in my mouth, sucking on the cut.

The door for CASTING was marked with a handwritten sign. I looked back down at the sides, one page stained with my blood, and steeled myself. If Cal was willing to fight dirty, then so was I.

I pushed the door open.

And nearly walked back out again. The room was packed with an uncanny valley of younger, thinner, better-complected, perkier-breasted Salmas, all with variations on the Cleopatra cut I'd worn most of my life. They glanced up as one, and then, not seeing anything worthwhile, back down at the pages in their laps.

I'd had more fun nightmares.

I plopped down in an open seat near the door. The Salma next to me was nervous; I could tell by the way she fidgeted, lips moving as she read. Even with Cal's dwindling star power, a speaking role in one of his films could launch a career. She was twenty-two, *maybe*, thirty pounds lighter than I'd been even as a teen. A bad dye job left her hair too dark for her skin; her bangs had been chopped short and it made her eyebrows look naked, an abandoned island on her forehead. I almost apologised to her for my bad stylistic choices.

I'd forgotten what auditions were like. The adrenaline so high, you could taste it in the air. I looked at all the dark-haired women, fun-house-mirror versions of the me that might have been. Each one hoping *this* was it, her big break, the moment she'd talk about in awards speeches and glossy interviews. She'd look back on this self and laugh indulgently: *I was just a baby then; I didn't even know.*

Perhaps Ankine had thought it, too, nervous and trying not to show it, wondering if this was her last audition as a nobody. Perhaps she'd been in my very same seat. I thought about that photograph of her dressed up as my sister. What had she seen in Tawney that called to her? What about Tawney did she want to take for herself?

I looked back down at the sides. I didn't need to read the words. I knew what it said. Even if I didn't remember all of it, my meltdown at Tawney's funeral had been covered by every news outlet in the country. Cherry Partridge's headline had read: *Sloppy Salma upstages sister's funeral.* My only bit of luck was it happened before social media.

You didn't need to make it about you, Salma, my mother had said the next day, when I'd finally come home, puffy-faced and dehydrated, refusing to look me in the eye.

'Beth Short?'

I looked up. The door to the inner casting sanctum was open. An intern glared down at a clipboard like it had personally offended him.

'They're ready for you.'

CHAPTER ELEVEN

Cal sat with his arms crossed at a table, behind a long line of water glasses. To his left, a Black woman with glossy box braids frowned down at her phone. On his right sat a white man with a waxed handlebar moustache. A white woman with purple glasses sat behind the camera, a copy of the sides in her hand. I'd be reading against her. In the tradition of such places, the casting room was an explosion of beige from carpet to ceiling.

I'd expected Cal to look like he did when Tawney was alive, the most handsome man I'd ever seen. I'd expected him to stay frozen, the way none of us but Tawney had. The lines around his eyes, the grey at his temples, hadn't hurt his good looks. But time had not been completely kind to him. His face was puffy, a thousand sleepless nights stacking up under his eyes. A slight sag to his chin. Possibly he hadn't cracked a smile in a decade.

In all the ways that counted, I didn't know him any more. My stomach twisted as I watched him frown down at the stack of headshots in front of him. I wondered if he recognised me.

But his face was blank when he looked up. 'We don't have all day.'

I cleared my throat. 'I'm Beth Short and I'm reading for the part of the Little Sister.' The training from my own years of PAA prep kicked in. My mother's words, drilled into me: *Polite, professional, passionate, that's how you make an impression.* I straightened my shoulders, looked down at the sides again.

In the script, Cal had made the Little Sister babbling, waffling between anger and hysteria. In turns, she accused other mourners of killing her sister; then she tried to throw herself into the casket. In Cal's film, no one tried to stop her.

The blood was beating in my head so hard I couldn't read the lines. I swallowed twice, focusing on my breathing.

Purple Glasses rattled off the scene directions in a dull monotone. *Interior. Daytime. WESTWOOD MEMORIAL CHAPEL. The LITTLE SISTER steps forward from a pew, interrupting a speaker. She's a boozy mess, stumbling. A hedonistic portrait of a spoilt Hollywood wild child with the barest whiff of class, Lindsay Lohan by way of Carmen Sternwood.*

Was that how he'd always thought of me? My eyes flicked up to Cal, but he was looking down at the script pages, bored.

Purple Glasses gave my cue: 'It's time for us to say our goodbyes . . .'

The pages were a blur but I didn't need them. I took a deep breath and let it rip, trying to keep my voice smooth and steady. 'Tawney, get up, somebody help my sister—'

Cal held up a hand. 'Stop.'

I lowered the page, my voice faltering. Cal leant back in his chair, studying me, his icy blue eyes focused. He stared so long I started to shift on my feet, brushing my bangs across my face.

'You flubbed the line.'

I looked down at the page, panicked. If he dismissed me now, my whole plan would fall apart. 'No, I didn't.'

'Look again.'

It took me two tries before I realised. I'd called her *Tawney*. I swallowed hard.

'Start over,' he commanded. Still no recognition. 'Slower. More emotional.'

Purple Glasses gave him a *look* but started again with the scene directions.

This time, I forced myself to slow down, slur the lines. Saying the words left a bad taste in my mouth, the ghost of old vodka and grief. It was hard not to cry. My fingers trembled against the pages, making a shivering sound so loud I was sure Cal could hear it.

'Okay,' Purple Glasses said after I finished. 'Thank you, Ms Short. We'll be in touch.'

The customary kiss-off. I opened my mouth to protest when Cal shook his head. 'I'd like to hear it again. More out of control.'

Purple Glasses stared at him with open incredulity now – clearly, I was all wrong for the part, why bother? – but Cal didn't blink.

This time, Cal let me get as far as shouting at a reporter that they'd killed my sister, with their bottomless pit of tabloid trash – God spare anyone from having to revisit the melodrama of their youth – before he cut me off.

'What are you misunderstanding about the cues?' His head tilted. Like he was genuinely curious. 'You lived it, didn't you? Show me what it was like.'

So, he *did* recognise me.

'Cal—' Purple Glasses tried to intervene.

Cal held up a hand. 'Go. Again.'

I made it twenty seconds before the loud scrape of his chair against the floor, then he was towering over me, filling my field of vision completely. Instinctively, I dropped the sides, backed up to the edge of the beige carpet.

But he didn't touch me.

Instead, his voice pitched low so only I could hear, he said: 'Do you remember the smell of the lilies? The chapel reeked of them. Close your eyes. Remember it.'

I blinked at him, my mouth half open. He was right – bouquets of lilies, the mourning flower, alongside Tawney's fuchsia roses. Thick, cloying *eau de chapel*. A fat bee dipped in and out of the flowers. I'd missed half of Tawney's eulogy watching it.

Tawney stuffed in a box. The last time I'd ever see her face, and she hadn't even looked like herself. Her skin waxy, lacquered with make-up so murder didn't show. It was even worse than the day I'd found her body.

Cal took half a step closer. 'What were you drinking that day?'

My mother upstairs, weeping as she dressed up for death, my father saying over and over, *I love you, I'm sorry, I'm sorry*. The give of the freezer drawer opening, the Belvedere bottle so cold it burnt my hand. Gagging in the bathroom as I forced myself to keep swallowing until the bottle was gone.

'Vodka,' I whispered.

'Close your eyes.' Cal reached out a hand, as if to shut them himself, and I screwed my eyes tight. 'What did it taste like? Describe it.'

My eyes still closed, I shook my head. No, I did not want to think about it. I did not want to think about vodka, or the funeral. It took years to shut that part of myself away.

'Tell me.'

I could feel his breath on my face, rippling my bangs. Saliva blossomed in my mouth. I hadn't had a drink in more than ten years, but I could feel the ice-cold vodka in my veins, I could taste its paint-thinner sweetness, and suddenly I wanted a drink *bad*, a cold, sweating drink of any kind in my hand, in my throat, warming my stomach.

My eyes popped open.

Cal smiled. 'Now. Do it now.'

This time, the monologue slid easily out of my mouth. I was saying Cal's words, *my* words, but I was also feeling the itchy tug of my black tights chafing my thighs. Staring at the stained glass as the pastor told me, *Life never really ends, not for those of us who Believe*, like he knew anything about it, and I needed out, GET OUT, because if I stayed there while they said all those things about my sister, she really was dead, and I was letting them put her in the ground. Me. I let it happen.

I was saying Cal's dialogue, but I was crawling over my father's knees as he tried to stop me, landing with a thump in the aisle, bawling. I was in a casting room in Venice, but I was standing in a chapel, letting loose all the fury and sadness and un-fucking-fairness of my sister's murder, all those feelings no one bothered to ask *me* about, to tell me

105

I was a saint for enduring the terrible thing that must be endured.

It wasn't in the script but it was the detail everyone remembered, my *you talkin' to me?* moment, and so I did it: I reached down, yanked off my ballet flat, and, screaming, threw it as hard as I could against the far wall.

In the chapel, it had overturned a vase of roses. In the casting room, it bounced off a wall.

'Okay, no improvising,' Purple Glasses warned.

In the chapel, I'd felt warm arms lock around me, Cal's grief-roughened voice in my ear, the first time I'd seen him since before Tawney died: *Let's get you out of here, Salmon.* Cal's arm around my shoulders, escorting me, one foot bare, through the chapel and into the grey sun.

I blinked. I was back. Cal was angled away from the camera so only I could see his face. I couldn't read the expression. 'Now,' he said, not quietly, 'if you weren't so old and fat, we might actually have something.'

I stood there numb as he walked back to the casting table.

I'd always be that little girl in the chapel. I was still there, drunk, high, terrified, the horror of my sister's body feet away, and nothing, nothing I could do about it.

You couldn't turn back time – not three minutes, not three days.

'Thank you, Ms Short,' Cal called, looking back to the headshots. The other three wouldn't meet my eye. 'You're free to go.'

Anger was a liquid gush, warm and welcome. Cal had ducked me for all these years, offered no closure, no mutual care in the wake of my sister's death. There had only been her funeral, and what came after, and then years and years of silence, while what happened – what *we* did – lived within me only.

No more.

'Excuse me.' No one looked up. I cleared my throat. 'The scene after the funeral,' I said.

The Black woman looked up from her phone. Her eyes had a familiar tilt, the expressiveness of her mouth an old memory lingering. But I ignored her; I had Cal's attention now. I could see it in the rigid line of his shoulders, the way he dragged one hand forward for a glass of water.

It was easy, too easy, to remember his effect on me at fifteen. Cal and Tawney: the most beautiful couple in the world. You either wanted them or wanted to be them. I envied my sister for the dramatic passion of it all, their terrible dance. After all, I'd been raised on the Hollywood appeal of bad boys: womanisers like Jack Nicholson and Warren Beatty, the hot-tempered flare of Marlon Brando and Sean Connery and Johnny Depp. Tawney was beautiful enough to tame one. It didn't matter that she'd break up with him, then run back. Rinse, repeat. I could only see the romance of the highs and lows.

But I wasn't that kid any more. I'd come this far. I wasn't going to lose it now. 'After Brandon Saturn' – I could've laughed at Cal's alter ego's moniker, but it wasn't particularly funny – 'takes the Little Sister out of the chapel, what happens next? I mean, where do they go? What do they do?'

Cal turned around. 'We're done here.' His tone was the murderous side of polite.

'Not yet,' I said, surprising even myself. 'I need to talk to you.'

Pushing Cal's buttons was possibly suicidal in nature. Purple Glasses grimaced. Moustache twisted a pen back and forth in his fingers. Only the Black woman, she of the familiar face – was she an actor? where did I know her from? – watched with stark, bright-eyed interest.

'Excuse me.' Cal pushed himself away from the table, brushing by me so forcefully I stumbled backward. He yanked the door nearly off its hinges as he left.

Without a backward glance at the casting panel, I followed. I found Cal bent over the water tank, pouring himself a tiny cup of cucumber mint water. He crumpled the cup in his hand, then grabbed another, filling it to the brim.

Without turning around, Cal said, 'Beth Short? You think that's cute or something?'

Of course he'd gotten the reference. 'I didn't think you'd see me if I used my real name.'

Cal gave a mirthless chuckle. 'You were right.'

I reached around him to grab a cup of water myself. Cal flinched as my arm grazed his. He backed up, put distance between us. 'Leave before I have security throw you out.'

This close, I could smell the musky cologne he wore. It flooded my nose like a smog. 'Where were you the day she died?'

Cal rolled his eyes. 'That's why you came here? I was with Cherry Partridge, giving an interview—'

'Not Tawney,' I said. 'Ankine Petrosyan. Your actor. Don't you remember her?'

Cal blinked at me, feigning confusion. But I knew better. 'Ankine? Why?'

I glared at him. 'I was the one who found her, Cal. Don't you watch the news?'

His shoulders tightened. 'Not unless I'm on the news, no,' he sniffed. Then he said stiffly: 'I'm sorry.'

'You didn't answer my question.'

Cal laughed, actually laughed. 'You're not serious.' Then, seeing on my face that I very much was, he rolled his eyes. 'I was on set. Multiple people can vouch for it, including my producer. Is that all?'

He'd looked me in the eye while he said it. 'All day? You were on set all day?'

Cal nodded. 'All day. Being a director is a *bit* of a full-time job, Salma.'

I tried something else. 'You're making a film about Tawney.'

Cal glowered at me, putting more space between us. 'And?'

And I think you might kill another leading lady. 'I want to be on set.'

The idea came to me after I'd yanked the flyer from PAA's board. It was the only way to keep an eye on Melany, protect her from Cal. And if he said no, I was prepared to go nuclear.

I'd finally sell our story to the press.

I lifted my chin. It was power I was feeling, but something else, too – an uncorking, a shift in the sands as I pulled up private pieces of myself I'd locked away for so long, a process he'd started by forcing me back into the memory of Tawney's funeral.

I could see the tension in his body, his shoulders hunching, his lips twisting into an ugly sneer. I waited for his temper to explode. But then, as suddenly as it had come, the anger vanished.

'All right,' he said.

I gaped at him. 'What?'

His eyes gleamed. He stared above my head, thinking it through out loud. 'A family consultant. It's a good idea, given the subject matter. You never can be too careful these days.'

I'd been so sure he'd say no. That he'd make me fight for it. Why was he giving in so easily? 'You're bullshitting me.'

Cal smiled, his teeth white and wolfish. 'It's a great idea, Salma. Really. Well done.'

Before I could ask him anything else, Cal signalled to the receptionist, explained that I would be working on the film set. I'd need a script overnighted. Cal asked me for my address, and I gave it in a daze. He explained the paperwork I'd need to sign before I left that day – an NDA, a freelance contract. Purple Glasses poked her head into the hallway, called after him. Cal held up a finger, the one-minute sign.

'We'll be seeing more of each other again soon, Salmon,' Cal said. The old nickname on his lips made me shudder.

As the receptionist passed me a fresh NDA – eyeing me suspiciously, as though I'd cast a spell on Cal; I could've told him I was just as confused – he said, 'He never does this. You're really lucky.'

'Yeah,' I said. 'Lucky.'

'Seriously.' He raised his eyebrows. 'I've never seen him do anything like this. I don't know what you said to him, but it really worked.'

I signed away my rights to ever publicly discuss the happenings of the film set, and then some. I didn't read the NDA as carefully as I should have. No one ever did.

And then I was out in the sunshine again, blinking into the blue Venice sky and wondering. Had it really been that easy? Had Cal really decided to let me onto his set, just like that?

And, I wondered as I walked to my car, if I'd won, why did it feel like Cal Turner had me exactly where he wanted me?

22ND JUNE, 1997

After we left the chapel, Cal drove me to the Formosa Café and forced me to sober up on chow mein noodles, even though I told him I didn't really want to be sober.

In the glow of the booth, his dark hair stuck up in greasy spikes. He smelt faintly musty, that curdled-milk smell of unshowered men. My heart cracked wide open, and alongside the grief I felt a fury at Tawney for leaving us.

No one carded me for the martinis Cal ordered.

Afterward, he drove us north, to Malibu. I'd asked him – begged him – not to take me home yet. My parents would be returning from the memorial soon. They'd sit me down, lecture me on how I'd embarrassed them. How I'd ruined Tawney's service.

Or maybe they wouldn't. Maybe they wouldn't say anything. That would be worse.

We were barely through the front door before he was fixing us drinks.

'You like whiskey?' Cal hollered from the kitchen. Before I could respond, I heard him say, 'Fuck it, she'll drink it.'

Cal emerged from the kitchen with two crystal tumblers filled with amber liquid and pressed one into my hands, sat next to me. I could feel the heat of his hip against my leg.

'Bottoms the fuck up,' he said, not so much clinking as ramming our glasses together.

After the third whiskey, Cal started crying. I was the one who pulled him onto my shoulder, who wrapped my arms around him as we sobbed together.

It's important – for me – to remember I made the first move. I touched him first.

I told him it was okay to be sad, we had to be sad. I babbled things that didn't make sense. I couldn't stop saying her name, an incantation to call her back to us. *Tawney, Tawney, Tawney.*

Finally, he blew his nose on his sleeve. He pushed his hair back, eyes swollen. 'Sometimes you seem wise beyond your years.'

'Eleven going on twenty-five,' I quipped at him, trying to make him smile when there was nothing to smile about. The director of *Morty's House* had said that about me, once. *Salma Lowe is one of the most accomplished child actresses out there – she's basically eleven going on twenty-five.*

I could hear the gentle lapping of the waves in the dark distance. Cal's head was propped on the back of the couch, his eyes chasing shapes on the ceiling I couldn't see. I was drunk. He was, too. Dirty and drunk and sad, my own Stanley Kowalski. I leant forward, traced his lips with the tip of my finger. Just to touch him. *Stop*, he said. But he didn't move. I stroked his ear gently, afraid to escalate it, afraid to stop. His ear was so soft, the tiny hairs like velvet under my nail.

My own experience of men had been mostly contained to wannabe producers cooing to me at parties, *Hey, little girl*, offering me powders that promised to make the world sparkly, a plummy role, a fast-moving car, until someone in the crowd coughed out, *Don't you know who that is? That's Dave Lowe's kid. Careful.* And then, later: *Tawney Lowe's kid sister!*

For some of those men, that cloak of celebrity would end it: *Whoa, sorry, babe, Dave Lowe's daughter, tell your pops hi for me.* For some of them, it was a red cape waved in their face. *Really*, they'd say, taking a step closer, counting each raven-shiny strand of hair on my head, *Dave Lowe's daughter. Tawney's sister.* And me not knowing better, enjoying the attention, the heat of it. Not able to pick the good attention from the bad.

You don't feel the tide pulling you in when you grow up like that. *Eleven going on twenty-five.* I was fifteen, not eleven. I thought I could handle myself. You don't even feel the danger. Worse, you start to believe the things you hear about yourself are true.

In that moment, I believed – sincerely – that I was in control.

Cal turned his head, blue eyes inky.

Then he leant forward and kissed me.

I'd been kissed before. My very first kiss had been on set with a co-star. His mouth tasted like Cheetos dust, and the director had laughed – *Atta boy!* – when he'd stuck his tongue down my throat without warning. A moment I couldn't get back. I'd been kissed since then, by boys at wrap parties, fumbling embraces and attempts to unhook my bra that missed the mark, or took so long he gave up.

But this was different. Cal wasn't a boy.

He hooked an arm around my waist and pressed me back into the cushions. When he touched me, every part of me lit up.

I was outrunning the sadness, the unthinkable part of me that was missing. I was liquid, my skin buzzing with the feel of his fingers, the scratch of his couch against my naked back, the night air cold on new parts of me, and then – sharp pain, like he'd bitten a secret piece from me.

I'd imagined something more romantic for my first time. A night up talking until sun cracked the horizon open, making love as dawn broke; that would've been a good first time. Even underneath him on the couch, before it became a thing I couldn't take back, I'd imagined he might turn his face into my hair, breathe me in, show me something of the shared experience of grief and lust and wrong decisions within which we were locked.

Instead: a strange, hurried handful of minutes, mostly silent except for his harsh breathing, the pound of my pulse like a bass line in my head. The sliminess of it, the wet crush of his body against mine. His smell all over me. There was a strange elation to the very adultness of it all.

I hadn't understood it, what it would mean. How much worse everything would be after the sweaty comedown, when he slid out of me and I watched the disgust and regret cloud his face. He wouldn't meet my eyes as he called me a taxi, told me we were drunk, told me to get lost, told me I was a mistake.

I hadn't thought that day could get any lonelier. I hadn't known it was possible.

CHAPTER TWELVE

E ven when the script arrived – in an envelope marked CONFIDENTIAL in big blocky letters – I still didn't believe Cal would keep his word. I stayed up the night before the table read, poring over the script twice. It wasn't an exact translation of Cherry's book; it wasn't a biopic. It was stranger, more surreal, Cal cloaking the truth in layers of filmic tricks. My real life through the looking glass.

The Hurricane Blonde died three times in the script. Once wasn't enough; Cal had imagined killing my sister three ways.

The cast was small. Besides the Hurricane Blonde, there was the Little Sister. Cal's alter ego was a private eye named Brandon Saturn, trapped in a bizarre pas de deux with himself, falling more in love with the Hurricane Blonde with each death.

When I got to the last page, I thought I'd missed something. I checked the pages again, making sure all the numbers were in the right order. I even double-checked the ridiculous CONFIDENTIAL envelope the script had arrived in.

But no. I wasn't missing anything. Cal's film had no ending. The action simply stopped. There was no resolution, no solution. It made me uneasy, although I wasn't sure why. Tawney died. There were no other possible endings.

I was still thinking about it as I drove through the studio gates, collecting a parking pass for Soundstage Seven from a security guard who waved me through without a second look.

I was back. After more than fifteen years away, I was finally back.

I rounded the corner of Sunset Boulevard and Yellow Brick Road and then there it was: Soundstage Seven. The blocky building looked like every soundstage I'd ever seen growing up, warehouse spaces you could transform however you liked. Within those four beige walls, magic was possible.

I parked in front of the twenty-foot-high elephant doors – so named for the days when actual elephants had to be loaded onto the soundstage for a scene – checked my lipstick one more time in the rear-view. My eyes flicked up to the wigwag, the light outside every soundstage that indicated whether filming was on. It was the first lesson an actor learnt on a soundstage: Ignore the red light of a wigwag – signalling filming was underway – at your own risk. Actors had been fired for less.

The wigwag was off.

Dave Lowe's daughter isn't afraid of a soundstage, I told myself, pretending it was true. Then I took a deep breath and pushed, stepping through the looking glass.

The soundstage set was still in process, chaos barely

contained. Filming wouldn't start for another week and a half or so, giving the actors time to rehearse, designers the chance to work their magic, and Cal the opportunity to micromanage his film into the ground. As I peeked around the jungle of wires that hooked up the lights, the sound, and the cameras at different angles, I could hear the buzz of a saw nearby.

In the centre of the room, a long rectangular table with a chair at one of the heads, Cal's nameplate propped in front of it. Melany was seated two chairs down from Cal. I searched for my own name and found I was at the other end of the table, as far from Cal as possible. That suited me just fine.

I slid into my seat, glancing at the tiny letters under my name: *Historical Accuracy Consultant*. I pushed the nameplate to the side so I could read the name across from me.

Cherry Partridge: Author of The Hurricane Blonde.

My nails dug into the table until I noticed, forced myself to relax. It wouldn't be pleasant, but then, neither was being in Cal's orbit. For Ankine, for Melany, I could stand it.

I flicked Cherry's nameplate to the side, revealing a pink paperback brick. The cover of *The Hurricane Blonde* featured Tawney's picture superimposed above a sprawl of green grass, a yawning dark door covered in caution tape. For the low, low price of $15.99, you, too, could be privy to the dark secrets behind that door, my family's worst day.

Behind me, there was a loud crack, and I jumped in my chair, heart racing, *God, what now, another bad thing, another body?* I looked around, expecting to see a crew member pinned underneath a piece of equipment.

Instead, I found Cal, rubbing his hands together – that had been the crack, his clap – and heading for the table.

'All right, crew,' he called, 'go time.'

He lowered himself into his chair. If he felt me watching him, he didn't look up. When Tawney had been alive, Cal wore the same thing every day on set – old jeans, baseball cap, a hoodie. But he'd evolved. Now he wore black pants, a black silk shirt rolled up over his elbows, expensive black loafers. Playing the part of the most dangerous director in Hollywood, I thought.

With Cal seated, the rest of the actors headed to the table. Melany was so absorbed in her conversation with another actor – a former teen heart-throb turned indie darling – she walked past me without stopping. I waved, and she did a double take.

'Salma! What are you doing here?' Her smile was genuine, although her eyes darted around like she wasn't sure she wanted people to see us talking together.

I forced a smile. 'Accuracy consultant,' I said. 'My family story and all that.'

Melany tugged on the sleeve of her leading man. 'Roger, have you met Salma Lowe?'

Roger grinned, leant across Melany to shake my hand. He was handsome in that improbably symmetric leading-man way; he'd have to work twice as hard to be taken seriously. '*Iron Prayer* was the film that made me want to become an actor,' Roger said, Aussie accent biting through. 'The way your father delivered that line, "Don't worry, kiddo, the sun—"'

I'd heard it a million times. 'Don't say it,' I said quickly. 'Bad luck on a film set.'

Roger looked bewildered and Melany opened her mouth, might've said more, but then Cherry swished by her, smirking at me. 'Salma, darling, how lovely to see you again. You're looking . . . robust,' she said in her sing-song voice, not leaving any doubt that by *robust* she meant *fat*.

The day was young. I comforted myself with the thought that she still had time to roll an ankle in her six-inch Jimmy Choos and snap off her porcelain veneers.

Cal clapped again, and everyone scurried to their seats. A low buzz of excitement took over the room. I spotted the actor playing the Little Sister right away by her blunt black bangs. The heart-shaped face was lovelier than mine had ever been. As she settled herself behind a nameplate that read *Lea Hallowes*, I stared at her with morbid fascination. I couldn't shake the feeling that I was looking at the daughter my mother wished she'd had.

Directly at Cal's right sat the Black woman from the casting session, still looking down at her phone behind her nameplate: *E. Majors*. Finally, when everyone was settled into their seats – Melany kept sending me wide-eyed stares, looking away when I caught her eye – Cal addressed the group.

'Before we get started today,' Cal said. 'I'd like to address a recent tragedy that has befallen our set.' He paused, his face unexpectedly serious. 'Recently, we lost a dear member of our film family in a tragic accident. I think you all know that film is my life. But I don't expect to mean that literally. I don't expect any of *you* to mean

it literally. I know this tragedy was a shock for us all.'
Cal glanced around the room. I followed his gaze. A few
of the crew members looked down. Roger looked self-
consciously sad – *pretty man in melancholy.*

But one crew member had taken it to heart. A short
white woman with acid-green highlights streaking her
dark hair and a grey Reading Rainbow sweatshirt was
choking back sobs. I watched her push her glasses up
onto her forehead, swipe her tears away. She was trying,
unsuccessfully, to stifle the sounds of her sniffles, and I
watched as more people turned from the table read to
watch her.

The woman at Cal's right hand looked up from her
phone, glaring. Reading Rainbow flinched and practically
sprinted from the room, covering her mouth with her
sleeves. Her muffled sobs followed her.

Cal waited until she was gone. 'If anyone would like
to speak to a grief counsellor, the studio has provided
us with a human resources representative. Julie, say hi.'
Behind his shoulder, a corporate suit with a power bob
leant forward, waggled a finger in greeting. 'Now, if we
could all have a moment of silence for Ankine.'

It was the first time he'd said her name in his little
speech.

I bowed my head, turning over Cal's speech. There'd
been nothing *wrong* with it – but it hadn't been very
personal, either. Ankine had been his leading lady. She
and Cal must've spent dozens, if not hundreds, of hours
together. No matter their relationship – wouldn't that
register as grief? Unless there was a reason he *wasn't*
grieving. I snuck a glance at Cal. He had his head bent,

overhead track lighting spotting silver threads amid his dark, glossy hair.

But someone was staring at me. I looked around, my shoulders prickling with the feeling of being watched. Cherry stared at me. She wore electric-peach lipstick, her mouth upturned in the suggestion of a smile. When she caught my eye, she winked.

I forced myself to look back down at my script, words swimming on the page. Underneath the table, I pinched the inside of my thigh until it welted.

Cal lifted his head, gave another thunderous clap. 'All right then. Before we—'

'Excuse me, Cal?'

This time I wasn't the only one staring at Cherry, who pushed back her chair, stood up. Cal didn't answer, just inclined a hand slightly – a king, granting permission to speak, then sat back, arms crossed.

'I wanted to say something, too,' Cherry said, a beatific smile. 'As you all know, this film is an adaptation of my *bestselling* true-crime book, *The Hurricane Blonde*. I can't tell you what it means to me to have you all gathered here today, to work on my book. If you'd like a copy, I'm offering free autographs.' Cherry held for applause. When it didn't come, she sat back down.

Cal's face bore a hint of amusement. 'What a generous offer, Cherry.' I watched Cherry's face redden and she sniffed, pushed her glasses farther up her nose, refusing to meet Cal's eye. I found myself staring at Cherry's nameplate again. *Author*. Not screenwriter or co-producer.

Perhaps Cal and Cherry's relationship was different, too, all these years later.

'For those *new* to our set' – Cal inclined his head to Melany, who blushed – 'a word. What sets my films apart – what *makes* my films art and genius and all those things critics say, is that we're not acting.' He shook his head. 'We're *experiencing*. We are a proxy for the human spirit. When you come to set, come prepared to push yourself further than you believe you can go. It's the only way to make your performance *matter*. If you can't give me your entire soul, well. Feel free to leave the project now.' Cal extended a hand to the door.

I rolled my eyes. Typical Method acting bullshit. Awards-season bait, talent outweighed by struggle. Some actors took it to dangerous extremes, gaining and losing weight for a role, doing irreparable damage to their bodies chasing glory. Pain compensating for talent.

But when I looked at Melany, her eyes were glued to Cal's face. Drinking in every word.

Cal started at the top. He read the stage directions, setting the scene. *Magnum Opus* was an episodic script, circling to different points in Brandon Saturn's life. In some, his path crossed with the Hurricane Blonde's in meaningful ways. In others, a near miss. It was romantic, perhaps, the wish fulfillment of all the ways their lives might've touched.

Except it was my sister. I knew too much about what her life with Cal had been like. And he'd only given the Hurricane Blonde thirteen lines – I'd counted – although she was in nearly every scene. Even in her own film, he'd made Tawney a ghost.

As the read went on, it became clear Melany wasn't up to speed yet. Where Roger and even Lea, cast after her, were already practically off-book – breaking character only to ask for Cal's opinion on a line delivery – Melany stumbled and flubbed, her embarrassment mounting as the minutes passed. I winced with each apology – *Oh my gosh, I don't even know what's with me today!* – expecting Cal to explode. But Cal surprised me, only giving her quick instructions to take it from the top.

That only flustered her more.

The third time she flubbed the same line, Cal stopped the production. My breath snagged and held. This was it. Here was the Cal I remembered, the tantrum-prone taskmaster. I looked around the table. Roger's head was down. Lea chewed a thumbnail. I didn't think it was my imagination that others seemed to be having the same anxious reaction.

'Sorry, Cal,' Melany said, darting a look at him. Her shoulders were hunched, her hair pulled back in a long braid, which she tugged nervously, artfully pulled tendrils framing her face.

There was a long, weighty moment where Cal stared at her blankly, his eyes unreadable. Then he smiled. 'That's all right, my dear, that's what table reads are for. Take three deep breaths, and go again. We all know you've got the talent; just relax and let it take over.'

I exhaled. The tension drained from Melany's shoulders, and she beamed at Cal, blushing. This time, she nailed the lines and glanced up at Cal from under her lashes, melting under his nod of approval.

If anyone else noticed the film didn't properly end, they didn't say anything. Cal stood up and smiled, thanking everyone for their time. I'd been watching him mark notes and I knew what came next: Cal, king of tinkering, would tweak the script with each table read. Then we'd start over. The actors stood up, chattering and stretching out kinked muscles from the hours-long process.

I could feel Cherry watching me as I put away my notepad and script – unlike Cal, I'd only managed one note: *Sobbing Reading Rainbow girl?* Cherry stood up, started toward me, and I didn't even bother to snap my purse closed before I ducked in the opposite direction, eager to hide from her the rest of the day.

It was a good plan, until I smacked into someone, sending an iPhone flying.

I knelt to pick it up, already apologising. 'Oh God, I'm so—'

Cal's right-hand woman glared at me, hand outstretched for the phone. 'Watch it, Salma.' She shook her head. 'Christ, you've always been a klutz.'

Always? She towered over me. I stood up slowly, staring at her face, that beautiful, nearly familiar face, no make-up except for a swipe of pink gloss that matched her silk shirt.

At Morty's House, we're all together, all part of one big famalee . . .

The premise of the show was simple, and unlikely: Morty, a curmudgeon accountant on the brink of retirement, had inherited a rainbow of three little girls, his grandnieces, after our parents died in a cruise ship disaster (specifics never specified). Polly, Greta, and Jenny. I'd played Polly, plucky and outspoken. Jenny had been played by Katie Ng.

And then there was Greta.

'Oh my God,' I said. 'Emmy Majors.'

Emmy gave a half-hearted smile. 'Emerald now, actually.'

Emmy had been the sweetest of us, quiet, always a book in hand between takes. Emmy – *Emerald* – no longer seemed bookish. Her long braids framed a heart-shaped face, her hazel eyes bright behind wire-framed rims. Her heels were true ankle-snappers, four inches high, and she wore an oversize fuchsia blazer over skintight jeans and a vintage concert T-shirt of a band I'd never heard of.

A lifetime ago, we'd been friends. I'd gone over to her house for pizza, and to watch the Disney movies of the week together. We'd practised kissing on our hands, made prank calls to the cute boys in our class – well, in *Emerald's* class; I had a tutor.

And then *Morty's House* ended. And so did the rest of it. Not real friends, after all, just kids in close proximity.

'I didn't realise you were still in the biz,' Emerald said. Her phone buzzed, and she looked down at it. 'But I'm glad. I heard some' – she looked up – 'rumours.'

'Oh?' I forced a laugh. 'That I was in rehab again? Absconded to a tropical island? Locked in a Scientology dungeon? All true.'

'Obviously. No, I thought I heard something about . . .' She hesitated. 'Something about you driving a bus.'

'Oh.' I blinked. Behind Emerald, Cherry was deep in conversation with Roger, squeezing his biceps rhythmically. 'No, um, that's actually true.'

Emerald's brow raised. 'Ah,' she said. 'I'll see you around, Salma.' Her phone lit up again, and she looked down, already moving away. 'Let me buy you coffee sometime, yeah? Catch up a bit.' She didn't wait for a reply.

Like all good producers, Emerald could make demands sound like favours. A new skill.

As she walked away, I wondered if we were both thinking the same dreadful thought: *this could have been me.*

CHAPTER THIRTEEN

I went to find Melany before I left. After her performance at the table read – that fawning look she'd given Cal – I needed to lay my cards on the table. I needed to warn her. A PA pointed me in the direction of the talent trailers, around the corner on Yellow Brick Road. As I walked, buses of tourists whipped by me on fifteen-seater golf carts, waving without knowing who I was. I waved back, breathing in sweet gasoline fumes.

The trailer was a gas-guzzling monster, a large piece of paper with THE HURRICANE BLONDE taped to its side. Maybe Cal expected his leading ladies to have a high turnover rate, so why bother with actors' names.

Or maybe it was one more of his Method expectations.

I took the steps two at a time, my hand raised to knock, and then I stopped. Listened.

I could hear voices inside – Melany's lilting soprano, then a deeper voice – Roger? Cal? – and finally, a third female voice.

It sounded like . . .

I shoved the door open without knocking.

The trailer layout was what I remembered. A small

kitchenette. Bookshelves and a Murphy bed pressed against one of the walls. A bathroom in the back. Melany and Cal were hunched over a laptop at the kitchenette table. I couldn't see what was on the screen, but then I didn't need to. I knew the sound of my own sister's voice.

'She drops her T's,' Melany murmured, jotting something on a notepad.

Cal's hand was on the back of Melany's chair, close enough to stroke the back of her neck. I stared at it, remembering the squeeze of Tawney's throat.

'What are you watching?'

At the sound of my voice, they both turned. Cal's hand dropped.

'Reviewing footage with the Hurricane Blonde here,' Cal said. He smiled at Melany.

I'd hated that nickname while my sister was alive. It was so much worse to hear it now. 'She has a name,' I snapped.

'It's all right,' Melany said, blushing. 'It'll help me get in character. I have big shoes to fill.'

I didn't know if she meant Tawney or Ankine.

Cal nodded toward me. 'Did you enjoy the table read?' His face was polite, like I was a new acquaintance and he was genuinely interested in my experience.

Like he hadn't fucked me the day they put my sister in the ground.

'Yes, thank you,' I said, finding myself meeting his formal tone. I searched for something to say, remembered the dark-haired ingenue who'd sat opposite Melany at the table read. Cal's Salma had cried twice on cue. 'The Little Sister is well cast. I understand why you went in a different direction.'

129

Cal's lip curled, just the hint of a laugh. 'Funny, Salmon,' he said. 'You always were funny.'

Melany's attention bounced back and forth between us. I saw her mouth, *Salmon*, as he said it.

I ignored the traitorous frisson I felt, hearing my nickname from his mouth again.

'I'll let you two visit,' Cal said, darting smoothly around me, placing a hand over a leather portfolio file open in front of him, blocking my view. As he got up, he tugged on Melany's braid. 'Wear it down tomorrow,' he said, and Melany blushed harder, nodding. She practically scalped herself yanking out the hair tie.

I craned my neck to glance at the portfolio. Glossy paper – photographs were my best guess. Cal was meticulous about framing his shots perfectly; it was his past as a director of photography. He closed the file, then squeezed by me, taking as much care not to touch me as if I'd been radioactive.

'Before I forget.' From the portfolio, Cal pulled a small white sheet of paper. 'Homework.'

He passed it to Melany, who practically kissed it, before putting it in her pocket.

Cal stopped at the door. 'Actually, Salma, do you have five minutes?' He checked his watch. 'I'd love to pick your brain.'

'P-pick my brain?' I'd have been less shocked if he hit me.

'Yes,' he said in that patient tone. So unlike the Cal I'd known. 'In my office.'

I looked at Melany as I tried to think of a plausibly polite refusal – no way was I going alone to his office. But Melany was no help. If anything, she looked jealous.

Cal's walkie-talkie lit up, crackling. *'Cal, they need you at set dec.'*

Sweet relief. 'Pity,' Cal said. 'Another time.'

As Cal left, Melany plonked herself in front of the mirror, pulling up her long blonde hair into a ponytail. She had a picture of Tawney tacked to the mirror, the same headshot that graced Cherry's book. She smiled at me in the reflection, turning so her chin was propped up by the back of the chair.

'So,' Melany said, her eyes glittering. 'What was she like? What should I use for my performance?'

I dodged it. 'What's your homework?'

'I'm not sure, it's – Oh.' Melany pulled it out of her pocket. I watched her face fall as she read it.

'What is it?'

Melany nibbled on the end of her ponytail. 'It's, um, instructions. For tomorrow.'

I frowned. 'Instructions?'

'Yeah, just like, um . . .' Melany swallowed. She didn't want to tell me. 'Things to help me get in character.'

'Can I see?'

Reluctantly, Melany handed me the paper. *Instructions* was generous. To me, it looked like demands.

1. *The Hurricane Blonde must always remain in character on set. No exceptions.*

2. *The Hurricane Blonde should seek director approval before meals or snacks. If the Hurricane Blonde is off-set while eating, she must send the director a photo of her proposed meal for permission.*

3. The Hurricane Blonde shall respond to the director's queries via text or email within thirty minutes. No exceptions.

4. The Hurricane Blonde must be off-book by the end of the week.

'I've got my work cut out for me,' Melany said with an uneasy laugh.

I looked up. 'Melany, this is bullshit. He can't ask you to send him photos of your food before you eat. That's insane.'

Melany turned back to her mirror, trying a different configuration of her hair, then letting it drop against her shoulders. 'If this is what it takes, this is what it takes,' she said, her voice resolute, chipper. She met my eyes in the mirror. 'Can you call me the Hurricane Blonde from now on?'

I handed the list back, shaking my head. Melany was already moving on, telling me the notes she'd made about the role, how Cal was helping her envision the Hurricane Blonde, and did it really sound like Tawney? Or was it maybe more like . . .

I tuned her out as I glanced around the trailer again. On *Morty's House*, each of us kids had had our own trailer, but we'd all piled into mine to study between takes. Sometimes Tawney would sneak us treats – donuts or bagels – never indulging herself. I never would have guessed, back then, that Emerald would land on the production side of things. Cal Turner's right-hand woman, of all people.

Emerald had been a good actor, even in the *Morty's*

House days, more intuitive and reactive than me or Jenny. One moment on set, she'd be smiling, impish, full of life and high spirits. And then the camera would switch off, or the director would move on to someone else, and her face would fall back into neutral, a carefully shuttered mask. In our trailers between takes, the three of us kids had played bullshit – BS when adults were around – and Emerald won nine times out of ten.

That poker face would have evolved over the years.

I gave Melany the occasional *hmm*, or *that sounds like a good idea*, as she unspooled her thoughts, still thinking about Cal's directives. Waiting for her to wind down so I could warn her.

Melany had already started cluttering her trailer with knick-knacks: I spotted picture frames on a far console, a stack of papers, a fancy candle. I walked to the console, glancing at the trinkets assembled there. A handwritten card, propped up, a shooting star on the front. I smirked at it, flipped it open.

Ankine! Now that you're famous, I expect a million-dollar trust fund. I'm not greedy. I will take payments in installments. Love ya, sis. Love, Brian.

My hands shook so badly I dropped the card. A note to Ankine from one of her little brothers.

I bent over, picked it up, rereading.

No one had come to clean out the trailer yet.

I set the card back onto the console shakily, then looked down at the piles of paper beside it. A blank NDA. Wardrobe measurements. Underneath, a thick brick of script. *Magnum Opus.* Someone had drawn a tiny heart next to Cal's name in purple gel ink.

133

'Salma?' Melany was staring at me in the mirror, frowning. 'Are you okay?'

I pointed at the script. 'Is this yours?' Miraculously, my voice didn't quaver.

Melany shook her head. 'I think it belonged to' – she lowered her voice, made a theatrical grimace – *'you know who.'*

I flipped through the pages. Purple gel ink notes covered the margins with increasing frequency. Ankine's thoughts, a little window into her psyche. Maybe even into her relationship with Cal.

'Do you mind if I take this?'

Melany shot me a funny look, then shrugged. 'I guess not.'

I tucked the script under my arm. But I still hadn't done what I'd come to do. Melany had her head bent over her script, lips mouthing the words as she practised.

I took a deep breath. 'Melany, be careful, okay?'

She looked up at me, her nose crinkled, a goofy little smile on her face. 'What do you mean?'

There was too much to tell her, and not enough to say. 'Film sets are . . .' I searched for the words. On the third season of *Morty's House* – I was thirteen – my producer, Carla, wandered into my trailer during a fitting, pinched a roll of my stomach between two fingers. *We'll fix this for you, okay? Trust me. You don't even have to worry.* Diet pills cut with amphetamines, uppers for the red carpet, champagne lunches – endless access to danger disguised as a good time.

'Just, um. If anybody ever says or does anything that makes you uncomfortable, come talk to me, okay? We can

134

figure out how to handle it together.' Melany stared at me blankly in her mirror. But that wasn't far enough. I was chickening out. 'And be careful around Cal especially. He's got a volatile reputation for a reason.'

Melany stared at me, then gave a little tinkling laugh. She pushed herself away from the vanity, throwing her arms around me. 'Salma, you're a doll, you know that?'

I stared at myself in the mirror, her golden head notched to my shoulder. She wasn't hearing me. But then, if I were her – on the verge of my big break, hungry for stardom, about to become the person I'd always dreamt I'd be – well. I wouldn't have listened, either.

It was on me to keep her safe – from Cal, from Hollywood, from herself.

CHAPTER FOURTEEN

Ankine Petrosyan had been surprisingly funny.

On the stage directions that introduced the Hurricane Blonde (*early twenties, proportions that get a girl in trouble*) Ankine had scratched out *girl* and written, in all caps purple, *WOMAN*. I could almost feel her rolling her eyes as she read. I wondered if, under different circumstances, we would have been friends.

Then I remembered the picture of her dressed up as Tawney a year before Cal's film. Maybe not.

I'd driven back to Glassell Park with the script on my passenger seat, stealing glances at it like it was a baby I hadn't properly buckled. I barely made it to the bungalow court before I was buried in it.

I skimmed through to the end, focusing on Ankine's notes. One caught my eye. On page fifty-three, the Hurricane Blonde broke it off with Brandon Saturn. She didn't offer an explanation. In the margins, Ankine had scribbled notes. *Does she haunt him because she left, or because she died?*

It was a good question. Tawney had clammed up whenever I'd asked her why she'd left Cal so abruptly.

I'd been enamoured of their relationship, mistaking the volatility for passion – I was fifteen. And then there'd been the co-star Eric Wainwright. The rumours. I pushed those disloyal thoughts out of my head. I was no better than a tabloid, speculating.

Maybe that was how Cal remembered his breakup with Tawney, a big question mark never answered. *Maybe he answered that question himself*, a little voice whispered.

On another page, near a description of the Jacaranda House, Ankine had scribbled the name *Elizabeth Wennick*. It rang a bell, and I frowned at the page, wishing it would give up its secrets. Wennick – where did I know that name?

I closed my eyes, picturing a photocopy of an official-looking document. MacLeish's police report. The owner of the Jacaranda House was listed as an E. F. Wennick. I chewed my lip. Ankine had done her research. Maybe it was a part of Method acting. But the film was about the past, not the present. I didn't like all the connections she was turning up close to my family. It felt like a noose drawing in tight.

I flipped forward to look again at the three different death scenes for the Hurricane Blonde in Ankine's script. It was an interesting technical choice, I thought, not giving the audience the resolution they wanted, the definitive proof.

It was also a chance for Cal to watch my sister die, over and over and over.

A word on page seventy stopped me. I paused, read slowly. I flipped forward, then back. The first and third deaths remained the same – a car accident, and then a representation of her real-life death, strangulation, culprit unknown.

But in Ankine's script, the second death scene had been changed.

I scrambled for my own version of the script, comparing. In my copy, the Hurricane Blonde in her second death simply disappeared, wandering away from Brandon into a darkened landscape, never to be seen again.

But in Ankine's script, there it was – in the stage notes. *EXT. The Hurricane Blonde, wearing a white bikini, walks down the steps of the pool, Brandon Saturn behind her. She looks peaceful; Saturn places his hands on her shoulders. Slowly, she submerges into the water. From underneath the water, we can see the outline of Saturn – watching. Watching.*

I blinked at the paper, not believing my eyes. I read the scene, then re-read it.

Cal had changed the script. He'd killed one of his Hurricane Blondes in a pool, and then Ankine died *in that same pool.*

I sat at my kitchen table in Glassell Park, but I was looking across town, to the Jacaranda House. Two women dead in the same spot, twenty years apart. Cal the biggest link between them.

I was glad I didn't keep any alcohol in the house. When I closed my eyes, I could imagine the velvet finish of a Gamay Rouge on my tongue, the heat of it in my throat. How easy it would be to use the alcohol to forget for a little while.

I snapped my eyes open. Cal fucking Turner and his goddamn Method acting, uncorking my thirst. But I wasn't that person any more. I wouldn't let myself be.

I put Ankine's script away and pulled up her Instagram. A new post announced a memorial. *Public welcome.* I scanned the details – Forest Lawn cemetery, Sunday, 8th October.

I was about to click out of her profile when something stopped me. I squinted down at the screen.

The last time I'd checked, she had about four thousand followers. Now, after her death, that number had shot up to nearly three hundred thousand. More comments had been left on her posts, many of them urging her to rest in peace, professing their admiration.

I couldn't believe it – but then, I *could*. In death, she'd found the fame she'd wanted while she was alive, I thought.

Hollywood loves a dead girl. She's always photogenic.

Two days later, I had my first real run in with Cherry.

By the end of the week, we'd moved from table reads to blocking shots, practise run-throughs on the semi-completed sets. With each rehearsal, Melany – the Hurricane Blonde – gained a little more confidence. And as she did, Cal beamed more approval her way.

More than once, I'd spotted them together, whispering and laughing in some private corner of the set.

I didn't like it. I didn't *trust* it. I caught myself staring at him for long swaths of the blocking, looking for any sign of a guilty conscience. He'd written a death for one of his characters that had come true, and then erased the evidence from his script.

Once or twice, he caught me staring. I flinched when he met my gaze, but I didn't blink. His face was closed to me now; I couldn't read his expression. Then, as if nothing had happened, he looked away.

For all my suspicions, Cal did appear to be a changed

person. He was still intense, focussed to a fault, and not particularly patient when either the cast or crew made a mistake. But he had learnt to hold his temper better, even to joke between scenes. Nobody walked on eggshells around him the way they once had.

The only time the façade fell was when Cherry butted in.

During the first blocking pass, Cherry found ways to comment on every artistic choice Cal made. Most of it was subtle: tapping her nails on the arm of her chair, clicking the top of her pen, shifting creakily when Cal posed something *just so*. Just enough to grab attention.

Cal ignored Cherry, keeping his focus on his actors. But I could see his shoulders tighten with each micro-interruption.

Cal was blocking the Little Sister's meltdown in the chapel – my favourite scene – when Cherry spoke up.

'Oh dear,' Cherry said. I looked up from my script. When Cal didn't react, she repeated it louder. '*Oh. Dear.*'

Cal had his hands on Lea's, the Little Sister's, shoulders as he walked her through the motions of the scene when Cherry interrupted. Cal's jaw clenched. He took a long beat before he turned to face her. 'Okay, Cherry, I hear you.'

Cherry leant back in her folding chair, re-crossing her legs to show them off. She had the slim thighs of a teenager still and she knew it, twitching them to draw attention. Below her skirt, I could see sunspots dotting her legs like polka dots. 'Sorry, darling, but I believe you've got that line wrong. Read it again for me?'

Lea looked at Cal for permission before complying. 'I can't be in here with my sister in a box—'

'There,' Cherry said, jabbing the air with one triumphant coral-painted finger. 'See? Page one-eighty-six.' She held up her copy of *The Hurricane Blonde*. 'The line should be, "I can't stand to be in a room where my sister is dead in a box."'

The Little Sister looked at Cal. I looked at Cal. The entire crew looked at Cal.

Cal smiled. 'It's the right line.'

'Well, shouldn't we be sure—'

'I know what I wrote,' Cal gritted out. 'It stays.'

Cherry turned, pointed at me. 'Salma, which was it?'

Now everyone on the soundstage was looking at *me*, Cal included. I felt a swell of panic. *No, no, not me, not for this.* I didn't want to get in between Cal and Cherry.

'I don't remember,' I admitted. 'That whole day is a bit . . . fuzzy.'

The funeral was, at least.

Cherry rolled her eyes, waggling the book in Cal's direction. In the lights, her hair glowed purple. 'I don't know why you bothered to hire her, baby, when you've got me right here. I wrote the damn book.'

Cal took his time crossing the soundstage to Cherry, drawing out each step so all eyes were on him. He held out his hand and Cherry smiled at him, handing over the book. Without missing a beat, he threw it across the room, where it clattered into a set and fell to the ground. Someone squeaked, and then it was silent.

'Call me "baby" one more time.' Cal's voice was quiet. 'Try it.'

Melany tried to smooth it over, giving him an appealing little smile. 'Cal, I think she's just—'

Cal whirled, glaring at her. 'Did I ask for your fucking opinion?'

Melany's mouth dropped open, and I could see she was fighting back startled tears. I realised I was trembling gently in my chair, my heart beating like a trapped hummingbird.

Emerald placed a hand on Cal's arm, whispering something to him. Whatever she said must've helped because Cal closed his eyes, took a deep breath, then said: 'Let's take five.'

The spell broken, the set came back to life, like it never happened. Cherry shoved herself out of her folding chair and stomped away. Cal kept his back turned, chatting quietly with Emerald.

I found Melany staring down at her script.

I squatted next to her chair, tried to get her to look at me. 'You're doing great,' I told her. 'Really – crisp line readings, you're nailing it.'

Melany huffed. 'Yeah, thanks.'

I chewed on my lip. 'Hey, he's an asshole. We all know it. Don't take it too personally.' *And don't go anywhere near a pool with him.*

Melany shook her head. She looked up, her eyes hot and glaring. 'I shouldn't have gotten in the middle. It was my fault.'

'You don't really believe that, do you, Melany?' It was out of my mouth before I realised.

'I told you,' she seethed. 'Don't call me that.'

I stood up. She was glaring at me like I was the problem. 'Sorry. My mistake.'

Melany held up her script. 'I need to practise my lines

before we go again. Do you mind?'

Well, she had Tawney's stubbornness down, that was for sure.

Dismissed, I headed outside, needing to clear my head. It had rattled me, seeing Cal like that again. I'd believed – *known* – he was dangerous. But seeing it again up close took my breath away. Cherry had been lucky he hadn't thrown the book in her face.

I pushed the door to the soundstage open, blinded slightly by the sunlight.

'Well, well. If it isn't the *accuracy consultant*.'

My vision cleared. Cherry stood on the landing, sucking on an e-cigarette like a lifeline. The door clanged shut behind me.

'Salma Lowe,' Cherry said, exhaling a plume of blueberry smoke. Her voice was velvet and unpleasant, like a sloppy kiss from a stranger. 'Time has not been kind to *you*, my dear.'

We bared our teeth at each other, the way chimps smile at each other in the wild. Both of us playing so very nice.

When I was twenty, fresh out of rehab for the first time, Cherry had run a story with the headline *Sloppy Salma up to her old tricks: Mama must be so proud!*

Admittedly, it hadn't been my finest hour: I'd crashed a rooftop pool party, slipped, and fallen into the water, cutting my foot on the flute of champagne I was definitely not allowed to be drinking. The photo accompanying the article showed my swimsuit twisted around a peekaboo nipple, my bloody foot in the foreground.

Those were all my bad choices. But the glee Cherry took in reporting them – that I couldn't forgive. I'd needed a couple of years to wise up: never read the headlines. Never read the tabloids *period*.

I cleared my throat. I'd pitied Cherry for a moment in there, with the full force of Cal's rage turned on her. It wasn't a comfortable feeling. 'Are you all right? After . . . that?'

Cherry exhaled a long stream of smoke. The sun illuminated her mascara, bright blue to match her linen blazer. 'A temper tantrum.' She shook her head. 'This film is going to have all kinds of scrutiny after that girl died. He'll thank me, once he calms down.'

That was one way of looking at it. Cherry had always been Cal's biggest champion, spending columns praising his films when he was still a nobody. She referred to him as *The boy genius, the wunderkind, America's next great auteur.* And then, after my sister's death had threatened to blow the wind the other way, she'd found a way to harness the controversy: a cover profile of Cal, dubbed *The most dangerous director in Hollywood.*

But she'd also opened a door for me. 'What was Ankine like?'

Cherry snorted. Up close, her perfume was a gardenia smog. 'Nightmare. An absolute nightmare.' My eyebrows shot up. It was a breathtakingly crass thing to say, and even Cherry realised it, blushing.

'A nightmare?'

But Cherry was a quick learner. She didn't take the bait again. 'A Method actress and a Method director – they brought out the worst in each other. Besides, *you* know what actresses are like,' she said, baring her teeth at me. 'Anyway . . .' Cherry deftly changed the subject, flashing that Cheshire grin I remembered so well. 'What's this about you working as a bus driver?'

It shouldn't have surprised me. And yet. 'I'm a historian. I run a true-crime tour in Hollywood.'

She gargled a laugh. 'I bet Vivienne's *thrilled*.'

'My mother—' I snapped, caught myself. The old Salma would've taken Cherry's bait. 'My mother supports my work.' I turned to the doors. 'I should go.'

'I'll bet,' Cherry said with a wink. 'We'll be seeing much more of each other soon.'

I stopped, my hand on the handle of the elephant door. 'I'll be here every day, so yes.'

Cherry grinned. 'No, dear. Your father's retrospective. I'll be interviewing your mother onstage. Such a tragedy, that a great man died so long before his time.' She watched me take it in, barely concealing her enjoyment. Then she pressed a finger to her lips, making a show of thinking. 'I wonder – now that he's gone, is your mother finally ready for the truth to come out?'

I slammed the door shut behind me, not bothering to reply. I hoped I'd closed the door before she got a look at my face.

All these years later, Cherry's aim was still deadly.

MARCH 1991

The first and only time I attended the Academy Awards, I was nine years old. I was my father's date for his third, and final, Best Actor nomination.

Tawney helped me pick out a dress that made me feel like a princess, frosting me in layers of icy blue tulle, silver stars. My mother smeared a kiss of pink lipstick on my lips before I left – *Like a big girl now, Salma* – and catching my reflection in the limo's windows, I'd turned my head this way and that, admiring the clips in my hair, the bits of pink goo on my mouth. I thought I looked older. More like Tawney.

I didn't think to ask why I was going instead of my mother, or Tawney, who was on the verge of teenage stardom.

At dinner with my father and Jack, I knocked back so many Shirley Temples I thought I'd be sick before we even made it to the Shrine Civic Auditorium. But when I stepped onto the glowing red carpet, my hand locked tight in my father's, and people I'd never seen before clapped my father's back, told him how talented he was, and *My goodness, who is this pretty girl*, I forgot all about the

Shirley Temples. I decided I loved being famous. I wanted to spend the rest of my life feeling exactly this way.

My father's charms hadn't yet started to erode, and if he wore sunglasses all evening to hide his hungover puffiness, he still had that famous sharky grin. For pictures, he would hoist me onto his shoulder, a girl-size parrot, and whisper that I was the prettiest girl there, the best date he ever had.

Women, especially, approached him on the red carpet.

'Who are *you*?' they'd coo, slipping close to me in a pretext of looking at my dress; more than one found an excuse to skim a hand over my father's biceps, a hip, the knob of his chest between shoulder and collarbone.

'This is Salma,' my father would say, his hands proud on my shoulders. 'She's going to be an actress someday. One of the *greats*, I promise you.'

And I believed him for a long, long time.

When my father lost the award, he took it like a champ, clapping and laughing for the other attendees. Not making a big deal of his disappointment. I thought the night was over, but he took me to a party hosted at the Bar Marmont, the swanky lounge in the Chateau. When he entered the bar – an intimate affair, only the best of the A-list – a cheer went up through the crowd. Dave Lowe was a good time, and everyone knew it.

Well-wishers pressed drinks into my father's hand – *You were robbed, Dave* – which my father accepted with a gracious bob of his head, a *What can you do?* grin.

When he noticed my eyes drooping, he parked me on the couch, and I curled up and drifted off to sleep amid the crowd. I was Dave Lowe's daughter. No one would hurt me.

When I woke up, hours later, I was alone. I sat up, rubbing the sleep out of my eyes as I looked for my father. I couldn't find him. I pushed through a forest of spray-tanned legs and pinchy high heels, brushed wool gabardine slacks, searching.

I told myself he wouldn't have left, not without me. Besides, everyone at the party was a friend of my father's, which meant they were my friends, too. I didn't start to panic until I'd circled the party twice. No sign of my father. A woman leant down, cleavage spilling out of her strapless dress, tipsy hands on tipsy knees as she cooed, 'Are you lost, little girl?' Her hand slipped, and she spilt something that smelt like gasoline on my dress.

I was working up a good cry when I spotted him, in shadow on the patio. His shoes first with their shiny wing tips next to strappy red pumps. The blue glow of a cigarette passed back and forth between him and a tall blonde who shimmied her hair over her shoulders as she laughed at something he said. As I walked toward them, she passed him the cigarette, then slipped one French-manicured hand against the front of his pants, cupping him.

I froze and watched. I didn't know what I was seeing, only enough to know I didn't like it. She squeezed then slid her hand back up. My father took one long drag on the cigarette, said something to her, then looked over his shoulder – a guilty reflex – and spotted me. He twitched away, straightened his jacket.

When he stepped into the light, he was all smiles. Like nothing had happened. 'Salma, baby,' my father said, opening his arms to hug me. 'Ready to leave?'

Later, at home, I found Tawney in her bathroom. The

door was locked, and I could hear the sink going. My sister opened the door, dry toothbrush in hand.

I couldn't get the words out, I couldn't get them right. Only the bad feeling it had given me.

But Tawney knew as soon as she saw my face.

My sister – sixteen, a woman of the world – shushed me, wrapped me in a hug, spine knobby and birdlike under my hands. 'Now you know,' she whispered, and it wasn't a question. 'It'll be okay, Salmon. The truth hurts but it's always better to know.'

'Does Mom know?'

Tawney blew out a big sigh, ruffling her bangs. 'Yes. Mom knows.'

That should've been a weight off, but somehow it wasn't. 'Jack, too?'

Tawney pulled at her baggy T-shirt, accentuating her waist. She'd started dieting the week before, after a particularly nasty tabloid photo zoomed in on her arms at a premiere. *More like Flabby Lowe.* 'Of course. Jack knows all the secrets.'

I never told my parents what I'd seen. Only Tawney.

For the next few days, there was a stormy tension in our household. Tawney filled me in, eventually; I wasn't the only one who'd seen my father with the blonde, a co-star on an upcoming film. A reporter was threatening a scoop. Tawney caught me listening at closed doors to the barely contained cadence of my parents' fights, only hearing snatches of words: *Can't believe you'd do this to me; C'mon, Viv, don't you think you're overreacting; should let them do it this time, what do you think would happen then?*

'Don't worry,' Tawney told me, sitting next to me on the silk rug outside their master bedroom, where I was sprawled on my stomach, ear to the door. 'She won't let them run the story. She never does.'

But that wasn't what I was worried about.

In the end, Tawney was right. My mother worked her Powell magic, or maybe Jack worked his. The story turned out to be unverifiable. A libel lawsuit in the making.

There was a price, though. There was always a price.

The next week, *Vanity Fair* ran a story instead about the Lowe family tragedy: a miscarriage. No one had even known my mother was pregnant. Privacy needed during this devastating time. A family portrait of all of us – minus Tawney, who refused to pose – my mother, the trained actor, looking serene and sad about a miscarriage that never happened.

The byline on the article was a cub reporter for *Vanity Fair*, a Hollywood beat stringer named Cherry Partridge.

CHAPTER FIFTEEN

The Cinerama Dome was the shape of an enormous golf ball chopped in half, puckered and dimpled. Less a kitschy throwback and more a remnant of 1960s Hollywood – the Manson and Polanski years – it was still home to premieres, and fond of nostalgic showings of classic cinema. It was a reminder of what Hollywood had been once and, for better or worse, would never be again.

As I waited in line to grab a ticket, I noticed a large poster with my father's face plastered over it, handsome and young; his retrospective already selling tickets weeks early. Beneath his photo:

VIVIENNE POWELL LOWE IN CONVERSATION
WITH CHERRY PARTRIDGE.

Maybe that explained why the Cinerama Dome was playing *Iron Prayer* every night for the next month.

He would've loved it. Dave Lowe, with his thinning blond hair and snaggle-toothed grin, wasn't the second coming of Cary Grant. Unlike my mother, my father hadn't been raised in a Hollywood family; he'd willed himself into superstardom, a combination of talent and natural charisma. The chemistry he was able to generate – on and off-screen – made him the thinking woman's leading man. He'd worked hard for that; I was proud of him.

I braced myself as the lights went down. I hadn't watched *Iron Prayer* since his death – a massive heart attack in the Beverly Hills Hotel bar two years before, instantly fatal. No less devastating than my sister's death, although the violence this time was only internal, his heart going off like a soft bomb inside his ribs. Seeing him on-screen was still a jolt, as though he might climb down and give me a hug, the tinkle of the ice in his glass behind my ear as I buried my face in his cashmere sweater.

The film's first shot was a lazy pan through the haze of a long-gone Los Angeles, curving its way through bustling jewellers' fronts, past the glowing neon of Grand Central Market, the burnt marigold of the Angels Flight trolley, landing, finally, in a velvet-boothed bar replete with dark-haired dame, *sex* and *danger* and *can't help myself* written all over her.

My mother.

A Raisinet was melting in my hands. I popped it in my mouth, licked my fingers clean, then wiped them against my jeans, not taking my eyes off the screen.

Vivienne ashed a glowing cigarette in a glass bowl, camera catching the graceful curve of her cheek as she looked away, doling herself out in bits. On-screen, she looked like a stranger.

Then the voice-over kicked in: my father, playing an FBI agent with a weakness for dark-haired, buxom, witty women. It wasn't a stretch. 'They tell you, never trust a

152

dame with gams that long, but I couldn't help myself . . .'

The sound of his voice squeezed my throat with tears. *How's my little Salmon doing today, swimming upstream?* On-screen, the titles ran, shadowed and slanting. DAVE LOWE. VIVIENNE POWELL. A few scrolls later: PRODUCED BY JACK PARLATO. All the important players there; Tawney and I set to enter, stage right, in a few years. A family preunion, of sorts.

In the film, Dave Lowe was charming, handsome, upright, and heroic, if remote. The father I'd known had let me tug on his curly hair when we played horsey when I was a toddler, had argued with my sister constantly, was always the first to apologise.

On-screen, my mother flicked a long lock of dark hair out of her face and said her most famous line: 'Well, Detective, when you decide you want to tango with the big girls, maybe you'll shimmy it my way.' That click of her tongue on *tango*, the slurp of her mouth on *shimmy*. Little nuances that added up to three seconds on-screen that would stand the test of time. Actors would kill for it.

In less than a year, she'd lose the Oscar for her performance; weeks later, Tawney was born.

It was on the set of *Iron Prayer* that my parents had fallen in love. But more than that, it was the start of their golden Hollywood mythology. My father, placing his confirmed bachelorhood at the feet of my mother: herself the elegant daughter of a director, the granddaughter of a studio head. A princess who reformed the former womaniser through her worthiness.

Truly, a Hollywood love story.

As a kid, I'd been obsessed with the film, watched it over

and over, trying to see the exact moment my parents fell in love. Was it when my mother slapped my father across the face after he told her the terrible truth at the heart of his investigation? Was it when he took her in his arms, cradled her under the soft amber lights of Union Station, and told her he loved her, the performance becoming true, truth being performed? Or was it a smaller moment: the twist of her half-smile, his throaty laugh. The movie was the start of *me*. It was better than a scrapbook.

And it was the secret sauce of the film, the way you urged them toward each other, even knowing it would mean utter disaster. *Because* of it.

Finally, the reveal: my mother, the obvious *femme fatale*, had been secretly good all along and truly in love with my father, trying to go straight. But it was too late. Driven insane by his jealousy and paranoia, my father forced tragedy along. In the end, my mother, the moll with the heart of gold, wound up bent-limbed in the trunk of a car, sinking to the bottom of a river. The world broken apart, never to be repaired.

My father was the only one who didn't know the truth at the heart of the double cross, wouldn't know it even after the credits rolled. She'd loved him all along.

But look: the last frame of the film. My father, the FBI agent, knelt in front of my mother's little sister, the last keeper of her secrets, a nymphet whose fluorescent tears shone in the dark. He tucked a blonde curl behind her ear – gruffly father-like, in a way that still sent a pang to my heart – and said the line that made his career: 'Don't worry, kiddo. The sun will come out tomorrow. It almost always does.'

I couldn't help myself. I mouthed the words, sniffling back tears.

I kept my head down and waited for everyone else to leave the theatre, an old movie star trick to preserve privacy.

As I waited, I noticed a bright white head in the second row, waiting, too. I squinted, but it wasn't until he turned his head to check the rest of the theatre that I realised it was really him.

I made my way down the rows. 'Hey, old-timer,' I called.

Behind his bifocals, Jack's eyes looked huge and cartoonish. His face lit up, and he creaked himself to stand, moving slowly, to hug me.

'What are you doing here?' Jack offered me a mostly empty popcorn bag, sitting down.

I popped a handful in my mouth. 'Same as you, I think. Taking a stroll down memory lane.'

Jack chuckled. He stared up at the rolling credits like the action was still going. 'She's beautiful, isn't she?'

I didn't pretend not to know who he meant.

Jack never married, although there'd been women over the years. No one for long. I had a vague childhood memory of a dark-haired woman, eyes cool as water, who seemed to be in the cobwebby corner of every holiday party and birthday. I couldn't remember her face, though there was the faint impression of a graceful name – Gretchen? Isobel? – and my father sidling up, *Jack, when are you going to put a ring on it? A woman like Isobel won't wait forever. C'mon, Jack* . . .

And in the end, he was right. She hadn't waited forever. We all pretended it was bad luck, commitment issues. Nothing else.

'I miss him,' I said instead. Jack looped his arm around me. In the dim dark, his cologne was enough like my father's that I could feel the tears starting again. I closed my eyes, rested my head against his shoulder.

'You never did call me back.'

'It's been a weird few weeks.'

Jack was silent. I knew he wouldn't push me. 'Anything you want to tell me?'

I took a deep breath, then I told him all about finding Ankine. Jack listened with his eyes on the screen, frowning. The credits had long since stopped rolling, but he stared ahead, as though he could still see my mother's image up there, thirty feet high. When he realised I was finished, he shook his head. 'Christ, kid, you've got no luck at all.'

'How did she wind up in Tawney's pool?'

Jack didn't say anything. Tawney's name hung heavy between us; she was the one thing we'd never found a way to talk about.

When it became clear he wasn't going to respond, I tried a different tack. 'What happened to Tawney's house after she died?'

Jack tipped his head back, thinking. 'Your mother sold it. A year or two after . . . everything.'

He couldn't even bring himself to say my sister was dead. 'To someone named Elizabeth Wennick?'

Jack went very still. In the silver glow from the screen, I could see his eyelashes fluttering. He opened his mouth, then closed it. He glanced at me, brow furrowed. 'I can't remember,' he said, and I thought he looked embarrassed. An old man, getting older. 'Where did you get that name?'

'From the police,' I said. It wasn't a lie. 'Just curious, I guess.'

Jack nodded slowly, looking ancient as he considered it. 'Wennick. Maybe it was Wennick.' He put his arm out. 'Help me up, let's skedaddle.'

Jack leant on me as he stood up, wincing as his spine cracked audibly. In the lobby light, he looked older than I was used to, frailer. An old man, come to revisit an old love. I went on my tiptoes to kiss him, his face like paper under my lips. 'Take care of yourself, old man.'

Jack squeezed my arm. Then his face got serious. 'You, too, love.' He took a deep breath. 'You can't change the past by digging it up, Salma. When you're my age, maybe you'll feel the same way.'

I watched him walk out of the theatre, limping a little. I wanted to ask him: *if that's true, why are you here?*

But I already knew the answer.

CHAPTER SIXTEEN

The next few days on set were a flurry. Cal asked me to sit in on wardrobe fittings, so I could give notes. No detail too small to agonise over. He watched my face greedily as I doled out little pieces of my sister: her signature lipstick shade, Naughty Peach. That she only put perfume in her hair, not on her body. In those moments, I had Cal's undivided attention, and the weight of it made me feel sick.

I made sure I was never alone with him. He didn't mention meeting in his office again. I tried not to leave Melany alone with him, either, tried to keep her always in my line of sight, unless I was with Cal. Then I could breathe a sigh of relief.

And as the days went on, principal photography moving ever closer, I turned over Cherry's comment. Ankine was *a nightmare*. What had she meant by it? I didn't trust Cherry, but it was a lead.

Most of the crew gave me blank stares when I asked if there had been anything off in Cal's relationship with Ankine. *There is no normal when you're talking about Cal Turner*, more than one told me. *He wasn't any different with her than anyone else.*

But no one used the word *nightmare*, either.

The head hairdresser had a complaint. 'Her hair was always turning green,' she said. 'I gave her special shampoo to use, but she wouldn't do it.'

I cocked my head, and she rolled her eyes. 'Chlorine. She swam laps every morning. Annoying as hell, I had to process her on a weekly basis. But she wouldn't give it up.'

Tawney had famously swum thirty laps every morning. Surely that wasn't a coincidence, either. But if Ankine was such a frequent swimmer, how had she drowned?

During a wardrobe fitting, I realised one of the neon-haired assistants was the woman who had run sobbing out of Cal's announcement about Ankine – I overheard someone call her Avril. She was fitting Melany for a sky-blue slip dress – the dress for death number three, strangulation – although she still didn't make eye contact or smile. Avril was jumpy, barely finishing Cal's and Emerald's notes before hurrying out of sight.

Almost like she couldn't stand to be in the same room with him.

I watched Melany and Cal together – possibly discussing her allotted calorie intake for the day – weighing the risks before I followed.

'Hey!' I called after her as she scurried down the hallway. 'Wait up!'

She turned and peered over her shoulder at me, her steps slowing. She'd exchanged the Reading Rainbow sweatshirt for a shredded black T-shirt. She fiddled with her fingers anxiously as I caught up.

'Can I help you?' Standing in front of her, I realised she was young – twenty-five, maybe. Her big green eyes blinked owlishly at me from behind her round glasses.

I should've come up with a cover story, I realised. Something sly to get her to talk to me about Ankine. But I wasn't exactly the second coming of Philip Marlowe. I decided to be honest. 'I saw you crying the other day when Cal was talking about Ankine. Did you know her?'

Avril's eyes filled with tears. 'We were . . . friends. Room-mates, actually.'

Oof. Brutal. I nodded sympathetically. This wasn't going to be the person to pump for information about why Cherry thought Ankine was a nightmare. 'It must've been hard for you. Her dying in a terrible accident like that.'

Avril's face darkened. 'It wasn't an accident.'

My pulse jumped. 'What do you mean?'

Avril choked back a sob. 'Cal was going to fire her. You know she was obsessed with the Hurricane Blonde? When she heard Cal was making the film, she told me it was the role she was born to play. Ankine would've rather die than lose the part. I think . . . I think she . . .'

Then she had her face in her hands, fully sobbing. I thought I understood what she meant. She thought Ankine killed herself. But purposefully drowning yourself in a pool – without weights in your pockets, something to keep you submerged – was hard. Maybe impossible. Even with asthma.

I waited for her to stop sobbing. 'So you think she killed herself because she thought Cal was going to fire her?'

Avril gaped at me. 'Why else wouldn't she use her

inhaler? She took it with her everywhere. Why didn't she use it if she didn't want to die?'

That was the million-dollar question. The police report hadn't included an inhaler at the scene. Why hadn't Ankine had it with her, especially while exercising? Avril broke into fresh sobs, and I stared down at her heaving shoulders.

'What makes you think that Cal was going to fire her?'

Avril pulled herself together to answer, still fighting sniffles. 'At the beginning, everything was great. They were always sitting somewhere with their heads tucked together. "We're going to light your character like this, which will tell the audience how they should read her." "The Hurricane Blonde would wear *this*. She does her hair like *this*."' Avril shook her head. 'He gave her homework. She loved it, at first. Then it started to get weird. *I* thought it was weird anyway. But she never complained.'

'But something changed.'

Avril chewed on her lip. 'They got into a big fight on set in front of everyone. A week before she died.'

I opened my mouth to ask more – *but what was the fight about?* – when Avril's face scrunched and she squeaked out a hurried, 'I've got to go.'

I tried to stop her when I heard a voice from behind me.

'How about that cup of coffee, Salma?'

When I turned, Emerald was there, smiling at me. She had her ever-present phone in one hand, a clipboard in the other.

I looked after Avril – if I hadn't known better, I'd

have thought the expression on her face was fear. When I turned back, Emerald had her eyebrows raised. That Mona Lisa smile.

'No time like the present,' I said.

Emerald's office was located a golf cart ride from Soundstage Seven, in a creamy bungalow crawling with purple bougainvillea. On the door, a sign announced: CAL TURNER, DIRECTOR. In smaller type below it: EMERALD MAJORS, PRODUCER. She swiped her badge against the scanner, then knocked the door open with her hip, gesturing me in.

Inside, two doors led to separate offices. Cal's door was closed. Emerald went to the cappuccino maker centered between the two, flicking it on, before ushering me into her office.

I'd thought we were going to go to one of the coffee shops on the lot. A private meeting in her office was a different type of conversation.

'Take a seat,' she said, gesturing at a deep leather chair. She plopped the coffee cup in front of me on the desk, which was also home to a gloriously untidy heap of papers. She glanced down again at her phone. It seemed like a compulsion.

I studied the film posters plastered on her wall: ones she'd worked on or starred in. Even, I noticed, one for *Morty's House*. Abe Lewis, our Morty, stood with his arms turkeyed up comically, as if to say, *What the hell have I gotten myself into?!* I stood front and centre of the trio of girls, hands on hips. Emerald peered shyly out above my shoulder.

'So,' Emerald said, setting the phone down and bringing me back to the present. 'What do you think of the production?'

In the week I'd been on set, I'd come to see Emerald wasn't just Cal's support. If anything, the crew looked to her opinion as often as his, on everything from line readings to wardrobe fittings. She *was* the film – maybe even more than Cal.

'Cal has a strong vision,' I hedged.

Emerald's mouth quirked up, amused. For a moment, she looked like the kid I'd known, the one who had wrapped a friendship bracelet around my wrist and told me she thought I'd win an Academy Award one day, but not before she won one first. I'd liked that kid a lot.

'That's all?'

I took a chance. We'd been friends, once. Emerald would be a powerful ally on set. 'Avril told me Ankine and Cal argued on set before . . .' I swallowed, decided to leave it there, *before.*

One perfectly arched brow raised. 'Did she.'

'What did they argue about?'

Emerald took a deep breath, suddenly all business. 'No idea. Creative differences, probably.'

Even in the short time I'd been on set, I knew there were very few things about which Emerald had *no idea.* 'Was it about—'

'This is exactly what I wanted to talk about,' Emerald said. 'I see you sneaking around, asking questions about Ankine. Hovering over Melany, making her so nervous she can't get a line out without looking at you. You're gonna fuck up my movie, and I'm not sure why.' She leant forward on the desk. 'So. Why?'

There went my hopes of gaining an ally against Cal. *Why? Because I don't think Ankine's death was an accident.* I felt a chill up my spine. It was the first time I'd fully admitted it to myself. But I couldn't say that to Emerald. 'I want to make sure Cal's sensitive to the material.'

Emerald's fingers drummed on the side of her mug. 'I see,' she said. 'This is about your sister.'

I didn't correct her. 'I saw Cal had a change to one of the deaths in the script. A drowning.'

Emerald froze, the coffee mug halfway to her lips. 'Who told you that?'

'One of the key grips,' I lied. 'I didn't catch his name.'

Emerald pursed her lips. 'Well, given the circumstances, we thought it would be . . . tasteless to keep it. So Cal changed the script.'

Sure. Tasteless. Not an admission of guilt. 'Ankine – what was she like? Did you know her well?'

Emerald looked up to the left. 'Not well. She was . . .' She paused, thought for a moment. 'Committed,' she said finally.

I waited for her to say more, then realised she wasn't going to.

Emerald's phone buzzed, and she frowned. 'I need to take this,' she said. She grabbed my barely touched coffee cup without asking, then whisked both cups into the other room, where I could hear her rinsing them out as she spoke on the phone.

As I waited, my eyes caught on the poster of *Morty's House* again. That Salma was all pigtails and sassy eye rolls. No matter how sober I stayed, I'd never be that clean again. *Run*, I thought at Little Salma, perky and shiny-skinned, no self-inflicted brain damage, no dead sister, an entirely different life possible still. *Run, now, run, run, run.*

But she wouldn't. I knew which choices she'd make. I knew how the story would go.

In the other room, Emerald snapped directions to some hapless PA. She'd be back in a moment. I looked at the heaps of papers on her desk. Then I reached out one finger and flicked through them, gently at first, then more quickly.

I passed by sketches for set design, lipstick swatches for wardrobe. I didn't know what I was looking for until I saw it: the pre-production cast and crew log. I glanced at the door. I could see a sliver of Emerald's back, still on the phone. I scanned the sheet as quickly as I could, looking for the day Ankine died. Then there it was: *Friday, 8th September.* I dragged my finger down the sheet, remembering her time of death from the police report – between 3 and 3:37 p.m., when I'd found her – 2:15–3:45: *wardrobe fitting, Roger Brossard, Emerald Majors, Cal Turner.* Initialed by Emerald herself.

Fuck. Cal *did* have an alibi.

I heard the click of Emerald's heels on the hardwood, and I pushed the paper back into her pile, shuffling it around so it wasn't so obviously on top.

'Salma?' Emerald was in the doorway, looking down at me. If she'd seen me slide the pre-pro schedule back, she didn't say anything. I smiled up at her, my stomach tight.

She could've lied. She could've signed for him to cover his tracks.

I shook my head, told myself I was getting into tinfoil hat territory.

'Everything all right?'

Emerald smiled but it didn't reach her eyes. 'Always some fire to put out. I should get back. But do me a favour, okay? If you have any more questions about anything – the script, Cal, Ankine – come to me first. I don't need anybody else distracted.'

Without waiting for an agreement, she turned and walked out. I cast one last look at the desk – what other clues did it hold? – before following her. Emerald stayed glued to her phone as she drove me back to Soundstage Seven, manoeuvring the golf cart with her knees.

'How long have you worked for him?' I half-yelled over the rumble of the cart.

Emerald kept her eyes glued to her phone, tapping away. 'Seven years. I started as his production assistant, worked my way up to producer. I'll be an executive producer in the next year.'

Seven years of Cal's mercurial behaviour. Jesus. Emerald, who I'd once seen cry when she realised *Morty's* shooting schedule meant she'd miss that year's Scholastic Book Fair. 'Wow, that's . . . impressive.'

I thought I heard her say under her breath, 'You have no idea.'

'Why did you stop acting?'

Emerald checked over her shoulder, then pressed harder on the pedal. 'At the time, it seemed like the best option.' I opened my mouth to ask a follow-up question – *what does that mean?* – but she beat me to it.

'What about you? What got you out of the game?'

My parents, a united front after my second rehab stint. My father looked resolute; my mother wouldn't meet my

166

eyes. 'I think it's best if you take a break from acting for a while, Salma,' he said.

'Temporarily,' Vivienne had added. 'While we work on some things.'

They meant well. I think they'd had fantasies of coming together as a family, helping guide me to a path of sobriety and strength. And then I'd either follow in their footsteps, or I wouldn't.

But they'd also meant I was bad for the family brand.

'Tawney,' I said. It was explanation enough. 'So why do you keep the *Morty* poster up?'

Emerald put the phone down, finally looked at me. '*Morty* was a big deal.'

I laughed. 'Em, even we knew it was a seriously shitty show, and we were kids.'

Her phone pinged. The cart sped up a tick. 'Yeah, well. It was the first audition I booked. I didn't even have to have Mommy or Daddy call in a favour for me, either.'

That stung. 'No,' I snapped back at her, 'clearly not. But you do work for one of the biggest assholes in Hollywood.'

Emerald clenched the wheel, shoulders hunched. 'Look, was Polanski nice? Was Hitchcock *nice*? I don't agree with all his methods, but you can't argue with the films he makes.'

Technically, Cal *was* a genius. He was able to capture a story simply in the framing of a scene. His films were more *alive* than other films; sometimes, more alive than life itself.

He made great films, maybe even important films. And

I also knew he hurt people along the way.

'Besides,' Emerald said, her face tipped back down to her phone, 'Cal takes care of his own. He's very loyal, in his own way. He just expects loyalty in return.'

I wondered what Cal's definition of *loyalty* entailed.

And then, thinking back to her initials on the set log with a chill, I wondered what *Emerald's* definition of loyalty entailed.

CHAPTER SEVENTEEN

I woke with a bad feeling in my stomach the next day, our first full day of principal photography. I told myself it was first-day jitters. I remembered it from my previous life on set. Excitement and nerves feel the same, I told myself. It's how you interpret them that counts.

I told myself that right up until I stepped onto the soundstage.

Crew moved quickly, frantically fixing last-minute details. One knocked me in the shoulder, didn't slow down to apologise. But I couldn't move. I was frozen.

I blinked, the white lights hot on my face as I took it in. On one side, Tawney's snowy leather couch, a marigold velvet settee reclining in front of her fireplace, a vintage Batchelder tiled in blue-and-gold sunbursts. Lighting technicians scurried up the curving marble staircase. I'd always thought of that staircase as Tawney's bridge to stardom. Upstairs, we were just girls trying on make-up together, practicing our expressions in the mirror. When she came down the stairs, heels clicking with each step, she was Tawney Lowe, movie star in the making. *Salmon, a girl's gotta make an entrance.* The doors to her master bedroom were closed, but sound technicians and grips padded back and forth, setting up for filming.

'Holy shit,' I whispered.

I was inside the Jacaranda House.

Cal stood at the base of Tawney's marble staircase, one arm draped against the handrail. He drummed his fingers along the staircase, looking displeased, barking instructions at those crew members unlucky enough to cross his path. I wasn't the only one with first-day jitters.

I kept my eyes peeled for Avril, trying to catch a glimpse of her to finish our conversation, but in the chaos, I couldn't find her.

Emerald slid past me, throwing a curt *Hello* over a shoulder. Today, she wore a leather crop top, peep-toe pumps, and dark jeans. But her face looked tired, and her eyes kept darting between Cal and the rest of the crew. I opened my mouth to reply, but she was already gone.

Melany emerged from behind a column. She wore a blue silk gown that was a near-perfect replica of the dress Tawney had worn to her first film premiere, her breakout role as an underage sex worker in a drama about the crib prostitutes in turn-of-the-century Los Angeles. It was a small part in a major motion picture; Tawney had only a handful of lines, but reviewers couldn't get enough of her. *Star in the making*, Ebert panted. *Can't take your eyes off her*. Her baby-pretty face on a grown woman's frame; men ate it up. Soon she was booking supporting parts, clothing campaigns, a major make-up spot. I always wondered how much those first images of her – torn silk negligee, teenage breasts spilling out of her corset – framed her career. Sex sold in a five-foot-six frame.

Cal looked up, and his eyes seemed to take on a darker,

colder blue glow as he appraised her.

I couldn't help staring, either. Melany was transformed. Her face – narrower than Tawney's – had been filled out with well-placed blush, her hairline brought forward with a careful application of prosthetics. She even wore a flipper over her teeth, making her smile a decent replica of Tawney's.

Still, I could spot the differences: the mouth not quite full enough, the make-up a little too bright. But I doubted anyone else could.

Except maybe Cal.

He circled Melany, who blushed head to toe under his gaze. I could see her nipples poke through the thin fabric of the silky dress and a wordless shudder ripple over her shoulders.

'No,' Cal said finally. 'No, it's not right.'

Melany twitched, but Cal turned and snapped at the make-up artists, who scurried over, carrying palettes. Cal directed them on each brushstroke, and another twenty minutes passed before he was satisfied.

But we weren't filming yet. It took another forty minutes for lighting to make minuscule adjustments to Cal's satisfaction. I watched Melany sweat under the lights, trying to stay in character. She reached up to brush away a bead of sweat.

'We just spent twenty minutes on that face,' Cal snapped at her, breaking from his lighting *tête-à-tête*. 'Don't fuck it up.'

Melany flinched, then nodded. 'Sorry, Cal.'

I bit my tongue.

Finally, a PA yelled 'Places' and I retreated to the

sidelines, settling into a chair next to Emerald to watch.

Cal was heading back to video village – the spot where the director, assistant director, and cinematographer supervised the action, watching the footage in real time to make adjustments between takes – when Melany shaded her eyes against the glare and said, 'Sorry, Cal, but can we take five? I need to use the restroom.'

'Oh shit,' Emerald muttered.

From the darkness of video village, there was the creak of a chair as Cal shifted. 'Just now you need to piss? We've been setting up for an hour, you couldn't give me a fucking heads-up then?'

Melany's face turned red. Her mouth trembled. 'Sorry, Cal.'

There was a pause, then: 'We're behind schedule already. Let's get the take first.'

Melany blinked sharply, her mouth dropping open. 'I'll be thirty seconds, I swear—'

'Take one step off your mark, and you're fired.'

The silence on the soundstage was so complete I could hear Emerald breathing next to me.

Melany wasn't blushing any more; she looked like she might faint. 'Okay. I'm sorry. Let's roll.'

We were shooting out of order. The shot was simple: Melany would walk down the staircase, her grand entrance. She didn't even have a line. No more than twenty seconds in total.

The first take was solid, Melany's footsteps measured and regal. But Cal didn't like the click of her heels on the marble, so we had to wait while wardrobe rustled up new shoes, tested them for Cal's approval. Melany sent pleading, hopeful looks at Cal as he listened to the click on the marble. If he remembered her request, he didn't show it.

The second take, Melany skipped a step, and we were back to one.

On the fifth take, Cal criticised her stride. 'You *have* walked down a staircase before, haven't you? Maybe I was wrong about you. Aren't you an actor?'

Melany flinched, running her hands over the goose-pimpled flesh of her arms. But she didn't say anything. I could see her lips moving, maybe giving herself a pep talk – maybe giving vent to Cal with a few well-placed and near-silent expressions.

I realised my shoulders were hunched, that I was cringing back into my chair. This was him. This was the Cal I remembered.

'Answer me,' Cal called from across the soundstage. 'That wasn't a rhetorical question. Do you know what "rhetorical" means?'

Melany's cheeks burnt. Next to her, Roger looked uneasy. The rest of the crew was going about business as usual, but I noticed a few stealing prurient glances at her humiliation.

'I'm an actor,' she said in a tremulous voice. 'Sorry, Cal. Let's go again.'

In the first hour of filming, Cal barely let a shot play out longer than thirty seconds before cutting, restarting from one. By the eighth take, there was desperation in Melany's eyes. Each time we reset, it was another four or five minutes before Cal called, *Action*.

On the twelfth take, Melany broke. 'Cal, please, can I get five minutes?'

Cal stood up from where he was hunched behind the

camera. He didn't seem angry. Instead, he walked up to Melany slowly, rested his hands lightly on her shoulders, a little smile on his face. He didn't say anything. He caressed her chin briefly. Even from feet away, it made my skin crawl. Melany's face brightened, and my heart sank. Then I saw his fingers dig more deeply into her jaw, the skin turning white. Melany's eyes widened, fearful, and she started to put her hands up to his wrist as his fingers clenched, then thought better of it.

I sat forward, ready to throw myself between them. Emerald caught my eye and gave an almost imperceptible shake of her head.

Cal leant in close and whispered something. I watched Melany's mouth tremble, a tear straggling down her cheek, and then there was the sound of a little spatter of liquid hitting the ground, Melany's humiliated, trembling face crumpling as she realised.

Oh God. My fingernails dug into the arm of my chair, denting grooves into the wood, and I stared at Emerald. She was looking down at her clipboard, but I saw a muscle in her jaw twitch.

'Problem solved,' Cal said, stepping back, admiring the puddle of urine at his feet. 'Can I get someone to clean up her piss?'

A PA sprung into action, mopping up the mess. I heard more than one crew member snickering.

I'd seen Cal angry before. Screaming at Tawney on set; sometimes in private, more often in front of the crew. That changed how the crew saw you, how they treated you. It made them uncomfortable. Even when Cal wasn't berating his fiancée, the relationship between actor and director felt too intimate when it played out with an audience. But nobody got mad at Cal, *America's next great auteur*. Instead, it was always Tawney's fault. Wasn't she difficult to work with? Didn't she ruin takes? Wasn't she the reason Cal was angry and, therefore, the problem?

My hands tightened into fists. 'Was he like this with Ankine, too?' My voice was a harsh whisper.

Emerald kept her eyes glued to her clipboard. She didn't answer. She didn't like me bringing up Ankine, I realised. No one breathed on set without Emerald's permission. It was her job to know all the details. But about Ankine, she clammed up.

It took another twenty minutes before Melany reappeared in a fresh blue silk gown, mascara blotted and reapplied. A tremulous *Silly me* smile on her face. Crew reset as Cal whispered to the actors. Roger shook his head vehemently, but Melany put a hand on his arm. *No, it's all right. I'm all right.*

'Places!'

It took three more takes to get the shot. Cal's mood had cooled, but I could see Melany was still jumpy, her confidence carved away with each new take.

When Cal called a wrap, I made my way to her. She'd retreated to her seat, keeping her head down as she studied her script. Up close, I could see goosebumps on her arms, but she gave me a megawatt smile as I approached. Like nothing had happened.

'Hey,' I said, bending down next to her chair so our heads were level. 'Are you okay?'

Melany forced a laugh. 'Never better.'

I hesitated. She was determined to pretend nothing bad

had happened. I couldn't force her to talk about it. But I couldn't ignore it, either. 'That wasn't cool, what Cal did. He put you in a terrible spot.'

The smile didn't exactly drop off her face, but it froze. 'It was an accident. My fault. I should've known better.'

I shook my head. 'Cal should never have—'

Melany interrupted me, her voice high, slightly strangled. 'I'm really busy, okay, Salma? I need to work on my line readings. Could you just leave me alone?'

I stood up, stung. I stared at the top of her head for a moment. She gripped her script so hard it trembled, and as I watched, a tear dropped onto the paper. I opened my mouth, about to say something else, thought better of it.

I didn't say goodbye. I was halfway to my car in the parking lot when someone called my name. When I turned, Emerald was jogging toward me, somehow keeping her balance in her pumps. I braced myself for a lecture – *Stop interfering, you don't understand*, blah fucking blah.

Instead, when Emerald caught up to me, she said, slightly breathless, 'Grab a drink with me.'

That was a surprise. I watched her face, trying to tell if she was serious. *'Now?'*

'Yes. Now.'

'I don't drink,' I reminded her.

Emerald looked tired, but she had a nervy energy jangling her. 'Then I'll drink for the both of us. C'mon, Salma, please?'

If there was something under her skin – something named Cal – maybe I'd get lucky and she'd confide in me. 'Okay,' I said. 'But you're buying.'

Emerald scoffed. *'Cal's* buying.'

'Even better.'

CHAPTER EIGHTEEN

Emerald drove us to the Chateau Marmont, her sporty little Porsche darting in and out of traffic, like a stunt driver. We were stopped at a red light, almost to the Chateau Marmont, when she finally said anything. 'I know how that looked.'

I watched her profile, the palms of her hands relaxed and easy on the leather steering wheel. The car purred and hummed, and every few seconds she'd release the brake and the car would leap forward a few inches before she stopped it again.

'It wasn't just how it looked, Em. It was how it *was*. You could have a lawsuit back there.'

'Not with Cal's NDAs, no.'

She had an answer for everything. 'You think people didn't make excuses for Roman Polanski, too?'

Emerald scoffed. 'Cal is hardly Roman Polanski. And he's absolutely not sleeping with any of his actors.'

Of course not. They're too old for him. I stopped myself from saying it in the nick of time, something dawning as I studied Emerald's face.

'You're in love with him, aren't you,' I said, suddenly sure of it.

This time Emerald's laugh was genuine. She flashed peroxide pearly veneers in a wolfish grin. 'Salma, I'm gay.'

The light turned green and she sped off, throwing me against the door on a hairpin turn. Emerald took the curve up to the Marmont's parking lot like it owed her money before she slammed it into park, tossed the keys to the valet, and we headed for the elevator.

There was a saying: *If you have to misbehave in Hollywood, do it at the Marmont.*

Money came here to rest, not stand at attention. The ruby carpets were threadbare but expensively vintage. Dark exposed beams threaded the ceiling between hand-cut crystal chandeliers, a soft-lit glow that erased imperfections. Even the brass keys to the bungalows and villas had an old-fashioned weight to them, as if to remind you that of all the gin joints in all of Hollywood, this was the only irreplaceable one.

But when I looked at it, I also saw the dark ghosts of Hollywood: Kirk Douglas allegedly raping teenage Natalie Wood in his suite before he offered her a part. Belushi's overdose. Sharon Tate setting up house at the Marmont before leaving for Cielo Drive, where in six months she'd meet her grisly end.

A classy little refuge for bad behaviour and tragedy.

Emerald led me to the bar. She ordered a gin gimlet, straight-up, then waited. I skimmed the bottles behind the bar – the smoky ambers, the fruit-spiked vodkas. All my old friends together in one place.

The sky wouldn't collapse if I ordered a drink. It wouldn't tailspin me back to rehab. I could feel Emerald watching me. 'Shirley Temple, please.'

Emerald snorted, shook her head. 'God. You ordered harder drinks when we were kids on *Morty's House.*'

'Things change.'

I recognised a woman at the end of the bar. Her hair was pulled back in a greasy knot, her face make-up-less and puffy, yet still gorgeous. She'd made a few big movies years ago, though I realised I hadn't seen her in much since.

Emerald caught me staring. 'She auditioned for the film.'

'No good?'

Emerald shrugged. 'She's just not what Cal prefers.'

'What does Cal prefer?' I didn't think I'd like the answer.

Emerald's eyes were on the bartender, watching him make our drinks. '*Tabula rasa,*' she said finally. 'He wants what all directors want. To create.'

But not all directors would humiliate their leading ladies on the first day of a shoot. I changed the topic. 'What was so urgent that we had to leave right now?'

Emerald sighed. 'New plans for the shoot tomorrow. We'll be off-site. I'd prefer it if you didn't come.'

This same shit again. I rolled my eyes. 'Seriously? Haven't I stayed out of the way? If your production is having problems, it's not my fault.'

Emerald shook her head. 'Cal's shooting the death scene tomorrow. You know. The real one.' She widened her eyes, struggling to find the exact words she wanted. 'I don't think you should be there.'

'Oh.' My breath escaped me. All protest died as I tried to imagine what it would feel like to watch Tawney's murder in real time, all the wondering I'd done about those moments pinned to something real, even if it was only Cal's imagination. *Or his memory.*

In the gap, the bartender brought us our drinks. He'd fixed my Shirley Temple in a martini glass, its noxious sunset tones somehow more depressing dressed up. A fat purple cherry drowned in the grenadine.

I took a sip of the drink. It would taste better with gin.

I'd pictured Tawney's death a million times in a million different ways. Cal's version couldn't be worse than what I'd already imagined. And after today, I didn't want to leave Melany without a friend on set. 'Well, thanks for warning me, but I'll be there. You can count on it.'

Emerald heaved a sigh, dragging her nail down the condensation on her drink. 'If you insist.' She clinked my glass and took a deep gulp, nearly draining the gimlet in one go.

Down the bar, I watched the actor tinker with her phone, occasionally looking up and pretending to be annoyed when people stared. But she could've picked a less conspicuous bar, I knew. She wanted to be seen. She wanted to be seen *here*. No one imagines their dreams will come true and they'll still be found lacking.

There'd been a snap on Ankine's Instagram of her at the Marmont, sipping blush-coloured wine. I imagined her here, tossing her hair, trying to look confident and bored, not overeager and ready to be discovered. If she'd lived, would she have been a success? Or would she have been back here in a few years, trying to cover the desperation of ageing and an increasingly outdated reel with lunchtime vodkas in places that still made her feel like Someone?

'Why don't you ever talk about her?'

Emerald took another sip of her gimlet. 'Who?'

But I knew she knew. Every time I mentioned her name,

she clammed up. 'You know everything that goes on on set. But you don't ever have anything to say about Ankine.'

Emerald flipped her long braids over one shoulder, eyes on her drink. 'She was playing Cal's favourite bimbo. Not exactly a lot to it.' She downed her drink, signalled the bartender for another. 'No offence.'

Was it Ankine she had a problem with, or Tawney? I wondered. 'Was she difficult to work with?'

The bartender pushed another drink across the bar at Emerald, and she smiled her thanks, toasting him. She took a long drink before she answered. 'All actors are difficult, in their way.'

'Was Ankine more difficult than most?'

Emerald's shoulders hunched just a fraction of an inch. 'What did you hear?'

I decided to be honest. 'Cherry called her a *nightmare*.'

Emerald snorted. '*Cherry's* a nightmare.' She took another sip of the gimlet, her soft pink tongue flicking a drop from her lip. 'Ankine was . . . committed. More committed than most actors. It drove me nuts but . . .' She shook her head. 'She could've been a good actor, one day.' Emerald opened her mouth to say something, thought better of it. 'Despite whatever you think, I'm sorry she's dead.'

I watched her, the long, graceful sweep of her neck, thinking of how our lives had changed since we were kids on the set of *Morty's House*.

'I believe you,' I said.

Emerald rolled her eyes. 'Well, isn't that a relief. Now I can sleep at night.'

I bit my lip, played with a suspicion that had been nagging me. 'I didn't see Avril on set today.'

Emerald downed her drink. 'I fired her.'

'*What?* Why?'

'Don't be such a child, Salma,' she scolded. 'You told me yourself. She violated her NDA. She knows better.'

I was speechless. 'You fired her.'

'Look.' Emerald leant toward me, against the bar. 'I believe in this film. You and some gossipy make-up artist aren't going to fuck it up.'

She signalled for the check while I stared at her.

The bartender slid Emerald the bill, and she looked down, her brows lifting in pleasant surprise. 'Comped,' she said, a self-satisfied smile on her face. Another perk of being Cal Turner's right-hand woman. 'Thank you.'

The bartender winked at me. '*Iron Prayer* is my favourite film.'

Emerald's mouth dropped and her head whipped to me so quickly it set her earrings swinging. My face heated as I thanked him. Emerald was already up, gathering her purse, before I had it out of my mouth.

I scurried to keep up with her long-legged stride to the elevator. As we waited, I cast one glance backward at the actor I recognised. She had her head down on the bar, making a pillow of her hands. I looked away, feeling queasy.

In the parking lot, Emerald pressed a bill into the hands of the valet, then yanked the door open, wedging her legs into the tiny car. It wasn't until she'd merged onto the freeway, north toward Burbank and the studio, that Emerald broke the silence.

'Stuff like that happens for you all the time, doesn't it.' There wasn't any bitterness in her voice this time, just a resigned amusement. 'Even though you haven't done anything in – how long?'

'Yeah, well.' I looked out the window as the palm trees whizzed sickly by above us. 'I can't really escape it. I didn't ask to be born into my family.'

'You could've been—' Emerald stopped abruptly.

'What?'

'Nothing.' Emerald eased on the brakes as we rolled to a stop in traffic. 'Doesn't seem like you're trying all that hard to avoid it.'

My head ached – the long day, the grenadine, this argument on simmer, all of it piling up. 'Emerald, why did you bring me there?'

'I told you, I wanted to warn you—'

I shook my head. 'Bullshit. You could've done that on set. You could've emailed me the call sheet for tomorrow.' Emerald was silent. I remembered the way she'd stared at her clipboard as Cal berated Melany into soiling herself. Like it was a lifeline. 'You think Cal went too far today.'

Emerald glared at me. 'You think I'd turn to *you* for a crisis of conscience? Because we were, what, forced to be set buddies as kids?'

That stung. 'I think you don't have anyone else to talk to.'

'Well, I'm not talking, am I?' she snapped. In the evening twilight, I could see the slump of her shoulders, the tiredness. Then, like she couldn't stop herself: 'Do you know what it was like, trying to break into films as a Black actor twenty years ago? Making movies is the only thing I've *ever* wanted to do, and no one would let me fucking

183

do it. No one until Cal.' She shook her head. 'It was so *easy* for you. And you threw it away.'

We were almost to the studio lot. I held my tongue, stewing. I knew she wasn't wrong. But I hadn't asked for famous parents, either. Emerald showed her pass to the security guard, soaring through the parking lot at a dangerous speed, rocketing past the famous water fountain. She took a sharp curve into the space next to my car, then turned and made direct eye contact with me, her lovely hazel eyes sharp.

'Look,' Emerald said. 'All I wanted to do was give you a heads-up about tomorrow. I still think you shouldn't come, but it's your decision.'

She yanked the keys out of the ignition, and I put my hand on the door handle.

But Emerald wasn't done.

'If you really want to know, though, that isn't why I hate your family.' My head whipped around so quickly, my hair lashed her face. 'I hate your family because you all seem to think a famous dead white girl is the worst thing that's ever happened in this city. I hate your family because instead of free drinks, you could be using that power to make a difference in the industry, really helping people if you wanted. *Instead*, you're demanding access to a film shoot because you feel entitled to it. Because you *can*. But mostly?' Emerald took a deep breath. 'Mostly I hate your family because you think you *earned* everything you have. When the truth is, you haven't earned a goddamn thing.'

She reached across and popped the car door open for me. 'See you tomorrow.'

CHAPTER NINETEEN

Even if Emerald hadn't warned me, I could've guessed the scene as soon as I pulled up to the hotel. The hotel turned set was located in the posh part of Hollywood, rooftop pool shimmering under the Hollywood sign's lusty gaze.

The most cinematic place to strangle a woman.

A single lobby elevator bank meant I spent twenty minutes in line with a mix of bored and fidgety crew and irritated tourists whose excitement at being part of a film in the making was quickly dwindling. One of the hazards of living in a company town: a film crew might co-opt your vacation at any moment.

A PA ushered me into an open elevator, reeking of stale sweat and anxiety. I closed my eyes, holding my breath as the elevator climbed, a few juddering jerks causing a nervous burst of laughter from the crew members stuffed into the carriage. I was wedged into the corner, a support bar jammed into my back.

Too late to back out now.

The elevator doors dinged open, and the crew piled out, tugging equipment after them. I was the last to leave, and as I stepped out onto the rooftop, blinking, I was blinded by the sunny glitter, the turquoise slip of the water like a vein opened in grey pavement. A lemon-yellow-and-white striped cabana on one side of the pool, a neat replica for the one my sister adored. She liked the kitsch of it, joked about having carved tiki statues fringing the grass, pink plastic flamingos. *They think I'm tacky anyway, Salmon,* she said with a wink.

I blinked, trying to clear my head. To one side, Cherry made a show of supervising unlucky PAs, loudly demanding first water, then a better vantage point. I spotted Emerald in the crowd, ponging between different teams, working her headset like an extension of her body.

If she saw me, she didn't show it.

I'd thought about her words all night, litigating the accuracy of them for myself as I tossed and turned, stressing about the shoot. *I didn't ask to be born into a famous family,* I argued. *I wouldn't have chosen it.* But she was right – I knew she was right. The advantages I had simply by being born who I was – I needed to make those mean something.

Under the umbrella, Cal coached Melany into the right tangle of limbs. He'd guide her to a position, tell her to hold the contortion, then photograph it, checking his work with a frown. *This death is not yet beautiful enough.*

I skirted the scene, watching. I had a superstitious feeling that if I stepped into the frame, I'd set something terrible in motion.

Even from feet away, I could see Melany, Cal's *femme*, shortly to be *fatale*'d, her neck ringed in purple bruises. There was a prosthetic clasping her throat, making it smaller than a throat should be, and every so often, as Cal gave her an instruction, I saw Melany's chest heave, trying to draw in more air. Then she forced herself to take smaller breaths, smaller and smaller, until you almost couldn't see her breathing at all.

'Could somebody grab me a chair?' Cherry complained loudly. I looked up. She was fanning herself with the call sheet, looking irritated at every crew member who crossed her path. Bizarrely, the sight of her comforted me – some things never changed.

Or maybe her presence was a reminder that this was only a film set.

When I turned back to the scene prep, Cal was staring at me. I could have sworn he winked. Then he looked back down at Melany, in a heap at his feet.

I stopped in my tracks, my heart thumping. I couldn't tell if I'd imagined it.

I took a few deep breaths to steady myself. As I did, the smell of suntan oil clogged my throat, and I gagged at the piña colada smell. That *smell*. I looked down. At Melany's feet, there was a spill of suntan oil, the orangey bottle kicked a few feet away.

Cal knew the details well.

I circled around to the other side of the pool, fascinated despite myself.

When I found my sister's body, it had been from the front, through the French doors that led out to her pool. I closed my eyes, picturing it. The last normal moments of my life. My outstretched hand turning the knob of the French doors, the soft mop of Tawney's hair spread out on the pavement. I remembered thinking she'd been sunbathing. Then I opened the door – and the twist of her limbs was . . . *wrong*.

I circled to the back of the shot, close enough to hear Cal's instructions. If we were shooting, I'd be directly in frame. I could see Melany bunched up against the chaise longue, her toes ever so slightly touching it. That was wrong; Tawney hadn't been touching anything.

'She shouldn't be touching the lounger,' Cal called out, echoing my thoughts.

I frowned.

'Can I get a PA on the suntan oil?' Cal said.

As I watched, a production assistant, barely out of her teens, quick-walked to the puddle. I realised what was going to happen a split second before it did. At the scene, there had been oily footprints, slick drag marks, indicating whatever struggle had ended my sister's life. Never enough to get a footprint out of, and besides, I'd never been entirely sure that it hadn't been from my mother and me.

It was one of the more reported-upon murders in recent history, of course – too many salacious, trivial details. But as with all murders, police had withheld a few details. The footprints were one of those details. I knew about them only because I'd been there, seen them myself.

The footprints had never made it to any magazine article, nor to Cherry's book.

But Cal knew about them.

On cue, the girl, frowning, began to stomp through the oil, tracking it over the set.

'Fewer steps,' Cal murmured, playing with Melany's hair, parting it this way and that over her face. 'It wasn't everywhere.'

A shiver started in my spine, my teeth rattling as adrenaline pumped through my veins. Cal had gotten so many of the details right. The pool of spilt suntan oil. The necklace of bruises around her slim throat. The positioning of my sister's body. The oily footprints.

Things he shouldn't know. Things he *couldn't* know.

I continued my slow circle, making myself dizzy. The scurry of the hotel staff peeking in on the scene, the production assistants buzzing around my dead sister.

But no, it wasn't Tawney, it wasn't *real*. The pool was different, slipped into the concrete like a Tetris block. It was all wrong, although the camera wouldn't know the difference.

It was all wrong, except for all the ways that it was right.

Tawney's hand outstretched just so, the claw of her fingers, like she'd been reaching for me.

Cal knelt next to Melany, gripped her hand roughly, and bent her fingers into shape. Next to the chaise longue, under the striped umbrella, a warming glass of Fanta that had started to collect bugs, left unattended in the sun.

Almost like he knew exactly what it looked like. Almost like he'd been there.

Cal looked up, caught my eye. Extended one finger in my direction.

In a daze, I stepped forward as he beckoned, avoiding the pools of suntan oil. A production assistant bumped me in her hustle to fish an errant jacaranda blossom out of the pool with a net. I stood in front of him and Melany, staring mutely down at them.

Cal gripped my hand and tugged me down until I knelt

next to him. My hand tingled where he held it. This close, I could smell the faint wisp of Melany's perfume, lilacs and cheap vanilla.

'What do you see, hotshot? Since you see so much?'

Melany held herself as still as she could, but I could see a ripple go through her every so often, the rise and fall of her breath. Cal followed my gaze and set his hand on her back, stilling her. Her eyes fluttered closed under the pressure of his fingers.

I could feel the warmth of his body radiating off him; I could smell him. I closed my eyes. I remembered the tickle of his breath against my ear, his hips pistoning against mine. His arm around Tawney on the red carpet. His face, twisted in anger, whipping a crystal tumbler against the wall of Tawney's trailer, the glass tinkling to the ground around her like sharp rain.

When I opened my eyes, he was watching me. It felt like a violation.

'This,' I said. I reached down and pulled Melany's hair away from her face so you could see the purple ring around her neck.

I stroked her hair back behind her ears, letting my fingers linger in the silky strands. The dye job was close to my sister's, almost the right tangle of golden and vanilla and reddish brown underneath. But Melany's roots were growing out, ever so slightly, so there was a paler gold strip near her scalp. I wanted to press my finger against it, proof that she was a different woman.

Ever so gently, I turned her head to the left. I was kind to Cal's Little Sister – I turned Melany's face in the wrong direction so their eyes wouldn't meet.

'That's better,' I said. 'That's right.'

Cal frowned, his body very still. He stroked the sides of his mouth – a habit I remembered with an electric shock. I held my breath, waiting to see what he would do.

After a long moment, he reached down and parted Melany's hair around her skull, arranging it over her shoulders, strands catching in his fingers. Melany winced, her eyes closed.

Then he gently moved her head back the other way, so she was facing the camera.

Exactly the way she'd looked when I found her, twenty years ago.

My breath caught in my throat. I began to shiver again, so hard Cal looked at me. He smiled.

'Better,' he murmured. 'Thank you anyway, Salma.'

I nodded, not trusting myself to speak.

It wasn't a coincidence. Maybe one piece – the way she was positioned, say, or the oil – could be a coincidence. But he knew too many details.

Cal Turner had killed my sister.

I'd always known he was capable of violence, of terrible things. And here was proof. And, I realised, if he killed Tawney – didn't that make him more than capable of killing Ankine?

Did that mean Melany was next?

I stumbled backward, trying to keep the bile from my throat. I'd need footage. I'd need photographs to show the police. MacLeish. Then I realised: Cal was documenting all of this himself. He was documenting his own guilt. It was insanity.

Or. Or he was so sure of his own power, his own

superiority, he could film the proof of the murder he committed, and never ever be called to account for it.

'Clear the shot,' the assistant director bellowed from video village, and I scurried out of the way. My hands were trembling so hard I almost dropped my phone. I turned it on – no service – and tried to hold it up casually as I snapped pictures.

But Cal was still kneeling next to the Hurricane Blonde, blocking the shot. I inched closer, trying to zoom in.

'Clear the goddamn set!' The AD was finally at the end of his rope. But I didn't have the shot yet. I looked toward video village, but Cal's proxy wasn't even looking at me. Instead, he was glaring across the pool at Cherry, who was now arguing with Emerald. Cherry's shrill voice cut through the Los Angeles traffic, but I couldn't hear anything Emerald said.

Cherry, Cal's alibi for the day Tawney died. A goddamn liar, I knew that firsthand. Had she been willing to lie to cover up a murder, too?

'Goddamn it, Cherry,' Cal said, straightening up, giving me the angle I needed, 'what is it *now*?'

While they argued, I darted forward, so close Melany's eyes snapped open. Behind me, I could hear Cherry and Cal starting to argue, loudly. I heard Cherry say, 'Be careful, baby. I made you, and I can undo you, too.' But I wasn't going to miss my opportunity. Instead, I zoomed in on Melany, taking as many pictures as I could.

Melany glared at me, but she didn't dare move. Not after Cal had done so much work.

'Cal,' she called. 'Cal, she's—'

But I turned away, practically running for the elevator,

shoving PAs out of the way. My hands shook, and I shoved my phone in my pocket. Finally. Proof. Proof that Cal had killed my sister.

I'd been right. All these years. I'd been *right.*

As the elevator doors slid closed behind me, I heard Cal bellow: 'Action!'

Even the great Cal Turner couldn't have orchestrated it any better.

CHAPTER TWENTY

My fingers trembled as I unlocked my car, and twice I dropped my keys on the ground, cursing. I couldn't stop looking up at the hotel rooftop, wondering if Melany would raise the alarm again. I half-expected the lobby doors to burst open, for Cal or Emerald to drag me back inside.

Cal killed my sister. He was *filming* the proof that he'd done it.

I wondered if Emerald knew. I remembered her signature on the pre-pro schedule, the one proving Cal's alibi the day Ankine died, and felt a chill. How far would Emerald go to prove her loyalty?

I burnt rubber on the way out, making turns at random, until I found an open lot a mile away, putting my emergency flashers on as I called MacLeish.

It tumbled out of my mouth before he could even say hello. 'I have it. Proof Cal killed Tawney.'

There was a buzzing under my skin as I waited for him to say something, anything. If anyone was going to believe me, it was John.

'What do you mean by *proof*?'

'Meet me in twenty minutes,' I said. 'Our place. I'll show you everything.'

Then I hung up without waiting for his reply.

I got there first. I was still trembling, the adrenaline pumping through my veins, as I waited. A fly buzzed over the donuts in front of me. My head jerked up each time the glass door clattered, and I slumped back into my seat, staring glumly at the sugar bombs in front of me, each time it wasn't him.

I wanted MacLeish's validation before I took my photos to Watkins – if he didn't believe me, there was no way Watkins would. While I waited, my phone lit up, and I was so on edge I nearly dropped it. My mother. I picked up, my eyes on the donut store door as I said hello.

There was a pause, then my mother said, 'Is something wrong? You sound funny.'

We hadn't spoken directly since she'd told me she approved of Cal making a movie about Tawney. We'd passed oh-so-polite missives to each other through Jack. I hadn't told either of them that I was involved with Cal's film. I was worried my mother would approve. 'Must be allergies. What's up?'

The door opened and this time, finally, it was MacLeish. I waved him over.

'It's about the retrospective.'

'Right. The retrospective,' I repeated, as MacLeish scooted into the booth, nodding in thanks for the donuts.

A pause. 'You didn't forget, did you?'

'Of course not,' I lied. 'Remind me when it is again?'

'Salma,' my mother said with a sigh. 'Two weeks. Cherry

Partridge will be interviewing me onstage. I hoped you'd come up with me.'

I watched MacLeish shove a chocolate donut into his mouth practically in one bite. I plucked at my skin, an old nervous habit from my teenage years, leaving red welts along my wrist. 'Yes. Of course.'

I could hear the sigh of relief down the line. Did she really want me onstage with her, or did she just want to avoid the awkward questions: *Why wasn't Salma with you? What does that mean for Dave Lowe's legacy?* 'Wonderful. Also, I have a fitting at the end of the week. I wondered if you might want to go with me to Anjelica's. You know, like the old days.'

Anjelica once called me *hippy*. I was twelve.

'Sure,' I said, watching MacLeish dissect the second donut with surgical precision. 'I'll be there.'

'Lovely.' There was another pause on the line. 'Thank you, Salma. I appreciate this more than you know.'

I wanted to tell her then that I'd done it. I knew who killed Tawney; I had proof. But I knew better. Until it was official, it wouldn't bring us any closer. 'I love you, Mom,' I said instead. I wondered when I'd last said it unprompted.

There was a pause, and then my mother's voice was soft, slightly choked, when she answered. 'I love you, too, baby.'

MacLeish was still chewing as I put the phone down. He raised his eyebrows, wiping chocolate goo off his fingertips.

'Cal killed her,' I said. 'Tawney, I mean. I think Ankine, too, although I haven't figured it all out. But I'm sure he killed Tawney.'

I told him all of it, the details of Tawney's death Cal had gotten too right. The spilt suntan oil, the exact right brand. The bugs floating in the plastic glass Tawney had been drinking out of. I took a deep breath, then told him the kicker: 'He knew exactly how her body was positioned, MacLeish. I tested it – I moved her body. He moved it right back. *He was there. He had to be.*'

MacLeish's eyes were solemn. 'Salma.'

I knew the look on his face. The old doubt: *You make things up, Salma. You see things that aren't there. Honey, you're sure you've been sober?*

I pulled up the photos of Melany. '*Look,*' I snapped. 'Now tell me I'm wrong.'

I watched, cross-armed and fuming, as MacLeish flipped back and forth through the photos. He zoomed in on one and stared at it thoughtfully for a while. Then he passed the phone back to me. 'You might have something here.'

There was a small part of me that had expected him to react in stunned silence at my Columbo-cleverness. 'What do you mean, *might have*? Don't you think I should tell Detective Watkins? MacLeish, he was basically telling me he killed my sister and there's nothing I can do about it. He's filming the evidence, for fuck's sake! He's planning on thumbing his nose at all of us, proving not only that he killed her, but that he can get away with anything. *Anything.*'

MacLeish was shaking his head, *No, no.* 'It's not what you know. It's what you can prove. Turner had an alibi for the day your sister was killed. Nothing found at the scene to implicate him. Now you think he might be a serial killer who kills twenty years apart? That doesn't make sense.'

'But, John, he *knew*—'

'You said yourself Turner's obsessive about his films. How many of those details could he have gotten somewhere else? The sunscreen, the flies – they'd be in police reports.'

I saw where he was going. I didn't like it. 'Of course, but the suntan oil, what about the body—'

MacLeish interrupted me. 'I'm sorry this happened to you twice, kid. Two dead women you've found, what are the odds? Anybody would start to see connections. Maybe even if they weren't there.' He shook his head. 'It's not that you're wrong. It's just too easy to poke holes.'

I gritted my teeth, forced my anger down. 'So what *would* it take to reopen an investigation into Cal?'

Across the table, MacLeish leant back, his eyes approving. He finally liked the question I'd asked. 'Something big, something that can't be explained away. For your sister, irrefutable proof he was at the scene. Petrosyan's already been ruled an accident; you need something that proves murder definitively. That's hard to do.'

Hard didn't scare me. 'What proves murder definitively?'

'New evidence. Proof that someone kept her from getting out of the pool, or denied her aid. To pin it to Turner, you'll need his alibis to fold. For a warrant, you need the means, motive, and opportunity. I told you my concerns about your sister's case, but consider this new girl.' MacLeish held up three fingers. 'Means: yeah, you could argue Cal has that. Close proximity to the victim. Knows her schedule, knows where she goes.' One finger ticked down. 'But opportunity – there's a hiccup. He's got a whole set willing to vouch for him. Now, let's say, for argument's sake, he can get all those people to lie for him. That's a stretch, in my experience, but let's say it's possible.' Another finger down. 'Finally. Motive. Why does he kill this girl? It delays his film. It's bad press. He has to start over with a new actress.' MacLeish frowned, one finger pointing up at the ceiling. 'I don't see it.'

I stared at his finger in the air. 'Cherry called her a nightmare. They argued. Cal's a control freak. He can't stand things not going his way.'

'All that may be true,' MacLeish said, 'but an attorney – and he'd have a good one, the best money could buy – would argue it would be easier to fire her. But that's just the start. Someone that famous—' MacLeish shook his head. 'Sorry, kiddo, but I don't see airtight yet.'

Cherry was his alibi for Tawney. I'd seen Emerald's logs of the pre-pro meeting from the day Ankine died. I'd need them both to crumble, if I had a chance of selling Watkins on my theory. Neither of them seemed much like the crumbling kind.

'Airtight,' I repeated. I hadn't touched my donuts. No appetite. I watched the fly circle my pink frosted, then surprised myself by asking, 'Do you believe me?'

MacLeish hesitated. I wanted him to say, *Yes, of course.* I wanted him to tell me, *Why wouldn't I?* I wanted him to tell me the truth.

I wasn't sure those were the same things.

'I've never wanted to give you false hope,' MacLeish said finally. 'All these years, all the families I've seen get hurt – it's hope, that's the worst of it. If we'd ever found enough to prove that anyone had killed your sister, and I mean *anyone*, kid, you'd have known about it.'

'So you don't believe me.'

MacLeish tilted his head, eyes sliding to one side. 'I believe Tawney was killed by someone she knew. Strangulation – it's brutal. It's *personal*. Why didn't anybody notice someone in the neighbourhood? Because nothing was out of place. It was a normal day – until it wasn't.'

I didn't understand what he was trying to tell me. 'So you think it could've been Cal.'

MacLeish sighed, looked away. 'He had the motive.' But there was that heaviness again.

'But?'

MacLeish said it almost reluctantly. 'Leaving aside his alibi for the moment – your sister and Cal, they were known for their blowout fights. Loud, public screaming matches, all those dustups caught by the paparazzi. If he'd come over in the middle of the day, and they'd fought, why didn't anybody hear it?' He squinted up at the ceiling. 'That's what I've always wondered.'

I shook my head. 'What if he came over there meaning to kill her? What if he surprised her?'

MacLeish shook his head. 'Surprised her by strangling her with her own towel? We found traces of her sweat and sunscreen on it. She'd been lying on it before she was strangled.' He held up a hand as I started to protest. 'You're right, maybe she got up and he strangled her with it before she could see him – *maybe*. It would require absolutely perfect timing. It's not impossible. But then – there's the alibi.'

I shook my head, over and over and over. MacLeish didn't know, he hadn't seen what I'd seen. Cal killed

Tawney. Cal killed Tawney, and then, years later, he killed Ankine. Maybe there were other women, too, murders the LAPD hadn't solved, or maybe never even found. I knew it, in my bones. It wasn't a wish, because I wouldn't have *wished* for this.

But no one believed me.

'I'm sorry, kid,' John said. 'I know it isn't what you wanted to hear.'

Kid. Baby. Sweetheart. Honey. Little girl.

'So who do you think did it, John? If you're so sure it wasn't Cal.' I glared at him.

MacLeish's mouth dropped open. He closed it. Looked away, out the window to Nom-Nom's parking lot. 'Neither of your parents submitted to a blood sample or DNA swab. They let us fingerprint them. But that was it.'

I stared at him, not sure what I was hearing. 'What are you talking about?'

'Look,' MacLeish said, his face granite. 'Crimes like these – nine times out of ten, nine point nine nine nine times out of ten, it's someone with a motive, a real one. There's love involved, which means there's hate involved, and when we think of that we start with two pools: the family, or the partner. I already told you why I don't think it was the partner.' MacLeish held up his hands, cutting my protests off before they began. 'Kid, I don't know any more than that. I'm not saying that's worth much. It's just a hunch. Just something that doesn't sit right with me.'

I stared at him. MacLeish stared back, pity on his face. He was out of his goddamn mind. My parents? My father had spent the night Tawney died vomiting in grief, barely able to stand. My mother visited Tawney's grave every week, changing out flowers. There was no way. *No* way.

After a moment, MacLeish slid out of the booth. He stood there, watching me. Then he said, 'You have a connection with Cal. You have a history. That's an advantage, if you can use it.'

I looked down. I'd thought he'd been my partner in this, all these years. But I'd been alone all along. I wouldn't call him again, I knew that much. I kept my head down until I heard the clang of the door, looking up in time to see MacLeish's back retreating out of the donut shop.

I was no closer than I'd been before to proving that Cal was guilty. But I knew the truth: Cal killed Tawney, and then days later, he'd slept with me.

'Oh *fuck*,' I said out loud, and then I was crying, crying hard like I hadn't cried since my father died, maybe since Tawney died. I sat there and let the hiccupping sobs come, pouring down my face, puddling on my blouse.

It could have been ten minutes or an hour before I finally pulled my face up from the clump of napkins I'd buried it in, and sniffled, trying to regain my composure. I watched a little boy poke his finger against the glass at the donuts, his other hand sandwiched against his mother's thigh. I swiped the tears from my cheeks, covering my fingers in dark rivers of mascara.

I could hear the little boy's feet scuffing at the linoleum, dragging as he walked. He had a blue-sprinkled donut in one chubby fist, his eyes on me as his mother dragged him past my booth. He peered in at me, tugging on her arm. I tried a watery smile but heard him say: 'Look, Momma, look, why is the lady sad?'

I stared at my donuts, thinking. *Why are you sad, Salma?*

Why are you sad? *Why aren't you pissed off? Cal's out there, killing women, and you're here, boo-hoo-hoo-ing about it? You know MacLeish is wrong. Stop feeling sorry for yourself. Stop being sad, and do something about it. Whatever you can do. Just fucking do* something *about it. Before he hurts anyone else.*

The voice sounded a lot like Tawney's. After this many years, I couldn't tell the difference between my own internal monologue and her voice. Maybe there was no difference any more.

I stood up, carrying my donuts. I walked over to the table where the little boy sat with his mother. He was busy smearing the blue frosting on his face, as happy to be painted as to eat the treat.

'Excuse me,' I said. The boy's mother looked up, staring. 'Would you like these? My eyes were bigger than my stomach.'

I dropped the donuts on their table and turned to leave. I was halfway through the doors when I heard her call after me, 'Hey, aren't you . . .'

But I let the door slam behind me before I heard the rest.

11TH JUNE, 1997

Tawney called me. When I picked up, she asked me if I was buzzed.

'No.' Not a lie. It was only my second beer of the afternoon.

I could practically hear Tawney thinking on the phone. 'All right,' she said. 'Can you take the car and meet me at the Jacaranda House? *Don't* tell Mom and Dad where you're going.' She hesitated. 'Tell them . . . tell them you're going to meet a friend or something.'

I took the turns from the Hollywood Hills as a game, trying hard not to tap on the brakes as I leant into the curves with my learner's permit. By the time I sputtered to a stop in front of the Jacaranda House, my veins were buzzing with adrenaline, almost a good substitute for coke, although I'd bargained with myself that Tawney wouldn't be able to tell if I did just a *little* bump in the car.

Things had been so strange since Tawney had broken off her engagement with Cal – she'd gotten more reclusive, shutting herself up in the house so paparazzi couldn't trail her, prone to crying jags that left me wondering why, if she missed Cal so much, she'd left him in the first place.

Some nights felt normal: Tawney would grab a bottle of wine – *our secret* – and make popcorn and we'd sit in her three-million-dollar mansion, on her white leather sofa that cost more than most people made in a year, and, like other sisters, watch *Death Becomes Her*, talk about boys while we hid out from the paparazzi.

This time, Tawney met me at the door. Her face was scrubbed of make-up, arms crossed over her famous chest in a slubby grey T-shirt and jeans. Light freckles dusted her nose.

'Did you tell Mom you were coming?' she asked as I hugged her. She pulled away abruptly and headed back through the house, out to the pool.

No VHS and wine tonight.

'Of course not,' I said, kicking my shoes off so I could dangle my toes in the water. Tawney had already rolled her jeans up, kicking her feet back and forth in the pool.

'Good.' Tawney sat half in shadow, so I could only partially see her face, but even so I could tell something was weighing heavy on her mind. With the clarity of a coke high starting to come on, I realised she'd been crying: her eyes were just the littlest bit puffy.

'Why do you care if Mom knows I'm here anyway?'

Tawney ducked her head. 'Because I needed to talk to you. Not her.'

'Is it Cal? Do you think you might . . . get back together?' I still couldn't believe she'd ended it with him for good. I knew they'd had their ups and downs, but so had our parents and everyone called theirs the love story of the century.

Her lips pinched together. Her eyes darted to the

privacy hedges that enclosed the yard. 'No. I don't think so. I don't know.'

My big sister fumbling for words wasn't something I was used to. I didn't like the way it made me feel.

Tawney scrubbed her hands over her face in frustration, and then said, in a voice more like her usual. 'What we had wasn't healthy, you know that, right? I loved Cal. A lot. But the thing between us . . .' She shook her head, staring gloomily into the pool. 'There were only bad endings for it. Even if I hadn't . . .' She bit herself off mid-sentence, actually clamped her lips together so she didn't say anything more.

I knew I should pay attention, but my brain couldn't track it, couldn't keep up. 'Tune in for the exclusive take on Tawney and Cal's breakup tonight at five,' I said, then giggled crazily, nearly slipping off the lip of the pool into the water.

Tawney's entire body went electric-shock straight as she examined my dilated pupils. She slapped the pool, splashing me. 'You're high, aren't you? I fucking knew it. Goddamn it, Salma, what's wrong with you?'

'Look, just because you want to live your life chained up even though you're young, doesn't mean I can't—'

In the dark, the palm trees above us swayed and Tawney held a finger to her lips: *Quiet*. I shut up and we both sat in the dark, listening. Tawney's eyes narrowed, and she stared at the rippling bushes with laser focus. I rolled my eyes.

'You're so paranoid—'

'Shh, quiet!' Tawney flapped her hand at me, head jerking back to the hedge. A frond twitched, then went still. The breeze. I was sure it was the breeze. But Tawney stared at it like it would crack under interrogation, if she willed it.

'Tawney Lowe, the world's most famous actor. Give me a break,' I snapped. 'Nobody's trying to get you. It's night, the photos would be shit anyway. Okay?'

Tawney listened and watched for another minute before her shoulders slumped, and she sighed. 'I swear to God, I feel like someone is *watching* me. I keep expecting that I'm going to wake up one morning and there'll be all these photos of me like – swimming, or in the shower or something. It's like they're in the house with me, even when I'm alone.' She shuddered. 'They're under my skin.'

Tawney, so dramatic. Her feelings coloured the world; I thought she was overreacting. The paparazzi were bad, but I thought it would pass. Once the story about her and Cal died down, so would the attention.

'Give it a few years,' I said, sisterly rivalry bubbling to the surface. 'Someone younger and prettier and more stacked will come along, and you'll be old news. Just ask Mom.'

'You are such a fucking—'

This time, there was no mistaking it. The soft *click, click, click,* of a camera shutter, the rustle of the hedge. Even in the dark, I could see Tawney's face turn white, and she pulled her feet out of the pool so quickly, she slipped, scraping her hand. 'Get inside,' she hissed. 'Now!'

She didn't have to tell me twice. I scrambled for the door, and she tugged it shut behind me, throwing the lock and the curtains. She dripped a puddle on the terracotta tiles, trembling as she hugged herself.

'I wasn't imagining that, was I?'

I had to admit no, she wasn't.

Tawney turned her head, peering anxiously through the

curtains. As she did, her hair fell back and I could see a reddish blotch on the side of her neck, about the size of a golf ball.

Or a mouth.

A shock ran through me. She'd been broken up with Cal for weeks. She hadn't done anything wrong, not technically. But the sight of it made me queasy.

Tawney was pale, and she had a funny look on her face, one I hadn't seen before. I wondered if she knew I'd seen. 'Salma, I have to tell you something. But if I tell you,' she whispered, her eyes dark and glittering, 'you'll hate me for it.'

I stared at the hickey. I knew what she was going to say. There was someone new; the tabloids had been right, there'd been someone all along.

'Wow,' I said coldly. 'Like father, like daughter, huh?'

Tawney's face fell, and then she was crying, big, gulping, ugly sobs. I didn't go to her. I turned and left the Jacaranda House, slamming the door behind me, ducking my head in case the paparazzo was still outside, waiting, never knowing how badly I'd failed her.

The next morning, I would call her and apologise. I'd tell her I loved her, and I was drunk and high, she was right about that, and I was sorry for being a shit. Tawney would accept my apology, making it sound easy and light and forgotten already, because that's who she was: the kind of sister who made it easy for me.

A few days later, she'd fight with my mother, so loud I thought they'd scream the rafters down. And then, what felt like minutes later, she'd be dead.

That was the last night I saw her alive.

CHAPTER TWENTY-ONE

When Melany picked up my call, I lied. I told her I had something of Tawney's to give her, to help her with her performance. I didn't feel bad for a second.

I told Melany to meet me at the museum behind Stars Six Feet Under at 8 p.m., three days after the hotel pool shoot. By eight, she'd be out of make-up. And at Stars Six Feet Under, the last tour would have ended. The gift shop, closed.

We'd be alone.

I got there early, waiting in the parking lot until I was sure everyone had left for the evening, before I went in the back door, tapping in the key code to keep the alarm off.

I'd had time to think after I'd talked to MacLeish. He wasn't wrong. It wasn't impossible Cal had learnt about the scene of the crime through other means – the coroner's file, for instance. Every time I closed my eyes, I saw that flutter of X's down the centre of Tawney's chest. The clutch of jacaranda blossoms kicking against her thigh.

Or maybe there had been police photographs taken of the scene – Cal could've bribed a police officer for them.

But it was so *intimate*. The pleasure Cal had taken in the

details, the arrogance of filming a letter-perfect recreation of a murder . . . It felt personal.

Much as I didn't want to be anywhere near Cal, I knew I'd have to stay in his orbit. Maybe I could convince Emerald and Cherry to meet with me off the set, find ways to chisel away at their alibis – if they were lying – although I didn't count on it.

But I needed to get Melany away from Cal, fast.

I flipped on the lights, pulling apart the heavy black velvet curtains that guarded the museum. Over the years, Dale had amassed a macabre collection of trinkets and mementos of the dead – letters from famous murderers or victims; Jean Harlow's handkerchief, stained with something brownish and gory; a patch from James Dean's motorcycle jacket, trimmings of leather visible underneath it.

Together as a collection, the museum was ghoulish. I knew that. A study in poor taste, linked by prurient interest, shock value, the gawking worst of human instincts. All true. But there was also a melancholy impulse there, one I understood to my core: the attempt to pin a piece of those loved and lost to the human realm, to create a story we could revisit. Memories weren't tangible. Mementos were.

In one corner, I'd built a shrine to my Dead Girls. I grouped their headshots on an altar, along with pieces Dale could find. The radio from the car where Thelma Todd, the Ice Cream Blonde, had died of carbon monoxide poisoning. Dominique Dunne's hair ribbon from *Poltergeist*. Dried flowers from Dorothy Stratten's marriage to the man who murdered her. A handwritten letter by Rebecca Schaeffer, a pill bottle made out to Lupe Vélez, a replica of the Black Dahlia's handbag.

At the top of the altar: Tawney, of course.

Melany poked her head around the black velvet curtain. I waved her inside, watched her take it all in – the Marilyn-centric wallpaper, the exhibit under glass. Me, standing quietly, hands folded on the altar of my making.

There was a look on her face between wonder and revulsion. 'This is spooky,' Melany said, forcing a laugh. Her eyes darted toward the black velvet curtain. 'Is it . . . is it just us here?'

I nodded. I knew how it looked, me asking her to come here at night, in the dark. I tried to break the ice. 'How did the shoot go today?'

Melany was leaning wide-eyed on one of the glass exhibits, her lips moving as she read the card beneath it. She didn't look up as she answered. 'Fine.'

I waited, but she didn't say anything else. As she straightened from the case, there was a gassy rumble, and Melany laughed a little, self-consciously. 'Sorry. Haven't had a chance to eat yet.'

'We could go—'

'No!' There was a bright panic in her eyes, then she smiled, like she was trying to wave it away. 'No, that's all right. I'll grab something at home. I have approved dinners at home.'

I frowned. 'Approved? What do you mean, "approved"?'

Melany looked embarrassed. 'Cal has me on a strict diet. Stuff to maximise my performance. It's really helped, I think.'

'Cal put you on a diet?'

She raised a shoulder, studied her nails, like it wasn't important. 'It's been good for me. I've lost twelve pounds since I auditioned.'

Twelve pounds. I stared at her willowy frame. She did look thinner. Her collarbones jutted. I felt dizzy. Cal was shaving her down to nothing. Trying to recreate my sister at her most unhappily skeletal.

Studios were no longer allowed to enact a formal weight clause in their contracts for female actors, the way they had once, but there were ways around it: well-placed comments and suggestions, different meals served at breaks, even outright threats of firing under the guise of *not being right for the part.*

I knew all about that. Tawney did, too.

'Melany, that's not healthy,' I said. 'You should—'

She cut me off, yanking on her ponytail, a sharp, irritated movement. 'What was so urgent I had to come down here? You said you had something for me?'

I took a step closer. I'd practised what to say to her in the days since I'd talked to MacLeish. I had it all worked out in my head. But seeing Cal's effect on her body rattled me. When the words came, they were rushed, shrill: 'Melany, you need to quit the movie.'

She gaped at me, her mouth dropped comically low. Then she started to laugh. 'God, Salma, you had me worried there for a moment.'

'I'm serious.' I hesitated. I reached out a hand and she flinched. 'I think Cal killed Tawney. I think he killed Ankine. I think he's capable of hurting you, too.'

Melany was staring at me now like I'd grown a second

head. Her brow puckered, and she made a soft whistly inhale between pursed lips. 'Oh my God, you're serious. You're actually serious.'

'He's a dangerous man, Melany. I know.'

Melany looked around the room, her eye lighting on a photograph at the top of my Dead Girls altar. It was the only piece in Dale's museum that didn't have a descriptive card. In the photo, a young woman looked into a mirror, a candle below her chin brightening only a sliver of her face, the lines of her clavicle. Her shoulder blades were sharp as fins in the semi-darkness, and she was hallowed by a Technicolor glow: sunset yellows and oranges. In front of her, a scattering of jacaranda blossoms glowed with light, like they were on fire, a camera propped in front of them.

In the self-portrait, my sister didn't look beautiful. She looked otherworldly. She looked like she'd never belonged to any of us in the first place.

'Look,' she said slowly, her eyes still on Tawney's photo. 'I saw you taking pictures. I can see that what's happening on the film set – I get that that's really *triggering* for you. Maybe you should talk to someone about it?'

I huffed out a breath I hadn't realised I was holding. Cal was her big break. On set, she seemed half in love with him. She wasn't going to turn on him unless she really understood – he wasn't the man she thought he was.

I took a deep breath, steeling myself.

'When I was fifteen,' I said, 'the day of my sister's funeral – Cal and I had sex.' The words stuck in my throat, threatened to choke me. I'd only ever told my rehab counsellors. 'Just the one time. But I was . . . I was a kid. Fifteen years old. He took advantage of the situation,' I

213

said, realising as I said it that it was true. I'd wanted him. But he'd been an adult. He'd known more about the human heart than I did. He could've protected me, and he chose not to. 'He's not a good man, Melany. I promise you.'

Melany's face drained of colour. I thought of all the small moments I'd seen between the two of them, Melany's set-crush obvious to anyone with eyes. I knew she wouldn't like it – but I had to tell her.

Finally, she shook her head. 'Sorry, but – it's a little hard to believe.' Her smile was pained. 'You and Cal? I just . . . really don't see the two of you together.'

I frowned. 'Well, it happened.'

Melany held up a hand. 'I'm not saying you're lying. I believe *you* believe it. But . . .' She paused, and I knew, I fucking *knew*, what was coming next. 'You had a troubled childhood. Maybe you . . . thought something happened. Maybe you got confused. I mean . . .' She gave me a sympathetic look. 'He's *Cal Turner*.'

'Right,' I said. My hands were balled so tightly into knots my nails were slicing my skin open. 'Why would Cal sleep with me when he could have anyone in the world? I don't know, Melany. Maybe you should ask yourself why Cal would cast *you* when he could've had any other leading lady he wanted.'

Melany looked like she'd been slapped. But only for a moment. 'Cal warned me. He said you were jealous. But no, I thought you were trying to *help* me. All this pathetic hanging around. Well, you know what, Salma? Just because you ruined your big break doesn't mean you can ruin mine. Sorry, but you need help. Like, lots and lots of it.'

I'd let my temper get the better of me. I'd never forgive myself if anything happened to her now that I knew for sure what Cal was capable of. I took a step forward. 'Please, Melany. I'm trying to help you. Call Emerald right now and tell her you quit. We can find another role for you, anything.'

Melany shook her head, like she couldn't believe me, like I disgusted her, then she swept out of the dark velvet curtains. I followed her into the gift shop, calling her name until the door slid shut behind her, the ping of Chopin following.

I stood there, stunned. Maybe I should've known she'd react like that. I knew what her big break meant to her. But even more than her life?

'Salma?'

My head jerked up. Dale was behind me, a worried look on his face. Fuck. The last thing I needed tonight was another lecture.

'Dale, I'm sorry, I just came to pick up—'

Even though we hadn't spoken in weeks – Dale had sent the occasional text with a misguided emoji: a crying-laughing cat to express his concern, or a big ear to symbolise he was there if I needed someone to talk to – Dale didn't hesitate, just reached his arms out and I stepped into them, thankful. I didn't even come up to his chin.

'You don't look so hot, girl.'

I laughed through a sniffle. Now that he mentioned it, I was sure my appearance hadn't reassured Melany, either – stretchy black pants and a grey sweatshirt I hadn't washed in too long. My hair was pulled up in a greasy knot, and I hadn't bothered with make-up. Vivienne would've been horrified that I'd worn this around the house, let alone stepped out in public in it.

'I call it "depression chic."'

That caught Dale's attention, and not in the way that I'd hoped, with a laugh. 'Salma, if you need someone to talk to—'

I waved him away. 'Still sober, scout's honour. Just . . .' I tried to think of what to say, how to say it. 'I seem to have found myself surrounded by ghosts. Real, non-Stars-Six-Feet-Under-tour ghosts.'

Dale nodded like he understood. When he finally spoke, his voice was soft and measured. 'I've started going back to Sunday meetings,' he told me, then waited. Not offering to take me. Just giving me a piece of information. 'You know there's a lot I don't believe in. "Easy does it" – what does that even mean? Recovery isn't easy. "Let go and let God" – no thanks, ma'am, I don't think He walks here.' He looked down at his black T-shirt, the silvery trail of snot I'd left. 'But there's one I think is as true if you're sober as if you're using. "We're only as sick as our secrets." That is true of everybody, sober or not.'

He gave me one more meaningful look, then turned away. He didn't shove me through any doors, just let me know they were open. 'Good night, Salma,' he called over his shoulder.

I stood in the gift shop, thinking. I wanted to tell him I agreed with him. I wanted to tell him I was trying to get rid of the secrets, only nobody else would listen, or believe me. I wanted to ask him, which secrets did he think I was still keeping?

CHAPTER TWENTY-TWO

My mother had scheduled our fitting for less than two weeks before the retrospective – barely enough time to make alterations for a regular celebrity, but for Vivienne Powell Lowe, anything was possible.

I was fifteen minutes late, and I knew, even as I tossed my keys to the Beverly Hills valet, I'd hear about it.

Sure enough, as I threaded my way through the tiny boutiques to the atelier of Anjelica June, my mother's preferred stylist and seamstress, I found my mother beside a rack of already pulled clothes. She pointed at her watch as I approached, and I rolled my eyes.

'Lovely of you to deign to join us,' my mother said drily. A champagne flute in her hands was half gone, tiny bubbles dancing up the side. I watched the bubbles wiggle their way to the top, remembering their sparkler taste on my tongue.

I forced myself to look in the other direction as I gave my mother a hug, flopped onto the couch.

The truth was, I hadn't slept. After Dale left me in the gift shop, I drove back to Glassell Park, where I took a sleeping pill but didn't fall asleep until three in the morning, then promptly shut my alarm off before remembering I was supposed to be in Beverly Hills at ten.

On the drive over, I'd called both Emerald and Cherry. Neither picked up. I didn't want to set foot on set again if I could avoid it. I didn't want to see Cal again unless he was in handcuffs or behind bars.

Now, in the atelier, watching my mother pick through the garment rack, MacLeish's words came back to me. My parents hadn't consented to a DNA swab or a blood test. Why not? I couldn't believe they were involved – but why wouldn't they make every effort to find their daughter's killer? Why leave the door open?

'Sorry. Traffic,' I said lamely. 'Have you been waiting long?'

My mother was dressed in wide, expensive slacks that made her legs look exceptionally long, a white short-sleeved blouse that showed off her firm arms. The film star, at rest. 'Just long enough for Anjelica to begin pulling you some options.'

In the corner, Anjelica frowned, pushing clothes back and forth on the rack. There were two bunches: one with the jewel colours my mother preferred, and another with worryingly bright patterns and colours like chartreuse and bubblegum. The dresses would've suited Tawney. But with my pale complexion – even in the Angeleno sun, my skin was so white it was practically blue – and dark hair, I'd look worst-dressed-list washed-out.

Anjelica had a faux French accent, a way with a needle, and an impeccable eye for designs that flattered my mother – not me.

Vivienne tipped her head back, not so much sipping the

champagne as letting it slide down her gullet, like shooting oysters. She set the glass discreetly behind her on a marble pedestal; out of addict sight, out of addict mind. 'Well, let's get started,' she said. 'No time to waste.'

She held out her hand. I stared at it – *Neither of your parents submitted to a DNA swab* – then I tugged my T-shirt over my head, stepped out of my jeans. I avoided eye contact with the angry red line at my waist where my jeans had cut into my flesh, the jiggly droop of my arms in the mirror. I avoided eye contact with my mother, too, afraid of her expression, or even her non-expression, at my pouched stomach, my doughy thighs.

It was a necessity of our industry to stay vigilant against the advance of cellulite, curves that showed up in the wrong spot or spilt out too far. My mother was possessed of a frame that bent to her will, excising five unwanted pounds with no more effort than pulling pages out of a book. For Vivienne, it had been second nature to stand watch over her body – why should it be any different for her children? Growing up, that's what I'd thought it meant to be a woman: to be constantly at war with your own body.

But my body was unruly, incapable of defying its own nature. No matter the diet, I stayed thick-hipped and pudgy in the middle, my face all bad, soft angles even on a good day.

And then there was Tawney. When she'd made her film debut, she'd been sixteen: baby fat still clinging to her cheeks, burgeoning breasts not yet caught up to the rest of her. *Tiny tits Tawney*, one gossip site dubbed her. Then, later, when she'd had her breasts augmented she'd caught criticism for that, too: *Today's stars set unhealthy body ideals.*

There was no good way to have a woman's body. Everyone had an opinion about it.

I'd caught my share of criticism in the tabloids. *Whoa, Nelly! Salma Lowe addicted to food?* But Tawney's body had been hard and coveted as a jewel. It didn't stop tabloids from examining every angle of her, by turns critical and fetishistic. If she gained weight, you could guarantee a paparazzo would highlight the slightest jiggle of her thighs, zoom in on her cellulite. If she lost weight – and I knew the ugly truth: the locked bathroom doors; the hours she spent in the pool offsetting a bagel; South Beach and Atkins and SlimFast and the Zone – tabloids would gleefully point out how *unhealthy* she looked.

No reprieve even in death: The coroner had leaked photos of her body on the autopsy slab – *What was inside her?* Tawney's body was always up for grabs.

And yet. I thought of the twelve pounds Melany had lost at Cal's behest, the envious look in her eye about my family's paparazzi coverage. There'd always be people who craved fame, even bad fame. It was one way to live forever.

My mother helped me into the first dress, a bubblegum-pink pouf that made me look like a sentient cupcake. I scowled at myself in the mirror as Anjelica tugged on the zipper that wouldn't close – *Sample sizes only, so sorry, Salma, I didn't realise they wouldn't fit you.*

My mother's eyes narrowed, and she frowned. I watched her try to imagine how to reconfigure my body to fit the dress.

Even if it had been the right size, the slim column tube beneath the tulle clung to me in the wrong places, the delicate fabric emphasising the jelly of my stomach, the dimples in my thighs.

I watched her face in the three-sided mirror. All the angles of her – the mole on her left cheek, the long, graceful arc of her neck. Why hadn't she ever believed Cal might have killed Tawney? How could she be so sure?

'Anjelica, I think not,' Vivienne said finally. Her eyes met mine in the mirror, the cool touch of her hand on my exposed shoulder, and she said, 'Darling, it's not the right dress, that's all.'

An assurance she wouldn't have had to make if it was true the dress was the problem.

The next few dresses – a chartreuse bias-cut slip dress, a vintage Schiaparelli that cowered in fear at the circumference of my waist, even a dove-grey skirted suit – were also not the right dress. Finally, Anjelica pulled a gun-metal lamé halter that skimmed my calves. The fit wasn't perfect – too much of me spilling out of the bust – but it was the first one we could both agree on.

I wondered what Emerald would say if she could see me here, trying on pretty, pretty princess dresses to be honoured for a film I'd had no part in creating. I pushed the thought out of my head.

'You look beautiful,' my mother said, a big smile on her face. She looked relieved.

I stared at the dress in the mirror.

I looked like a movie star. I looked like Dave Lowe's daughter.

Dave Lowe, who had withheld material that might have mattered to Tawney's murder investigation.

Stop it, Salma. You know what happened. You know

who's really responsible. Besides, I reassured myself, my parents had had nothing to do with Ankine's death. It wasn't possible.

Anjelica finished taking the measurements for the alterations she'd need to make, then I stepped down from the three-sided mirror, plopping myself into the corner of the pillowy leather couch. Next to me, the pedestal where my mother had set her champagne flute, a small golden puddle at the bottom. No more than a taste. Not even a full drink.

With the tip of one finger, I pushed the flute as far from me as I could.

Unlike with me, nearly every option Anjelica pulled suited my mother. Vivienne Lowe wasn't hard to dress, and Anjelica had been doing it for years. But my mother could find fault with a misplaced stitch, a too-low-cut neckline, a jewel tone that read as overly wintry.

If Tawney had still been alive – if she'd been here for this fitting – if nothing else had been different in my life in this moment except the presence of my sister – maybe it would have been bearable. I imagined her curled on the couch, feet under her, a champagne glass in her hand. 'Too widowy,' she would've called out about the black crepe silk my mother liked. 'You're still a young woman, Vivienne. We're looking for your next husband, you know.'

No one – not my father, not Jack, certainly not me – had made my mother laugh more.

If Tawney had survived – who would she have been? Who would I have been? Maybe we'd have grown apart. Maybe she would have reunited with Cal, married him. Maybe she would've quit acting. All our lives would've been different. That was the only thing I knew for sure.

My mother examined herself in the mirror, turning a critical eye on her white and navy polka-dotted dress. 'No,' she said finally. 'Not this one, either.'

Anjelica clucked her tongue. 'I have one more theeng in zee back room.' She disappeared through a discreet door in the wall, a soft click closing her off from us.

My mother turned again to the side, examining the polka dots, and I screwed up my courage. 'Mom.' Vivienne looked up. 'Too widowy,' I tried, making a face like one Tawney made when she joked.

Vivienne stared at me, bemused. 'What an odd thing to say, Salma.'

Anjelica returned from her closet of secrets, holding a black garment bag like it contained the crown jewels. She threw me a quick wink as she passed, and I sat up straight, paying attention now.

I couldn't see the dress as she unzipped the garment bag, but my mother clapped in delight. Her face flooded with pink, and I thought I could see tears in her eyes. 'Oh, *Anjelica*, you *doll*.'

I sat forward as they carefully extracted a black velvet backless dress. My mother shucked off the polka dots, disappearing into the black velvet, taut stomach only lightly silvered with decades-old stretch marks, and then Vivienne was ensconced in the tulip flare of the dress, hugging her tightly as if she was made for it and not the other way around. She turned to me, cheeks glowing.

'It's beautiful,' I said.

Anjelica plucked at my mother's body, *hmm*ing. 'It fits you nearly perfect still, no? Perhaps we shall even have to take it een.'

My mother giggled, swatted Anjelica. 'Don't flatter me too much, you old witch.' My mother had found a rapt audience, and she knew it. They were like teenagers, giddy over the proportions of my mother's waist. 'Those were the best days of my life.'

I watched my mother twirl girlishly in the mirror. I was missing something. 'It's very pretty, but . . . why so special? Is it from a film or something?'

Anjelica refilled my mother's champagne glass, and Vivienne took a swallow that was half the flute, her face aglow. 'It was hand-stitched for the 1974 Academy Awards by a little-known French master, a protégé of Coco Chanel. It was calculated to the very centimetre of my waist; I wasn't allowed to eat anything but broth and non-cruciferous vegetables for months.' My mother smiled, shook her head. Like it was a good memory. 'I was so afraid of popping a stitch.' My mother glided her hands up her slim white throat, shuddering at the memory. Anjelica made the sign of the cross. 'Finally, I'll get to give her the premiere she deserves.'

I frowned, my brain skittering to a stop.

The Academy Awards had been in April the year *Iron Prayer* was nominated. Tawney had been born weeks later. *Too pregnant to be in public*, she'd joked. *Publicist's orders.*

Fasting for months before she gave birth?

'*Alors*, you did not go?' Anjelica was adjusting my mother's hemline, looking up at her with a trio of slim metal pins curled in the corner of her mouth.

'No.' Vivienne's fingers fiddled with the bust, the two strips of crisscrossing fabric that held the dress up against all forces of gravity and nature and ageing and changing waistlines.

'Mom,' I said, then stopped. I wasn't sure how to ask what I was thinking. I stared at my mother's midsection, taut under the velvet. I could probably span it with just my hands now.

How could my mother have been near-term pregnant with a twenty-six-inch waist?

Unless, I thought with a sick feeling, she *hadn't* been pregnant.

It wasn't possible.

In the mirror, my mother watched me, a slight smile on her face. Waiting for me to go on.

I looked at Anjelica, feeling hot, nauseous. My mother caught my glance, then something drooped in her face, and for a second, cool, collected Vivienne Powell Lowe was replaced by a hot burst of panic and fear.

But only for a second. Vivienne cleared her throat. 'Anjelica, the Dior pumps we tried last week – they'd be darling with this, don't you think? Could you go scrounge them up?'

Her cheeks were red, and not just from the champagne. I waited until Anjelica was in the back room. But I couldn't find the words.

There was an idea kicking around in my head. A crazy thought about Loretta Young, who had 'adopted' her own child, and the mysteries of my parents' marriage, my mother's ambition, my father's insatiable hunger. The refusals to give blood samples.

In the mirror, a small muscle twitched in my mother's face. I watched, fascinated. She looked so beautiful in the dress. She looked so happy. I wanted to go back in time three minutes, clap my hand over her mouth when the dress arrived. *No, no, stop now. Don't say it.*

If Tawney had been here. If Tawney had been alive. My brave sister wouldn't have hesitated.

You're only as sick as your secrets.

'Mom,' I said slowly, my voice barely a croak in the silently opulent room, 'how could you have fit into that dress when you were pregnant with Tawney?'

In the three faces of the mirror, I watched my mother's face crumple, turning ashen. Then she reached down and threw back the rest of the champagne in her flute. She finished the glass, poured herself another, then stole a covert look at me, holding up the bottle in offering.

I ignored that.

'Mom,' I said. Or tried to say. My voice came out so strained and thin, I could barely hear myself. I cleared my throat. 'Mom, was Tawney your daughter?'

That broke my mother's fugue, and she glared at me. 'Of course she was my daughter,' she snapped. 'She was *my* daughter. She belonged to *me*. I knew the moment I saw her.' My mother shook her head, a pulse jumping hard at her throat.

When the next words came, they were slow, halting. 'You know what your father was like. Even when we . . . even at the beginning. There were always other women, so many other women.' She shuddered, and I felt the competing urges to hold her in my arms and to press my hands over her mouth, stop her from saying anything more.

There was a rushing in my ears. 'So, what, Dad had an affair? With Tawney's mother?'

My mother's hand clutched the flute so hard I was

afraid it would crack. 'An *affair. Please.* Not even that. A mistake, just one time.' She turned her head and I studied her profile, the pieces of her face coming apart like a Picasso. 'I found out in February. Your father and I had been married three months. He sat me down, told me there was going to be a baby. He asked me what I wanted to do. It was my choice, Salma. She was *always* my daughter.'

I had the pieces, but I couldn't turn them into a picture I understood, I couldn't make it all fit. Except this: I wondered if one day I'd carry it lightly enough to tell MacLeish I thought I knew why my parents had refused the DNA sample.

'How could you not tell me? All this time. You never told me. Who was her mother?'

My mother flinched. 'In every way that mattered, I was her mother. I chose her. She was my beautiful golden baby, as much mine as you are. The woman who gave birth to her – she wasn't worthy of Tawney. *She didn't deserve her.* Some groupie floozy, wouldn't stop hanging around him, wouldn't stop throwing herself at him. She didn't want to raise a child. She just wanted your father.' Her long nails clicked against the beading on her dress, and for a moment, it was the only sound in the room. 'Tawney was *my daughter.* Our *daughter.*'

Our daughter. I thought I understood better now. My mother had loved Tawney, I knew that was true. But she'd also found the only weapon at her disposal in the face of betrayal; she'd found a way to hew my father more closely to her, to turn heartbreak into a padlock for her love.

Every day she looked at my sister and saw the woman

my father had had an affair with. How awful. How unbelievably unfair. 'Oh, Mom,' I said, reaching for her. I thought my heart would crack.

Her head snapped up, and she glared at me. Vivienne Powell didn't *do* pity. Pity was reserved for the weak. Vivienne Powell was not weak.

'Stop that,' she scolded. 'Your father and I had a very happy marriage.'

A better daughter would have told her: *I understand, and I'm sorry. I'm sorry you felt you had to pretend Dad's infidelity was your own, too. I'm sorry you tried to scrub his sins and hurts away by adopting the baby as your own. I'm sorry, I'm sorry, I'm sorry.*

But I wasn't just sorry. She'd lied to me for years. Even now, after Tawney was dead, and my father was dead, she'd never told me the truth.

I brushed tears off my cheeks, closed my eyes. Tawney: teaching me to smile with my tongue tucked behind my teeth, Cindy Crawford–style; picking me up from the Viper Room, trying to protect me from paparazzi; forcing me to clean out the jacaranda blooms from her pool while she sipped lemonade in a lawn chair. My beautiful, moody, capricious sister. Even if I could've picked another, I wouldn't have.

'Why didn't you tell me?' I asked again, my voice barely a whisper.

Vivienne shook her head wordlessly, and Anjelica bustled back through the door, the Dior shoes tucked under an arm, seemingly oblivious to my tears. Perhaps she was used to women sobbing in her atelier.

I'd spent so long thinking I was the problem in my

family. I was the bad one, the one who couldn't keep her life together, the one destroying *the Lowe family brand* – the legacy we'd been lucky enough to shoulder, our burden and our gift. *Think of the family, Salma. What will the fans think?* And all the while, they'd been hiding *this*.

I stood up, grabbing my purse. 'Salma, please don't leave,' my mother said. 'Please, please, stay, we can talk about it more. Later, darling. After the fitting?'

Because she wouldn't talk about it in front of Anjelica.

I didn't answer her. I didn't look at her as I gathered my phone. I'd forgive her one day. I knew that. It's what families did; you forgot, and forgave, because you didn't want to waste the love in hatred or resentment. Because time was not infinite, and I knew that. But as I swiped away my tears, as I fumbled for the valet slip in my purse, as I stepped out of the door over her plaintive wails and protests, I wasn't sure when that day would be.

CHAPTER TWENTY-THREE

I parked the car a few blocks away from Tawney's house and found myself walking along the sidewalk, dragging my feet, until I was squarely in front of that hideous pink stain on her asphalt. I squinted up at the Jacaranda House, dark and closed.

My sister. That hadn't changed, even if it had a different weight now.

The drive from Beverly Hills to the Jacaranda House hadn't been long enough for me to sort out my thoughts. I'd cried as I drove, the tears streaming down my face as regular and unthinking as breathing. I had only the strong sense that I needed to be near her, the way I knew how to be. The Jacaranda House, the last place she'd been happy.

It was almost possible to believe my sister was alive there still, bricked up inside the walls like a blonde Fortunato in 'Cask of Amontillado.' It did not seem possible that anyone else could ever live there. Although according to the police report for Ankine's death, one E. F. Wennick did.

I looked over my shoulder, then keyed open the gate. I stepped up to the big windows at the front of the house, cupping my hands around my eyes on the glass as I peered inside. The curtains were drawn but sheer; I could see the outline of a large couch. Tawney's fireplace. The last time I'd seen it, I'd been – I stopped myself. The last time I'd seen it had been a few days before, on Cal's set. A replica almost good enough to be the real thing.

It was getting harder to keep reality straight from the Hollywood fiction.

I leant back into the glass, squinting. The decorating taste was a step up from Ikea generic, though not such curated tastes as Vivienne's. It looked nearly the same as when Tawney'd been alive, just skewed enough to feel a little off, a little wrong.

I took a step forward into misdemeanor and walked to the side of the house, stopping only when my toes were up against the edge of the pool. The spot where I'd tried to resuscitate Ankine.

I stared at the pool, shimmering in the afternoon sun. There was Tawney, giving herself a bounce as she dove in, her body sleek as a seal's underwater, trying to hold her breath to make it to the far side in one go. It was how she started her morning laps, every time. A test for herself. She rarely made it in just the one breath, although she always got close.

When I stayed over, pulling myself out of bed groggy and hungover, I'd creep to the window, watch without her knowing. The command she had over her body, the grace and power – it was a marvel. My body, still changing, had always been a stranger to me.

The whole world knew Tawney's body.

Why had two women died here, alone, in this happy place? Why – *how* – had Ankine even been here in the first place? It didn't make sense. To feel closer to my sister, maybe – but then, when she'd been struggling, why hadn't she gotten *out* of the pool? Had she been incapacitated, had Cal thrown her in?

I didn't hear the French doors open until I heard a sharp gasp. A woman had come out of Tawney's house – all these years later, I couldn't think of it any other way – gardening shears in hand, which she nearly dropped with a little cry when she saw me.

'Shit,' I said. My first thought was how bad it would look – *Salma the Snoop caught red-handed breaking into dead sister's home!* – and then I realised, as I stared at the woman – Elizabeth Wennick – I knew her.

The striking silver-blonde hair, the long, graceful neck, nearly translucent skin dotted with freckles, wearing late middle age well – I *knew* her. The woman outside the Jacaranda House the day Ankine died.

I looked at her, the open French doors behind her, the gardening shears in hand. Not a nosy neighbour. She lived here.

'I'm sorry,' I started, 'I'll be going—'

'I know you,' she said, interrupting me. 'You were here the day that poor young woman drowned in my pool.' Even though her voice was low and pleasant – she would've been a star elocution pupil at PAA – it caused the hairs on the back of my neck to stand up. She reached out her hand, the non-shears-holding one, for me to shake. I hesitated, but her expression didn't change. Finally, I stepped away from the gate, back into the realm of the Jacaranda House, and grasped her hand, papery and cool.

'I'm Elizabeth Wennick.'

I know, I thought but didn't say. 'Salma,' I said automatically, though I remembered she knew my name, too. *You're Salma? You're Tawney's sister?* 'That was a terrible day.' I looked at the pool, remembering.

Elizabeth looked up at the bobbing jacaranda tree above us. 'Yes,' she said simply.

I gnawed on my lip, shifting. 'Did you know her?' I kept my eyes on Elizabeth's face, the one that seemed to pull me like a magnet.

Elizabeth shifted the gardening shears to the other hand, the one that had shaken mine. 'We were friends,' she said. Before I could follow up on that, she brushed her fingers over her lips again, tracing her mouth into a little pinch, then said: 'You're her sister, aren't you. Tawney's sister.'

It was too much. My eyes welled. Elizabeth noticed, her eyebrows shooting skyward.

'I'm sorry,' she said. 'I didn't mean to upset you. I just feel . . . close to her, living here.'

I took a step back. Over the years, my sister had collected stalkers. When she was alive, there had been the weirdos – men, mostly – who sent her shitty requests, like pleas for dirty panties, or hair from wherever she wanted to cut it.

But the stalkers Tawney collected now that she was dead tended to be women. They liked to see themselves as well-meaning, and maybe they were – to an extent. But over the years, their interference had ranged from gentle to awful. Notes that showed up at my door, a stranger telling me they'd talked to my sister and she had a message for me and actually the message was that she had been reincarnated in this person's body and it would be appreciated if they could move into my house, or maybe my mother's house.

Those had been the benign ones.

I took another step back, so I was up against the gate, my hand on the top so I could swing it backward. I thought about playing dumb, then thought better of it. 'I am,' I said, hurrying away from the topic. Tawney, my sister, my *half* sister, but no, I'd never think of her that way, never, never. 'You said you were friends with Ankine – how did you meet?'

The corner of Elizabeth's mouth twisted into a gentle smile. 'Halloween, strangely enough. She came to the house dressed as Tawney.'

I remembered the Polaroid MacLeish had shown me. 'You didn't find that . . . ghoulish?'

'I thought it was a nice tribute,' she snapped. 'I invited her inside. We started talking. She was such a nice young woman. Then, later, when she was cast in that film, she asked if she could use my pool. She told me she wanted to get in character by swimming laps, like Tawney used to.'

I didn't like the way she was using my sister's first name, so intimate. Elizabeth's eyes were locked on my face, like she was looking for something. But if she was, she wasn't finding it. She looked down at the shears in her hand, as though unsure why she had them. 'Would you like to come in,' she said, the shears long against the side of her body, 'for a cup of tea?'

Behind Elizabeth, through Tawney's French doors, I could see the flutter of a curtain, a shadow from a light left on. How many years had I been passing by this place, never once imagining that I'd have the opportunity to go inside? It wasn't likely to come again.

But I still had the good sense not to wander into empty houses with women who might or might not be obsessed with my dead sister, especially not when they were clutching three-foot-long garden shears.

Besides, what I wanted was to go inside and find my sister alive and well. I wanted a miracle, not a home tour.

A cloud passed over the sun, and the Jacaranda House, with its familiar contours, those places I knew so well yet hadn't seen up close in years, took on a malevolent tinge. Once, I'd thought of this as a happy place.

But bad things had happened here. Bad things *kept* happening here.

'Another time,' I said.

Elizabeth gave me that dreamy smile again. 'The Jacaranda House will wait.' Elizabeth saw my face. 'That is what Tawney called it, didn't she?' There was a strange little smile on Elizabeth's lips, her eyes sliding off my face like water. 'The two of you.'

Jesus Christ, she made my skin crawl. 'I have to go.'

Elizabeth's face screwed up. 'Wait, please. I have something for you.'

That was not a good sign.

'I really should—'

'*Please.*' The way she said it, so sincere, made me hesitate, and in that split second, she dashed back into the house, the shears clattering to the ground behind her.

I could've left. I could've run.

But maybe she'd found something of my sister's in the house. Something my family had missed. The months after Tawney's death – minus her funeral, and Cal – were a vodka-dimmed blur. The particulars of Tawney's estate, if I'd ever known them, had escaped me.

If she had something belonging to Tawney – my *sister* – I wanted to see it.

Don't be an idiot, Salma. Go.

But then Elizabeth was squeezing back through the door, pressing a crumpled white card into my hand. On the front, in pretty, looping handwriting that wasn't my sister's, one word: *Vivienne.* I blinked twice.

'Would you get this to your mother for me?' Elizabeth sounded hopeful. 'Please.'

I looked back down at the card. 'It's not . . . it's not from Tawney, is it.'

'Oh.' Elizabeth looked flustered, as though the possibility that I might mistake the moment hadn't occurred to her. 'No, it's not.'

I looked up at Elizabeth. Her eyes were placid but a little desperate. The lines on her face were soft, gentle. She looked like a woman who laughed a lot, in other circumstances. But that didn't mean she wasn't like the rest of them: trying to use the Lowe family, feeling like she knew something about us because we'd made a film that mattered, because she'd read up on the most tragic chapter of our lives.

Even after everything that afternoon, all my family's lies – I still couldn't pass along the card. Not without knowing what was inside.

'No,' I said, pushing the card back at her. Elizabeth looked down at it, unbelieving. 'I can't. I'm sorry. I have to go.'

She called my name as I hurried out of the gate, back to my car.

I slammed the door and sat behind the wheel for a moment before I looked back. I couldn't see Elizabeth any more. I stared at the Jacaranda House, my very own personal haunted house.

Ankine had known Elizabeth Wennick, who was, it appeared, obsessed with my sister.

My sister.

Nothing had changed, I decided as I turned the key in the ignition, navigated out of the neighbourhood. If my parents could lie to me for my entire life about my sister's parentage, I could push it down, forget that it was a thing I knew.

I almost believed it.

CHAPTER TWENTY-FOUR

After having been so close to the Jacaranda House, Soundstage Seven felt strange by comparison. I dragged my feet going back to the studio – Cal was a murderer; even among crew and cast I didn't want to be in the same room with him.

But there was the Melany of it all to consider.

Pulling into the soundstage, I realised it was the first time I could remember not feeling the magic of being on set. Things were so muddled now. I was uncovering secrets, all right, but I wanted to tell Dale so far the truth had only made me feel more sick.

Emerald caught me at the craft services table, her face sour. 'I'm surprised to see you again,' she said, as I smeared a bagel with cream cheese. She glared at me as I stuffed half of it in my mouth, took my time chewing.

'Hello to you, too.' I chewed, swallowed. She hadn't returned my calls. I still wasn't sure how much I could trust her. 'Wouldn't miss it. What's on deck today?'

Emerald's bracelets jangled as she crossed her arms. 'Really. Because we haven't seen you in *days*.'

Off to the side of the soundstage, Melany was psyching

herself up for a scene, earbuds in, lips moving to whatever she was listening to. She'd seen me as I entered but pretended not to. I felt a sick little pang in my stomach as I remembered I'd told her my deepest secret. *It's a little hard to believe.*

My phone buzzed. Jack. I silenced it. In the days since I'd discovered my family's shameful little secret, I'd missed no fewer than twelve calls from Jack and my mother. Mostly from Jack, the family smoother.

'I didn't want to leave Melany alone,' I said.

Across from us, Cal and Roger, his leading man, were deep in conversation, and as I watched, I realised it wasn't just a conversation – it was an argument. It made me uneasy. It didn't bode well that Cal's hold on his temper was already in short supply.

Emerald sighed. 'Salma, whatever you may think of me, you have to know I wouldn't let anything bad happen on set. Cal can be extreme in his measures to get a performance, but the most important thing in the world to him is his art. You have to believe me when I say he wouldn't jeopardise a film on that basis alone.' She paused. 'I'm not the heartless bitch you seem to think I am. I don't want to see anyone get hurt.'

Cal and Roger's argument got louder, more agitated, and Roger was shaking his head, *No, NO,* then Cal put his hand on Roger's shoulder. Cal towered over the shorter leading man. But Roger wasn't intimidated; he shrugged off Cal's hand. I watched Cal's face turn red, and though I couldn't hear it, I could tell he'd had the last, angry word.

I looked up through my bangs at her. She had a serious,

compassionate look on her face. 'Someone *else*, you mean.'

Emerald kept her eyes glued to the soundstage – Cal manoeuvring lighting into place to cast a softer angle, make-up giving the last few adjustments to Melany's face. Then everyone stepping back, the scene about to start. 'Yes,' she said. 'Someone else.'

I looked around. There was one person missing. 'Cherry decided to stop coming to set, too?'

Emerald snorted. 'You missed it. Cal fired her when we were shooting on location.' Emerald must've seen my thunderstruck face. 'It was a long time coming.'

So I'd been right. Cal and Cherry *were* on the outs. Maybe that explained why she hadn't returned my calls. 'Can I ask you something?' I said.

Emerald rolled her eyes. 'You never *stop* asking me things.'

'Why aren't you filming on location?' It had been tickling at the back of my brain for days now, since I'd met Elizabeth, but I hadn't realised it. Cal was a perfectionist. And he fetishised authenticity. Even if they would've had to completely redo the house – which I doubted, based on what I'd seen through Elizabeth's window – it would've been cheaper than recreating it on a soundstage. And, more important for Cal, it would have been the *real thing*.

Not every homeowner would agree to onlocation shoots, of course. But Cal Turner was one of the Big Names, still. He had star power, and Los Angeles was a town that kowtowed to its stars, like local royalty. It was hard to imagine many people saying no to him, especially given the house's history.

I darted a glance at Emerald. Her mouth was pressed into a tight line, the same way it always was when I asked about Ankine. Like she was stopping herself from saying anything. 'We asked,' she said shortly. 'They said no.'

'*No?*' That surprised me. Especially given Elizabeth Wennick's obvious obsession with my sister. *Especially* since Ankine had been a friend. 'And they knew what the film was about?'

'Oh yes,' Emerald said. 'Cal went to speak to the owner herself. When he showed up, she wouldn't even talk to him.'

Hmm. That was something new.

'Places,' a PA called from off-side the soundstage, and everyone scampered to their seats except for the talent. Melany took a step forward into the spotlight, her face tilted upward like it was the sun. Just offstage, Roger looked vaguely ill, holding a prop in his hands. I squinted. It was a towel. He was holding a towel.

Like the one used to strangle my sister.

Emerald started to head to the nook opposite video village where she watched the shots across from Cal. I put my hand on her arm, a tight feeling in my chest. 'Emerald, what are we filming today?'

She stopped. She wouldn't look at me. 'Last-minute script changes,' she said. 'I would've warned you, but you didn't take to it when I did that before.'

Oh shit. I looked between Melany, eyes closed, preparing herself, to Cal, slouched insouciantly in his director's chair.

There was no time to do anything. I watched Emerald walk away, then I sank down into my chair – next to

Cherry's now-permanently-vacant one – and waited, a bad feeling gathering under my skin.

'Action,' Cal called.

The room went silent except for the whir of the camera, Cal's commands to Melany – *More thoughtful, imagine someone you love, that's it, that's right.* Roger *now* – the white lights baking down on them, illuminating the baby wisps framing Melany's face like a halo.

I watched Roger approach Melany from behind, fedora tipped over one eye, towel in his hand. My mouth was full of hot saliva. I was going to be sick. Close, close, then he looped the towel around her neck, yanked it tight, and pulled until I could hear Melany struggling for air, gagging and choking. Even though she knew it was coming, she was a good actor and it sounded real. Too real.

I closed my eyes, tears flooding my throat. No, no, no, I didn't want to see this.

Then, blessedly, I heard the towel *whump* to the ground, and the sound of Melany sucking in air loudly.

'Cut,' Cal snarled. He popped out of his chair, crossing the soundstage until he was in front of Roger in three long strides. Melany rubbed her throat gingerly. 'What the hell was that?'

'You got the shot,' Roger said, his face hard. 'I didn't need to drag it out.'

Cal's face was twisted into an ugly sneer, and he towered over his leading man. 'I decide when the shot ends. *Me.*'

Roger's eyes narrowed. 'Right.'

They glared at each other for another moment, then Cal yelled, 'Back to one.' He stalked back to video village as Melany and Roger reset.

But on the second take, Roger eased off even more. I could see the towel slack in his hand. Melany didn't make any choking noises, although she did her best impression of being strangled, her eyes bulging, face purpling as she held her breath, simulating lack of oxygen. She clawed her nails into Roger's arm. Cal let them get barely two seconds into the shot before he called cut again.

Cal was in Roger's face before Emerald could get to him. 'Pull that again, and I'll make sure your career *ends*—'

'Goddamn it, Cal, she's an actor,' Roger snapped. He had his hands out, keeping a distance between him and his fuming director. 'You hired her to act. So let her fucking *act it.*'

Melany put her hand on Roger's arm. She turned to Cal, then said: 'You do it.'

Roger stared at her in open disbelief. 'Sorry, but has everyone gone insane? You're going to let this bloody wanker choke you out? He's clearly getting off on it.'

Cal sneered. 'If she doesn't feel it, how will the audience?'

'It'll make the scene stronger,' Melany said coolly. 'I'm not scared.'

'Are you fucking kidding me?' The words exploded out of my mouth without warning. The quartet at the centre – Cal, Roger, Melany, and Emerald – all turned to look at me.

I could read Emerald's face – *What are you doing, sit down, I'll handle this.* Melany and Cal both glared, though Melany's expression was more hateful. Still, I tried to appeal to her. 'Melany, this is crazy, you don't have to do this.'

'It's fine,' Melany said, turning to Cal with big, pleading eyes. 'Really. I want Cal to do it. He'll have the fedora on, right? You can zoom in on the towel and my face.'

I exchanged a glance with a queasy-looking Emerald. But Cal was determined, practically purring. Roger threw his hands up and stomped off the soundstage, throwing himself into his chair so hard it thumped.

My heart beat hard as I sat back in my chair, slowly. I couldn't believe this was happening. I couldn't believe we were all letting this happen.

'Action,' the assistant director called.

Melany tipped her face up to the lights again as Cal, cloaked in Brandon Saturn's fedora, his face to the floor, snuck up behind her. His hands hovered in the air next to Melany's shoulders, and I stared, entranced, at the pulse jumping under her skin in the hollow of her clavicle. Then his hands moved up, up, up, until they circled her throat. I watched as his gloved hands tightened on the towel, looping it around her neck, and Melany's face turned first pink, then red, then purple, a vein beating so hard in her temple I thought it might burst. Her eyes watered, and her lips parted, a long wedge of drool flying out between her teeth. He pulled his arm around her neck, snaking it snug against her windpipe, and kept it there for another fifteen seconds while Melany choked and gagged and struggled, before she slumped back against him, eyes rolling, and Cal released the pressure on the towel, breathing heavy as he said, *'Cut.'*

It was only when I saw Melany breathe that I breathed again, too.

Without the pressure of the towel around her throat, Melany staggered forward, gasping sharply for breath, both hands braced against Tawney's couch as she sucked in lungful after lungful of air. Cal didn't stop to ask if she was all right before heading to video village to watch the footage on playback. I bit my nail as Cal watched it, muttering with the assistant director and Emerald. Emerald's face was studiously neutral, but when the group broke and she walked back to her seat, her eyes flicked up to me. I knew what was coming.

'Again,' Cal said. 'Melany, try not to brace yourself this time. Just relax your whole body, okay?'

Melany licked her lips, nodded. I looked at Emerald – *we're really letting this happen?* – but she had her chin propped in her hand, was staring resolutely ahead.

Cal strangled Melany for five interminable takes before he was satisfied.

On the fifth take, I saw it – what Cal had been waiting for. Melany finally relaxed enough to not tense before Cal's towel circled her neck, and the dance between them pirouetted between murderous and carnal. The twitchy, shivery tremble of her jaw, her hands helplessly scraping at her assailant – Melany might've been minutes from suffocation, but it was compelling. You couldn't look away from her.

I hated it.

I hated it, because now I knew I'd have this picture in my head every time I thought of my sister. I'd always wonder if this had been exactly how she'd died – cradled in Cal's arms. It would always be a certainty and a question, a new nightmare I'd have to live inside.

And I hated it because I knew what it meant. Since Cal got the shot, it meant the ends justified the means. He was free to abuse any actor – specifically, any *woman* – and we'd all excuse it in the name of art.

But what I hated most of all was that it *worked*. He'd gotten the take, the performance, he wanted, one that would make the film stronger. And because he had, he would feel empowered to do it again. And again. And again. And we would let him – all of us, me, Emerald, everyone on set – because of the final product.

Would it matter to his biggest fans – many of them women – that he was capable of casual cruelty, and abuse, and maybe even worse? Or would his art always justify the means, and his behaviour? If I came forward and told the world what I knew – my suspicions, what had happened between us when I was so young, even what I'd seen on set – would it matter to anyone? A few would stop going to his films, I believed that.

But probably only a few.

This time, when Cal cut the scene, I wasn't surprised that it was followed up by, 'Moving on. Let's take five.'

When Cal released her, Melany sank all the way to the floor, taking great, heaving gulps of air, her shoulders shaking as she tried to collect herself. Wardrobe rushed to her, whispering something to her, but her eyes were closed and she was massaging her neck in comforting loops, over and over.

Emerald passed by me. 'See?' She didn't make eye contact. 'He knows what he wants.'

I didn't particularly give a fuck what Cal wanted.

Cal was shaking hands with the crew. From the sidelines, Roger glowered, his face pinched. When Cal headed for craft services, I followed him. I caught up to him hovering

246

over the water bottles, a tiny, self-satisfied smile on his face.

'Salmon,' he said, his lip curling. He gave me a little salute, in a jaunty mood, then grabbed a water bottle and started to walk back to video village.

Before I could think better of it, I reached out and grabbed his arm. I could feel every place our skin touched alive with electricity, an unpleasant buzzing sensation clicking under my flesh like a wire about to pop.

This time, the feeling wasn't lust.

'You're an asshole,' I hissed at him. 'I hope you know that.'

Cal wrenched his arm out of my grasp. He sneered at me, his handsome face ugly and unkind. 'Don't be a child. That?' He jabbed his finger back behind him, at Melany, who was now staring blankly out from her folding chair. 'Those ten seconds will book her a bigger job, one where she has more lines. Then maybe, after that, a supporting role. And on and on and on. If she's smart, those ten seconds will be the launching pad to every dream she's ever had. Why don't you go over there and ask her yourself if she hates me? I bet she'll tell you she's *grateful*. She understands. Everyone else on set understands. *You're* the only one who doesn't, Salmon.'

Then he spun off on his shoe, a whistle on his lips and a bounce to his step.

Melany had a large red mark around her neck, and she massaged it, fighting back tears. But then one of the crew, a grip, came up to her, said something. Even from a distance, I could tell he was congratulating her on the take, telling her how well she had done. Her face lit up: *Thank youuuu*. A hand pressed to her chest, a slight blush. Imagining her future unfurling ahead of her already.

Like Ankine. Like Tawney, once. Like every dead girl from my tour.

I felt sick.

Cal was right. I was the only one who didn't understand it.

CHAPTER TWENTY-FIVE

When I got home, I couldn't shake the sight of Cal tightening the towel around Melany's throat. The expression on his face – it wasn't even angry, or hateful. Instead, he looked focused, set on a goal.

Almost . . . orgasmic.

And Melany – she'd put herself willingly in his path. After everything I'd told her, everything he'd done to her – she was still under his sway. I remembered what Emerald had told me, that she wouldn't let anything bad happen on set if she could help it. I wanted to believe her – but there was Ankine to remember. She hadn't been able to help Ankine.

I flopped onto my couch, eyes closed, resting my head against the sofa's back. I knew Emerald had been disturbed by what had happened today on set. I could see it in her face. But what I didn't know was how willing she'd be to speak up to Cal. Tell him he'd gone too far – for no other reason than the potential bad press the incident might generate. That was something Cal couldn't afford now that Ankine had died, bad press.

My eyes snapped open, and I stared at my ceiling, the

popcorn ridges and subtle earthquake cracks.

Maybe there was someone who would be willing to speak up against Cal. Someone with a grudge. Emerald had told me herself.

I reached for my purse, fumbled my phone out. Cherry picked up on the second ring. 'My goodness, my phone hasn't been this busy since Angie dumped Brad. Desperation is never an attractive look, Salma.'

I took a breath. 'I heard Cal fired you. I thought maybe I could buy you a drink to cheer you up.'

On the other end, I heard the suck and crackle of Cherry's vape pen. 'I see. The enemy of my enemy, *et cetera*. Well. As long as you're buying.'

I smiled. Cherry was sharp, I'd give her that. And, I hoped, she'd have an axe to grind.

Musso & Frank's was an old Hollywood institution, and a very public one at that. Cherry's choice. Perhaps it was the old gossip columnist in her who couldn't refuse the chance to write her own headlines: *What's Sloppy Salma dishing at Musso & Frank's?*

I found parking a few blocks over. I stepped over my father's star on Sunset Boulevard not far from Musso's, sandwiched between a Rat Pack singer and a famous stuntman.

Cherry had already settled herself in one of the front booths, tossing a megawatt smile my way, waving like we were old friends. 'Martini?' she asked as I slid into the booth.

I gritted out a smile. 'Still sober. But don't let that stop you.'

I wanted her nice and liquored up before I pumped her for information.

'Isn't that cute,' Cherry said, already studying a laminated menu. Musso's didn't make you wait: our server was asking for our orders not thirty seconds after I sat down. He mostly succeeded at not rolling his eyes when I ordered a ginger ale.

As he left, Cherry beat me to the punch. 'So,' she said, 'come to gloat?'

Maybe a little. 'To commiserate. Cal firing you like that – it's terrible. Really. You wrote the book on my sister.' This part grated, but I powered through it. 'Nobody knows her better.'

Cherry's mouth twisted. She knew I was buttering her up, but she was vain enough to still be flattered by it. 'For the record,' she said, 'he didn't fire me. It was a mutual splitting of ways. Creative differences.'

'Oh?' I raised a brow, putting a hint of surprise into it. PAA would be proud. 'That isn't what Cal's saying.'

Cherry's eyes narrowed. I could see she didn't believe me. Her mouth opened, and then our server was back, sliding her martini in front of her. I thanked him as Cherry watched me.

'What's he saying?'

I shrugged, taking a sip of my ginger ale. 'That he fired you.'

Cherry shook her head. 'He wouldn't dare.'

I crossed my arms, stared her down. 'Then how did I know you'd been fired, Cherry?'

Cherry slid her hand into her purse, pulled out her vape pen. Her fingers were shaking. Our server appeared again.

'Sorry, ma'am, no vaping inside,' he said to her apologetically.

'It's for my health,' Cherry snapped, then rolled her eyes, took a deep drag, and shoved the pen back into her purse. She glared at me. 'I knew you'd come to gloat.'

I hesitated. I had to handle the next part delicately. Cal had screwed Cherry over, but I wasn't sure yet if Cherry's loyalty was all burnt out. 'This obsession with Cal.' I shook my head. 'I used to wonder if you were in love with him. But that's not it, is it? You made him. When no one else would give him a look, you said he had talent. When my sister died, and people might have turned on him, you said, "No. Of course he didn't do it." You kept him from being a pariah. He's your little piece of Hollywood history. And look how he thanks you.'

I took a deep breath. 'Or maybe you saw a chance to make him even more grateful to you. Only at some point, he stopped listening to you, didn't he? And when you were let go from *Vanity Fair*, did he pull any strings to help you? It doesn't look like it. He won't even let you give input on *your* movie.'

Cherry held up her martini stem thoughtfully. The light shone through the cloudy nimbus of olive juice at the bottom. She tilted her head back, finished the drink, then signalled our server for another. 'His art is his own. Understandably.'

She hadn't looked so understanding back on set. 'Back at the hotel pool set you told Cal you could 'undo' him. What did you mean?'

Our server returned, slid another martini under Cherry's nose.

'What did you mean when you said you could undo him, Cherry?'

Cherry *hmm*ed noncommittally. 'Nobody likes bad press.'

I chewed on my lip. Behind us, a man was plunking out a mediocre version of 'As Time Goes By' on the baby grand. The restaurant was filling up with Musso's regulars, classy drunks who crowded the bar before happy hour. Like most of Hollywood, Musso's was a happy marriage between the die-hard locals and the wide-eyed tourists. I took a swing – a big swing. 'I think you meant you'd retract your alibi for the day Tawney died if he didn't start listening to you.'

Cherry gave me a long look. Then she snorted, shook her head. 'Let me get this straight. You think I helped cover up a murder by providing Cal with a false alibi? Not only would that be *morally* wrong, but I'd be covering up the biggest story of my lifetime.'

That was true. It was something I'd considered, too. Why would Cherry interfere with a story that would've been front-page fodder for months, if not longer?

Unless.

'Not if you couldn't prove it.' Cherry's brow arched, and she lifted her chin. I took it as a sign to keep going. 'You'd already been sued for libel once – that story about the sex workers targeting producers. *Vanity Fair* wouldn't have taken a chance again, would they? You were on thin ice. So if you couldn't break the story – why not make it?'

Cherry was hard to read; several decades of Botox did that to an emotional register. She took a very long swallow of her martini, sucking the olive off the sword. I watched her chew each bite with precision before she answered.

She blew her ginny breath in my face when she answered. 'You're suggesting I committed a crime. Perjury. Accessory after the fact, actually.'

I held my breath.

It wasn't a denial.

'And if that's true,' she said, twirling the plastic sword against the table – *en garde!* – 'why would I out myself now?'

Truth. Justice. A murderer behind bars. But those weren't the right answers. 'Because you make Cal's narrative. You always have. Take that power back, Cherry.'

'Well,' Cherry said, then stopped. She took her time, pursed her lips as she studied the table. 'That would be an attractive offer. *If* I'd been lying about Cal's alibi. Which I wasn't.' Then she signalled our server for another drink.

I leant forward, desperate. 'Cal optioned your book so you couldn't make the movie *you* wanted. Imagine that; he'd rather pay one million dollars than let you take the credit. We both know it.' I shook my head. 'The times are changing, Cherry; slowly, but they are. His bad behaviour *will* get him in trouble someday. If it's not for Tawney, it'll be Ankine. If not for Ankine, then another woman he torments on set. What then, Cherry? What then for *you*?'

Cherry and I stared at each other, while I willed her to do the right thing. Cherry looked away first. 'Being a controlling bastard isn't a crime, Salma. Now, unless you have something else to offer me, I'll be going. Three martinis on an empty stomach is quite the limit for me.'

She drained her martini, then stood up, shrugging her coat over her shoulders. 'Listen. A piece of friendly advice.

All you need is a rebranding. Hollywood loves a fuck-up when they become a success. You'd be welcomed back with open arms like that.' She snapped her fingers, painted a coraly orange. 'Ball's in your court, kiddo.'

I shook my head. 'Thanks, Cherry, but I don't think the world needs to hear more from Sloppy Salma.'

For a heartbeat, there was something almost human in her face, gone as quick as it came. 'I didn't lie,' she said slowly. 'But that doesn't mean I was Cal's keeper that day.'

My heart leapt into my throat. 'What does that mean?'

Cherry sniffed. 'He and Georg took part of the photo shoot off-site, away from the Beverly Hills Hotel. My presence wasn't required. But Georg was with him the entire time. They had a rocky start, but they had . . . interests in common.'

I didn't want to know what that meant. 'Where's Georg now?'

Cherry gave a mirthless smile. 'Dead. Six years ago. A heart attack while driving near the Chateau, in fact. I suppose we'll never really know for sure. Will we?'

I watched her walk away, pushing through the doors of Musso & Frank's, walking almost a straight line. In the end, Cherry stuck me with the bill.

CHAPTER TWENTY-SIX

Ankine's public memorial service, the one her family had posted about on Instagram, overlapped with another shoot day. That was fine with me. I'd needed a bleach shower after meeting Cherry at Musso & Frank's; her naked willingness to sell her version of the truth to the highest bidder was a reminder of all the things I'd hated about supercilious fame. And every time I closed my eyes, I could see Melany's throat wrapped by Cal's towel, the pop of her eyes as she struggled.

I needed a break from all things Hollywood.

Plus, I owed it to Ankine to pay my respects, though we'd never met in life. I picked out a simple black dress and black motorcycle boots and pulled my hair back in a low chignon.

I pulled the door open, ready to head to the memorial, and nearly fell backward when I realised someone was on my doorstep already, hand up and poised to knock.

'Jack,' I said. 'What are you doing here?'

Jack was dressed King of Hollywood–casual: a purple batik shirt and khakis so pale they were almost white. His kerosene-blue eyes were sombre, scanning my face. 'Can I come in?'

I looked at my watch. Ankine's service started in forty-five minutes – it was at least a thirty-minute drive to the cemetery. Not much of a margin to spare. 'I'm on my way out,' I said, drawing the door shut behind me. 'Another time.'

'Salma.' Jack laid a hand on my shoulder. I bit my lip. I'd ignored too many of Jack's calls to sweep it completely under the rug, and I knew it.

It was going to have to happen sometime.

'Fine,' I said curtly. 'Ten minutes.'

I escorted Jack back inside, and he slid onto my couch. I stayed standing. I hadn't seen him since I'd found out. I could tell by the look on his face, he knew I knew.

'So what is it you would like to say to me?' I crossed my arms over my chest.

Jack kept his head bowed. Finally he said: 'I'm sorry. Your mother's sorry, too. We should've told you.'

I gnawed on my lip. The apology did mean something to me, but not enough. Not after thirty-four years of lies. 'I don't see her here, apologising.'

'Would you have talked to me if we'd come together?' Jack looked up, genuinely curious.

A fair point. He could see the answer on my face, because he nodded.

'That's what I thought.' He seemed to register my all-black outfit for the first time. 'What are you wearing? You look like you're going to a funeral.'

'It's Ankine Petrosyan's memorial today.'

Jack looked at me blankly, which pissed me off all over again.

'*Ankine*,' I repeated. 'The woman who wound up dead at Tawney's house. Remember?'

Jack looked genuinely bewildered. 'Why are you going?'

'Because two women are dead,' I snapped. 'No one else seems interested in finding out what happened to them, but their lives matter to me. I have to find out what happened to Tawney, Jack. I can't stop trying.'

A darkness passed over Jack's face but he clamped his mouth down on whatever he'd been about to say, jaw twitching. Then: 'You know what happened to her, Salmon. She's gone. That's the only answer.'

Cold spread from my toes to my stomach. I felt like I'd been punched. I'd always assumed that my family, that *Jack*, understood why I couldn't just let it go, this thing that had upended our lives, this dark wedge at the centre of our family. 'That's not good enough. Not for me.'

'Nothing will bring your sister back.' Jack reached out a hand and squeezed my arm, and for the first time, his touch made me flinch. If he noticed, he pretended not to. 'She's dead. You can't fix it.' He squeezed my arm again. 'It's time to move on, Salma. You'll be better off. I promise.'

As if he knew what was best for me.

I stepped closer, towering over him on the couch, something mean and slippery inside me. No matter what I did, how many years I spent making amends, I'd never be more than the fuck-up I'd been as a kid. As if the last decade of my life and who I'd become now didn't matter.

But they were the liars.

'Like I was better off not knowing the truth about my sister?' I hissed. 'I can't believe you lied to me, Jack. *You*, of all people.'

There were tears in Jack's eyes, and he was leaning back against the red cushion of his seat, shaking his head, *No*, *no*. But it was true, and we both knew it.

Most of the time, I could forget that Jack was getting older. He still had a thick shock of now-bright-white hair. His eyes were still lively. But there were other, smaller things that made me aware that the band was winding down for him. The tremor in his hands as he pushed the menu aside. His trick ankle that wobbled him off-balance as he sat.

He was my family. As much as my parents. As much as Tawney. And as he sat there, cowering beneath me, I could feel all seventy-six years of him.

'I know why you did it,' I said. 'I know you did it for *her*. But you lied to me, Jack. *You* chose to do that. And I think it's time for you to go.'

'Salma—'

'Go,' I repeated.

He got to the door, then he turned. 'Are you still coming to the retrospective?'

I closed the door in his face.

Ankine was laid to rest in a cemetery midway between Los Angeles and the San Gabriel Mountains, on a curvy slice of road made green only by the constant vigilance of the cemetery staff. It was the only place in Los Angeles unlikely to get a ticket for irresponsible use of water – no one wanted to imagine their loved ones six feet under a desert.

The memorial service was public and open, and I had assumed, correctly, that Ankine had already been interred and celebrated by her family in a private ceremony. This was meant to be a chance for a wider group to mourn her. And it worked: the cemetery was packed. I had to squeeze my way through the crowd to find a good spot to stand.

A cynical take might be they wanted to keep the publicity cycle going. But I didn't feel like being cynical. For this moment at least, she was important to a lot of people. Her life, as short as it had been, mattered.

Her family had put up a wreath and a picture of her face – an old photo, her hair dark and curly. I spotted one of her brothers, who I recognised from Ankine's social media. Her father was there, arm in arm with an elegant-looking woman – her stepmother, I assumed – whose face had the watery look of endless crying.

I pegged a group of young women near the front as aspiring actors – they had that shiny, PAA look to them. They wore a Vivienne Lowe–endorsed mask of grief, but I thought I could see something else, too. Envy. Ankine was famous now. Death was still a game to them, one more avenue for notoriety.

As my eyes travelled over the crowd, they stopped on a short woman, dressed in black slacks and a black button-down that gaped slightly across the chest. As I stared at her, Detective Mykella Watkins caught my eye and nodded. I nodded back.

Ankine's stepmother had a microphone and she was doing an admirable job of staying stoic through her memories of her daughter, although her voice wobbled. 'Ani was a light in the darkness, the best daughter, the best friend . . .'

I tried to make myself listen, but my eyes kept scanning the crowd. I knew from my own funereal experiences, speeches about loved ones lost were more frequently about the love the living still felt for them, not the person themselves. I'd seen it before when I was researching for my tour: we want there to be one story about a person, one clean narrative for us to hold on to. There never is. Only a prism that catches a certain reflection, depending on the light, depending on the viewer.

No sign of Cal. I hadn't expected him. But there, tucked in the back, was someone else from the set. Emerald had wrapped a silk scarf around her head, Grace Kelly–style, and she wore oversize glasses, but I recognised her in a heartbeat.

I pushed through throngs of mourners who might or might not have known Ankine and settled in beside her. Emerald didn't spare me a glance.

'I didn't expect you to be here. You never mention her,' I said.

Emerald was quiet for a moment. 'My mother raised me to be respectful.'

Ankine's stepmother wound down her speech by pressing a kiss to her fingers, then touching them to the enormous headshot of Ankine graveside. Her fingers trembled, sending a light ripple through the paper, and she mouthed, *Love you, baby girl.*

Emerald's posture was rigid. I looked down – she'd swapped the ankle snappers for a pair of buffed leather boots, travelling all the way up her thighs. When she spoke, her voice was so low I thought I misheard her. 'It's my fault she died.'

I held myself very still. 'What do you mean?'

Beneath the scarf, her face was a mask. It was starting to drizzle, a light, stormy mist that made my wool-blend dress feel clammy against my skin. Emerald heaved a sigh, pulling her scarf tighter under her chin. 'You think I don't see what Cal's really like. He pushed her and pushed her. You see what he's like with Melany? Well, Melany *complies*. Ankine was . . .' She searched for the word. 'Opinionated. She was on my set. I should've seen what was happening.'

My heart skipped a beat. *Motive*. 'Em . . . are you saying Cal killed her?'

Emerald huffed. 'Don't you think if I really believed he'd hurt a woman, I would've told somebody? You, the police, anybody?' She shook her head. 'I'm saying . . .' Her voice broke, and she cleared her throat. 'I'm saying she killed herself. I'm saying I think Cal pushed her too far, and I let it happen.' She looked at me. 'Okay, Ms Nosy? I feel responsible. Because I *am* responsible. I'm the producer. This happened on my watch.'

We fell silent. Ahead of us, one of Ankine's brothers had refused a turn at the mic, shaking his head over and over. The mist was turning into rain, and a few mourners started to disperse. I noticed Detective Watkins watching us.

I studied Emerald. *Would* she tell me if she thought Cal was more directly involved? The girl I'd known on *Morty's House* all those years ago would have. But this new Emerald – I couldn't be sure. She had so much to lose. But I could feel for her, too. I thought of our different paths in Hollywood. Emerald was right. I'd been handed everything on a silver platter and still managed to fuck it up. Emerald had worked her way up in a grueling, racist, misogynistic field, a proud good-ole-boys club that still enjoyed the world at their fingertips. How was Emerald supposed to stem the tide of *that*?

'It can't have been easy,' I said, watching her. 'Any of this. *Cal* can't have been easy.'

Emerald laughed bitterly. 'You can't imagine.'

The ceremony was ending, and people were drifting away in the rain. She pulled her sunglasses off so I could see her eyes. Her face looked tired, and without make-up, I could see her stubby lashes poked straight out of her eyes, making them look smaller. Mortal, maybe.

'Salma, even if you were right? Cal's not going to go to jail. Men like him never do. I'd be careful if I were you.'

'What do you mean?'

Emerald hitched her purse higher on her shoulder. She didn't answer my question. 'You've been a distraction to filming this entire time. You yelled at him yesterday. Cal fired Cherry for less. He doesn't do things out of the goodness of his heart. If he's keeping you around, it's because it serves *him*. Watch yourself.'

Then she turned and walked away, stopping next to the freshly tilled plot of land that covered Ankine. She stood there for a long moment, looking down at the ground, then she made the sign of the cross and left.

I stood there, watching people go up to Ankine's grave to pay their respects, thinking about what Emerald had said. Her warning about Cal rang true. It didn't seem likely that he was allowing me on set simply for the pleasure of my company.

But then, why else?

I was almost back to my car when I spotted someone else I knew. With her acid-green highlights tucked back into a solemn bun, I hadn't recognised Avril until I was almost behind her. Avril stood at the grave, her mouth moving as she cried, saying something to her friend. I waited until she turned, and then I lifted a hand in acknowledgment. Avril practically sprinted for me.

'Isn't this just, like, the saddest day?' Her lip trembled, and she sniffled, smearing snot across the sleeve of her navy-blue sweater.

I nodded. It was. For Ankine's family, I knew it was.

'Can you believe Cal didn't even bother to show?' Avril's pale face was angry, her sloping shoulders hiked up to her ears. She shook her head. 'Bastard.'

I could, in fact, believe it. 'I'm sorry you got fired.'

Avril rolled her eyes. 'For the best. I couldn't be on that set without thinking about her.'

I remembered our interrupted conversation, the argument between Cal and Ankine. 'Avril, you told me Cal and Ankine argued. What about?'

Avril shuddered. 'The pictures.'

'Pictures?' I frowned at her. I'd expected her to tell me about the lists, like Melany received. 'What kinds of pictures?'

Avril winced. She looked around. She didn't want to tell me. 'Pictures of . . . your sister. Dead.'

I recoiled. 'The coroner's office photos? Why would he show those to her?'

But Avril was shaking her head, *No, no.* 'No. It wasn't like that.' She grimaced. 'They weren't from the coroner's office. They were from the *crime scene*.' She stuck her tongue out. 'I couldn't believe she was okay with it. He asked her to pose like them. Over and over, until she got it just right.'

That stopped my brain short. I was frozen. I tried to find words, failed.

Avril's tearstained eyes widened. 'It was so fucked-up. Ankine told Cal she wanted to focus on her life, not her death. Cal freaked out, blew up at her in front of everyone. "It's *my* movie, it's *my* story." The crew started calling her Dead Girl Walking. She went along with whatever he said after that.'

I was barely listening, stuck on the photos. The idea of Cal posing an actor to the photos of my dead sister was disturbing. But – how had he gotten the photos? Had a paparazzo gotten a shot of Tawney after she died? If so, why hadn't I seen those reprinted?

Or had Cal gotten the shot himself? Or – I remembered Georg – had he outsourced the job?

I switched topics, tried to process what she'd told me. 'Were you on set the day she died?'

Avril nodded. 'Doing make-up briefs. Cal came in to approve them around noon.'

My heart sank. Another person putting Cal on set the day Ankine died. 'So he was on set all day.'

Avril tilted her head. 'Well, not . . . *all* day.'

'What?' I stared at her.

Avril bit her lip. 'He left after he approved the briefs. He had a meeting with the studio bigwigs at one. Then he came right back after, because I saw him at the set dec meeting with Emerald. They were arguing about "couch integrity," whatever that means.'

'When was this?' The words rushed out of me so fast, Avril took a step back.

'Like . . . he left at noon, maybe? He was back by two, two-thirty.'

Ankine's time of death had been reported at 3 p.m. But

she'd been in the pool, dropping her temperature. What if the coroner had been wrong? Even by just an hour? 'Avril, are you positive?'

Avril looked taken aback. 'Yeah . . . I mean, why?'

I shook my head. I looked around for Watkins, but she'd already left. 'Avril, if I asked you to tell someone that – someone important, even – would you do it?'

'Sure,' Avril said, looking bewildered. I pulled my phone out, ready to look up Watkins's extension at her precinct, ready to put Avril on the phone with her that second.

But I had a bevy of colourful notifications. Text messages from Jack, my mother, a handful of others. News headlines from *The Hollywood Reporter*, the *Los Angeles Times*. That was odd. I hadn't been at Ankine's memorial that long. I was about to ignore them, when a headline from *TMZ* caught my eye.

Source claims Salma Lowe, daughter of Dave Lowe and Vivienne Powell, cops to affair with dead sister's fiancé. Read all the juicy details!

Oh. Fuck.

CHAPTER TWENTY-SEVEN

I drove straight to Soundstage Seven from Ankine's memorial, ignoring several lights shading from yellow to red, ignoring everything but the crazy thrumming of my heart. *No, please. Please, no. Not this. Not this. Not this.*

My worst secret. Laid bare for the world to see.

Halfway to the studio, I pulled over on the side of the road, threw my door open, and dry heaved, tossing up only bile, a few wilted salad greens. I wiped my mouth – Melany had done it, she'd really fucking done it – and then I forced myself to open up my phone, wincing as I tapped on the *TMZ* headline.

SOURCE CLAIMS CAL TURNER HAD AFFAIR WITH DEAD FIANCÉE'S UNDERAGE SISTER.

A source close to Salma Lowe, one-time child actor and daughter of Dave Lowe and Vivienne Powell, revealed that Lowe claims she had an affair with Cal Turner years ago. Lowe's sister, the murdered starlet Tawney Lowe, was Turner's ex-fiancée. A source – who spoke with TMZ *on promise of anonymity – said Lowe claimed she was fifteen at the time. 'I think she even carries a torch for him still,' the source said. 'It's sad. I feel bad for her.'*

Turner, the twice Academy Award–nominated director of such films as Hardboiled, Love's Long Midnight, *and more, could not be reached for comment.*

The rest of the article was a summary of *Iron Prayer*, my sister's death, Cal's illustrious career. There, in black and white, the exact footnote I was to my family. I scrolled back up to the top, double-checking the byline – Katy Wilson. I'd never heard of her. I was almost surprised it wasn't Cherry.

I sat there, staring vacantly out the front window. It could've been minutes, maybe an hour or two. It was out in the world now. The secret I'd guarded the most closely; the piece of my life I was most ashamed of. Out in public, for everyone to see. And it was even worse now than when I'd been a kid, because this time I was sober for the experience. I'd spent so long trying to build my new life. Trying to be someone else.

All just a reminder that no matter how hard I tried, I couldn't outrun Sloppy Salma. She fit around my neck like an invisible noose, letting me forget she was there until I was already choking.

Why had Melany done it? Why, why? For a couple hundred bucks, for a scoop? It would be bad publicity for the film – it wouldn't help her. It didn't make any sense.

At the cemetery, I hadn't even clicked on the headline. Instead, I stared at it so long, not blinking, not breathing, the words twisted themselves into pretzels.

'Are you all right?' Avril had said.

I hadn't answered. I'd turned and run back to my car, slamming the door shut behind me, my heart hammering so hard in my chest I thought I'd die.

Slowly, I turned the key in the ignition, nosing the car back out into the street. It would take me about thirty minutes to make it to the studio; I had plenty of time to figure out what I'd say to Melany on the way.

When I pulled up in front of Soundstage Seven, the wigwag was on, bright red and angry. I didn't hesitate. I broke the first set rule, shoving the door open, puncturing Cal's darkness with sunshine.

The door banged behind me so loudly in the silent, focused room that I stopped in my tracks, too. On the centre of the soundstage, Roger was in scene as Brandon Saturn, handsome face agape under the lights. The assistant director was out of his chair, face turning purple as he charged me.

No sign of Cal.

Melany sat cross-legged in a folding chair, her legs barely covered by a slinky peach robe. When she saw me, she shrank backward into the chair. That made me angrier.

Coward.

I stormed over to her chair, not caring that we had an audience. 'How could you do this to me? Seriously, Melany, what the fuck?'

Melany's fingers gripped the sides of her chair. Her eyes darted around, looking for help.

'No,' I said. I stopped short of grabbing her chin, forcing her to look at me. That was Cal's way, not mine.

'No. *Answer me.* How could you do this? *Why* did you do it?'

'I don't know what you mean,' Melany said.

I leant in closer. 'You were the only person I've ever told,' I whispered. 'Do you understand? *Ever.*'

Melany's blue eyes filled with tears. 'You were going to ruin it,' she whispered. 'You were going to ruin the whole film.'

I almost laughed. She was worried about the fucking *film*? I'd told her because I was trying to protect her. Cal had humiliated her, strangled her. I'd shared my most vulnerable moment *for her* and this was what she'd done. *I think she even carries a small torch for him still.*

I shoved her chair backward. Melany wailed as the chair rocked, nearly dumping her, before it settled safely.

'Jesus Christ, Salma!' Roger leapt from the soundstage, was at Melany's side, pushing me away. He glared at me, like *I* was the problem, like *I* was crazy.

But he didn't need to bother. I wasn't going to touch her again.

A hand on my elbow, gentle. Emerald's eyes were large as I turned to face her. She'd traded the silk scarf from Ankine's memorial for a black blazer. She looked sorry for me.

'Come with me,' she said. Then she pulled me off the soundstage and back into the sunshine.

Emerald was silent as she ferried me across the studio in her matte-black golf cart. We whipped down Yellow Brick Road, going well over the speed limit. Finally, she stopped in front of a row of bungalows, covered in thick yellow and purple bougainvillea vines. I recognised it as the office space she shared with Cal.

She escorted me into the bungalow, turning right instead of left, to Cal's office. She knocked on the door, didn't wait for an answer before she pushed it open.

Inside, Cal sat at his desk, a sour expression on his face. I could feel the hatred radiating off him, and I took a step backward, almost out of the doorway. His fingers drummed on the desk. Julie Cheong, the studio corporate suit he'd introduced as grief management for Ankine, had been mid-sentence when we entered. Her eyebrows jumped when she saw me.

And, seated in front of the two of them, vape pen twirling in her fingers as she smiled up at me, satisfied as the Cheshire cat: Cherry Partridge.

Emerald moved to stand next to Cal, but he held up a hand and she froze.

'Thank you, Emerald,' Cal said, eyes on me. 'You can go.'

Emerald's head jerked back, like she'd been slapped. She looked from Cal to Julie to Cherry, then me. But there was no arguing with Cal, and she knew it. She gave me a long, worried look before she shut the door behind her.

'Have a seat, Salma.' Julie gestured at the chairs. Cherry sat closest to the door. I'd have to crawl over her to escape.

As I sat, Cal swivelled his chair. Behind him, a lacquered black safe, an electronic keypad protecting it. I craned my neck to get a better look. It was the only piece of furniture in the room with a visible lock. I remembered the photographs Avril had told me about. Was that where Cal kept them? What other secrets did the safe hold?

'You remember Cherry,' Cal said. There were at least six feet between us, and a heavy slab of desk, but I could practically feel his breath in my ear. 'My new executive producer.'

My head snapped to Cherry, who lifted a brow in acknowledgment. But she didn't look at me.

They'd made up. I wondered how Cherry had done it, what she'd threatened, or promised.

Julie hovered behind Cal like a corporate angel. 'Ms Lowe, opportune timing. Cal and I were discussing the *TMZ* story. I presume you've seen it?' I nodded. Julie shook her head. 'Those are some really serious allegations, Ms Lowe.'

I shook my head. 'I wasn't the one who leaked it to *TMZ*. I didn't want the story out there, either.'

'So then who was it?' Julie looked serious, and sad. *We're not mad, just disappointed.*

There was a thick silence. Julie had her eyebrows raised, waiting for me to answer. Cherry shifted in her seat, getting a better look at my face. Across from me, Cal steepled his hands on his desk.

The hands he'd strangled my sister with. The hands he could still hurt Melany with. She'd betrayed my trust in the worst way, but I couldn't leave her to him, even if our fight raised eyebrows.

'I don't know,' I said. 'But it wasn't me.'

'But you do maintain the allegations are true?'

I met Cal's eyes, sick with shame. I wanted to be anywhere else. 'You know it's true,' I whispered.

'She's lying,' Cal said.

'Everyone saw us leave together, Cal,' I said. 'Tawney's

funeral – every magazine in the country noted it.'

'You were a fucking mess,' Cal said. 'I was doing the *gentlemanly* thing. I sobered you up and took you home. That's all.'

I gaped at him openly now, speechless. Cal's hand stroking my face, slipping his thumb into my mouth. *I'm drunk, I'm really drunk. You should go home now. Just go.*

Cal turned to Julie. 'Maybe it's my fault. She had a little *fixation* on me. I was flattered, at the time. But she was fifteen. Nothing happened.' He looked at me. 'Maybe you got confused. Maybe you imagined something, and you forgot it wasn't real. All those years as an addict can be hard on the memory, I hear. I never touched you, Salma.'

'I didn't imagine it, Cal,' I said. 'We'd both been drinking, but I know what happened. I'm not . . .' I could feel the tears building again. 'I don't want this story out there, either. But I'm not lying, Cal. You know I'm not lying.'

Cherry cleared her throat. I'd almost forgotten she was there. *Why* was she there? 'Maybe I can shed a little light,' she said, her voice nearly apologetic. 'After Cal dropped Salma off, we met up at his home. We spent the night together.'

I gaped at her. 'Really, Cherry?' The words burst out of me. 'He says jump, you say how high?' Cherry dusted an invisible speck of lint from her jacket as I stared. I wondered if Cherry had even finished reading the *TMZ* article before she called Cal with her offer. 'Well,' I said finally into the silence. 'At least you didn't sell yourself cheap. Emerald Majors worked for him seven years and still hasn't made executive producer. Brava.'

Cherry ignored me, spoke directly to Julie. 'It's embarrassing for me to say this,' she said with a little laugh. 'I was covering Cal for a story. It was a lapse in my journalistic ethics. But I was there with him, that night.'

Journalistic ethics. Cherry didn't have *any* ethics.

I looked at Cal. Cherry to the rescue, again. I reached across the desk, grasped his hand with my own, and squeezed. Cal's face blanched at the contact, staring down at our fingers intertwined, then wrenched his hand away like he'd been burnt.

'It happened,' I whispered. 'It did.'

Cal leant back in his chair, cradling his hand like I'd damaged him.

Cherry finally looked at me. The smile on her lips was frosty. 'You said yourself, you don't remember that day very well.'

My mouth dropped open. 'What are you—'

'At the production blocking read-through,' she said, faux-gentle. 'Remember?'

I remembered the moment: Cherry asking for my opinion on the funeral scene. I'd refused to back her up, told her I couldn't remember. But that was hours later, I wanted to say. I remembered *this*. I knew it wouldn't matter.

'Thank you for sharing that difficult truth, Cherry. Ms Lowe, this is very disappointing,' Julie said, her face severe behind her glasses. 'Allegations of this kind are seriously damaging. You may have caused irreparable harm to Cal's career.' Cal looked smug behind his desk. Cherry looked down at her lap, like she was trying to be polite.

'Cal, I don't imagine you feel comfortable with her on your set now.'

'No,' Cal said, his blue eyes triumphant. A little smile on his face. 'I do not.'

Julie pulled up her walkie-talkie. 'Security needed in Bungalow 989 to escort Ms Salma Lowe off the premises.'

I stood up, my knees shaking. 'That isn't necessary. I'll go.'

'I have to warn you, Ms Lowe,' Julie said. 'If this story continues to spread, the studio will sue for libel on Mr Turner's behalf. That won't go well for you.'

I nodded stiffly, heading for the door. I knew what kind of pockets the studios had.

Julie's voice stopped me one final time. 'I also think you should consider what you've done,' she said. 'Do you know one of the main reasons women don't come forward after they've been raped is because they're worried they won't be believed? False allegations hurt every woman, Ms Lowe, not just the men they're directed at. Now that you're not going to be working on set, I hope you use the time to reflect.'

Security deposited me back at my car, watching me while I gathered my keys out of my purse. Emerald was waiting for me.

'I'm sure they can see me off the lot,' I snapped, annoyed she insisted on witnessing my humiliation.

Emerald's face was soft. 'Is it true? When you were fifteen . . . ?'

I glared at her. 'What? You can't believe Cal would sleep with me?'

Emerald shook her head. 'I believe you. Salma, I do believe you.'

'Yeah? Why don't you go tell Cal and the studio that. They just fired me.'

I knew what she was going to say before she said it. 'It was twenty years ago. I believe you, but . . .'

I understood. *But* Cal was powerful. *But* there was no evidence other than my word – and I wasn't exactly reliable, was I? *But* there was a multimillion-dollar movie project in the balance.

The truth mattered so much less than those *but*s.

'You know what,' I said, throwing my door open, 'don't worry about it. It doesn't even matter.'

Then I pulled away from the curb and left Emerald and Cal and Melany and the entire soundstage behind.

CHAPTER TWENTY-EIGHT

Jack and my mother pulled up to my curb an hour and a half before the retrospective started. I hadn't spoken to Jack or my mother in days – not since my argument with Jack. They pulled up in Jack's shiny car, the size of a Tic Tac – I'd be packed into the back seat, like a kid on a road trip – and I let them wait a few minutes while I fixed my hair, my face, took my time smoothing out the lines of the dress Anjelica had delivered the day before.

Dave Lowe's daughter was going to make him proud, even as his secrets choked me.

In the passenger seat, my mother wore the black velvet dress – I glared at it, feeling, irrationally, like this was all the dress's fault. My mother gave me a tremulous smile, Jack beside her looking debonair in a navy-blue suit, chequered scarf tied around his neck.

If you didn't know better – hell, even if you did – you'd mistake them for a couple.

'This car looks like a mid-life crisis,' I said in lieu of hello, crawling into the back seat.

'Mid-life,' Jack said, glancing at me cautiously in the rear-view. 'Bless you, Salmon.'

We drove to the Cinerama Dome, where I'd gone to see *Iron Prayer* what seemed a million years ago. As we inched along the freeway – top down, the smell of wildfire singeing my nose – I ran through the program, trying to calm my nerves.

There'd be clips of my father's greatest films – including, of course, *Iron Prayer* – and a few pre-taped tributes, from actors and directors on what my father's work had meant to them. Then the Q&A, moderated by Cherry. Finally, a special display of photographs, memorabilia, and more – most of it on loan from my mother's collection of their life together.

It wasn't unlike Dale's morbid museum, except this time the artifacts were carefully selected to construct a rosier view of my parents' marriage: loving, faithful, consistent.

No secret love children. No decades' worth of lies.

When we arrived, Jack tossed the valet the keys, comped for the evening, of course. It was funny how Hollywood gave away privilege to the people who needed it least. My mother checked her face one last time in the mirror – slicing away a sliver of wayward lipstick with a ruthless thumbnail – then took the hand the valet offered. Without asking, Jack headed to concession to grab popcorn and a box of Raisinets for me. We had three seats in the first row reserved. I left the one with the best cushion for Jack's bad back.

When Jack returned, wordlessly handing me the box of candy, I ducked my head and muttered a nearly inaudible thanks. As the lights went down, I tried to ignore the feel of his elbow next to me, the shades of guilt for the silent treatment drowning out the leftover hurt of our fight.

The last time I'd felt this alone had been after Tawney's funeral, sitting on the curb in front of Cal's house.

The lights went down and a few audience members whooped in excitement as a spotlight came up.

Cal Turner walked to centre stage.

I looked at Jack sharply, and he shook his head: *Kid, I didn't know.* From the gasps and screeches around the room, I took it I wasn't the only one for whom Cal's appearance was a surprise.

Cal shone in the spotlight. His navy-blue suit was cut tight to his body. He looked sombre and focused and handsome, not at all like the monster who'd sat across from me and told me I was crazy, who had strangled my sister, kept photographs of her corpse, choked Melany until her face turned purple.

'I met Dave Lowe when I was a kid from the Valley with a dream, trying to break into the industry . . .'

From the second-floor balcony, someone yelled out, 'Perv!'

The theatre erupted into buzzy whispers. I slid down in my seat, shoulders hunched. Jack put a hand on my wrist. Cal glared into the audience, like he could see who had said it, and after a few tense moments, I could hear a security guard talking to the person who'd yelled. I didn't turn around.

Cal waited one more breath, then continued with his speech.

It wasn't fair. Ankine and Tawney were dead. But Cal got to be on a stage, extolling the virtues of my family's talent. It didn't make any sense. As he praised my father – *Ingenuity, truly embodied the human experience for us all* – I wondered how Cal lived with himself. He'd killed my sister. I believed he'd killed Ankine, too, or at least helped push her to a brink she couldn't get back from. How did he reconcile it within himself? Was he so far gone he didn't even understand what he was doing wrong?

Cal's head turned and my insides seized as his gaze drifted over me, a shiver tracing all the way down my spine. He caught my eye and held it for a moment. Then he turned to the screen.

'There's someone who should be here tonight,' he said, bowing his head. Behind him, the screen projected my sister, my father's arm around her. In the photo, Tawney was maybe eighteen, a wide smile on her face. Short jean shorts, a T-shirt knotted above her navel. Her long blonde hair lifting in the breeze. 'She should be up here, giving this speech. Not me.'

I'd pulled my hands into fists, knotting so tightly I broke skin. I blinked back the hot sting of tears. *Why isn't she, Cal? Why isn't she here?*

'I wish I could've heard that speech,' Cal said. His voice was soft. Around me, the crowd melted with sympathy. No one yelling *perv* now. 'Tawney could always make me laugh.'

He turned and gazed at the photo, drinking Tawney in. Then he blew her a kiss. The crowd swooned. Jack squeezed my wrist, like an anchor. I was shaking my head over and over, *no, no, no.*

'Without further ado,' he said, 'I give you . . . Dave Lowe.'

From everyone but Jack and me, the applause was

thunderous. Cal had been redeemed.

The carousel of my father's greatest hits played out on-screen. There were my parents, falling in doomed love in *Iron Prayer*. There was my father, playing a modern cowboy with murder on his mind in *Vengeance on a Pale Horse*. The video quality got better as my father grew older, and I could better see the strain on his face from years of alcohol, womanising. The camera candidly cruel about each crease, every sagging jowl. I felt the sting of tears, watching him on-screen. A cop. An everyman. A Roman emperor. My father, who lived a hundred lives in his too-short one.

I snuck a glance at my mother, on the other side of Jack. Tears streamed down her cheeks as she watched her husband on-screen. In that moment, I forgave her, too: she'd done something terrible and something beautiful all at the same time. She'd given me my sister, even if she hadn't given birth to her. Even if she'd lied.

When the lights came up, there wasn't a dry eye in the house.

I wiped my face with my napkin, succeeding only in smearing my make-up. Jack offered a handkerchief and I took it, giving him a grateful, watery smile. Theatre ushers hauled three leather chairs into place before waving my mother and me onstage. As I stood up, Jack reached out and squeezed my hand, gave me a wink. It buoyed me more than I expected.

When the lights came up, Cherry was already seated in a chair, legs crossed underneath an eye-popping leather minidress. I hadn't seen Cherry since she'd lied for Cal, called me, tacitly, a liar. I felt a surge of anger as Cherry smirked to the crowd, her purplish-red hair tickling her chin, then extended her hand, Vanna White–style, to intro my beaming mother. The applause was thunderous, so loud my mother stood up and gave a half curtsy.

Vivienne Powell Lowe was even more luminous than she'd been forty years before. A living Hollywood legend. Encounters like these were what kept our city stocked with starry-eyed hopefuls. If you could see Vivienne Lowe in the flesh, why, who's to say you couldn't be her?

Graciously, Cherry extended a hand to me. The applause was more tepid this time. I ignored her, settling myself in my chair.

'Ladies' – Cherry leant forward in her seat, her eyes sparkling – 'thank you so much for being here with us today as we celebrate the life of a great man.' Behind her on the screen, an enormous picture of my handsome father, with his bourbon scent and easy laugh. My eyes misted a little. *My brave girl, my smart girl, my good girl.* I blinked back tears. My mother threaded her fingers into my own, and the audience *coo*ed and *aah*ed.

The moment would've been more meaningful. But I couldn't forget Cherry onstage. Cal somewhere in the audience.

Cherry's first questions were softballs to my mother. *What was it like working on* Iron Prayer? *Did you know as you were making it that it was going to be one of the greatest films of all time? What was it like, falling in love on set?*

It was easy for my mother to charm, and she spun out eloquent, funny anecdotes that set the crowd clapping. But as she spoke, I was doing math in my head. Tawney had been conceived right around the filming of *Iron Prayer*. The set my mother described – a creative utopia where ideas thrived, with evenings spent sharing bottles of Syrah and secrets, the golden-hour glow she sketched – the reality had to have been more complicated, messier, more painful. But that wasn't the story Vivienne wanted to see, or to share. I wondered if my mother could even remember the truth any more, or if she'd painted over the picture so many times she thought it *was* the truth.

'Yours is one of the great love stories of Hollywood,' Cherry said. On the screen behind her, a gorgeous shot of my parents, arm in arm at some red carpet, then a slow slideshow of their life: as newlyweds, with my sister in a bassinet, my sister and me at a film premiere. More *aah*s, scattered applause. I looked around. I wondered how the crowd would feel if they knew the truth.

'He was the love of my life,' my mother said softly into her microphone. 'I've never loved another man.'

I could see, in the audience, Jack's hand curl into a fist on his armrest, just for a fraction of a second. The great, big, unnameable secret we all just manoeuvred around without acknowledging. The worst-kept secret in the world.

But not my family's only secret.

'Dave and I had a love that was hard for people to understand,' my mother continued. 'It was bigger than Hollywood, but it was also so much about our work. Most people aren't lucky enough to find soulmates in their love *and* creatively.'

In the back row of the theatre, shaded into darkness so I couldn't see, there was a muffled exclamation, the slap of a seat folding up. Then an abrupt square of light as one of the doors opened, slammed shut. Jack's head swivelled, then our eyes met. He shrugged. *No idea.*

'Tell me about your work,' Cherry said, leaning forward in her chair. 'Twice nominated for an Academy Award, winner of a Golden Globe, you also run your own acting academy—'

My mother tinkled a laugh, soft as a bell. 'Oh no, dear. This isn't *my* retrospective.'

'Don't be so modest, Vivienne.' Cherry's eyes sparked, her pleather miniskirt audibly crunching as she sat forward. 'You're a legend in your own right.'

A small roar of approval went up from the crowd. Vivienne's smile tightened, her knuckles white on the mic. 'What a doll you are. And I appreciate the acknowledgment. But no. Tonight is not about me.'

The way we make ourselves smaller for men, for love, as though it's worth it in the end. As though we'll be rewarded for it.

Cherry didn't like being told *no*. 'No need to hide in his shadow, dear.'

I'd had enough of Cherry. I picked up the microphone I hadn't yet bothered to use, and said, 'You know something about hiding in the shadows, don't you, Cherry?'

Cherry blinked, then looked down at her cue cards, shuffling a few. My mother put a hand on my knee, warning me.

'Care to elaborate on that, Salma?' Cherry said. 'As a matter of fact, I believe I saw your name in the news again, just the other day.' She waited, eyebrows raised.

Without meaning to, I looked to the side of the stage, where I could see Cal watching our interview with a water bottle in hand, a hot cloud of anger and resentment seething off him even from a distance. I flinched.

Cherry had dared me. If I said anything publicly, I'd give the studio an excuse to sue. I wouldn't give her the satisfaction. 'I meant,' I said slowly, 'that that's what you writers do. Observe from the shadows.' I glared at her.

Cherry smiled, and winking so lightly I wondered if I imagined it, she said: 'I prefer to think of what we do as *making the narrative.*'

Making the narrative. It's what I'd urged her to do in turning against Cal. She'd shown me.

Cherry turned away from me, clearing her throat. Asked the big one. 'Vivienne, you've suffered more than your fair share of tragedy. How do you cope with it?'

Behind her, my sister slinked on-screen, the dialogue cut. It was a scene from the film she'd made with Cal. I held my breath, watching her wiggle from camera left to centre, her dress a shimmery pale turquoise stretched tight over her most famous assets. The movie had been a flop. But you could see Cal's love for my sister in every frame. The camera practically caressed her every move. Somehow, she looked more alive than life under his lens. I was struck, too, by how young she looked. Younger than I ever remembered her being.

My mother smiled sadly. 'I learnt a long time ago you can't linger on the *why*. I would feel the same if she'd been killed in a car accident, or died of an illness. The truth is, my daughter died years before her time. The *why* won't bring her back.'

My mother took a deep breath, collected herself. She looked up at me, her eyes glittering, and her face softened, then a mask descended on it. I recognised that, too. My mother liked the crowds, liked to play the game more than I ever had. But Tawney was the line. That grief was private. That grief belonged to *us*. I squeezed her hand. 'Tawney was a beautiful soul. It's my most fervent hope that she's remembered for much more than simply the way she died.'

The crowd clapped as my mother wiped her eyes.

But even as I clapped, I couldn't stop thinking about what my mother had said. The *why* of Tawney's death wouldn't bring her back. Jack had said some version of the same thing: *You can't change the past by digging it up, Salma.* I knew that. But without that *why*, I was stuck, a loop that could never be completed. Maybe that wasn't true for anyone else, but it was true for me.

Cherry closed the interview by thanking my mother for her time, before announcing the exhibit – and the bar – open.

There was more thunderous applause and my mother stood, dragging me with her into a curtsy. Behind us on the screen, my sister – dead now almost as long as she'd been alive – blew a kiss at the camera and twirled off-screen, as if inviting us to follow.

And I would. I always would.

CHAPTER TWENTY-NINE

My father's face – a still from *Iron Prayer*, his signature down-turned smirk in a white suit – was eight feet high in the lobby turned exhibit. The smirk followed me around the room.

My mother had a beatific smile plastered on her face as we waited for the crowd to file out of the theatre. 'I had no idea Cal was going to give that speech.' Her voice neutral.

'Mm.' Across the way, the bar beckoned to me like an ex-lover. The bartender mixed drinks underneath a television playing a clip from *Iron Prayer*: my father's famous last lines, his hands resting in that little girl's golden-blonde curls. The clip then looped to my father's other well-known films: *Vengeance on a Pale Horse*, an adaptation of a Hemingway novel whose name I could never remember; even his later work in buddy-cop comedies: *Ride Along* and *Ride Along 2: These Mean Streets*.

'I thought it was quite heartfelt,' my mother said. 'And frankly, I think it was a good showing of support, for you both. After that sordid little story.'

She gave me a pointed look, and I stopped breathing. So she'd seen the *TMZ* story. *Ask me*, I thought. *Ask me if the story is true. Ask me, ask me, ask me.*

Vivienne sighed, then turned to Jack. 'Tabloids always find a way to drag a good man down. There's no money in stories about *good* men. Jack, what did you think of Cal's speech?'

The moment was over.

Guests filtered into the lobby from the theatre, a swarm crowding around my mother and peeling her away from Jack and me. Cal and Cherry held court in the corner, surrounded by a phalanx of adoring adolescent acolytes. If I could avoid them tonight, then the event would be a success in my eyes.

Jack took the opportunity to pull me over to one of the glass cases housing family-approved Dave Lowe artifacts: personal letters written from film sets; his signature round sunglasses from his later years (when the lines around his face deepened); vertical cases where headless mannequins modelled some of his most famous costumes, even one containing the suit he'd worn when he took me to the Academy Awards.

Jack's face was miserable. 'Salma, I'm sorry. I can't stop thinking of it. Someone should've told you. No excuses. But I suppose we all thought it would be better . . . for you kids not to know.'

I opened my mouth, closed it again. He'd lied to me my entire life. But I loved him. Like Tawney, and my parents, as imperfect as we all were, I loved him. And it was a lesson I'd learnt too many times already: nothing – no one – stays forever.

'I'm still upset,' I said. 'I think I'll be upset for a long time. But I'm still fond of you, old man. That doesn't change.' He squeezed my hand, and I muscled up a ghost of a smile. 'Come on. Let's go check out Vivienne's handiwork.'

I pulled us to the display case labelled DOMESTIC LIFE. There was a picture of my mother, taken by my father, with a baby Tawney on her hip, golden and wailing. It was odd to see the photos now, knowing the truth. My slim mother looked exhausted but happy. I felt the urge to trace the radiant smile on her face as she held my chubby, screaming sister.

Then a picture of the four of us together. My father held Tawney's hand, while my mother cradled a dark-haired newborn me, the Powell nose already evident. My father grinned brilliantly at the camera. My halved family. My mother was slightly puffy, rumpled by the weight of two children. Next to us, two gawkers clucked over the pairs of baby shoes, one for me, one for Tawney, both achingly small and vulnerable.

'Mom looks tired. Happy, but tired.' It was true – there were dark circles under her eyes, a heft to her chin and bosom from the pregnancy. I looked back and forth between the photos; it was so clear now that my mother had been actually pregnant with me, and not with Tawney. I couldn't believe no one else had seen it.

Jack shook his head. 'She's beautiful.'

I looked at his reflection in the glass: the slightly ridiculous neckerchief, the too-tan skin. Dave Lowe had been my mother's choice. If it was up to me, I'd have wished Jack could find someone else who made him happy, someone who loved him back. He deserved it.

But then, I knew a thing or two about being possessed

by a love you couldn't let go. *Move on, Salma*. Neither of us could.

Someone tapped Jack on the shoulder, pulled him away to talk shop, leaving me on my own. The next case was dedicated to *Iron Prayer*, moving backward in time. I zipped through the photos – my father devilishly handsome, with his arched eyebrows and off-kilter grin; my mother young and sleek, her hair a long dark waterfall, a very serious expression on her face as she absorbed a director's note.

I found myself scanning the photos feverishly, looking for any plausible candidates to be my sister's mother. A groupie, my mother had called her. I scanned the background, searching for attractive women in Dave's orbit. But my mother had picked the pictures. They only showcased the principal players: my father, my mother, Jack, the director, one with the little girl who played my mother's sister. No sign of any groupies who might've thrown themselves at a susceptible Dave.

Gradually, I became aware of a muffled buzz growing from the other side of the room, culminating in a large, collective gasp. I turned in time to see my mother, drenched, wipe liquid out of her eyes.

I couldn't understand – had someone bumped her? No one had bumped Vivienne Powell in her life. I looked around. Behind the bar, my father's loop had fed back around to his closing line in *Iron Prayer*. A small group of film geeks stood in front of it, red cups in hand, enraptured. The crowd parted and I could just make out a tall blonde, her back to me, towering over my mother. Jack had his hand out, skimming her shoulder, trying to shield my mother. The blonde twisted away from him, holding a dripping glass. She'd thrown the drink in my mother's face.

I hurried over, my heart beating in my throat. Where the hell was security? Who would want to ruin my father's night? I elbowed past gawking strangers, not bothering to excuse myself as I shoved people out of the way.

Even before I could reach her, I could hear the fight. The woman who had thrown her drink was screaming, tendons bulging in her neck. 'You ruined my life, Vivienne! You ruined my *daughter's* life!'

My mother was stunned, speechless, face drained of all colour. Jack spoke quietly to the woman, saying something too low for me to hear, making pacifying gestures like she was a wild animal. I finally broke through the crowd, passing by Cherry, craning her head to see better, before I made it to my mother. Vivienne sagged against me.

My arms around my mother, I glared at the blonde woman, this interloper – and realised I was looking at Elizabeth Wennick.

Elizabeth's soft face was twisted by anger, a long witchy finger extended, jabbing at the air in front of my mother's face. A wet splotch from her drink soaked the front of her grey T-shirt. 'Vivienne, tell them. You tell all of them, right now. *Make it right.*'

My mother whimpered and turned her face into my shoulder.

'Security,' Jack was yelling. 'Security!'

The room was nearly silent now. All eyes on us. I flinched as I noticed more than one iPhone raised, capturing the scene for social media. Cherry had her phone up, recording.

'You know what you did,' Wennick said again,

pleading. 'You have to tell them. Tell them she was really *my* daughter! For once in your life, tell the truth!'

My mother flinched into my shoulder, muffling sobs. Behind Elizabeth, two security officers grabbed her arms, tried to pull her backward. My head was pulsing, and I wondered if I would faint.

Her daughter. Tawney's biological mother.

I stared at Elizabeth, struggling against the security guards, twisting her head as they pulled her away so she could continue keeping eye contact with my mother, her eyes hard and dark.

Instinctively, I pulled my mother back from the crowd, turning her away from Elizabeth as I stroked her hair. I kept my eye on Elizabeth as the security guards escorted her out. Even with my mother's back turned, she stared at her. I couldn't tell if she'd even noticed me.

I recognised the look on Elizabeth's face. No – I recognised her *face*. My brain rearranged her features: the silver-blonde hair a touch more golden, the face rounder, tanner. That perfect ski-slope nose. I'd been transfixed by her face the first time I'd met her, mesmerised by her prettiness.

But it wasn't her beauty that my brain had been evaluating, I realised. It wasn't that at all.

Some groupie, my mother had said. *A floozy.*

It didn't make sense. If Tawney had lived, she'd be forty-two now. I didn't think Elizabeth looked older than her mid-fifties, give or take a few years. She couldn't be my sister's mother.

'This was *his* night,' Vivienne whispered into my shoulder. 'It was supposed to be his night.'

I patted her shoulder mechanically, not saying anything. Behind the bar, the reel of my father's clips started over, rebooting with *Iron Prayer*, his most famous line. Dave's hand on the tiny blonde's shoulders, stroking her curls. The smattering of light freckles over her nose – that perfect ski-slope, Tawney Lowe special nose.

'Oh my God,' I said. 'Oh my God.' I dropped my arms from my mother and stepped back. I stared at Vivienne's bent head. She was sobbing harder than I'd seen her cry since my father died. Security shoved Elizabeth through the doors, her heels skidding on the marble floor in protest. She was still yelling. Jack pulled my mother away.

I looked around in a daze. The tension in the crowd eased, replaced with laughter, the relief of having survived an uncomfortable moment. A few people were replaying the footage they'd captured on their iPhones, maybe feeling like they'd gotten their money's worth.

No one else had had their world knocked off its axis.

I stared at the screen again. My father's hand on Elizabeth's hair. Her toothy smile, pretty face with the baby-fat cheeks. Long coltish legs, caught in the transition stage between childhood and womanhood. She couldn't have been more than thirteen, fourteen years old.

'Salma. *Salma.*' Jack snapped his fingers in front of my face. I jerked. He'd been saying my name and I hadn't heard. 'You're crying.'

I shook my head, putting my hands up to my wet face. The room was spinning. My mother was recovering, dabbing at her eyes, and even making a joke to the person next to her: *Crazy fans these days. Probably a social media prank!*

I pushed past Jack. 'Mom.' She didn't look up. 'Mom, we need to talk.'

When she turned to me, Vivienne's smile was strained. 'Not now, Salma. Whatever it is, it can wait. Jack, can you escort me to the powder room? I need to clean up.'

She turned away, but I grabbed her arm. This couldn't wait. This absolutely could not wait. 'That was her, wasn't it? Tawney's . . . biological mother?' I dropped my voice to a whisper. 'The little girl from *Iron Prayer*. Wasn't it?'

My mother's smile froze, her lips pulled back from her teeth like the rictus of a corpse. But otherwise, she didn't react. She didn't even turn around. 'Salma. We can talk another time.'

'But—'

She yanked the sleeve of her gown out of my grip. 'It's your father's night. We will talk about it *tomorrow*.'

I'd wanted her to deny it. I'd wanted her to tell me I was crazy. Even though I knew I wasn't.

I took a step backward, melting into the crowd. *Dave Lowe's daughter.* I hadn't realised I'd said it out loud until the woman next to me gave me a smile and patted my arm.

'You must be very proud, dear.'

I tucked my head down and headed for the doors, almost running by the time I got there. Air. I needed air. I stumbled out onto Hollywood Boulevard, the evening breeze a blast in the face. I could hear my mother call my name behind me. *Don't ruin your father's night!*

A child. Tawney's mother was a child. My father had slept with – no, *raped* – a child.

Across the street, the sign for the St Leo Hotel

flickered in neon lighting that had seen better days. The St Leo Hotel was one of my tour stops: it had been Ellen Howard's preferred assignation spot for rendezvous with her producer paramour, the one she'd later murdered. Another one of my Dead Girls, the dark sisterhood to which Ankine and Tawney now belonged.

The St Leo had a bar.

My father had raped a child. My sister's mother had been a child.

And my mother knew. Jack knew.

They'd kept his secret, all these years.

The words played in my head on refrain as I clicked my way across the street, not stopping as I reached the soggy hotel air conditioning, as I bellied up to the bar. They didn't stop until I had the first drink – a double – in my hand.

CHAPTER THIRTY

Being booked for destruction of property wasn't quite as bad as being booked for a DUI, but it was all a matter of how you looked at it.

I'd stayed at the St Leo Hotel until it closed at midnight, downing six or eight vodka cocktails called Lou's Revenge: flaky-salt rim, lime cordial, celery bitters. Cool, salty, unapologetic. But even the warm magic of the vodka hadn't been able to blot out my thoughts completely.

My sister's mother had been a child.

When the St Leo closed, I'd swayed back into the Hollywood night. There were other bars still open. But I didn't want a bar.

I crossed the street. The Cinerama Dome was dark save for the marquee, a grey eyesore. I crept to the lobby door – locked. I rattled it once, for good measure. On the other side, I could see my father's costumes, the enormous headshot a beacon in the dark. He smirked at me.

The tears came again, but this time, anger, too.

How could he have done it? How could my mother and Jack have let it happen? And to sit there while he was celebrated – all the time knowing the truth. The hurt he'd caused.

I dropped to a squat, sobbing, my hand on the asphalt to steady myself. I stumbled forward, and my fingers found the rock, curling around it as I pulled myself up, choking on my tears. Then I pulled my arm back and hurled the rock through the lobby windows as hard as I could.

The sound the glass made as it crashed was bigger than anything I'd ever known. I stared as it all came crumbling down, a glittering mess of shards spraying into the air like snowflakes.

A police cruiser was parked down the street. It had been dark, but I'd been so far gone I wouldn't have seen it anyway. It was only when its blue and red lights started to go, diving across the lanes to get to me, that I realised.

I let them push me into the cruiser without a word. It was only in the back seat that I realised the glass had cut me, too; I'd bled through Anjelica's dress, crusty red-brown streaks spilling over my foot. As a kid, I'd used every trick in my arsenal to get out of my consequences. *My father is Dave Lowe, maybe you've heard of him? Call him, and we can straighten this out . . . Just let me go home and go to bed . . .*

When they asked me my name, I gave them Salma Powell, unwilling to even mention my father's name.

From the back of the cage, I could see the dark Hollywood night blur and skitter past. I wondered if my mother was still out there, celebrating Dave Lowe's night. I kept my head down when they marched me through the station, as they fingerprinted me, chastised me for giving the wrong name.

And when they escorted me to a relatively clean, gently sticky cot and instructed me to sleep it off for the next few hours, I said *thank you* and listened to the rattle of the lock shutting and that was all.

I'd finally found something even vodka couldn't blot out.

It had been years since I'd had a drink – my tolerance was nothing. I should've been asleep, or blacked out, swaying on my feet. Instead, curled up on the scratchy sheets, I listened to the chorus of the same conversation on repeat – *I didn't do anything, Officer, I was just having a nice night, I promise I won't do it again, if you just . . .*

I understood. My brain was dancing lazy circles around the same thoughts, too.

Cal killed Ankine. Cal killed Tawney.

My father raped a child. My mother covered it up.

And I'd broken my sobriety. Sloppy Salma revived: drunk, disorderly, derelict. All the things I'd worked so hard to change in myself – and I'd ended up back here, again.

There was a rhythmic stomp in my head, and my stomach felt tight and uneven. At one point, I rolled over on the cot and retched into a bucket someone had left behind. The vodka was easier to get rid of than the truth.

I'd known my father had an appetite for women. How could I not – the overheard but hushed arguments, the constant patchwork of my parents' marriage. At my father's funeral, the front pews had been a rainbow of beautiful women of various ages, sobbing into handkerchiefs. A moment that should have belonged to my mother broken apart and sliced into pieces for everyone to grab. It had been woven into the fabric of my life since before I understood it.

But this wasn't a woman. This wasn't an affair. This was a girl. A *child*.

I must've nodded off because I woke to a guard calling out, 'Rise and shine. Let's call someone to pick you up.'

I sat up slowly, my head spinning gently. I could still feel the liquor in my veins. That would be easier to excise than the shame, which sat heavy in me like a stone. My sinuses felt heavy, like I'd been pushed underwater. I was still in the lamé dress from the night before, the dark silver pleating crushed and stained brown at the hem. *My mother will kill me*, I thought, then barked out a dark little laugh.

No, she wouldn't. There wasn't anything she could say to me now.

At the front desk, I plucked the phone from the cradle, then hesitated. It was nearly 4 a.m. I didn't want to call Jack. I didn't want him to confirm what I knew in my bones to be true. I wanted to live in this space for just a moment longer, where I could pretend I didn't really *know*.

In the front office, a young man in handcuffs sat on a bench, his head in his hands. Cops chatted quietly with witnesses or suspects, no way to tell which. The desk cop snuck little glances at me, still in the dark silver halter dress I'd worn to the retrospective, my heels scuffed from where I'd stumbled.

Finally the front desk sergeant glared at me. 'Use it or lose it,' she said, her hand hovering over the dial button.

I punched in the numbers. I didn't want to do it, but I had to. He was the only person who I could be sure would come pick me up from a police station at four in the morning.

He picked up on the third ring, his voice sleepy. 'Parlato.'

'Jack?' My voice squeaked, and I pinched the inside of my wrist. The pain focused me. 'I need . . . I need you to come get me.'

There was a pause, and then Jack said, his voice tender and brisk: 'Tell me where. I'll be there in fifteen minutes.'

I replaced the phone in its cradle, then looked up at the desk sergeant, circling items on a piece of paper. 'Excuse me,' I said, 'would it be possible to charge my phone for a few minutes?'

She looked me up and down. 'This isn't a library. We don't offer free services just 'cause you need 'em.'

'Please.'

There must've been something in my voice that made her pay attention, because she peered at me, then a familiar expression came over her face. 'I know you, don't I? You're the daughter of what's-his-name, *Iron Prayer*?'

'Yes,' I said, trying to hide my grimace. 'Good old what's-his-name.' *Dave Lowe, the child rapist.*

'Tell you what,' she said, 'you say the line, you can charge your phone.'

My vision throbbed at the corners. The vodka was sluggish in my veins, and I'd forgotten how much I disliked, truly, the feeling of being drunk, like you were swimming inside your own body. But I was grateful that the booze buffeted me from the worst of what I was about to do.

I cleared my throat. It took two tries. '"Don't worry, kiddo. The sun will come out tomorrow. It almost always does."'

She beamed at me. 'That's the one! My favourite.'

In the end, she charged my phone. Anything for Dave Lowe's daughter.

I waited on the curb, toggling my feet back and forth to alleviate my pinching shoes, when I heard the strains of Mina's 'Un anno d'amore' as Jack parked his vintage white Stingray.

'Hey, good lookin',' he called out of the rolled-down passenger-side window.

I smiled weakly and stood up, holding my dress so he couldn't see the bloodstain on the hem. I'd managed to blot off most of it in the ladies' restroom before he got there – the cut wouldn't need stitches, but it stung.

Jack was still in his satin purple plaid pyjamas. True to his word, he'd come straightaway.

My knight in shining jammies had also covered up a rape.

I kept my head down as I slid into the passenger seat. Jack patted my knee as I curled against the door. I flinched, then shifted, trying to make it seem like I was stretching. But I knew he noticed.

Jack cleared his throat as he pulled away from the curb, taking the curves old-man careful. 'You took off from the retrospective in a rush.'

I closed my eyes. The gentle sway of the car sloshed my stomach. 'Yeah.'

'We were all pretty worried, Salmon.' Jack forced lightness into his voice. 'Where did you go? Why didn't you call us?'

Tears dripped down my nose. I pushed them off my

face with my fingers, wiping them on my dress, trying not to let Jack see. But I knew he did – he murmured, 'Oh, baby,' quietly.

I sniffled. Found my courage. 'Who was that woman?' I didn't have to specify who.

He jerked the wheel, rocking the car. 'Damn squirrel,' he said, forcing a laugh. 'I don't know, Salmon, some crazy fan, I'd guess.'

After my phone had charged, I'd looked her up. I'd dropped it the night before and realised the screen was cracked to bits, but it still worked. She'd been credited for *Iron Prayer* under the name Betsey Wennick, a connection I could've made if I'd known to look for it. Seeing her name was as much confirmation as I'd ever need. I was right.

There were other things I'd picked up from her credits, too, a little insight into her history. She'd gone from starring in America's favourite neo-noir to one B-movie two years later, then a handful of scattered, nothing credits. No one had noticed she'd fallen through the cracks.

'No?' My mouth was cotton dry. 'It wasn't Elizabeth Wennick, who played Mom's little sister in *Iron Prayer?*'

We pulled up to a light. In the yellow glow, his face was old and drawn, orangey skin sagging. 'Well, maybe you're right, Salmon. You've got a good eye for these things.'

I kept my eyes on the road. If I looked at Jack, I'd never be able to say it. 'Funny you didn't recognise her. She looks just like Tawney, all grown up. But then, that makes sense, doesn't it? Seeing as how she's Tawney's biological mother.'

I could hear Jack's breathing, a harsh, laboured noise. 'Salmon, what are you—'

302

'When I was a kid,' I went on, trying to find the words I'd started to put together on that cot, 'I always felt like I'd fucked up everything about our family. Mom and Dad were legends; Tawney was so talented and so beautiful. Her whole future ahead of her. She was a *Lowe* to make the Lowes proud. And then there was me. Dumpy, bad-in-front-of-the-camera, substance-abusing, fucked-up *me*. The one bringing down the family name.'

You're still fucked-up, a dark voice inside me said. *You thought you could out-run yourself. Now you know.* I rolled down the window, turning my face into the arroyo breeze of the freeway. So many lies, over so many years. People who love you are never supposed to lie to you, but they're usually the ones who do it the most.

'But maybe,' I said, '*maybe* I'm fucked-up because this family has been fucked from the start. And I can't help thinking, during this terrible mess I've uncovered, how *helpful* it would have been to have someone explain it to me years ago. So I knew I wasn't crazy. I'm giving you this one chance to do what you should've done years ago. Just one, Jack. If you lie to me now, I'll never speak to you again. Do you understand?'

This time, when I looked at him, I could see the streetlights reflecting off the tears coursing down his face. I made my body full of stone. It wasn't hard to do.

'I'm sorry, Salmon,' he whispered. His lip trembled. 'We all thought it would be better – *easier* – for you, if you didn't know.'

I rubbed the bridge of my nose. 'Easier for *you*, you mean.'

'Yes,' Jack agreed. 'It was easier for us.'

I twisted my fingers together. We were flying down the freeway without traffic. We'd be at Glassell Park soon. 'Nobody contemplated going to the police? She was a *child*, Jack. Tawney's mother was a *child*.'

'Your mother is Tawney's mother,' Jack said, not looking at me. 'She was her mother her whole life.'

I knew why no one had gone to the police. My father's talent and career were too valuable; my mother and Jack loved him too much. Elizabeth had been deemed expendable, collateral damage.

It was the same reason Julie Cheong had been so eager to believe that I was making up my affair with Cal. It made everyone's lives easier.

'Your mother—' Jack stopped abruptly. Collected himself. 'Your mother was worried it would ruin your relationship with your father. Especially after Tawney died.' He coughed, massaging his chest.

'Did Tawney know?' I remembered that conversation I'd had with her before she died. The fight with my mother. That night at her pool, I'd been sure my sister wanted to tell me about a new love affair – but maybe this had been weighing on her. My heart hurt all over again, thinking of how I'd been so cruel when maybe she needed a shoulder.

I can't love you when I don't even know who I am.

'If she did, she never said anything to me.'

I tried to imagine Tawney finding out, keeping quiet about the information. I couldn't picture it. If she knew, she hadn't told Jack.

'Is it better, now that you know?' Jack pressed. I didn't say anything. He knew the answer. 'Your father was a flawed man, Salma, but he loved you and your sister very much. He

304

did the best he could by you. What's one mistake against a lifetime of work that's mattered to so many people?'

He took the exit for Glassell Park, threading his way through narrow streets. I didn't answer him.

'Thanks for the ride,' I said, my hand on the handle as Jack parked the car. My godfather reached out, grabbed both of my hands, and brought them to his trembling lips. I gasped, tried to yank away.

'Forget this whole night, Salma,' he said. There was a dark urgency in his voice that made my skin crawl. 'Put it out of your head. Choose to remember him as you knew him.'

His grip was starting to pinch my skin. I looked down. His knobby-knuckled hands were holding me so tightly, it sent little throbs up my arms. 'Let go of me, Jack.'

'You'll only break your mother's heart and destroy your father's legacy – and for what? *What?* It's already happened. We can't change any of it now. Please, Salma.'

'Let go of my hands, Jack,' I said.

He looked down, almost in surprise, and let go.

I got out of the car. This time, Jack didn't try to stop me. I leant back down into his window. A little old man with white hair and blue eyes in rumpled purple silk pyjamas, driving his goddaughter home from the drunk tank. A little old man who had aided and abetted his best friend's worst sins. 'If it was me,' I said finally, 'and not Elizabeth Wennick – if this had happened to *me* – would you be telling me to keep quiet?'

Jack didn't hesitate. 'Of course not, Salmon. I would've killed him with my bare hands.'

CHAPTER THIRTY-ONE

I woke up, fuzzy-headed and sticky-eyed, to the bleating of my morning alarm. Sobriety is no picnic, but I'd forgotten the rush of shame that came after a night of drinking: *did I say something terrible? Do they finally know how awful I am? Oh God, what did I do?*

But this was worse. I let it pin me to the mattress, the full weight of my actions. Twelve years of sobriety down the drain. Property destruction – I'd be on the hook for that, financially. Sloppy Salma wasn't my past. I could no longer pretend she wasn't a part of me.

Even that wasn't the worst of it. Four hours in the drunk tank and a few hours of sleep had sobered me up enough to remember the night before with perfect, terrible clarity. My father. Elizabeth Wennick. All the terrible things my family had covered up in the name of – what, fame? *Love?* I wasn't sure any more.

Then there was Cal.

I closed my eyes. I could see Cal's hands on Melany's neck as he moved her head to and fro. The towel looped around her neck. The eggplant bruises on my sister's throat. Ankine, twirling in the pool.

Just forget it, Jack had said, as if that was possible. But it wasn't without a certain appeal, either. I could build a barrier between myself and the knowledge of what my father had done, and maybe, eventually, it would feel like some once-heard but nearly forgotten piece of Hollywood lore. A bad thing that had happened to someone else. That's what Jack and my mother had done.

It was what they'd done with Tawney's murder, too. Pushed it to the side, I realised now with a sick feeling, because dwelling on it would bring with it the *other* bad thing. Maybe they'd even been worried that more publicity about her murder would out their secrets.

I couldn't forget. I wouldn't.

I had Avril's word that Cal had left the studio the day Ankine died. But what did that prove? He could've been in the meeting with studio bigwigs, as he claimed. He could've gone to lunch. Hell, he could've been with Ankine at the Jacaranda House, and still not murdered her.

And it was the same with Cherry's story. Even if I could get her to repeat what she'd told me – Cal had left with the photographer the day Tawney died – which I seriously doubted now, there were too many holes.

Airtight, MacLeish had warned. I needed more.

I wondered if anyone had ever died of a hangover before. *No, but people* have *died of broken hearts, Salma*. It wasn't much comfort. I reached for my phone. As I swiped up, one jagged shard from my cracked screen pricked my finger open, a bead of blood welling up and smearing the screen, filling the cracks in it like a river irrigating a valley.

I dialled before I could lose my nerve.

'Majors,' Emerald said, all business.

'You really believed me? About Cal?'

There was a long pause. In the background, I could hear the noise of the soundstage. I closed my eyes, listening. I'd never step foot on one again. I was sure of that now. 'Yes,' she said. Then, wryly, 'You've never been that good an actor.'

I huffed an almost-laugh. 'Can you meet me somewhere for coffee?'

'I'm on set.'

'Please, Em. I wouldn't ask if it wasn't important.'

In the background, I could hear someone asking for Emerald's attention, a muffled exchange about props. She answered, then came back on the line. 'The Smoke House. 2 p.m.' Then she hung up.

I checked my watch. I'd slept seven hours after I got home. That left me two and a half hours to come up with a plan for Emerald and get all the way over to Burbank.

It would have to do.

The Smoke House was located right across from the studio lot, which meant it had a history of feeding hungry off-duty actors like Bing Crosby and Bob Hope. Back in the sixties, it wouldn't have been uncommon to take a booth next to extras still in costume as knights or Spartans. The walls were lined with black-and-white photos of stars gone by. I was sure, if I looked long enough, I'd find my parents.

I didn't try.

Emerald arrived at 2 p.m. on the dot. Her braids were pulled up into a crown on the top of her head, and she wore dark pink lipstick. She grimaced as she slid into the sticky red booth.

'I only have thirty minutes,' she said. 'If we're lucky.' She looked more closely at my face. 'Rough night?'

I winced. I'd twisted my paper napkin to nervous shreds to keep myself from checking to see if my night had made the news.

I'd deal with my sobriety after Cal.

Thirty minutes. No time to waste. 'Do you know where Cal keeps the photographs?'

Emerald stared at me blankly. 'What photos?'

I watched her face, trying to decide if I believed her. She'd been such a good actor. *What other options do you have, Salma?* I took a deep breath. 'Cal has photos of the crime scene. Of . . . Tawney. Not the police photos,' I added, seeing she didn't realise. 'His own personal photos. He was there that day, Em.'

Emerald opened her mouth, and I could practically see the denial springing from her lips. I held up a hand, stopped her.

'Maybe I'm wrong,' I said. 'But there's only one way to find out. Where would he keep something like that? Something valuable, that he wouldn't want anyone else to see?'

Emerald didn't even have to think about it. 'There's a safe in his office. It's locked with a code.'

I remembered the black lacquered safe I'd seen in his office. I felt a tingle moving up my arms. I was doing it. *Finally, Tawney. All these years.* 'Do you know the code?'

Emerald shook her head. 'No one does. Only Cal.'

I'd worry about that later. 'Em, can you help me get into his office?'

She shook her head again. 'I really don't think—'

309

'If I'm wrong, I'll never bother you again,' I said. 'I promise. But if I'm right . . . Em, if I'm right, then you know what we need to do.'

Emerald's eyes drifted down to the table. I could see her making calculations in her head, arguing with herself. But I also knew she knew I was right.

When she looked up, her face was still at war with itself. But she said: 'You really promise you'll never bother me again?'

I gave her a smile I could feel with my entire body. 'Scout's honour,' I said. 'Never again.'

CHAPTER THIRTY-TWO

Monday morning dawned bright and eager. I woke up forty minutes early, forced myself to lie in bed an extra hour, even as my restless legs jiggled the sheets.

I checked my phone. Nothing yet.

After I'd left Emerald at the Smoke House, I'd called MacLeish. I'd told him I had one last favour I needed.

'Last, huh?' He hadn't sounded like he believed it.

But it was. If this didn't work, then I had nothing left. I'd explained the plan, twice.

'Spell the name for me,' he'd said finally. I'd bitten back a smile of victory – I still didn't know if it would work.

'*MYKELLA WATKINS*. Hollywood precinct. Let me know what you find.'

'I hope you know what you're doing, kid,' MacLeish had said.

'I do,' I'd said. For once. 'You just wait for my text tomorrow.'

MacLeish had called back twenty minutes later, told me Watkins was on the docket for rotation today, 10 a.m. to 7 p.m. shift. I'd squeezed my hand into a tight fist, knocking it against my thigh in celebration. There were no guarantees my plan would work, but at least there were no barriers.

I should've felt better, I'd thought after I hung up. I had a plan. I would feel better, I told myself, once Cal was arrested for murder. Once Tawney and Ankine had justice, I would start to feel a little bit better. I wouldn't just be Sloppy Salma.

Then I thought of Elizabeth Wennick and wondered if I ever really would feel better.

I took my time getting ready, blow-drying, then straightening my hair, pushing my bangs back and forth across my forehead.

I checked my phone again. Still nothing.

Emerald had promised she'd text me when they started filming. I had to trust she would keep her word.

I made myself breakfast, burning the toast and watery eggs, and downed so many cups of coffee I was practically levitating from my chair.

Finally, at nine-thirty, my phone dinged. A single emoji from Emerald: a red light.

Filming had started.

I checked my face one last time. *Hysterical*, I thought, and watched my face shift into the wrong shapes: my eyebrows pulling down, my teeth clenched as if in pain. But it wouldn't matter. This performance would convince not because I was a good actor but because everyone was ready to believe it: Salma Lowe, fuck-up, *fucked*-up and hysterical. It wouldn't take much to convince anyone – especially Cal – of all that.

The role I'd been playing my whole life.

During the drive to the studio, I thought of Ankine's family. If I was correct, her brothers would find out what had happened to their sister soon. It wasn't much comfort, but it was the only comfort left before the endless maw of grief. It was more than I'd had for twenty years.

Emerald had put me on the parking list as Beth Short. The guard waved me through without so much as a second glance.

I pulled my car into one of the last spots near Soundstage Seven. The wigwag blared red. I waited, watching it. It didn't go out, which meant Cal was deep into a block of filming.

Good. He'd be more upset when I interrupted him.

I checked my watch. I'd spent part of the day before tracing the route from Hollywood to the studio – at the outset, I'd have about twenty-five minutes before Watkins got here, maybe less, depending on when the studio called the police.

I took a deep breath, then shoved the elephant doors open, letting them smack against the wall with a satisfying clang. Yellow sun poured into the dark mouth of the soundstage, and I heard a small ripple of confusion run through the crew. I felt a little shiver of triumph, then reminded myself I hadn't fixed anything yet.

I stepped around the corner. All action on the soundstage had halted. Cal glared from video village, looking for the culprit who had committed the most rookie of rookie mistakes, but he couldn't yet see me. The lighting crew, though, could. *Drunk*, I told myself. *Hysterical. A hysterical, drunk woman no one takes seriously.*

This wasn't going to be pleasant.

I took a deep breath, then stumbled forward. I made my steps unsteady, faltering. I made a louder commotion than I needed to, then, bracing myself on an expensive piece of rigging, gave it a yank. *Rrrip*.

Cal couldn't miss me if he tried. No one could.

In the centre of the soundstage, Roger stared at me like I'd grown a second head. I remembered his face when I'd gone after Melany, and I felt a pang: surely, I'd tarnished the Lowe name for him. *Sorry, Roger, but you know what they say: never meet your heroes, or their clumsy daughters.* Melany tucked herself behind a piece of the set, watching me with large eyes, like I might come after her. *You'll thank me someday*, I thought, though I wasn't sure she ever would. Behind her, I saw Emerald slip away, out the back. Cal half-raised himself out of his chair, a dark sparkle to his face.

He was looking forward to dressing me down.

'Oh shit,' I said. 'Were you guys in the middle of filming? Oh God, I'm sorry. I didn't mean . . . I jussssht needed to say something to Cal. Real quick.'

My foot slid on a replica of Tawney's vintage rug as I stumbled over to video village, and I nearly went down, catching myself as I fell. *Don't overplay it.* The key to appearing drunk was trying to seem sober – all my years as Sloppy Salma had taught me that much.

Cal was remarkably calm, looking more amused than put out now that he'd seen me. I liked that, too; I knew that as far as Cal was concerned, amusement was a warning sign of the gathering storm. I was ready for it.

'You,' I said, pointing my finger at Cal, crooking it. I wanted witnesses, lots of witnesses. 'You have a lot to answer for.'

I was making it as easy as possible for him. Hysterical out of the gate. Easy to dismiss.

'Okay, *Salmon*,' Cal said, standing in front of me, arms open wide like Jesus on the cross, drawing out my nickname so that, even inebriated, I could be sure he was mocking me, 'what do I have to answer for?'

I took a deep breath. This part, I didn't have to act. 'You killed her,' I said. Tears came to my eyes unforced. Cal's posture didn't change but he swayed a fraction of an inch away from me. *Who do you think I mean, you twisted fuck?* I thought but didn't say. Instead, I said: 'You killed my sister. I know you did, and I'm going to prove it.'

The set was so quiet you could hear a pin drop. I knew better than to believe the crew was on my side, or that they believed me. After all, they'd seen me attack Melany. But it wasn't their reactions I was looking for.

Cal heaved a sigh, loudly. 'You're drunk.'

I suppressed a smile. 'No,' I protested. 'I am sober as a . . . as a . . . as a *stone*. Sober Salma, that's what they call me.'

But Cal was determined, for a moment at least, not to take the bait. 'Go home, Salma. Sleep it off.'

My eyes travelled out over the set. Most of the crew stared at me. A few looked away, uncomfortable with the scene. Someone in the back was speaking on a phone quietly, darting a glance at us. Calling security, I hoped. I turned, clocking Cal's replica Jacaranda House until I could see the curving marble staircase. 'Do you think my sister would be proud of this?' I said softly. 'She'd hate it. All this "most dangerous director" bullshit – she'd hate *you*.'

Whatever Tawney had loved in Cal was long gone. Maybe if she'd lived, he would've been a different person. But she hadn't. And he wasn't.

Cal had wiped any expression off his face, like he wasn't there. A big blank. For a moment, I worried I'd overstepped it. Then he started a slow clap. 'Good for you,' he said. 'You must've wanted to say that for a long time. You think Tawney would've hated me? Do you think she would've been *proud* of you? Giving tours off Hollywood and Vine?'

Cal took a step closer, crowding me. His go-to intimidation tactic. But I was ready for him. I reached forward and grabbed his arm. Cal flinched, as he did every time I touched him, and I felt a small throb of triumph. He tried to shake me off, but I clung tight, moving up his arm, using my nails.

Then I made a mistake. I'd been waiting for the moment for so long. I couldn't help savoring it. I pulled Cal closer. 'I know about the crime scene photos,' I hissed. 'You sick fuck. Soon, everyone is going to know what you really are.'

Cal's eyes widened, just a flare, just for a moment. Then it was gone, and he was in control again. 'Okay,' Cal said. Was it my imagination, or was his voice unsure, slightly shaky? Had I rattled him after all? 'Security, please escort Ms Lowe off my soundstage.'

Behind him, Emerald slipped back through the door, sending me a discreet thumbs-up. I let go of him. 'No need,' I said, slurring my words again a little. 'I'll see myself out.'

I stumbled off the soundstage, two security guards following me as far as the elephant doors. I rounded the corner, heading for my car, until I was sure they weren't watching me any more. I kept walking, only instead of heading for my car, I headed to Bungalow 989: Cal's and Emerald's offices. Then I texted MacLeish: *now.*

CHAPTER THIRTY-THREE

I pushed open the door, which Emerald had unlocked for me. *Your chance to atone*, I'd told her as we left the Smoke House. *It might help.* I kept the lights off, scurrying to Cal's office door, also propped open by Emerald.

I checked my phone – MacLeish had texted back simply *Done* less than a minute after I'd texted. If I'd mistimed it, Detective Watkins would show up to me rummaging through Cal's dark office, and this time, I wouldn't have the luxury of a private cell, after Cal told her I was now officially trespassing.

Now or never, Salma.

I pushed open Cal's office door. Framed posters from previous Midas Productions films were plastered over the walls, a flare of bright blues and oranges and flashy smears of blood. I manoeuvred around Cal's desk, dropping to my knees in front of the safe. An electronic keypad greeted me, and I flipped open my phone, googling the make and model for the length of the pin.

Four digits. I tried Cal's birthday first. No luck. I squinted at one of the posters, then tried the release date for his first film, *Break Neck Kids*.

Still nothing.

I closed my eyes. It could be anything. I'd known that, but I was so sure that if I got this far in my plan, I'd figure it out. *So close, Tawney. I'm so close to fixing it.*

I popped my eyes open. Then I punched in 0721 – the date of Tawney and Cal's wedding that never happened. It had been the key to her pool, too. Still.

The safe swung open with a green light and an electronic chirp. I stared down at a stack of black portfolios, like the one I'd seen Cal carry out of Melany's trailer weeks ago. I pulled the first one out, bracing myself as I flipped it open.

Inside, a luxurious black-and-white photo of a gorgeous woman reclining on a couch. Her eyes were closed, and she was completely nude except for a ribbon pulled tight around her throat.

But it wasn't Tawney.

I flipped through the book. They were all variations on the same theme – a beautiful woman, totally naked, except for some artistic demise, many, though not all, strangulations.

The models might not have been dead. But they were meant to look it.

On the last photo, an inscription:

For a fellow connoisseur. May these bring you eternal pleasure.
Georg

I put the portfolio to the side, picked up another. It was more of Georg's photos, those gorgeously dead women.

I shoved it to the side, too, picking up the final portfolio. This had to be it. This had to be Tawney's photos.

I turned the page. Another glossy black-and-white photograph. This time, it was Tawney. Alive. A grainy, night-time photo: the two of us, obfuscated by darkness, toes in the pool.

I remembered that night, but I hadn't remembered it looking like that. Even in the moonlight, I could see Tawney's face was pinched with worry, her forehead creased, her mouth downturned. I looked unbearably young, my cheeks still baby-plump, my bangs chopped too short in a cut that didn't suit my face. It was the last photo of us. I stared at that Salma, wishing I could freeze her in time. *Don't get older, please. Don't go forward.*

I tried to remember that night: the smell of jacaranda and chlorine by the pool, Tawney's anxiety that bordered on paranoia. The memory was more muddied now, threaded through with other images. I read once that every time we remember something, we're only remembering the last time we *remembered* it.

But she hadn't been wrong. Someone *had* been taking photographs of us. Tawney hadn't been paranoid.

I flipped forward through the pages, looking for others. But it was the only one of Tawney in any of the portfolios. Where were they? Emerald said Cal kept his treasures in the safe. If not here, where?

I slid my hand into the safe, checking to see if perhaps they'd fallen into a crack somehow. My fingers touched plastic, and I drew it out, my hands shaking. A cylindrical tube. More precisely, an inhaler.

I flipped open the cap. The mouthpiece was covered in Tawney's signature lipstick, Naughty Peach.

Ankine's inhaler.

My phone dinged. I looked down, expecting to see an update from MacLeish about Watkins.

Instead, it was Emerald.

Get out!! C coming!!

I shoved the portfolios and the inhaler back into the safe. I swung the door closed just as I heard it – the creak of the main office door opening.

I held my breath, my heart beating so hard it rocked me back and forth. From Cal's office, I heard the creak of a floorboard, the metallic jangle of keys, as someone moved quietly into the darkened space between the offices.

I felt a deep well of panic. Cal could trap me in here, easily. Was it better to hide, hoping he might not find me? Or to run, hoping I could escape into the sunshine before he caught me?

I crept to his door, listened. The footsteps moved to the other side of the bungalow, where Emerald's office was. I heard the creak of her door open, then it slammed shut. I exhaled, waiting a few seconds. Nothing.

I took a deep breath, steeling myself, then slipped into the centre vestibule between the two offices. Emerald's door was closed. I tiptoed to the front door, trying to move silently. My lungs weighed ten pounds, each breath an effort. I was halfway to the door, and then –

'So you're *not* drunk.'

I froze. The hairs on my arms stood up, and I turned slowly. Cal was tucked into the darkest corner of the office, near Emerald's espresso machine. In the dark room, with bright white light trickling in only gently between the slatted window shades, I couldn't see his face. But I knew.

Cal took a step forward. In one hand, he held a folder. He held it up. Smiled that wolfish, *I've got you now* smile. 'Looking for these?'

I ran.

CHAPTER THIRTY-FOUR

I didn't make it to the door. Cal tackled me, sending me flying. I cried out as my chin crashed onto the floor, blood filling my mouth where I'd bitten my tongue. I could feel Cal's heart beating against my back.

I hadn't been this alone with him since the night of Tawney's funeral. The night we had sex.

Outside, someone on a walkie-talkie called for a steady-cam dolly. The sputter of a golf cart ferrying someone by. Cal kept me pinned underneath him.

If he wanted to, he could grab my throat, squeeze the life out of me. Like the women in the photos I'd seen. Like Tawney. My skin buzzed with the realisation.

How long had it been since MacLeish called Watkins? How much longer?

'Why couldn't you leave well enough alone?' Cal grumbled on top of me. He sat back a little, easing the pressure, though I was still trapped underneath him. 'You've always been a nosy little bitch.'

I squirmed, trying to kick him off me, and Cal pinned me so hard against the wood floor it knocked the air from my lungs. Cal leant forward, so his mouth was against my ear.

'Was Tawney sleeping with Eric Wainwright? Is that why she left me?'

I twitched. Of all the things I'd expected Cal to say. '*What?*'

'You heard me.' Cal's voice was filled with hate. Was this what had been fueling him all these years? The question of my sister's fidelity? 'I know she told you. What did she tell you?'

'*That's* what you want to know?'

His voice was quiet, almost desperate. 'I can't finish the damn film until I know the truth.'

As if there was one objective truth. I thought of all the pieces of Tawney's private life I'd seen – the photos with Wainwright. Tawney's hickey that night by the pool. There was no way to know the complete story now.

'Is that why you killed her?' I whispered. 'Because you thought she'd left you for another man?'

'I didn't kill her!' Cal's voice was a thunderous boom in the office.

I didn't believe him. 'What about Ankine? Elizabeth Wennick was letting her swim laps in her pool every morning. Did you set that up? Did you take her to the Jacaranda House that day?'

Cal scoffed. His knee found my kidney. I gritted my teeth. 'She wanted to be famous,' he said. 'And now she is. When people watch my film, they'll think of her, too. I made her dreams come true.'

Ankine's face, waterlogged and pale, rose in my mind. Then my sister, laughing, twisted around his arms at the Chateau Marmont. Or was it for me, fifteen years old, shivering, too fucked-up and shell-shocked to cry, sitting on his curb, waiting for the cab to pick me up and take me back home? Who was I doing this for, and did it matter any more? Was I ready to let Cal kill me to find out the truth?

'Let me go,' I whispered. 'Please, Cal. Don't hurt me.'

Cal shifted on my back, almost like he was uncomfortable. 'Jesus, you really *do* think I'm a monster.'

Outside, I heard a soft murmur, a security guard or PA giving directions. I strained my ears, trying to tell if it was Detective Watkins.

But Cal wasn't paying attention. '*You* threw yourself at *me*. It wasn't my fault. You must admit, you had quite a reputation back then. You didn't exactly come off like a nice little virgin.'

He was so heavy on me, it was hard to breathe. I coughed, shaking my head. 'Is that what you think? That it was wrong because I was a *virgin*, not because I was fifteen?'

'Fifteen going on twenty-five,' Cal quipped. 'Or don't you remember?'

Outside, I could hear footsteps getting closer, the beep of a walkie-talkie. If it wasn't Watkins, then she wasn't coming.

I felt a hot spike of shame. With him on top of me, I could smell his aftershave. I remembered the feel of his stubbly chin under my fingers, my tongue. I remembered all of it.

Outside, someone rattled the locked doorknob.

'Hello? Is anyone in there? Cal? It's Detective Mykella Watkins. I'm responding to a report of a disturbance on set – open up, please, I'd like to speak to you for a moment.'

I opened my mouth to call out, or scream, and Cal

clapped his hand over it. Fire lit up along my spine as he pushed me down into the floor. His fingers were thick over my mouth, tipping my head back at a sharp angle. I grabbed a hunk of his flesh in my teeth, tugged so hard Cal yelped.

I heard the click of a belt, then Watkins said in a strong, clear voice, 'That's it. I'm coming in.'

Several things happened at once.

Watkins slammed the door with her hip, loosening the lock. At the same time, Cal stood up, striding to the door. My lungs expanded and I gasped, rolling to the side.

'Thank God, she just attacked me,' Cal said as he swung the door open. Sunlight poured into the office.

Watkins stepped forward, Taser in hand, looking from Cal to me and back. Cal held up his hand as proof, keeping the folder with his precious files tucked against his side. I watched from the floor, still trying to get my breath back. I'd broken the skin with my teeth, and a pinprick of blood was welling on his palm.

Watkins's face was neutral. 'What's she doing on the floor?'

I dragged myself up to sitting. 'He killed Ankine,' I gasped.

Cal rolled his eyes. 'She's been harassing me with this shit on set for weeks,' he said. 'You can ask my crew. She interrupted a *very* important shoot today. She's delusional. She attacked me.'

Watkins's eyes flicked to me. 'Ms Lowe, I warned you to stay away.'

Cal held up his bitten hand – *See? I'm not the bad guy here* – and the folder in his arms slipped a centimetre, revealing a glossy corner of a photo. My last shot – I leapt at Cal, Watkins yelling out in surprise. Cal blocked me with an arm, cracking me across the cheek, and I saw stars as I went down. But I'd loosened his grip on the photos, which fluttered to the ground next to me.

Even in the haze of pain, I could make out Tawney's face: vacant-eyed, the pool behind her. Tawney, before anyone, even I, knew she was dead. The scene undisturbed by caution tape, or any of the signs of an investigation.

I'd been right. All these years, I'd been *right*.

Cal was on his knees, frantically gathering the photos. Watkins put her foot on one, trapping it, her head tilted.

'That's private property,' Cal snarled. 'I'll have your fucking ass if you touch them.'

'I'd reconsider threatening an officer of the law,' Watkins said mildly. She reached down to pick up the photo. She studied it for a second, then turned it outward, so we could both see it.

It was Tawney's pool. A blurred motion in the pool of a woman splashing. At first glance, I thought it was Tawney – more creepy proof of Cal stalking my sister with the help of his own personal paparazzo.

But there, foregrounded in the corner of the shot – a cylindrical tube, red and white and identical to the inhaler in Cal's safe.

'September eighth,' Watkins said, pointing to the date stamped in the corner. 'Mr Turner, who took this photo, and how did it come to be in your possession?'

I stared at the photo. Long shimmering blonde hair. Sharp cheekbones slicing out of the water, the not-quite-right nose. The expression on Ankine's face somewhere between determination and panic.

'That inhaler,' I said. 'You can find that inhaler in Cal's safe.' At the very least, Cal was withholding evidence in an investigation. At the most, he'd either noticed she was struggling and withheld the medication, or made the choice not to give it to her – after all, Tawney had swam thirty laps every morning without one.

Watkins's eyebrows shot up. Her hand moved to her belt, unhooking a pair of handcuffs.

Cal's face twisted. 'I didn't touch her. She could've gotten out of the pool anytime. She was an adult. I didn't make her do anything. She was getting into character. She needed to get it *right*.'

I felt a chill creep over me, imagining the scene against my will. Cal, the Method director, forcing Ankine into the water, trying to recreate my sister in someone else's body, refusing to believe the past was gone and over. That even in a film, you couldn't live inside it. I wondered what the truth was – if he'd held Ankine down, if he'd kicked away the inhaler, if he'd simply been there, watching her die, and done nothing. I doubted I'd ever know for sure.

The most dangerous director in Hollywood. No longer just a headline.

'Mr Turner,' Watkins said slowly, 'you have the right to remain silent. Anything you say might be used against you—'

'You can't be serious,' Cal said. He glared. 'I'm in the middle of shooting a film. You can't make me leave.'

Watkins jingled the handcuffs. 'I can ask you again nicely, or you can make this difficult – your choice.'

I thought Cal might take the handcuffs, then he straightened. Watkins put her hand on his shoulder. It was the moment I'd dreamt of for so long – Cal in custody, an answer to my sister's murder.

It was my answer.

I followed them, limping, to the parking lot, where Watkins pushed Cal into the back seat of the Crown Vic while he glared at me. Sixteen years before, it had been me being led away from him in handcuffs. The tides had finally turned.

He'd killed Ankine. And my sister. He'd killed her because he thought she'd left him for another man. That was the answer. Cal had protested, but he was a liar and I knew it.

As I watched them drive away, I told myself justice always felt bitter-sweet.

CHAPTER THIRTY-FIVE

Dale came to pick me up thirty minutes before the meeting. His green Honda Civic was comically small around his bulky frame, and it rocked back and forth when he stepped out, like it was shaking off a workout. I watched from the door, fingers tapping on my purse strap, as he waved at me. I forced myself toward the car, each step easier than the last.

I hadn't attended a meeting in years.

But even as I kept my eye on the headlines rolling gleefully in – *Inquest into starlet death opened*; *Cal Turner implicated?* – I was restless. The day after the news broke, I found myself paused in front of a bar, staring longingly at its swampy cool interior.

I'd thought I would feel more relief. But all I felt was numb. Lost. Tawney was still dead. Ankine was still dead.

My father had still raped a teenage girl.

I'd gone over to Jack's for dinner once, with my mother. Jack had given me a gruff hug, told me he was proud of me. My mother told me she couldn't believe Cal had done it, even though of course he'd done it, but what a talented man, what a *waste*.

No one mentioned Elizabeth Wennick.

At the end of the night, Vivienne hugged me and said: 'Now there's no secrets left between us.'

We were never going to talk about it. This was what it meant to be a Lowe: to prise the family legacy over the family secrets. As far as my mother went, the conversation was closed. Jack would do whatever she wanted. Before I left, Jack made me promise to come to dinner another night, after my meeting with Dale.

Dale clapped me on the shoulder as I sat, the Delfonics pumping in the air. His face split into an electric white grin. 'Looking forward to the coffee?'

I smiled back, despite myself, despite the nervous twist of my stomach. I hated meetings. 'Best in LA,' I said. It was shit. The coffee was always shit.

Dale drove us west, heading for the water. We didn't talk, and I cranked my window down, closing my eyes against the gentle slap of salty ocean air. The Delfonics played on.

Dale picked a seat near the back, and I sat with him. *My name is Salma and I'm an addict.*

Hi, Salma.

Dale didn't push me. When he got up to speak, to talk about the things that led him to use, and the things that kept him from doing it now, he didn't nudge me. He let me sit there and listen to the rock bottoms, the relapses, the little joys, the tiny triumphs.

I hated it as much as I remembered.

I'd thought, for a long time, the funeral had been my rock bottom. My outburst, Tawney in the ground. What happened with Cal. But that was too clean, too easy.

The truth was, I'd hated Sloppy Salma. But I'd envied her, too. The abyss wasn't without its charms. The total abdication of responsibility, for one.

Using, I had an excuse for being a mess, a bitch, a bad daughter. I had a disease. It wasn't my fault. Sober, I was a nightmare if I gave vent to any of those messy parts, any of those too-big feelings I didn't know what to do with.

As an addict, I could sob about Tawney to anyone who would listen, wake up on strangers' lawns, mascara painted round my face, laugh it all off. The consequences hurt less. The bad things weren't me; they were the drugs.

I sat in the circle of the meeting, scratching my toe along the floor. In a way, this was rock bottom. There was nothing left for me to do now. I'd thought once I had the answers, my grief would lift, or change. But now I had answers; Cal was in custody; my sister was still dead.

The only thing I could do was accept the unacceptable.

Cal had been the boogeyman in Tawney's story – in *my* story. He'd been the faceless answer to what had happened to her that day – to my entire family – to me.

But I realised, sitting there in the damp basement of a Santa Monica Episcopalian church, he wasn't the only answer. Cal wasn't the answer to my grief, or at least, not all of it.

I closed my eyes. The group leader was telling us we had to give ourselves up to a higher power. That there was no other, better way, there was no escape. Beside me, I could feel Dale exhale, his mountain-size shoulders rocking.

I didn't believe in higher powers. But I believed in the truth, and its power.

I pictured Elizabeth in *Iron Prayer* – toothy, childish,

starting to come into her own beauty. How old had she been – fourteen, fifteen, tops? My father would've been – I did some quick math – thirty-four. The same age I was now. My stomach turned. *Rape*. Even if she'd wanted it, or thought she did.

I'd been fifteen when I slept with Cal. Legally, I knew the word *rape* could apply to my own circumstances. But I'd never used it. That word scared me. The world knew me as a victim already, left behind, broken beyond repair. And, I'd argued to myself, it wasn't a simple thing that had happened between me and Cal. There'd been manipulation, and mutual attraction, perhaps, but also grief, and alcohol. A potent cocktail of bad decisions.

Before, I'd thought of what happened between us as a multifaceted prism, endless ways of looking at the same scenario. One flick: I was legally, emotionally, and physically a child. In the eyes of the law, there was no doubt about what had happened between us.

Another: ethically, he was in the wrong, as well. He was more experienced: with women, with sex, with the world. He knew about consequences. He should've been the responsible one, not the teenager.

But when I thought of that night, I thought of the want I'd felt for him, the simmering sadness that had dimmed only when he touched me, the genuine desire I'd felt.

Complicated. That's how I'd thought of it all. Before Elizabeth.

There was the burst of chatter that signalled the end of the meeting, when we all made pledges to do our best to stay sober, meet up again the next day or week or hour, depending on our needs. I exchanged smiles – one or two old-timers I remembered from years ago, who gave me a *welcome back* nod, and nothing else. No shame, no blame, no judgment. Maybe I was back because I was strong. Maybe I was back because I'd been weak. Either way, I was welcome.

Dale drove me home again in near silence. I liked that about him, his ability to not force conversation. I was still thinking of Elizabeth, and Tawney. I had the truth now. I was the only one in my family who seemed to wonder about what to do with it. What would Tawney want me to do?

Dale pulled up to the curb. I thanked him, unbuckling my seat belt, but he put his hand on my shoulder again. 'How are you doing?'

I thought about it. 'I thought I'd feel different,' I said. 'I thought I'd feel better.'

Dale knew what I meant. 'You're mourning again.'

I shook my head. 'I never stopped.'

'No,' Dale said. 'You're mourning the idea that you could still fix it.'

Tears flooded my eyes. He was right. I'd known that solving my sister's murder wouldn't bring her back, of course. But maybe I'd believed it would fix me.

I choked down the knot in my throat. 'Same time next week?'

Dale's face split into another smile, and he inclined his head.

I hated the meetings. But I hated being an addict more.

As Dale pulled away, I climbed the driveway to my bungalow, set back from the street.

You're only as sick as your secrets.

There were more similarities between Cal and my father than I'd realised. Handsome men with the world at their feet. My father had been more charming than Cal, but he also wore his flaws more visibly. Enabled by the world around them, because of their looks, their talent, their perceived value. In the end, they'd both hurt too many women. But unlike Cal, my father was dead. I didn't have to reckon with whether he deserved jail time.

Elizabeth Wennick was still alive. I'd let myself put her out of my mind for too long.

I called Jack. I told him I couldn't make it to dinner. I had somewhere I needed to be.

There was a long pause. 'Are you all right, Salmon?'

There had been too many lies for too many years in our family. 'No,' I said. 'But I will be soon.'

Jack said cautiously, 'Salma, if something's wrong, you need to tell me right now.'

I shook my head, realised Jack couldn't see. 'Something's been wrong in this family for a long time. I'm going to set it right.'

Then I hung up, grabbed my keys, and headed to the Jacaranda House.

CHAPTER THIRTY-SIX

The house glowed like a beacon in the white afternoon sunlight. We were past jacaranda season, and the trees, once lush and purple, were now knobby and gnarled. But I could almost smell the ghost of the blossoms, a sweet honey-musk funk.

The soft slaps of my shoes against the asphalt rang like gunshots in the still neighbourhood as I keyed in Tawney's gate code to the Jacaranda House.

I rang the doorbell. I heard the clatter of feet down Tawney's staircase, a pause in front of the door as someone looked through the peephole. Elizabeth Wennick swung the door open a sliver, enough to cast a finger of light across her nose with its soft freckles. Tawney's nose – how could I have missed it?

She looked at me.

'Hi,' I said. 'Can we talk?'

Elizabeth didn't say anything. I remembered her face at the retrospective – the wounded-animal quality of it. The things she'd suffered at the hands of *my* family.

Maybe she blamed me for it, too.

'I want to talk to you about – Tawney.' I wanted to say

my sister, your daughter, but the words stuck in my mouth. 'Please.'

The door shut in my face. I heard the slide of the lock, the click of the door opening. Elizabeth kept her head bowed as she held the door open, the sun swallowed in the house's inky darkness. I stepped inside Tawney's house for the first time since the day she died.

As my eyes adjusted, I could see Elizabeth had kept the bones of Tawney's house the same as I remembered. The same terracotta tiles on the floor. The walls the same colour. My eyes found the faint gold stain on a tile, where I'd dropped a bottle of nail polish mid-pedicure.

I felt light-headed. I was dizzy with history.

Elizabeth guided me to the couch – a grey-blue velour, not Tawney's snowy white leather. She stared at me expectantly, waited for me to say something.

Now that I was in the house, I'd lost my nerve again. What could I possibly have to say to her that would help? There were truths here that I could feel at the edge of my vision, like outlines of fish under the water. I didn't want to pull them up, I didn't want to see.

Above the mantel, a picture of my sister. A print done by a famous photographer – not Georg. I shuddered, thinking of his photos. I knew it was a print, because my mother had the original. Tawney was fresh-faced, straight from the pool, her hair slicked back and wet. A laugh tugging at her lips, her skin unlined. Twenty-three forever.

I'd always think of her as my big sister, even though I was so much older now. My big sister, my protector, the one who would have gone to the ends of the earth for me.

I could go a little farther. For her. I had to.

'First,' I said, knuckling my fingers into her soft couch, 'I want to say, I'm sorry. I know it isn't enough. But I'm guessing no one in my family has ever apologised to you, and I wanted to start there.'

Elizabeth tilted her head. 'What did she tell you?'

I licked my lips, which had gone dry. 'Vivienne? Not – not much.'

But Elizabeth was shaking her head. 'No. Not *Vivienne*. Tawney. What did she tell you about me?'

So Tawney *had* known before she died. I decided to be honest. 'She didn't tell me anything.'

Elizabeth's face fell, and she looked away, fighting tears.

'You must've hated my family,' I said, watching her closely. 'After what my . . .' I had to swallow before I could say it. 'After what my father did to you.'

'I sent her letters, over the years. But she never wrote back. I always wondered why she never wrote back,' Elizabeth said. Her voice had a practised quality. I wondered how many times she'd rehearsed this speech, waiting for the day to tell her story.

'How did you two . . . finally get in touch?'

'I wanted to keep my baby.' Elizabeth glared at me. 'I bet your mother never told you that.'

My mother didn't tell me anything. 'I don't blame you,' I said. 'You were a kid.'

'I wanted to keep her,' Elizabeth repeated. 'They took my baby.' She tossed her head, and a gold medallion peeked out from under the collar of her shirt. She saw me noticing and tucked it back in. A sobriety chip, fashioned into a necklace. 'Opioids,' she said frankly. 'I became an addict after she was born. I didn't need a lot of encouragement.'

Another piece of the puzzle fell into place, how and why she hadn't fought for custody of my sister.

'It took me twenty years to get clean,' Elizabeth said. 'Twenty years. But the first thing I did when I knew it would stick – I went to that acting studio.'

I hadn't expected that. 'PAA?'

Elizabeth nodded, a blotchy red stain spreading over her pale skin. 'Your mother told me the truth, eventually. She'd never given my letters to Tawney, not one. Not *one*. She never knew her own mother loved her.' She looked angrier about the letters than what my father had done, than even the loss of her child. 'I wrote her a letter, one final letter. I brought it here, delivered it to the mailbox myself. I sent her' – Elizabeth's eyes closed – 'a picture of her in my arms, right after she was born. If she hadn't written back to me, I would've lost it forever.'

'What did she say?' I leant forward, hungry for any piece of my sister. I wanted to hear my sister's voice again, even from this stranger's mouth.

Elizabeth gave another dreamy smile. 'She invited me here for lunch, to talk. At first, she didn't believe me.' Her face darkened. 'She was kind about it. She said it sounded like a soap opera.' I chuckled; it sounded like Tawney. 'But by the end of lunch, she was starting to believe. She invited me back. We met here six times before she . . .' Elizabeth looked down, holding back tears. 'Before she died. It's why she left me this house,' Elizabeth said, her eyes burning bright. 'It was the only place we'd gotten to spend time together. The only time when she really *was* my daughter.'

I closed my eyes. I tried to imagine what those lunches

had been like for Tawney. I was more than a decade older than she would ever be, and it was all still a mess in my head. 'What did you talk about?'

Elizabeth dabbed at her eyes, a smile brightening her face. 'You. The movies. That *man* she was seeing.'

I remembered Emerald telling me the owner of the house had refused to let Cal film here as soon as she heard the name. 'Cal,' I said. 'Her fiancé.'

Elizabeth shook her head. 'He didn't deserve her. She told me things about him . . . things she didn't tell anyone else. Not Vivienne. Not *you*.' Elizabeth's chin lifted. I wasn't sure I believed her, but even the possibility of it made me almost breathless with jealousy. 'I told her to leave him. Now they're saying he killed her.' Elizabeth's eyes filled with tears. 'Did he kill her because I told her to leave? Was it my fault? I just wanted to be a good mother.'

Elizabeth was sobbing in earnest now. I handed her a box of tissues from her coffee table, my heart aching. She should've gotten a chance to raise her child. But then I wouldn't have grown up with Tawney, wouldn't have been her sister. Not in the same way.

Without her, I wouldn't even be me.

It was a relief when the doorbell rang.

'I'll get it,' I said, giving Elizabeth a little bit of space, expecting FedEx, some other mail delivery.

Instead, when I swung the door open, it was Jack.

CHAPTER THIRTY-SEVEN

Jack wore a hangdog look. He was dressed in dark jeans, a simple white cotton shirt. His hair was a spray around his face, and he seemed out of breath.

'Jack? What are you doing here?'

Jack shoved past me and into the Jacaranda House. 'What are you doing talking to her? I thought you knew better than that.'

Elizabeth stood up, putting the couch between her and Jack. She had her hand up, *stop*. 'I can't believe you brought him here.'

'I didn't,' I snapped. 'Jack,' I said, 'you didn't answer my question.'

For the first time, Jack looked around. He seemed surprised to find himself there, and I watched him deflate slightly. 'You're making a mistake,' he said. 'You don't know what you're doing. You'll just confuse yourself. You know who Tawney's mother is. That hasn't changed.'

Elizabeth looked at Jack, her mouth pulled tight. '*I'm* her mother, and my girl knew it. She even said she told Vivienne that. That she wished I'd been her mother instead.'

My head jerked. Had that been the fight all those years ago? Tawney saying something so terrible to our mother?

'Were you there when she was sick as a kid? When she was crying, when she needed you?' Jack's teeth were clenched. His face was red, almost purple. A vein throbbed in his neck. 'You signed those rights away. You were happy to do it.'

The hurt on Elizabeth's face looked so much like my sister that it took my breath away. Jack must have seen it, too; he took a step back.

Elizabeth shook her head. 'That isn't true,' she told me, almost pleading. Somehow, I was in the middle of this, the spectator who needed to be convinced. 'I didn't know any better. I was a kid.'

I held up my hands. 'I believe you,' I told her.

Jack sat down on the couch. He looked old again, so old. He held his head in his hands. 'Didn't you already get your answers? You know who killed her. You know.'

Elizabeth glared at him, her eyes blazing, Tawney's face in her face. 'Vivienne did it. Cal Turner might've been the one who strangled her. But Vivienne killed my baby all the same.'

Jack looked up at her. He bared his teeth like a wild animal. His voice, when he spoke, was low and dangerous. 'Haven't you hurt her enough already? Now you're accusing her of murder, too?'

Elizabeth's tears were the flood of decades unleashed. 'She knew he was hurting me,' she sobbed. 'I was fourteen. She didn't do anything to stop him. She knew, and she didn't stop him.'

Oh God. I closed my eyes, tried to close my ears. I

didn't want to hear this. I didn't want to hear any of this.

With my eyes closed, I didn't see what happened. There was the sound of couch springs, then a loud crack and a cry of pain. When I opened my eyes, Elizabeth was curled up on the floor under Jack, her ankle tangled between his feet. He was yanking her up, shaking her like a rag doll, teeth clenched, his pupils blown.

'Jack, Jack!' I scrambled to Jack, tripping over the coffee table and sprawling toward Elizabeth. My shin ached, and I'd had the wind knocked out of me, but Jack let go, his breath coming in shuddering gasps. Elizabeth was limp, trembling.

Jack stared down at his hands, as if he couldn't quite believe what he'd done. 'Sorry, I'm sorry,' he wheezed. 'I lost control of myself.'

I'd never feared Jack. I knew he was capable of ethically bad things – the lies, the bribes, the threats. But I'd never seen him physically act in anger.

I looked around the room, dazed. Their tussle had knocked over a lamp and the room was shaded in weird darkness. I dragged myself to my feet and, limping a little, yanked the blinds open. Sunlight poured in, and Jack looked up, toward the pool, then flinched, turning his back to the French doors. His eyes lit around the room, and I saw them find Tawney's portrait above the mantel. His eyes zipped to the floor.

And that's when I realised.

He didn't want to look at the pool.

He didn't want to look at my sister.

He hadn't even said her name in years.

If Tawney had found out, if she'd threatened to go

public with the news, or asked something from my mother that she couldn't give – asked her to leave my father, maybe – what would my mother have done? Not with her own two hands. But what would she have set in motion?

I helped Elizabeth to the couch. She was in a world of her own, rocking and moaning.

My mouth was dry. For the first time, I was scared, really scared. Not of what Jack might do – but what he would tell me. 'Jack?'

He looked up at me, the blue of his eyes so light I could practically see through them.

'Jack,' I whispered, 'what really happened to Tawney?'

A burglar, Salma, a stalker, a fluke, Cal Turner. Anybody else. I didn't want to stop loving him. I didn't know if I could.

'We were just supposed to talk.' Jack sounded dazed. His arms sagged where once they'd been full of muscles. Twenty years ago, he'd been strong, fit, a man barely past his prime.

A man capable of strangling a young woman. Especially if he caught her by surprise. If she trusted him. If she believed he loved her enough he'd never hurt her.

On the couch, Elizabeth moaned and rocked, her hands between her knees.

'What did you do?' I whispered.

'Just supposed to talk,' he said mechanically. 'Make her understand it was better for all of us to forget it ever happened.'

'Not better for Elizabeth,' I said, and Jack's head snapped to me like a shot. Elizabeth stared at the picture of Tawney above the mantel. I wasn't even sure she heard us.

'That's what she said,' he said in a daze. 'That's exactly what she said. You sound just like her, you know.'

He turned and faced the pool, one hand on the latch to the French doors, the other twitching at his side.

'She said no one had considered Elizabeth in all this, that she'd been hurt over and over and none of us had done a damn thing about it. I agreed with her, actually,' Jack said, turning his face to mine, pleading for understanding. 'You should know that. What your father did to that little girl, it made me sick. And he had your mother, right there, adoring him. A fucking waste.' Jack turned to the side and spat, actually spat, on Tawney's – Elizabeth's – floor.

'But it would have ruined her life,' Jack said. 'Your mother would have died of the shame. I couldn't let that happen to her.'

I took a deep breath, said it fast before I lost my nerve. 'So you killed her. Because you *thought* she might talk.'

Elizabeth started to hyperventilate on the couch.

'No!' Jack glared at me. 'You don't understand. I told her exactly what I told you, that your mother would die if this came out, that we couldn't do that to her.' Jack's gaze drifted back out to the pool. The twitch in his hand had turned into a rhythmic pulse, a squeeze.

Like he was choking the life out of someone.

'You know what she did? She laughed at me. She said: 'Old man, nothing you do is going to make her love you.' Salma, she *laughed* at me.' His voice broke, on the verge of tears, and he spread his hands helplessly. 'She turned, to go inside. The towel was in my hand before I . . . She didn't even scream. It was over so fast. It was over, and I couldn't take it back.'

But I could see it, I could imagine. Tawney and her quicksilver tongue, her accuracy, her sometimes-cruelty. She'd always disdained the dance we did around the strange ménage that was my mother, my father, my godfather. She hated pretending we all didn't see what was happening – my father's infidelities, Jack's unrequited love. She'd used it to twist the knife at exactly the wrong moment.

And so my sister had wound up dead. I watched Jack's hand, squeezing. I wondered if he realised he was doing it, pantomiming Tawney's last moments on earth.

My sister dead over these sordid family secrets, a thoughtless little comment. Not Cal. Not Cal, after all.

I closed my eyes, pressed my hand against a wall to steady myself. I could swear, *swear*, I caught a hint of Tawney's smell on the air, clove and orange blossom. And with my eyes closed, and the smell of her in my nose, perfuming my head, I could almost believe she was upstairs, fixing her make-up.

But she was dead. Jack killed her.

Jack's voice was small, and I could tell, even with my eyes closed, he was crying. 'You don't know how badly I've wanted to undo it. I'd give anything if I could go back and change that, Salma, believe me. There's nothing I regret more.'

But I was frozen – from my toes to my heart, frozen completely.

Jack was still babbling. 'If you want me to go to the police, I'll go, I'm an old man now, what does it matter anyway. What can I do? Tell me what I can do to make it right.'

I couldn't put it all together, I didn't know what to do.

Make it right? How could we ever make it right? I blinked my eyes open. 'Did she suffer—'

Then Elizabeth was up from the couch, rocketing toward Jack, her face red, mouth open in a ragged scream. She charged Jack, hurling her body at him. She was a thin woman, and in other circumstances, she wouldn't have hurt him. But Jack was an old man, and caught off guard, and as he stumbled backward, Jack's trick ankle collapsed underneath him.

He went down, cracking his head against Tawney's fireplace. Elizabeth fell with him, rolling to the side, wheezing. Elizabeth had dodged the fireplace, but Jack lay in a dazed heap, his face white, ashen. As I watched, he reached back, touched his head, and his hand came away red.

I was by his side before I realised I'd moved. The gash behind his ear was so thick, it looked like a dent in his skull. I gagged as blood seeped from the wound. His mouth opened and closed in surprise, like a fish suddenly thrust into the air.

Elizabeth was sobbing next to him – no help, no help at all – and I fumbled for my cell phone, shakily calling 911 and giving them the address for the Jacaranda House.

'Did I hurt him?' Elizabeth kept asking, over and over.

Jack was shaking, not speaking. He slumped against the foot of the mantel, pale, too pale. His face turned, and then he was looking out at the pool, blue eyes fluttering.

I'd thought, before, if I'd been there with Tawney when she died, or my father, that I would've found the right words to say, the right ways to tell them I loved them. Even if I couldn't change a thing. I would've been able to tell them, at least, the words in my heart.

But as Jack ebbed into unconsciousness, his eyes drifting, all I could get out, between sobs, was his name, over and over, a tiny prayer on my lips. I couldn't help him. I didn't know what to say to him now.

But Jack had a word for me. He looked up, his blue eyes straining and wet, searching my face. One hand, the one I wasn't clutching between my own, reached for my face, a thumb drifting over my chin. His last word, as he drifted off into an unconsciousness he wouldn't wake from, was *love*.

16TH JUNE, 2004

The second time around, I was a model rehab prisoner. I knew the routines, and I was good at them: docile and polite to staff. I had no problem with authority, unlike some of my fellow inmates. I didn't mind being told what time to crawl into bed, or that drugs were bad for me. In group, I could produce tearful insights about the malformation my childhood had wrought, the reasons I was here. The truth was never a good enough answer: *I got too fucked-up and pissed off someone with more power than me. I'll probably do it again, given the chance.*

I'd shuffle pliantly from my sessions with my counsellors – I had two, one for my addiction and one for my family – to the yoga studio, where a petite dark-haired staff member performed non-consensual Reiki on us in turn. I detoxed, and I painted crappy renditions of my feelings for art therapy, and I didn't make waves.

I was biding my time. I was waiting to die.

The seventh anniversary of Tawney's death wasn't a visitors' day. I don't know who Jack bribed, but there was a knock at my door before dinnertime.

'Come in.'

When Jack opened the door, I was facing the wall, curled up in a ball under my sheets. He sat heavily on the bed. I knew it was him because I could smell his cologne: tobacco, lime, rich, and a bit acrid, like burnt leather. The bed depressed under the weight of him.

We sat like that for a long time before Jack said anything.

'I brought you something.'

The only thing he could've offered me that I wanted wasn't possible. But still, after a moment, I looked up at him. I hadn't showered in a few days, despite the urgings of my counsellors. Tawney's anniversary was always bad. But it was worse to be alone.

Jack sat on the edge of my bed. He wasn't smiling. It was a bad day for him, too. For all of us.

I stirred, shifting to face him. Jack held up a yellow laminated card.

I squinted at it. It took me a moment to recognise it. 'A library card,' I said flatly. 'Gee, thanks.'

Jack pretended not to hear my sarcasm. 'People like to think of their lives as stories,' he said. 'That's why we like movies, I think. Kid, the stories you've been living in lately are shitty.'

He shocked me into a dry, raspy chuckle. My first in days.

'Find a new story,' he said, handing me the card. 'It doesn't mean the old ones are gone.'

I rolled my eyes. Even by cheesy adult standards, this was pretty corny.

Jack stayed for another hour, although we didn't talk any more that day. When he left, he'd leave the card behind. I'd resist it for two days before I went to the rehab's computer terminal and asked for instructions on how to order a book from the LA County Library.

The first book I checked out was by a director. Peter Bogdanovich wrote *The Killing of the Unicorn* for his lost lover, an actor named Dorothy Stratten. Dorothy was twenty when her estranged husband murdered her.

Dorothy was the first, but it didn't take me long to find the others. Tawney's dark sisterhood. The ones keeping her company while I couldn't. Thinking about them was the only thing that made the grief a little bit easier – not gone, not fixed. Just the tiniest bit lighter.

Jack never asked if I'd used the library card, and I never told.

At the door of my rehab cell, Jack paused, then he said, the only time I'd ever heard him quote *Iron Prayer*: 'The sun will come out tomorrow, kiddo. It almost always does.'

CHAPTER THIRTY-EIGHT

Tawney and my father had been laid to rest together in the Pierce Brothers Westwood Village cemetery, under a tasteful but prominent marble monument my mother had commissioned herself. Locked together for all eternity. Tawney had always joked that no cemetery would let a nice girl with fake tits be buried in consecrated ground; but as it turned out, that wasn't true at all.

They were neighbours to Natalie Wood and La Marilyn herself, with her permanently kissed-pink crypt. A few of my Dead Girls rested here: Dominique Dunne and Dorothy Stratten. I'd brought them bouquets of sweet alyssum, and I laid them in tribute before I headed to my sister and my father's monument.

In the corner, nearly tucked away, a white marble angel stood guard over my father and sister. An inscription on the side read simply: NEVER FORGOTTEN. Beneath the marble angel, two small plaques. I knew there were two more graves in the plot – one for my mother, one for me. Nothing for Jack.

But Jack wasn't dead. Not yet.

I set down the bouquet of fuchsia roses at the side of

the monument I always thought of as Tawney's side, even though I didn't know where her ashes rested compared to my father's. Then I took a seat on the bench across from it, pulling my legs up underneath me.

'Happy birthday, Tawney,' I told the monument. The stone didn't say anything back. She'd been dead nearly as long as she had been alive, and gone from my life longer than she'd been in it.

After a few minutes, I knelt before the grave, pulled up the weeds that had grown around its base. Every week, my mother brought fresh flowers and placed them in the votive. Cheerful daffodils bowed in the breeze. Every week my mother came.

This year, there was also a fresh spray of enormous white lilies, so big I'd mistaken them at first for a permanent cemetery plant. It was only once I was kneeling that I could see the seed pearls threaded into the shape of a T in the centre of the design. There was a card, but I already knew who they were from.

In the end, the inquest had determined Ankine's death was inconclusive. It couldn't be proved that Cal had directly withheld the inhaler, or forced her to stay in the pool. Cal was exonerated, to the delight of the thousands of fans who had signed a petition – circulated by one Melany Grey – in support of his innocence. Industry rags opined that with the upwelling of publicity, *Magnum Opus* was slated to be one of the biggest films of the year. A return to form for a director on the outs. There would always be more chances for a man like him.

Watkins visited me once, to break the news. *Circumstantial*, she said. *Culpability hard to prove. Too*

much evidence lost; all we can prove is that he was there.
I'd nodded and nodded and nodded.

I knew what she was saying. It wasn't *airtight*.

That wasn't all. Watkins told me Cal wouldn't be charged with Tawney's murder, either. She watched me for a reaction as she said it, and I was careful to keep a neutral expression. For once, my face did the right thing.

And when it was announced that Cherry Partridge, his new executive producer, would replace Emerald Majors after seven years of partnership – well. That didn't surprise me, either.

At Tawney's graveside, I stared at the enormous spray of flowers Cal had brought. Of course he'd sent the most ostentatious, expensive arrangement he could find. He wanted to broadcast his grief, keep himself at the centre of Tawney's story.

Footsteps crunched behind me on the gravel path. I sat up, brushing grass from my knees, as my mother swept by me. She'd chosen a white linen wrap dress for the occasion. In her hand, she held a bulb of blue-white hydrangeas.

'Happy birthday, baby girl,' she whispered as she arranged the hydrangeas around my fuchsia roses, fluffing the petals through her fingers. She kissed her fingers and put them to the monument, pressing the kiss into marble.

The last time I'd seen her had been the only time I'd visited Jack in the hospital.

My mother gave me an uncertain smile. 'You look nice.'

I resisted the urge to glance down at my dress, say something self-deprecating. 'Thank you.' I licked my lips, squinting into the sun. Somewhere, a bird screamed, and little insects made a heated buzz in the grass around us.

The April day was burning into a scorcher, yellow and deep. 'How's Jack?'

My mother's shoulders sagged. 'The same. They don't think he'll wake up, but they're not sure. You should go see him. They think it's possible he may be able to hear us.'

A traumatic brain injury. It was the first time an ambulance called to the Jacaranda House had bothered with sirens as it pulled away, screaming out of the neighbourhood to Cedars-Sinai.

Elizabeth and I had waited around to give another statement to the cops. When they'd asked what happened, Elizabeth looked panicked. But I'd already decided.

'An accident,' I'd said smoothly. 'He slipped and fell. A terrible accident.'

We both knew my silence came with a cost.

'Maybe,' I said to my mother.

Vivienne's face dropped, but she nodded.

There were a million questions I could've asked. I could've asked why she'd gone along with what my father had done; why in the world had she stayed with him after she'd known?

But I knew the answer. She loved my sister, and she loved me. But we weren't the love story of her life.

'I miss her, Salma,' my mother said, her voice soft, like she was reading my mind. 'Every day, I miss her.'

I stared at the white boat of Cal's flowers. It was now. It was finally happening now. 'You never told anyone.'

Vivienne shook her head. 'You don't understand,' she said. 'It was a different time.'

It was a different time. It was such an easy answer because I'd never be able to prove she was wrong. But human kindness, empathy – those had never changed with time.

'I didn't realise there was a time when raping a child was all right.'

'You weren't there,' my mother said, her voice a scratchy almost-yell. She never raised her voice. Never on-screen, never off it. 'If you could have seen her. Swanning about that set, twitching her hips. Making come-hither eyes at your father. That girl was never a *child*, Salma. She knew what she was doing,' she said, her hand against the monument.

My mother lifted her chin, eyes blazing. It was the story she'd fed herself for the last forty years. I wasn't going to take it from her now.

'Mom,' I said softly. 'What happened to Tawney? How did she die?'

I wanted to hear it from her own lips. I wanted to see her face.

She looked away. 'I don't know.'

'Mom.'

'I don't know!' She yelled it. When she looked at me, Vivienne's face was bone white, her nostrils flared. She was trembling. 'I don't know, Salma, I don't know. *I don't know.*'

Or maybe, I thought, she didn't want to know. She hadn't wanted to know for twenty years. She hadn't *let* herself know.

I took a step forward, felt her tremble against me. She was still my mother. 'It won't bring your sister back,' she said, muffled into my arm. 'Nothing I can do will bring her back.'

I released her, wiped my streaming nose and eyes.

My mother put her hand against the marble angel, stroking the angel's inscription. 'If people found out what happened between your father and that girl, it would ruin his legacy. Not just his, but the legacy of *Iron Prayer*. You know what that film means to people, to history. It's art. It's bigger than our family. She would've destroyed all of that.'

Vivienne lifted her chin proudly, her eyes flashing. 'It's why he loved me. He knew he could count on me. Always.' She studied me. 'You're like me, you know. You're tougher than you think. And now you know the truth, all of it. The legacy is yours to protect now, too.'

I pulled my keys out of my pocket and walked up the gravel road back to my car, the pebbles crunching under my feet.

'Salma, wait,' my mother said. 'Stop.'

My mother ran to catch up and grabbed my arm, jerking me to face her. Her eyes were searching, and I winced as her almond red nails dug into my biceps. 'Salma, listen, please.' She was out of breath. 'Should one moment of weakness define a man's life? An entire life, everything he's ever done, every movie he ever made? Is that more important than the father he was to you?'

I stopped.

There wasn't a good answer to that question, or at least not an easy one. There never was. Maybe wherever my sister was, she knew all the answers. But I didn't believe that. She'd been a bright flicker, and then gone. I didn't believe she had the answers any more than I did.

I didn't know how to parse out the things I knew: my

father loved me. He'd been a good father in the ways he knew how to be. And Jack, even more so. They'd made movies that meant something to people.

And they'd done unspeakable, vile, awful things to people.

It wasn't a moment of weakness. It was a lifetime of secrets. It was two lives, destroyed. It was deciding, for themselves, whose truths mattered, and whose truths didn't.

It was the murder of my favourite person who had ever lived.

I pried her fingers away from my arm, and when she called my name, I didn't turn around. I kept walking.

CHAPTER THIRTY-NINE

When Emerald invited me to the private screening of Cal's film, I refused.

'He won't be there,' Emerald insisted. 'I wouldn't subject you to that. Besides, I think there's something you'll want to see.'

I thought about it. It was likely there'd be more bad memories than good. But I'd started to trust Emerald, or rather, we'd started to trust each other. We'd grabbed dinner a few times since the film had wrapped, even watched a movie or two together, arguing in a friendly way over our differing tastes. We were starting to pick up the pieces we'd dropped all those years ago on *Morty's House*.

I drove to her house in the middle of the day on a Saturday to watch the rough cut. Emerald's house was mid-Wilshire, only a few miles from the Jacaranda House. I wondered if my compass would ever point anywhere but straight at Tawney.

I hadn't been back to see Elizabeth since the day I found out the truth about Tawney's death. I'd promised I'd go back when the memories weren't so fresh.

I wasn't yet sure if I was lying.

Emerald pulled the door open. Compared to her outfits on set, seeing her in a sweat suit felt practically blasphemous. 'Welcome back,' she said.

I sat on the couch while Emerald poured herself a glass of wine. She raised her eyebrows at me, and I shook my head.

'I brought my own.' I patted my purse. Family-size Raisinets.

Emerald dimmed the lights and joined me on the couch. It was her last film with Cal, and I knew she'd pulled strings for the print. 'Ready for this?' she asked without looking at me.

I took a deep breath. 'As ready as I can be.'

It was still a rough cut of the film – too long, the titles hadn't yet been added. We opened in Brandon Saturn's office, about to be hired for his most unforgettable job: the Hurricane Blonde. On-screen, Roger's handsomeness was somehow bearable.

I made a little noise as the Hurricane Blonde stepped into frame, her back to the camera, her first rapid-fire flirtation with Brandon. It was a scene I hadn't been on set to witness, and for a moment, I forgot this was Cal's film, and simply gave over to the magic of moviemaking.

Then the Hurricane Blonde turned to face the camera.

It was Ankine.

I gripped Emerald's arm. 'How . . . ?'

'Film test,' Emerald said. '*Shh*. Watch.'

I held my breath. Ankine was only on-screen for one exchange with Brandon Saturn and then she was gone, flouncing out his door, never to reappear again.

She'd been on-screen maybe thirty seconds. But still,

she made an impression. I wondered what she could have done, who she could have been, if she'd lived.

The next time Brandon encountered the Hurricane Blonde, it was Melany, a nifty sleight of hand for the audience: who was the *real* one?

On-screen, Melany was luminous, the camera lingering on her face. But all I could see in her was hunger. She'd sold my darkest secret to *TMZ*. But there was another part of me that understood it, even if I couldn't forgive it. Our tastes might have been different, but I knew a fellow addict when I saw one.

When the story first broke about Ankine and Tawney, Melany had given an interview in support of Cal. 'Cal Turner has never been anything but professional in his conduct with me,' Melany had said, sombre in a *Take me seriously* suit. She'd recently signed on as a sidekick in a superhero movie, slated to make gazillions. 'He's helped launch my career. No one champions women like Cal.'

'*Bitch,*' Emerald whispered under her breath after Melany's first big scene.

I was grateful when she fast-forwarded through each of the Hurricane Blonde's deaths.

Finally, the big denouement: Brandon on the trail of the Hurricane Blonde, always one step behind. He chased her through Los Angeles, only catching glimpses of her before she was hidden around another corner. Brandon caught her outside one of the old, run-down theatres downtown. An old brick building, boarded up, a flickering neon sign. Nowhere for her to go. Trapped, the Hurricane Blonde ducked into the building, leading Brandon through a dark maze.

Until.

I could feel Emerald watching me.

A beacon in the dark theatre. No sign of the Hurricane Blonde among the rows. But a glowing movie screen. A figure coming into focus, spreading until she took up the whole frame.

Tawney. Actual footage of my sister. Flickering, silent clips. Some from her movies, others were interview clips. Still others were moments on the set of *Love's Long Midnight*; a few clips from home movies Cal had shot in their happy moments. My sister, barefaced and giggling under the sheets. Getting ready for a premiere.

It took my breath away, seeing new moments all these years later. So many years after I'd lost her, and there was still more for me to discover.

I thought about love and all the terrible ways it binds us to one another. Love could be a trap if you let it, I thought, but no, that wasn't true. *Grief* could be a trap if you decided to live in it instead of alongside it. Love was never a trap. It was a gift, even if it was one you didn't get to keep.

Jack and the things he'd done out of loyalty to, or love of, a woman who would never love him back. My mother, all the excuses she made as my father hurt her over and over, and she let him call it *Love, love, love*. Elizabeth, the ghost at my sister's heels for all these years. Tawney, bound to Cal until she hadn't been, until she'd decided to put her life together differently, alone, and then hadn't had enough time to do it. Even Cal – all these years later, and Tawney was still the ghost haunting him.

And me, stopping my own clock to grasp what was left of my sister for as long as I could.

They were all decisions we'd made, each of us. We'd live with the consequences.

The film snapped off.

'So?' Emerald was impatient.

I wiped the tears away. 'It was all right,' I said. 'A little bloated.'

Emerald laughed. There was a little electric buzz radiating off her, and I could tell she'd practised whatever she was about to say to me. 'I didn't just invite you here for the movie.' She took a deep breath. 'I want to open my own production studio. Make my own movies, my own way. I could use someone like you on my team.'

Of all the things I'd expected her to say. 'You can't be serious.'

'My partner. You'd be co-owner of it, with me.' Her hazel eyes flicked away from me. I realised she was nervous.

I couldn't stop shaking my head. I'd said goodbye to all that. I'd gotten out. 'That's ridiculous. I'm not meant for this life. Remember? I tried it once and couldn't hack it.'

'Don't be an asshole,' she snapped. 'If you'd wanted my job – I mean, if we'd interviewed at the same time, it would have been yours. No question. You could probably have my job now, if you got to the right people.'

'C'mon, Em, you know that's not—'

'It *is*, though. That's how this business works. It would have been yours. Dave Lowe's daughter?' She snapped her fingers. 'Whatever you wanted. Yours.'

I felt a burst of hot shame. She wasn't wrong. 'Okay. You're right. But so what?'

Em's face shifted. 'I'm not making an offer to be nice.'

She took another swallow of wine. 'Do you know how many box office hits I've produced in the last decade? Eight. I'm not even thirty-five yet. But a single Black woman, going it on my own? I know the kind of funding I could scrape up. Any production company with a Lowe attached to it would not have that problem. Think about it, Salma, all the movies we could make together. Great films. And even better, we'd have the influence to keep assholes like Cal Turner in line. We could make a real change.' She stretched a hand over the table, almost touching mine. It was as close to pleading as I imagined Emerald got.

I was at a loss for words. 'I don't know what to say.'

She sat back. I could tell she was disappointed that I hadn't jumped at the chance, and I understood why. It was the best deal I'd ever been offered in my life. 'Say yes. What else are you going to do, go back to your tours?'

Emerald didn't know it, but I'd given my last tour weeks before. Dale had graciously given me back my schedule. At first, it had been easy to get back in the swing of things. I made it through Dominique Dunne and Dorothy Stratten and Thelma Todd and Lupe Vélez like I was greeting old friends. The Black Dahlia hit a little heavier. By the time I pulled up at the Jacaranda House again – scanning for Elizabeth, though I didn't see her – I knew it was my last tour.

I'd collected the Dead Girls on my tour, the ones I'd built up around Tawney like a brigade of fallen, glamorous sisters. The ones whose stories ended in a question mark, the ones whose lives were cut short, the man responsible receiving a slap on the wrist. I'd believed I was doing something important in telling their stories.

But I would tell this story one last time. They were no longer my stories to tell.

I had ushered everyone off the bus. It was still the headline stop, perhaps even more so after Ankine's death. But even after only a few months, she was fading; her name wasn't in the news any more, bookings for the tour were down. No one had asked me about her in days.

In my riders, I saw a sea of people who longed to believe in a fairy tale. Even one with darkness and death at the end. Maybe it was the fairy tale of Hollywood, where the good guys eventually win, where hearts only stay broken for a two-hour running time. It's an easier world to live in, after all; celluloid lives in black and white that ignores all the greys.

It was time to let my Dead Girls rest in peace. It was time to find my way back to the living.

When I drove back to Stars Six Feet Under to drop off my riders, I gave Dale my notice. He didn't seem surprised, although perhaps a little sad. He told me he understood. He told me he'd see me at the meeting next week.

Emerald had accused me once of resting on my family's laurels. In a way, she was offering me both the opposite and more of the same. Attached to her company, I'd always be Salma Lowe, Dave's daughter, Tawney's kid sister. But then, I didn't think it was possible to leave my name behind completely, either. Or my family legacy.

'Thank you for the offer,' I said. 'I need to think about it.'

Emerald's eyes narrowed. She searched my face before sighing. 'Fine. You let me know.'

I left her house not long after. I was still thinking about Emerald's offer as I drove home to Glassell Park. It was still early. I sat on my couch, watching the light outside die down.

I closed my eyes and let myself dream, surrounded by a carnival of *my* Tawneys. Not Cal's. Not the Tawney of the movies. My sister, as I knew her.

The elegant line of her neck at her first film premiere, as she turned and vamped for the cameras. I thought there'd never been anyone more beautiful in all of history. Badgering her until she ate cheese pizza with me in front of the TV on nights our parents were out, whining until *Jesus Christ, okay*, my sister agreed to let me watch forbidden R-rated movies. The late-night conversations when we shared our dreams, the women we hoped we would become.

Neither of us had grown up into the women we'd hoped.

The vision shifted, scenes of *Iron Prayer* flicking by. I watched my parents circle each other, playacting love until it came true. And then, stage left: Elizabeth. In the film, she played a too-bossy-for-her-years spitfire. Even though she only had a few lines, she made an impression. She played her part.

I wanted to pull them all away from one another, unspool their lives backward until the reel snapped off. Push my parents away from each other, scoop Elizabeth away from all of them, keep them safe from one another. But if I did that, there would have been no me. No Tawney.

I watched my parents' dance, always drawn back to each other, life mimicking art. I tried to think about what I could do with the things I now knew.

I could call MacLeish. Tell him everything. Ask him for advice about what to do and how to do it. I didn't know what kind of proof we would need. I knew there was no way my mother would readily admit to what I had discovered, and Jack couldn't. *Oh yes, Officer, we have been covering up a murder for twenty years, how did you guess?* But Jack was nearly a vegetable now. It was only my mother who would pay. Maybe she deserved to. But I couldn't do it.

I could call Cherry, give her all the juicy details, or enough of them. She'd need proof, too, but less of it. It would be the punishment most painful for my mother, airing the dirty laundry of our family. But would it be justice?

And then there was Emerald. What she was offering me was a dream, one I'd had so long I barely even recognised it any more. A way out from under Sloppy Salma. Cherry had said it: Hollywood loved a comeback story. Even better: the chance to make real *change* in the industry. Couldn't that be the Lowe family legacy?

The Lowe name would be worthless with such a big scandal attached.

I sat and thought, turning each piece over and over. Every path wound up hurting someone I loved. Tawney was dead, my father was dead, Jack as good as.

So many people believed Tawney's story belonged to them. The Tawney groupies. Cal, who had put himself at the centre of it all these years. My mother and Jack had done a version of that, too: editing the truth until they had a version they could live with, letting the world believe a lie.

And even me – Tawney had been my favourite person. She was the centre of my world. I'd thought I was getting to the bottom of her story – but what I'd found was that it had been someone else's story, too, all along.

My whole life, I'd believed I was weak, that I wasn't as strong as my family.

But what if the opposite was true?

It'll be okay, Salmon.

You're only as sick as your secrets.

It was the work of only a few minutes to find Elizabeth's phone number online. I took a deep breath and dialled before I lost my nerve. On the other end, the phone rang and rang and rang, a line pulling me forward into the future. Into whatever would come next.

I was ready.

ACKNOWLEDGEMENTS

First, I'd like to thank my agent, the tireless Sharon Pelletier, for all her work on this book (and, truly, my mental health). It takes an actual village to write a book, and during a global pandemic, it also takes an agent with the listening and soothing capacity of a saint to make it happen.

It's not an exaggeration to say *The Hurricane Blonde* wouldn't exist without Danielle Dieterich – thank you for the phone calls, and the notes, and the reading of so many (SO MANY!) very-not-good drafts of this novel. Thank you for not giving up on me, or the book, or Salma, and for pushing me to get her where she needed to go.

Thank you to my Putnam team – Elora Weil, Emily Leopold, Ashley Tucker, Sally Kim, Alexis Welby, Ashley McClay, Alice Dalrymple, and Monica Cordova – for making my dreams come true. It's an honour and a joy to publish with you. Thank you to my UK publishing team at Allison & Busby: Lesley Crooks, Libby Haddock, and Fiona Paterson. It is a lifelong dream to have a book of mine go abroad, and I couldn't have asked for a better home for *The Hurricane Blonde*.

Thank you to Kristina Moore for taking my words places I only dreamt they'd go. You are a rock star and a badass.

Thank you to Layne Fargo and Wendy Heard and Megan Collins, my stabby coven, for brainstorming tirelessly about this book for years, and for lifting me up about this project over and over.

Olivia Batker Pritzker, how do people write books without you? I can't. Thank you for the feedback and the hand-holding and the cheering and the margaritas, and telling me when it's time to 'knifehand' a manuscript. My LA writer friends – Hannah Martin, Jenna Dorian – you inspire me constantly.

My COVID crew, my friends I'm lucky enough to call sometime-roommates – Jessica Miller, Bridget Altman, Cindy Shuai, Tiffany (now) Strickland, Melisa Baloglu, Faizah Rajput – thanks for putting up with all the various iterations of a friend-writerincrisis.

Nic – this book has our time together threaded into its DNA. Thank you for brainstorming with me in a gorgeous LA park, and for turning parts of a global disaster into something beautiful for a little while.

Tara, Sam, Leah, Shelby – thank you for the cheering on. This book, and I, needed it more than usual, and I'm so lucky to count on you guys, to know you and love you.

Honestly – I probably also need to thank my therapist, Stacey. We had 'book therapy' for almost two years straight, and the fact that I'm still even relatively sane is a huge credit to you.

It's fun for me to remember all the places this book – and Salma – has travelled with me, even during COVID

369

times: I spent a glorious week pounding limoncello martinis (very unSalma-like!) while working on revisions at the Abruzzo Tour d'Eau in Carunchio, Italy. I saw ABBA in hologram concert in London while trying to figure out how to have my midpoint hit *the actual midpoint, and not sixty-five thousand words in.* And I'm typing this, turning over copyedits, from a glorious *palapa* steps from Lake Chapala, México. Salma, you've been an excellent travelling companion.

Mom, Dad, my number one cheerleaders – I'm grateful for you every day. I promise one day I might write something you don't feel weird about. But let's be real – probably not. Thank you for loving me and being proud of me anyway.

And for Paul Vangelisti, noir poet, forever mentor and inspiration – thank you for the stories, and the laughs, and the *stories*. Down these mean streets, a poet must go . . .

DISCUSSION GUIDE

1. *The Hurricane Blonde* is narrated in the first person, and we as readers have an intimate look at Salma's suspicions and feelings. How did that perspective impact your reading experience? Did you find Salma to be a reliable narrator?

2. Discuss the interplay between the past and the present in the novel, particularly looking at the flashback chapters and how they interact with the narrative. Is Salma stuck in the past? And is her recollection of the past accurate? How does history change the way the story in the present day unfolds?

3. Who is the true villain in *The Hurricane Blonde*? Is there more than one? Consider the ways that both action and inaction harm various characters in the novel. Look also at the ways that characters are punished for their crimes – if they are.

4. The end of the novel is ambiguous regarding how Salma will choose to move forward in her professional

and personal lives. What choices do you imagine she makes? What do you think her life will look like after the novel's end?

5. Why do you think that Salma chooses to run the Stars Six Feet Under tour? Why does she remain submerged in the world of fame and cinema, even after her sister's murder? What do you think the stories of the women portrayed in the tour represent, and how do they parallel the modern day?

6. The novel explores both the danger and the draw of Hollywood. How far are each of the main characters willing to go in order to remain in the orbit of fame? Is it ultimately worth it?

7. Take a look at Salma's reputation and how it changes throughout the course of *The Hurricane Blonde*. What does it show about the standards women in Hollywood are held to? How does Salma both live up to and defy the stereotype that the public has placed upon her?

8. Why do you think the public continues to be obsessed with Tawney's short life and her death? In particular, why do you think Ankine is so devoted to taking on Tawney's persona? And what are the dangers she faces in doing so?

9. Take a look at the role of the media and tabloids in *The Hurricane Blonde*. How much power does the media hold? How do the narratives told by the press take on

a life of their own and impact events? Does the 'truth' truly matter, or do the stories shared by the media become a form of truth?

10. Discuss the meaning of the title. Aside from referring to Tawney's nickname, does 'The Hurricane Blonde' summon other themes or images from within the text?

A CONVERSATION WITH HALLEY SUTTON

Where did the idea for *The Hurricane Blonde* come from? When did you first think of it?

The more experience I have with writing novels, the more it seems to me my ideas for novels are both quick – all of a sudden, I put something together in a new way and attach to it – and also the product of several years of obsessions and vague what-ifs mashed together. When I was considering premises for my second book to pitch to my editor, I didn't really have a concrete idea in mind. My agent, the phenomenal Sharon Pelletier, recommended that I send her a list of premises to consider. The very last idea on my list – I don't remember the others! – which I added in a sort of why-the-hell-not? attitude, was: *Murder-bus tour guide discovers a body on her tour.* Sharon immediately pointed to that as something fresh, so that was really the spark.

But that idea also came from my experiences when I first moved to LA as a grad student and would take weekend true-crime bus tours to get to know various parts of the city. It was a really unique way to look at some of the history – or even, the dark mythology – of Los Angeles, and an interesting education for a burgeoning crime writer.

And in grad school, I fell in love with the weird mythology of Hollywood. This was facilitated by a wonderful professor of mine, a poet (who also wrote noir poetry) and translator named Paul Vangelisti. Paul had worked at *The Hollywood Reporter* back in the 1970s and had all these great behind-the-scenes stories of Hollywood big shots (buy me a drink at a reading sometime and I'll spill the dirt, very much off the record). I loved his stories – I believed him – but I also just liked the modern mythology of it all. Around the same time, I read *Hollywood Babylon* by Kenneth Anger – not the most humanitarian of books but a lot of soapy, insane, libelous fun.

Once I had that thread of a premise – murder-bus tour guide, etc. – these other obsessions started to coalesce. What if the tour guide was a flamed-out child actor? What if she came from an epically famous family whose fame was also concealing a terrible secret?

What was your experience of writing *The Hurricane Blonde*? This is your second novel, following your debut, *The Lady Upstairs*. Did the writing process differ from book to book?

With *The Lady Upstairs*, I had Jo's voice spring into my head almost fully formed, and then I spent about three and a half years workshopping, rewriting, reenvisioning her story. But I always knew exactly how she *felt*. And I had all the time in the world to figure out her story and get it right.

With *The Hurricane Blonde*, I was really getting to know Salma as I wrote the book. I knew where I wanted the book to go, and I knew what I wanted the book to explore. I even knew huge biographical portions of Salma's life: her childhood, her place in her family, her deepest shames and secrets. But it took a couple of years for me to get to know her voice, how she experienced the world.

Everyone warned me that writing a second book is very, very hard – and that was *before* the pandemic. As it turns out, *everyone was right*. But I'm also so proud of this book – it was such a labour of love, and I learnt so much about myself and my own writing process writing it.

Why did you decide to set the novel in Hollywood? How did Hollywood lore impact your writing? Were there any particular Hollywood true-crime cases that inspired you?

I'm fascinated by Hollywood mythology. It's American folklore, in some sense: you have these impossibly glamorous beings made immortal through film, and the archetypes – the seductive blonde, the girl next door, the handsome rogue, the overlooked hero, even the villains – that basically get embodied by new people every few years. I'm fascinated by that. Not just the truth of their stories – but how we tell their stories and why. What does it facilitate for us to read celebrity gossip, to root for or against certain marriages or life choices? It's not unlike, in my opinion, our fascination with true crime – whatever catharsis of emotion we experience in taking on these other stories as our own, as personal to us.

In terms of true crime, I was inspired by a variety of cases, including Dominique Dunne, who was strangled to death by an ex-boyfriend on her lawn in broad daylight when she was twenty-two years old. (Not-so-fun fact: her murderer was sentenced to six and a half years for her murder, and released from prison after serving three years, seven months, and twenty-seven days of his sentence. When I first heard that, I was so mad. I'm still mad.) And Rebecca Schaeffer – a young actor who was shot and killed at her front door by a stalker in the 1990s. The women that Salma includes on her tour are almost all based on real crimes or events, and I spent time delving into their stories, researching cases, and reading books that covered these events from a more mythological, even prurient, standpoint: Amber Tamblyn's *Dark Sparkler*, *Death in Hollywood* by Peter Underwood, *The Tales of Hollywood the Bizarre* by John Austin, and many, many more. I also spent a fair amount of time researching bad behaviour by men in Hollywood – Phil Spector, Robert Blake, Roman Polanski.

Why are you drawn to writing thrillers? Are there certain elements of the genre that lend themselves to the stories you want to tell? Do you have any other favourite thriller authors?

I'm drawn to telling stories about people exploring the darkest parts of their hearts, that most human of human impulses. I think I'm drawn more toward noir-tinged stories than thrillers explicitly. Two of my favourite definitions of noir really sum up big interests of mine in the stories I write. The first is from Laura Lippman: 'Dreamers become schemers.' I mean, isn't this more or less the story of America in a nutshell?! And the second comes, I *believe*, from Steph Cha, and I'm paraphrasing: in noir, getting to the truth always carries the heaviest price. I think that is such an artistically interesting concept to consider and it resonates when you think about crime – both fiction and factual crime. Knowing the truth does not put the world back together again. That's especially a theme I had in mind for *The Hurricane Blonde*.

Truly, there is an embarrassment of riches when it comes to considering crime writers working today: Megan Abbott, Layne Fargo, Wendy Heard, Megan Collins, Attica Locke, Wanda M. Morris, Barbara Bourland, Ivy Pochoda, Ashley Winstead, Steph Cha, Kellye Garrett, Laura Lippman, Alex Segura, Tod Goldberg, Vicki Hendricks, Sara Sligar, S. A. Cosby, Rachel Howzell Hall, Sara Gran, Amy Gentry, Eliza Jane Brazier, Tana French – I could go on and on and on.

I am in serious *awe* of these people and am very much not cool about it when I cross their paths at readings or conferences (or even on Instagram, yeesh).

This novel has both past and present plotlines. Why did you choose to tell the story this way? Were there any challenges in depicting the past? Did you do research for those particular sections of the book?

Once I figured out that the crimes at the centre of *The Hurricane Blonde* would span decades, it seemed to me that showing select moments from Salma's past was the best way to give full weight to her story. In this book, as in life, all the actions of the present are impacted by the weight of things that have come before – both extremely literally, in terms of Tawney's murder, but also in terms of Salma's tabloid past informing who she is, why she does what she does, and the coping mechanisms she's adopted to deal with her grief and shame. It didn't seem to me like I could fully flesh out Salma's story without the reader seeing some of those specific snapshots looking into her past.

I grew up in the '90s, so some of the research I did for the book involved looking backward at my own past. But the truth is, Salma and I grew up very differently, so I did more research into what her life would have been like as a child actor, what forces would've shaped her. I spent time researching tabloid culture in the late nineties and early aughts, the rise of the paparazzi, and the casual misogyny of the press during the nineties. (There's a podcast called *You're Wrong About*, which had a series of episodes on reconsidering maligned women of the nineties – I consider Tawney to be the fictional sister of these ladies.)

The bulk of the research I did for the book was in fact into Hollywood history; basically, every part of the book is informed by things that have come before. Vivienne's acting studio is based on actual businesses; even the crimes themselves are patterned (at times, loosely) on real Hollywood events and true crime. I did a lot of research on Hollywood lore, paying not total attention to what was factually true, but to what stories made it into the cultural narrative and why.

The Hurricane Blonde **examines the dynamic between powerful men and the women who work with them. Did current events have an influence on your writing?**

Yes and no. Yes: we're absolutely in a moment – have been for a few years – where these stories are surfacing more publicly. But also – that doesn't mean these stories are new. There's a story Salma tells about Clark Gable and Loretta

Young in the book – that's a true story. The idea of the 'casting couch' is a term we've used to refer to the rampant abuses of power in a sexual arena, and that was around long before Harvey Weinstein's trial. Some of the greatest directors in cinematic history are guilty of *terrible* abuses of power – sexual or not – in the name of 'art.' All of Cal's alleged misdeeds with his actors are based on actual incidents and the demands of directors on their talent.

I think the difference with current events is that we're naming these things and hopefully taking them more seriously. Hopefully. And one of the things I was interested in exploring in this book are the degrees to which women are oftentimes complicit, or made to be complicit, in these abuses of power – whether out of fear, or ambition, or a belief that that's simply how things are done. And that's, unfortunately, not exclusive to Hollywood power dynamics.

Were there any characters or scenes that you particularly enjoyed writing? Or any that were uniquely challenging?

This entire book was uniquely challenging, but one of my biggest challenges was getting to know Salma. With Jo, in *The Lady Upstairs*, I felt like she arrived fully formed. Salma was more cautious, less splashy. I worried about her more, I felt more protective of her. I would say the scenes I most enjoyed writing tended to be the flashback scenes of Salma's past. Those tended to be the ones where I could lean most heavily into my favourite parts of Hollywood lore and rumours. Threading those into the narrative in little ways was like a fun game of hiding Easter eggs that I was playing just for my own amusement.

Honestly, it was hardest to write the scenes of Salma grieving. Maybe it was just the collective grieving and horror of the past three years, but that was a painful place to spend time in, emotionally. But her grief for, and love of, her sister is so central to the book that it was inescapable.

What's next for you?

I'm at work on a fictional, scripted thriller podcast for Audible with Megan Collins and Layne Fargo, and I'm so excited to be trying a new way of storytelling! I'm finding the constraints of a new medium really fun for creativity, even as it has its own challenges. I'm not sure when that will wind up being released.

I'm also at work on my next book, which will take us out of Los Angeles and abroad to some fabulous locations. Coming out of COVID, I want to write a book that is exceptionally *fun* and global (because I'm dying to travel) and wild and big. I'll say more when there's more to say!

HALLEY SUTTON is the author of *The Lady Upstairs* and *The Hurricane Blonde*. She lives in Los Angeles where she immerses herself in Hollywood trivia. She holds a degree in creative writing from the University of California Santa Cruz, and a master's in writing from Otis College of Art and Design. Her writing has appeared in *Ms*, *Daily Beast*, *CrimeReads*, and *Los Angeles Review of Books*.

halleysutton.com